DISCARD

HEARTLESS

OTHER BOOKS BY
ALISON GAYLIN

Hide Your Eyes
You Kill Me
Trashed

HEARTLESS

Alison Gaylin

AN OBSIDIAN MYSTERY

OBSIDIAN
Published by New American Library, a division of
Penguin Group (USA) Inc., 375 Hudson Street,
New York, New York 10014, USA
Penguin Group (Canada), 90 Eglinton Avenue East, Suite 700, Toronto,
Ontario M4P 2Y3, Canada (a division of Pearson Penguin Canada Inc.)
Penguin Books Ltd., 80 Strand, London WC2R 0RL, England
Penguin Ireland, 25 St. Stephen's Green, Dublin 2,
Ireland (a division of Penguin Books Ltd.)
Penguin Group (Australia), 250 Camberwell Road, Camberwell, Victoria 3124,
Australia (a division of Pearson Australia Group Pty. Ltd.)
Penguin Books India Pvt. Ltd., 11 Community Centre, Panchsheel Park,
New Delhi - 110 017, India
Penguin Group (NZ), 67 Apollo Drive, Rosedale, North Shore 0632,
New Zealand (a division of Pearson New Zealand Ltd.)
Penguin Books (South Africa) (Pty.) Ltd., 24 Sturdee Avenue,
Rosebank, Johannesburg 2196, South Africa

Penguin Books Ltd., Registered Offices:
80 Strand, London WC2R 0RL, England

First published by Obsidian, an imprint of New American Library,
a division of Penguin Group (USA) Inc.

First Printing, September 2008
10 9 8 7 6 5 4 3 2 1

LIBRARY OF CONGRESS CATALOGING-IN-PUBLICATION DATA:

Gaylin, Alison.
    Heartless/Alison Gaylin.
      p. cm.
    ISBN 978-0-451-22497-2
    1. Women journalists—Fiction. 2. Actors—Fiction. 3. Soap operas—Fiction. 4. Murder—Fiction.
    5. Mexico—Fiction. I. Title.
    PS3607.A9858H43 2008
    813'.6—dc22   2008017396

Set in Janson text
Designed by Alissa Amell

Printed in the United States of America

For Marissa
I love you more than ice cream . . .

Acknowledgments

Boy, this was a tough one. But it would have been absolutely impossible without the help of the following wonderful people: Karin Reininger and Antonio Flores Lobos for making the Spanish *mucho mas mejor*. Dr. Sung-Hee Lee and Dr. Sheldon Gaylin for answering the world's strangest medical research questions with seemingly straight faces. Lee Lofland and Theresa Braine for answering all other research questions—you guys are great.

Deborah Schneider, Cathy Gleason and Britt Carlson for all their great work on my behalf, Ellen Edwards and Becky Vintner for terrific, spot-on editing. Kara Welsh, Tina Anderson, Kristen Weber and everyone else at NAL/Obsidian . . . thank you all so much.

A whole boatload of thanks goes out to my friend and hero Abigail Thomas, as well as my excellent writing group Paul Leone, Claudette Covey, Jo Treggiari, Jennifer May, Ann Patty, Rik Fairlie and Bar Scott, not to mention fellow First Offenders Karen E. Olson, Jeff Shelby and Lori Armstrong, as well as the many smart and patient friends

I forced into brainstorming sessions. I owe all of you big-time. Drinks are on me.

Marilyn and Shel Gaylin and Beverly Sloane for their tireless support.

And most especially Mike and Marissa. *Muchas gracias y muchos besos, mis queridos.*

"El que pega, paga." (He who strikes, pays.)
—Mexican saying

PROLOGUE

"**Y**ou want to?" Jordan asked.

Jordan had this sultry, slurry way of speaking that made it sound less like a question and more like an exotic name—*Yawanna*. And that mouth . . . God. It made Naomi blush a little, watching it move around the words.

It had to be the beer and the pot because Naomi never thought like this. Sometimes, the girls at Santa Beatriz would look at pictures of Justin Timberlake or Enrique Iglesias or maybe some guy from a *telenovella*, and they'd say, *Le quiero.* . . . I want him. . . . And yeah, Naomi would nod and all, but she wouldn't get it. Not really.

At seventeen, she'd been with a guy just once. It was horrible. She wasn't big on dating either, and Justin, Enrique, all those two-dimensional boys in magazines, on TV screens—they did nothing for her at all. For a while now, Naomi had been secretly thinking there might be something wrong with her because she couldn't even *understand* what it meant to want another person—want him the way you'd want new clothes, the way you'd want a glass of ice water after hiking straight uphill in the sun.

But now . . . Now she understood.

"I promise," said Jordan. "You'll love it."

Naomi's skin heated up. Her face flushed a deep red that she was certain he noticed, even from across the bonfire and with the desert sky darkening into that end-of-day color, that melony pink. She could blame it on the beer or the heat from the fire, but still he would know. The way he was looking at her, he just *would.* . . .

But then Corinne said, "Doesn't it make you puke?" And suddenly, it was as if the other two people around the fire—Naomi's American friends, down in San Esteban for summer break—had materialized out of nowhere.

Corinne's boyfriend, Sean, handed Jordan the joint, and he took a hit. "Puking is part of the experience," Jordan said. He was half holding his breath to keep the smoke in, so the words kind of snuck out of his throat. God help Naomi, he even inhaled sexy. She flashed on the Baggie he held in his other hand, at the shriveled gray disks inside, and thought, *Right. He's talking about peyote.* That's *what he means by "the experience."*

"I'll try it," she heard herself say, shocking everyone around the fire, especially herself. Naomi was a lightweight. One beer, three hits of pot and already she was a red-faced, trembling basket case with an embarrassing crush on Corinne's cousin. The last thing she needed was hallucinogenic cactus buttons.

"Are you sure, Naomi?" said Sean, as if he were reading her mind.

But when she looked at Jordan, when she saw the way he smiled at her, the way his eyes glittered under those half-closed lids . . . Oh, she was sure. So sure that she'd say it again, over and over, and then eat everything in the Baggie without taking a breath, even if it made her puke her guts out and go completely insane. She'd do it all if she could just get Jordan alone for a few minutes, if she could get close enough to touch the side of his face, to feel those soft lips against her neck, to explore these brand-new feelings. . . .

"You won't be sorry," Jordan said. And Naomi knew he was right.

So strange how life worked. How it could be chugging along, same old boring life it always was, and then something, some small part of it, would turn just a little and a screw would fall out. . . .

Jordan was visiting from New York. But unlike Sean and Corinne—both of whose grandparents lived here year-round—he wouldn't be staying in San Esteban for the summer, or even for the week. Guys like this—they were always *just passing through*, weren't they?

Naomi had met him earlier that day, in the *jardín*. She'd been walking to the *biblioteca* with her aunt Vanessa. "Corinne should be down here soon, right?" Vanessa had said.

And then, just like that, Corinne's Texan accent: "Naomi!" As if her aunt had conjured her or something. When Naomi turned, there was her friend, just in from Austin, standing next to a cute American boy who was not Sean and had to be at least nineteen. "This is my cousin Jordan," she'd said. "He's visiting from New York. He goes to NYU. I'm going to the doctor because I forgot my allergy pills, and Jordan is coming with me because he is sooo sweet. Aren't you, Jordan?"

"That's embarrassing, Corinne," he said.

Jordan was about two inches shorter than Naomi, but that didn't bother her. At five foot eleven, she towered over most Mexican guys. He had long eyelashes, shiny brown hair and a dimpled smile. He smelled like cocoa butter and soap. He wore khaki shorts and flip-flops and a white T-shirt that set off his tanned skin, made it glow a little. Definitely a hottie, but there was something else about his face—a sort of sadness. Naomi couldn't explain why, but that was what got to her the most.

"Hi," Jordan said. To Vanessa. Of course.

Naomi had been living with Vanessa for two years, ever since her mom had died, and she was used to her aunt getting all the attention. She'd always been what guys call smokin' and at fifty-five she still was, with her toned body and her sculpted cheekbones and her flowing, highlighted hair, but it was more than that. Vanessa was famous. A supergroupie back in her youth, she'd written a bestselling tell-all seven years ago that had landed her on all the talk shows and made enough money to buy her a mansion in San Esteban, plus keep her in liposuction for the rest of the foreseeable future.

Like all famous people, Vanessa had that airbrushed look, that sheen of perfection that made people stare. And when people actually recognized her, when they knew she was famous for screwing, like, every male rock star from the seventies who wasn't Freddie Mercury, well . . . then they were even more interested.

"Naomi's aunt is Vanessa St. James," Corinne told Jordan.

"Right."

"She wrote *Backstage Passes and Hot Licks*," Corinne said. "I *so* loved that book!"

"Corinne, your parents should not be letting you read that trash," Vanessa said.

Naomi couldn't help but roll her eyes. Vanessa used that line with everybody, regardless of their age.

"Nice to meet you, honey," Vanessa said.

"Actually," Jordan said, "we've met before. I was visiting my aunt Patty. Four years ago? Remember?"

Vanessa peered at him. "Oh my goodness . . . Yes! You were just a little *boy* back then!" She broke into an electric smile. Her fiery gaze slid up the length of his body, resting just before it hit the face. "You have really grown *up*!"

Naomi wanted to gag.

"How long are you in town?" Vanessa asked.

"He's leaving tomorrow," said Corinne.

"That's a shame."

Jordan said, "You live here all year-around?"

Vanessa didn't respond—and then, with a visible start, Naomi realized he was talking to her. "Uh . . . yeah. I do."

"You speak Spanish?"

She nodded.

"I'm hanging with you, then. Corinne doesn't even know how to get a taxi."

"Shut up, Jordan. That is not true."

Naomi felt herself smiling. "You guys want to do a bon-fire tonight?"

"Definitely," said Corinne. "I can't wait."

Jordan said, "Me neither." He caught Naomi's eye, and while Vanessa asked after Corinne's grandmother Patty, the two of them stood there, staring at each other as if they were the only two people in the world. Jordan's eyes were a shade of gold, and seemed so much older than the rest of him. As he watched Naomi, the sadness within them grew and deepened into something else, something bigger. . . . *What's wrong?* Naomi wanted to say. *You can tell me, and whatever it is, I will understand. I will help.*

"See you later," Jordan said.

"Sure."

After they walked away, Naomi took in the spot where Jordan had stood, a warmth spreading through her like a rash. "Better be careful," said Vanessa. "That one's a heartbreaker."

*   *   *

Naomi stared at the two peyote buttons in her hand. They looked like slices of two hundred-year-old squash, with little purple hairs poking out the sides.

"I can't believe you're going to eat that," said Corinne.

Naomi ignored her, which was easy to do, seeing as less than twenty feet away, Sean was making sounds like a dying yak. He'd eaten his buttons around half an hour ago and that he was now violently puking—a six-foot-five-inch football player with a neck the size of a Christmas ham—was not what you'd call good advertising for the peyote experience.

"Don't worry," said Jordan.

Naomi looked at him. His face was serene. "If there's nothing to worry about," she said, "why don't you take it?"

He smiled. "Already did."

"But you're not . . ."

"Throwing up? You don't always." His mouth tilted into a half smile. "If you eat yours now, we can still peak at the same time."

That pretty much sealed the deal.

Naomi held her nose, then popped both buttons into her mouth and chewed them up, fast as she could. As it turned out, peyote tasted the way cat crap smelled, only worse. She gagged instantly. *I will not throw up in front of him.* Naomi thought of a framed concert photo in Vanessa's bedroom— Ozzy Osbourne, taken just after he'd bitten the head off a live bat.

At least peyote didn't bleed.

"There's something about you, Naomi," said Jordan.

The vaguest compliment she'd ever received, and yet at this moment, the most wonderful. . . . *Don't throw up, don't throw up.* She swallowed the last awful bit and took a swig from Corinne's bottle of water.

"Thanks," Naomi said, but she couldn't look at him.

What if she looked at him and puked, and he took it person-ally? What if he got so grossed out he never spoke to her again? She closed her eyes tight, rubbed the lids with the palms of her hands. This had always calmed her down, ever since she had been a little girl, and after a time (ten minutes? twenty? forty-five?) the nausea passed, and she was safe.

She opened her eyes, gazed across the fire at Jordan.

"Whew. Thought I lost you there for a second." He grinned—but in his eyes, still that deep, mysterious sor-row. The combination was close to overwhelming. Naomi's heart swelled so big, her ribs could barely contain it. She inhaled the sweet smell of burning mesquite as the dried cactus worked into her system, and the sun melted away, the sky turning a deep soft purple, the air starting to cool and swirl. . . . *Please get up and sit next to me, please, please, please.* . . . "I'm cold," Naomi said. But the voice she heard was not her own. It was the voice of a ghost.

"Oh, man," Sean was saying. "I can see . . . Right here, in the dirt, it's like . . . some kind of latticework structure leading down into the center of the earth, like a secret civi-lization or . . ."

Corinne said, "Excuse me, but did you just seriously say, 'latticework structure'?" and then Jordan stood up and moved behind Naomi and sat down next to her, putting his arm around her shoulder. *Thank you.*

"Better?" he asked.

"Yes."

"Hitting you yet?" His voice was warm against the side of her neck. His hand stroked her arm, and when she looked down at it, she saw thousands of shimmering fish scales.

"Uh, I think so."

He exhaled, the breath breaking on her skin and curling, like a wave. "Puts you in touch with the nagual," he said.

"Huh?"

"You know. Castaneda's nagual. The indefinable. The left side of the . . ."

Naomi gulped. *Castaneda.* Who was that? Oh, right . . . Vanessa had a whole shelf of those books, but not once had Naomi thought of reading one. She couldn't even remember Castaneda's first name. She tried envisioning the books, the author's name on the spines, but all she could recall were the two huge pink crystals Vanessa used to keep them in place. . . . What a stupid high school girl she was.

". . . because Don Juan said the true warrior . . ."

Naomi gritted her teeth. Why wasn't he talking about latticework structures? At least she *knew* what latticework was. . . . *Think of the spines.* . . .

"I'm talking too much, aren't I?" said Jordan. And suddenly, the name appeared in her brain, sparkling as if a thousand silver stars were glued to the letters. . . .

"*Carlos* Castaneda!"

Jordan said, "You are really cute."

Naomi turned to see his face much closer than she'd expected—about two inches away from her own, a slight smile playing at the corners of his mouth. She ignored all the scales, gazing only at the eyes, those sad golden eyes. He gave her the lightest, softest kiss imaginable, and then he leaned back and just looked at her, saying nothing, the heat of him lingering on her lips.

"Wow," she said. Like a gargantuan dork.

The scales glistened in the firelight—kind of gorgeous really, in an exotic, god-of-the-sea way—and Naomi wanted to melt into Jordan right there. She wanted to lose her own shape and turn to liquid, soak into those scales and become a part of him forever and ever as he moved through the ocean waves, and oh, was Naomi ever glad she wasn't saying this out loud. Seriously, *wow* was bad enough, but *this* . . .

Naomi caught a sudden chill up her back, as if someone was watching her, someone in the darkness, and when she glanced around the fire, she saw Corinne and Sean were gone. *When did they leave? A minute ago? An hour?* Time wasn't moving the way it was supposed to. It half rushed, half oozed, like those clocks in Salvador Dalí paintings.

"Are you okay?" Jordan asked.

"Yeah." She closed her eyes, started rubbing them again. "I'm . . . I'm fine. I'm just . . . I . . ." Naomi's heart was doing this weird jumping thing. It reminded her of Vanessa's washing machine, how it always hopped up and down on the tile floor once the spin cycle started, shaking her aunt's entire laundry room and kitchen. *Jesus H. Christ*, Vanessa would say, *it's like there's an obese robot doing the pogo in there.*

That was what Naomi's heart felt like—a chubby little robot, hopping around inside her chest, only scary-fast. She started to think, *What if my heart explodes?* Because that really did happen to some people, didn't it? They could be doing something perfectly normal—shopping for groceries or whatever—and one of their internal organs would up and explode.

"Naomi?" Jordan said.

She was sure she'd read about this on the Net. Exploding organs, caused by some rare, undetected childhood condition. Undetected. Meaning you didn't *know* about it—*nobody* knew about it until it was *too late*. She heard herself say, "I think I need to see a doctor."

"A *doctor?*"

What if Naomi had a rare, undetected childhood condition, and her heart exploded from it right now? What would it feel like, that half second just before it happened, that moment of *knowing?*

"It can hit you hard the first time," said Jordan.

"I'm . . . I feel like . . ."

"I know. I feel weird too. Just try and go with it." Jordan took one of her wrists, gently moved her hands from her eyes. Her vision was blurry from all the rubbing, so she blinked a few times. Her hands and arms were glowing pink, like they were made from neon. "Take a deep breath," Jordan said, "in and out. . . ."

Naomi did. Her heart slowed a little. She looked at the fire and saw . . . just a fire. No scales or neon or tentacles.

"Better?"

"Yeah," she said. "Thanks." And for a long time, they sat there, just breathing.

"Jordan?"

"Yeah?"

"Do you . . . do you have to leave tomorrow? I mean . . . could you maybe stay a couple more—"

"Listen, Naomi," said Jordan. "I wasn't going to say anything but . . ." His words trailed into the smoke.

"What?" *You can tell me and whatever it is . . .*

Jordan sighed. It was a labored sigh, the way a sick person would breathe. When he finally spoke, his voice trembled. "This town. San Esteban. I know it's beautiful on the surface, but it is really fucked up. There's . . . weird stuff going on, stuff I'm guessing you don't know about."

That wasn't what she'd expected him to say at all. "What kind of stuff?" Her heart started to jump again. With each word, it wedged farther into her throat.

"I never should have come back here. And you . . ." he said. "You're young. You need to be careful."

She could now feel her heartbeat in her ears, her lips, her throat. She swallowed hard to tamp it down. "You're trying to mess with my head, aren't you?"

"I'm sorry. Forget I ever said anything. I'm just . . . I'm tripping, is all."

She turned, looked at Jordan's face. She started to tell him it was okay, just don't do it again. But then two long white fangs emerged from his mouth, a forked snake's tongue darting out between them. "Sssssssorry," he hissed.

Without thinking, she was up on her feet, running away from the fire, away from Jordan, who was hissing her name. Scrubby plants scratched at her legs and loose dirt flew into her face, rocks pushing through the thin soles of her sandals. It was as if the whole desert was trying to hurt her, and then there were those footsteps nearing, Jordan howling, "Come back!" Jordan the Fanged Snake.

Naomi kept running, but her heart . . . It started slamming into her ribs, slamming hard, as if it wanted out now. Naomi thought, *It's about to explode.*

It was the last thought she had before everything went black.

Naomi dreamed of an angel standing over her. *You are safe,* the angel said. And then there was a spotlight aimed at her face. When she cracked her eyelids, Naomi saw the spotlight was the hot sun, and she was thirstier than she'd ever been in her life. Her tongue felt like a wad of dried clay, too big for her mouth. Her eyes stung terribly and her skin throbbed—her face, her neck, the tops of her legs. She had no idea about the time, but from where the sun was in the sky, she figured it was at least ten in the morning. And Naomi was lying on her back with a third-degree sunburn in the middle of an agave patch, somewhere in the desert that bordered San Esteban.

"Hello?" she called out. Her voice was barely above a whisper.

Corinne and Sean—they had to be looking for her, right? Unless they'd gotten lost too. And Vanessa . . . she would be freaking out for sure.

Naomi struggled to her feet as last night flew back at her—some of it, anyway. That whole exploding organ thing . . . What had she been thinking, doing peyote with a college student? What had made her think she could *handle* that?

"Great," Naomi said to no one. Her lips stuck to her teeth. She ran her tongue over them. They were cracked and crusty and tasted like salt. She recalled, for a moment, what Jordan had said, about weird stuff going on in San Esteban. She thought about his sad, knowing eyes, how he had called after her as she'd run away. . . .

Best not to think about Jordan anymore.

She had to find the path, the dead bonfire, something she could identify so she could get on the trail that led to town. She had to make sure everybody made it back okay, and apologize to Vanessa and cry on her shoulder until her aunt felt needed enough to leave Naomi alone.

Then, finally, Naomi could do what she really wanted to do, which was smear aloe vera all over her body and drink every bottle of water in the house and get into her bed with the stuffed turtle she'd had since childhood and sleep for a week or, better yet, the entire summer.

She stumbled between the cactuses and through a sparse area, dusted with tumbleweed, empty Pepsi cans and a few sick-looking prickly pears, Bimbo Bread wrappers stuck to their quills. She tried to remember landmarks around the bonfire. She and Corinne always made their bonfires in areas that were easy to distinguish—near something tall like a jacaranda tree or a century plant—so they'd be able to find their way back to it should they wander. But this time, they'd let the boys choose the place. Dumb idea.

She kept walking, trying to ignore the vicious headache, that swimmy feeling, like she might pass out all over again.

Finally, she saw something that might have been the bonfire. It was about thirty feet away, near a blooming century plant, even though she hadn't remembered one of them being there last night. Century blooms were incredibly distinct looking—they shot into the air like cell phone towers, thirty, forty feet high, bright yellow blossoms clinging to their sides like an afterthought. . . . Usually, if you set up camp near one, you remembered it. But then again, there was a lot about last night she didn't remember. She moved closer, hoping for the bonfire with her whole body. Before she realized it, she was in a desperate, stumbling run.

Ten feet away, though, she knew it wasn't the bonfire. *Could be a pile of old clothes,* she thought. Until the smell socked her in the face.

She heard the hum of flies first. Then she saw the splayed legs, the outstretched arms, the blood, so much of it, so dark it was close to black. . . . He was still wearing his flip-flops, but the rest of him was . . .

"Jordan!" It came out a scream—an animal scream that ripped open her raw throat and tore at her insides and used all the breath in her body. . . . A scream that made her think she might lose her mind right here in this spot—because it couldn't get worse, nothing could ever be worse than what she was looking at. . . .

And then she saw Jordan's heart.

ONE

Hayley Caldwell threw herself on her father, Matthias's, lifeless body. As she tried in vain to pull the fire poker out of his chest, her hot pink backpack landed awkwardly on his face. "Please don't die, Daddy!" she shrieked. *"We were supposed to be a family again!"*

"Cut!" yelled Jerry, the director. "Beautiful, Tiffany. Let's take a ten-minute break, and then we'll do it once more, without the backpack."

Warren Clark, aka Dr. Matthias Caldwell, opened his eyes. His hand wrapped around the poker, he struggled up to standing and groaned, like an unusually good-looking zombie. "I need a new shirt," he said. "There's way too much blood on this one. It pulls focus from our faces."

"But, Warren . . . We're trying to go for realism, here, and with this type of killing—"

"This isn't *Reservoir Dogs*, Jerry." Warren glared at the director. The klieg lights sparked in his blue eyes. His back was perfectly straight, the poker jutting out from his powerful chest in a way that almost seemed accusatory. "Think about it," he said. "We've got *Pampers ads*."

Jerry's shoulders dropped. He glowered at his feet. "Good point," he said finally. "I'll . . . I'll talk to wardrobe."

Always the alpha male, thought Zoe Greene, who was covering the shoot—Matthias's shocking final scene on *The Day's End*—for *Soap Opera Headquarters* magazine. *Even on his last day at work, Warren Clark's got to have his way.*

God only knew why she found that so attractive.

As Warren started off the set, he looked right at her and winked—a perfectly acceptable gesture for an actor to give a known member of the soap opera press, she knew. But how could he be so confident that people would take it that way? Didn't he think they might *possibly* see it as a sign that he and Zoe had been secretly sleeping together for the past four months?

Zoe made a point of pulling out her steno pad and pen, of turning to the show's publicist, Dana LeVine, and asking, "How do you spell the director's last name?" As if to prove she was all-business, that there was nothing, absolutely nothing going on between her and Warren Clark, no matter how hard her heart happened to be pounding right now, no matter how much blood was rushing into her cheeks. *No, Dana, my interest in him is purely professional. How could you even think that Warren and I . . . ?*

"S-m-i-l-o-w," said Dana. "By the way, that . . . little interchange between Warren and Jerry? It wasn't for the record."

Zoe rolled her eyes. "Give me a little credit, Dana. *Headquarters* has Pampers ads too." She jotted down the director's name.

"I know, but your boss—"

"She won't find out about it."

Dana smiled. "Thanks, Zoe. You're one of the good guys."

"Yeah. It's a curse. . . ."

Tiffany Baxter (aka Hayley) headed past them for the dressing rooms, wearing a look of boredom so pure, it bordered on comatose. Zoe watched her—this dewy fifteen-year-old girl with a salary triple her own and, no doubt, a boyfriend she could tell her coworkers about—thinking, *Would it kill you to smile?*

"You want a quickie with Warren?" Dana said.

"What?"

The publicist peered over the tops of her red-framed half-glasses. "Quick interview. While he's waiting for the new shirt."

"Oh . . . Yeah, sure. That would be great." *Get a grip. Now.* Part of it was the absence. Absence, abstinence . . . whatever. After opting not to renew his contract with *The Day's End,* Warren had promptly jetted down to Mexico, where he'd spent three weeks at his second home in San Esteban. *Last chance to take my paid hiatus,* was how he'd put it, but to Zoe the time apart was agonizing. There had always been something addictive about her physical contact with Warren, a need to be with him that trumped pretty much everything she'd ever thought about herself. (Sleeping with the star of the soap she covered wasn't just unethical. It was completely ridiculous.) After nearly a month without him, though, her logic was shot. And Zoe was suffering the worst sort of withdrawal.

It was a good thing she could write *Headquarters* puff pieces in her sleep, what with these loops running through her head—Warren's voice, Warren's hands, Warren's lips and tongue and breath and heartbeat. His size, his power, the way he could lift her so easily . . .

Whenever anyone mentioned his name at the magazine—and that was often—Zoe would feel it coming on, that *blush.* It was so embarrassing—like she was growing up in reverse, coming *out* of age. She couldn't believe no one noticed, especially *Headquarters'* editor-in-chief, Kathy Kinney. Nothing got past that woman.

"Come with me," Dana said. "You okay? You look—"

"I'm fine."

"Flushed."

"It's the blood," Zoe said quickly, "on Matthias's shirt. I'm kind of squeamish."

Dana smiled. "It's not *real*, you know."

As the publicist led her past the set and down the narrow flight of stairs to the actors' dressing rooms, Zoe took a deep, steadying breath. Not for the first time, she wondered what was making her react this way. Was it the excitement of this clandestine relationship—or was it the dull safety of the rest of her life?

Five years ago, her day-to-day had been anything but boring, anything but safe. Would she have fallen this hard for a soap star back then, when she was covering crime stories for the *Daily News*, when she was living her dream and the blood was real and there were no Pampers ads?

She was better off now. Stultifying as *Headquarters* could be (and really, how many times could you write about the *same* character dying and coming back from the dead before some part of your brain snapped in two?), it beat what her so-called dream job had brought into her life, into the lives of innocent people. . . . She shut her eyes, willed the memory out of her head. "I hate blood," she told Dana. "I really do."

"Your eyes are incredible." As pickup lines went, it wasn't the most original. Plus, Warren Clark was too blond, too perfect, *much* too confident . . . not Zoe's type at all. But the timing . . . It was the timing of that line that had hooked her.

Each editor at *Headquarters* covered a different soap, and Zoe had just been switched from *One Life to Live* to *The Day's End.* He was her first *Day's End* interview. She'd known who Warren Clark was, of course. But outside of a one-minute conversation four years prior in the press room at the Daytime Emmys with event flacks hovering around him like a cloud of gnats, they'd never again met or spoken face-to-face.

Zoe had been sitting next to Warren on the leather couch in his dressing room, interviewing him about Matthias' recent bout with amnesia—and oddly enough, right up until he fed her that line, she'd felt as if *she* was the one in charge.

Zoe asked him a few preliminary questions, then looked deep into his eyes with that serious, I'm-hanging-on-your-every-word gaze she knew daytime actors loved—the one her boss, Kathy, called the "Barbara Walters thousand-yard stare," the one that got them right in the *soul*, practically *forced* them to open up, and asked, "Warren, have you ever thought about what it would be like to forget every—"

That was when he had said it. Interrupted her, as if his mind could no longer contain the observation. *Your eyes are incredible.* Then he'd looked away. Pulled his gaze off Zoe and threw it to the floor and said, "I'm sorry. That was inappropriate, wasn't it?"

"No. I mean . . . it's kind of . . . surprising, but—"

"I couldn't help it."

"You couldn't—"

"Because I want to drown in them."

"Oh . . . um . . ."

"Your eyes."

"I—"

"See, I figure if I'm going to be inappropriate, I may as well go the whole nine yards."

And Zoe just sat there, smiling like a fool. She was such a sucker for good timing.

Four months had passed since then. Four months and three weeks. Had Warren really missed Zoe when he was in Mexico? He'd texted her that he did, but did he mean it? Did he *feel* the lack of her? Did he crave their bodies together the same way she did?

Or was it just the secrecy of their relationship—the *we-really-shouldn't-be-doing-this* aspect—that got him off? Now that he'd quit the show and there was no longer a conflict of interest with her job, would his feelings cool down? And where would that leave her?

"I don't know what we're going to do without Warren," Dana said.

"Me neither." Zoe cleared her throat. "I . . . I mean, does it have to be so definite? Couldn't the writers have left Matthias's death a little more open-ended than a fire poker in the chest?"

She shrugged her shoulders. "Warren thought the character had run his course."

Zoe looked at her. "That decision isn't up to Warren, though."

"Come on, honey. Every decision involving Matthias is up to Warren, you know that. They'd never recast Erica if Lucci left *Kids*, they'll never recast Dr. Caldwell. Some stars are bigger than their characters."

Zoe copied those words onto her steno pad—*Some stars are bigger than their characters*—thinking for the millionth time what a strange turn her life had taken. *A hot, secret affair with the male Susan Lucci.*

She and Dana were in Warren's dressing room, sitting on the same leather couch, where Zoe had conducted that first interview. The couch dominated the place—oxblood, overstuffed—like something you'd find in a wealthy psychiatrist's office. It was the one semiluxurious thing in this small, spartan room, and it was there for practical reasons. Warren often worked late and needed to take naps, and he couldn't sleep on something uncomfortable. Otherwise, there was nothing but a sink, a makeup mirror with a chair in front of it, a small table stacked with highlighted scripts and unopened fan letters. The walls were bare. "I never want to be one of those actors who make their dressing room into a home," was how he explained it.

Of course, his apartment wasn't much more personal. He had some tasteful abstract paintings on his walls, a black-and-white photograph of the Chrysler building, a plasma-screen TV. But no pictures of friends or family or himself, not even in the bedroom. Her whole career as a journalist—whether she was interviewing high school valedictorians or murder victims' families or soap actors—Zoe had always searched her subjects' homes for personal pictures—the happiest moments of their lives, captured and framed. You could tell a lot about a person that way, but not Warren. He captured nothing.

Warren's closet door was open, but it held just one outfit—the street clothes he had worn that day. *At least he doesn't have to move a lot of stuff out*, she thought . . . and then she noticed something hanging behind the clothes, on the back wall of the closet.

It was a cross—plain dark wood, save for a red shape, painted at its center. *How long has this been here?* Zoe tried to remember the last time, if ever, she'd seen the inside of Warren's dressing room closet. She got up, moved toward it.

Up close, she saw that the red shape was a heart—not a Valentine, but a fairly realistic painting of a human heart, bulging veins and all. A crown of black thorns squeezed the top of the organ, which oozed deep red rivulets at the points of contact. Zoe grimaced. "Is this a prop?"

Dana shook her head. "He must have brought it back from Mexico." She got up, took a few steps nearer and peered into the closet. "God it's . . . it's awful, isn't it?" she said. "That isn't for the record."

"Obviously."

"Maybe it was a present from someone special. You know, so he couldn't throw it away?"

Zoe nodded. "Not much regifting potential."

They heard footsteps, and instinctively, Dana closed the closet door. Within moments, Warren stepped into the room, shirtless and thumbing his BlackBerry. The publicist said, "There you are," and Warren jumped a little.

"Christ, Dana, you scared the hell out of . . ." His gaze rested on Zoe, and her pulse sped up. "Zoe Greene." He said her name as if it were his favorite dish.

"How was San Esteban?" Zoe breathed. "I hear you went there on vacation?"

He gave her a weary smile, then poked at his BlackBerry a few more times and set it down on top of the highlighted scripts. "Not a halfway decent bagel in that entire freakin' town."

Seconds later, Zoe's cell phone vibrated against her hip. She plucked it out of its carrier and glanced at the screen: NEW MESSAGE. Zoe scrolled to her text messages, clicked on the new one, sent from Warren's BlackBerry.

Dana asked Warren, "You got time for a quickie?"

"Long as your husband doesn't mind."

Dana giggled. "Interview. With Zoe."

"Sure," he said.

The message said, DINNER 8:00 LEONE'S? Zoe looked up at Warren and, as imperceptibly as she could, nodded. Then she pulled her microcassette recorder out of her purse and clicked it on. "Why did you decide to leave daytime?"

"I'd like to spread my wings creatively—do some stage-work, films, maybe even direct," he said. "My ten years on *Day's End* have been very fulfilling, but . . ." He took a breath, and Zoe caught a glimpse of something new in his eyes—a flatness, as if a door behind them had just slammed shut. "I'm ready to move on."

"Won't you miss the show?"

"Of course." He smiled, and the flatness was gone. Maybe she'd just imagined it. . . . "I'll miss these interviews, too. I'll miss . . . all of you wonderful people in the soap opera press."

"What a charmer, huh?" said Dana.

A male voice called out over the speaker system, "Matthias to wardrobe! Your new bloody shirt is ready."

"Sorry to cut this short, ladies," Warren said.

Zoe picked up his BlackBerry. "Don't forget this."

As she gave it to him, their hands touched. It was like the smallest sip of water after three weeks in the desert.

"I really will miss these interviews," Warren said softly.

Zoe's throat clenched a little. She swallowed hard, but her expression managed to stay neutral; her cheeks were cool. She removed her gaze from his face and glanced at the screen, at the list of e-mails he'd received. She saw her own name in the "FROM" field, wondered if Dana had noticed, too, how she would explain it should Dana ask. . . . *Oh, I was just doing some fact-checking on an earlier interview.* . . . Then Zoe noticed another name—both under her own and over it, again and again and again. . . .

Vanessa St. James. It sounded familiar.

On the TV in Zoe's cubicle, Claire Caldwell was telling her philandering husband, Dr. Matthias Caldwell, that he'd ruined her life, as their daughter, Hayley, looked on, cheeks glistening with silent tears. "I should have known better than to trust you!"

A whole lot of emoting was going on—that was for sure. Normally, Zoe would have sent Warren a teasing text message about it. (*Should I have known better than to trust u?*) But at the moment, she was focused on her computer.

Via Nexis, she'd found dozens of articles, photo spreads and news items on the name she'd seen on Warren's Black-Berry, Vanessa St. James. And, while she hadn't gone through all of them, she'd read enough to know that *Rolling Stone* had dubbed the fifty-five-year-old supergroupie "the eighth wonder of the world," that Gene Simmons had once offered to buy her a small Caribbean island and that, at Zoe's age, she had incapacitated all four members of Mötley Crüe for a week.

Despite her reckless youth, she seemed to have aged stunningly. Zoe stared at a PDF she'd downloaded from an eight-month-old *People* "Where Are They Now?" piece—Vanessa reclining on a chaise longue, wearing nothing but a white string bikini, a silver cross around her neck and an all-too-knowing smile. . . .

What is her connection with Warren?

She heard the electronic trill of her desk phone, muted the TV and picked it up to her boss's voice. "How'd the interview go, sweetie?"

Zoe winced. *Sweetie* was not a word you wanted to hear from hard-edged Kathy Kinney. *Sweetie* was always bad news.

"Interview?"

"With Warren Clark."

Zoe inhaled sharply. "Fine. I mean . . . not terribly memorable, but . . ."

"Did Warren tell you why he was leaving the show?"

"He said he wanted to spread his wings creatively."

"Did he say *when* he decided to spread 'em?"

"When? Uh . . ."

"I ask, sweetie, because I just got off the phone with a friend of mine—a lawyer who handles *Day's End's* contracts. . . ."

"Okay."

"Warren reupped five weeks ago."

"What?!"

"You never knew about that."

"No." It was true. She'd never known. *Ten years on a soap is enough. I'm thirty-five. Now's the time. . . .* He'd told her over Chinese takeout at his place, but when? *I've been thinking about this for a while now, and . . .* Four weeks ago.

"I've been hearing rumors," Kathy said.

"What—was he fired after re-upping?"

Kathy snorted. "Who the hell would fire Warren Clark?"

"Well, then what—"

"I heard he's leaving *Day's End* because of a woman."

Zoe coughed.

"In Mexico."

"Mexico?" Zoe stared at her computer screen, as if she expected Vanessa St. James to answer her.

"All I can say is, she must be an *earth-shattering* lay if she could make him back out of a contract like *that* one. . . ." Kathy kept speaking, but Zoe didn't hear. She was too busy reading the tiny caption under the bikini photo. . . .

ST. JAMES RELAXES AT HOME IN SAN ESTE-BAN, MEXICO.

Kathy said, "I need you to find out who the Mexican babe is and how close they are. If he's marrying her next week, I'd better not find out from *Soap Opera Digest.*"

Zoe gritted her teeth; her jaw stiffened. "I'll ask around," she said.

TWO

Zoe had been best friends with Steve Sorensen for six years, ever since their mothers—members of the same mystery book club at the Tarrytown library—had set them up on a blind date. As an undergrad at Cornell, Steve had been a star hockey player, and at thirty-three he'd managed to more or less maintain his big, imposing build. He shared a lot of surprising things in common with Zoe—from a fascination with cheesy seventies rock operas to a preference for anchovies on his pizza—and he was good-looking, too, in an all-American, Wheaties-eating kind of way. But Steve was also dependable, protective, honest—all qualities that ensured Zoe would never be attracted to him. And, despite the gleam that sometimes crept into his eyes late at night after a few too many Heinekens, the feeling seemed mutual.

Like Zoe, Steve had been a metro crime reporter when they'd met, but unlike Zoe he still was—at Manhattan-based daily the *Trumpet*. The curiosity she'd worked so hard to drum out of herself, that urge to get to the bottom of any story—Steve still had that, which was the main reason why she hadn't mentioned Warren's name to Steve during the four months Warren and she had been involved. Steve would have kept her secret, she knew, but she couldn't take all the inevitable questions—especially *why*, which would have been at the top of his list. Steve wasn't exactly a soap fan.

Two hours before she was supposed to meet Warren for dinner at Leone's, Zoe was sitting with Steve at their favorite bar—a loud, cavernous place called Katie O'Donnell's on Fiftieth and Third. Katie's was packed, like it always was at happy hour. Some woman's elbow kept knocking Zoe in the back of the head, while a pin-striped Wall Street type leaned against Steve's broad back like a lover, repeatedly shouting, "Excuse me!" at the oblivious, head-shaved bartender. For years, Zoe and Steve had been meeting here for Friday night happy hours. They loved it because it was cheap and close to both of their workplaces, but Zoe was beginning to think she was getting too old for this scene. Maybe she could stomach a couple extra dollars a drink or ten more blocks of walking if it meant she could pivot a few inches without some junior lawyer's beer-stained tie flopping into her eyes.

Steve was oblivious, though. He lived on the Lower East Side, in a rent-stabilized apartment the size of *Headquarters'* bathroom, next door to a constantly arguing family of five. For him, this place probably seemed like a spa.

Right now, he was talking about a story he was working on—an exposé involving one of the higher-ups in the mayor's office taking bribes from a strip club owner with mob connections. Zoe was having a hard time keeping all the names straight—it had been years since she'd purposely stopped following the news, plus she could barely hear Steve over the din of customers. Still more distracting though was Zoe's thought process. She'd absorb a few words, and then her mind would wander to Warren, to the rumors Kathy had heard, to Vanessa St. James in her string bikini. . . .

"She had three screaming orgasms in a row," said Steve. "And still she wouldn't give me anything."

"*What?* Who?"

"Desiree. The stripper. My *source*." He stared at her. "You haven't been listening to me, have you?"

"I have, but did you just say—"

"Screaming orgasms are drinks, Zoe. Vodka, Baileys and Kahlúa."

"Oh, right. Sorry. It's just so loud in here, I think I missed the . . . the drink part."

He sighed. "Anyway, I wished you were at the bar with us."

She tried a smile. "Actually, I prefer my screaming orgasms in the privacy of my own home."

"Seriously . . . you would have known what to say to her. You could always get sources to open up."

I'll miss . . . all of you wonderful people in the soap opera press.
"Not always."

"Huh?"

"Nothing." She took a long pull off her glass of wine—a nice pinot noir that took the chill out of the air-conditioning and soothed her nerves a little. "Call Desiree now. Tell her you hate to bother her, but you've been put on probation and you're scared to death your boss is going to fire you over this story. Tell her she'll never be named, you'll get on-the-record sources to back her up. Promise her Deep Throat–level anonymity . . . and be prepared to give it to her. But tell her you need her to talk because *your job depends on it*."

"And that will work because . . ."

"She's scared to death of her boss, too. Talking to sources is like dating, Steve. You get a lot farther if you have something in common."

He raised an eyebrow at her. "I never have anything in common with my dates."

"Which explains your decadelong dry spell." She yanked his cell phone out of his shirt pocket and handed it to him. "Call her."

"I will." Steve placed the phone on the bar. "Later." He gave Zoe a long, probing look that confused her a little. "Okay. I give," he said finally. "What did he do?"

"What are you talking about?"

"The dude—the one you've been with for the past . . . what? Three months? You guys have a fight or something?"

Zoe gasped, audibly. In an attempt to avoid responding right away, she took a massive gulp of her wine, but it went down the wrong way and she started to choke. Steve pushed the Wall Streeter aside and started slapping Zoe on the back, as the bartender asked, "Does she need the Heimlich? I know the Heimlich," and the woman with the elbow shoved a glass of water under Zoe's nose, saying, "Drink, drink," in a slow, soothing voice.

Finally, she managed to croak, "I'm okay," and everyone calmed down. Everyone, that is, except her. "What makes you think I've been seeing somebody?"

"You're my best friend, Zoe. I'd be a pretty lame reporter if I couldn't figure *that* out."

She exhaled. For about three and a half seconds, she considered lying to Steve—telling him something like, *Well, guess what, Seymour Hersh. You're wrong.* But the fact was, Zoe was hurt and confused and sick and tired of covering it all up. The truth bubbled up inside her, as it often did when she was with Steve, and this time, she didn't force it back down. Why should she? What did she owe Warren Clark? "It's been four months, not three," she said. "And I've got a pretty good idea he's going to dump me tonight."

*   *   *

"Stand him up." Those three words had been Steve's entire reaction to the twenty or so minutes Zoe had spent describing her four months in the thrall of the male Susan Lucci, from "Your eyes are incredible" all the way up to Vanessa St. James.

Simple as that advice was, Zoe had to admit there was a certain beauty to it. *Stand him up before he dumps you. Never speak to him again. Don't give him the relief of saying goodbye.*

Only a guy could come up with a suggestion like that. But Zoe couldn't bring herself to follow it. She was not a guy. She had to see this thing through.

After three pinots at Katie's with Steve, Zoe was now sitting alone at the table that Warren had reserved for them at Leone's—their usual spot in the back, next to the fireplace. She was working on her fourth pinot and feeling no pain. Scratch that. She *was* feeling pain—lots of it—but after three and three-quarter glasses of wine, it was at least the type of pain she could live with.

Warren was fifteen minutes late. Zoe was starting to wonder if maybe *he* was standing *her* up, when she noticed him by the front door, involved in some kind of hushed, intense conversation with the head waiter. She watched him for a while before he caught a glimpse of her, ended whatever it was he was saying and hurried across the restaurant to their table.

"Hi, beautiful." He took the chair across from hers. His face was flushed. Above his smooth upper lip, she noticed a faint sheen of sweat. "Have you been waiting long?"

Zoe finished the rest of her glass of wine and dabbed at her mouth with her napkin. She started to tell Warren she'd been waiting for fifteen minutes, but then she decided, what was the point? He knew how long she'd been here. He had a damn watch. So instead, she called the waiter over and ordered another glass of wine.

"You okay?" said Warren.

She looked into those sky blue eyes of his—so pure a color it was sort of ironic when you thought about it—and she felt as if she were on camera, playing out some awful soap opera scene. Her gaze went from Warren's symmetrical face to the dripless red candle in its sparkling crystal holder on the immaculate white tablecloth, to the basket of dried flowers and herbs (fake, she was sure; they were that flawless), placed in the center of the white brick fireplace—a fireplace that was never lit, no matter what time of year—and it occurred to her that nothing here was real, nothing at all. *I should have known better than to trust you. . . .*

"I'm sorry I'm late," Warren said. "It was my last day on set and everyone wanted to say goodbye."

Another waiter—the same one Warren had been speaking to at the door—showed up with Zoe's pinot, a huge smile plastered on his face, as the busboy poured glasses of ice water. "Are you two ready to order?" the waiter said, his voice cheerful to the point of parody.

Warren said, "Give us a minute," as Zoe lifted the wineglass to her lips and drained it like a vampire.

The waiter stepped away. This latest glass warmed her face and made her feel kind of floaty, anesthetized. She could barely feel her lips moving, yet she heard her own voice, calm and dull, as if she were cold reading a line from a script. "I know about her."

The blue eyes widened. "What are you talking about?!"

Zoe sipped her ice water. "You reupped your contract five weeks ago and changed your mind a week later," she said. "I know why."

"It's not . . . I did that because . . . because I . . ."

His voice trailed off. She watched him—the slight twitch at the side of the mouth, the hand gripping the wineglass so tightly, as if he were juicing it for lies. "You thrive on secrets, don't you, Warren? You and I are secret, but that's not enough. She's the secret you've been keeping from *me*."

"Zoe, that is not—"

"You like to keep things hidden. Everything's got to be in the dark, tucked away . . . Like that cross at the back of your dressing room closet."

Slowly, Warren put down the glass and stared at her. His mouth tightened, and Zoe saw it in his eyes again, just as she had during the interview. *That flatness . . .* "Why were you looking in my closet?"

The waiter stepped up. "Shall I bring you the *special* appetizer?"

"This isn't a good time," Warren said.

After the waiter left, he repeated it, louder. "*Why were you looking in my closet?*" The stare bored into her, chilled her.

What is wrong with him? Zoe's mouth was dry. The skin tingled on the back of her neck, and for the briefest of moments, she was afraid of Warren—or at least, of the way he was looking at her. "The . . . the door was open," she said slowly. "But your dressing room closet is really *not the issue here.*"

His gaze started to soften. Soon, the flatness dissolved. "I'm sorry," he said. "I'm just . . . I'm confused."

The fear lingered, but before too long the wine had taken care of it. *You're hurt. You're paranoid. You're a little bit drunk. . . .*

Zoe said, "You're in love with Vanessa St. James."

"*What?*"

"You went to San Esteban to be with her. You're leaving *Day's End* to be with her. You're leaving *me* to be with her, so why don't you just tell me and get it over—"

"Oh, my God, you think—"

"I don't think. I *know*."

He was actually smiling.

Zoe said, "How . . . how can you . . . ?"

Warren called the waiter over and said, "We'll take the special appetizer."

"No, we will not." Zoe started to get up.

"Please sit down."

"Forget it."

"Please."

Zoe could feel several sets of eyes on her—other customers, that horrible waiter. . . . She dropped back into the chair and glared at Warren.

"Vanessa St. James," he said, "is old enough to be my mother."

"Give me a break. I've seen her picture and I've seen all your text messages to her so don't even try and—"

"She is my *friend*. She's . . . she's been having some family troubles, and she was confiding in me." He took a breath. "Now, as for leaving my job. Man . . . I didn't expect it to go down like this."

The demonic waiter placed a covered dish in front of her. "Your special appetizer, *miss*," he said.

"I don't want an appetizer."

"Take the cover off," Warren said to the waiter.

"I told you, Warren, I—"

"Take the *damn cover off now*."

Quickly, the waiter removed the cover. The plate beneath was empty, save for a small silver key glistening at its center. Zoe stared at it, then at Warren. "What is this?"

"It's yours," he said. "It's a key to my house. In San Esteban."

"Oh . . ."

"Yeah, I reupped. If you'd seen my new contract, you'd understand why. But one night . . . Remember that Monday, when you spent the night at my place? You had to leave at five in the morning because you wanted to get home to shower and change for work?"

Zoe nodded.

"I watched you that night. I watched you sleeping. I touched your face and you smiled in your sleep—like a reflex—and I thought, 'I don't want her to go home. Ever.'"

Zoe looked into his eyes. *No flatness, no closed doors, only light . . .*

"That's what made me change my mind," he said. "There is no other woman, Zoe. Just you."

"Warren, you're . . . you're asking me to . . ."

"I'm heading back down there tomorrow. I know it's sudden, but you have some time off, right? How about you take your three weeks, spend it with me in San Es?"

Zoe stared at him, her eyes starting to well up.

"If you like it," he said softly, "maybe you don't have to use the return ticket."

A tear trickled down her cheek.

He leaned across the table, brushed it away. "Is that a yes?" he said softly.

"Yes," she said, "yes, yes, yes, yes . . ." until he kissed her, and she didn't have to say the word anymore.

Zoe and Warren skipped dinner. They took a cab back to his place—a sleek, thirty-story building on Fiftieth and Tenth overlooking the Hudson River—and though they managed to do nothing more than hold hands during the ride over, the walk to the elevator proved excruciating . . . especially considering the lengthy wait Zoe knew was in store for them once the doors closed; Warren lived on the top floor.

Warren pushed the button, and then he turned to Zoe with that look in his eyes that always moved her. It was so real, she could physically feel it—that want turning to ache. Then his lips were on her neck, and his hands were on her waist and sliding under her blouse, and all Zoe could think of was how long it had been. *Three weeks, three years, three centuries* . . . She glanced at the numbers over the door; the elevator was between floors four and five. "Stop it."

"Huh?"

"Stop . . . the elevator."

Warren leaned back for a moment, his hands still moving on her, and grinned. "You're ser—"

"Yes."

Without another word, Warren hit the EMERGENCY STOP button. Then he yanked his black T-shirt over his head and threw it on the lens of the surveillance camera. He grabbed Zoe around the waist and lifted her up, pinning her against the closed elevator doors. God, but he was strong. Her pulse raced. Her entire body throbbed for him. Before she even realized it, her shirt was off, and she felt the cool metal doors against her back and his hard chest pressed into hers. His lips moved on the hollow of her throat, his voice thick and shaky from wanting her. "We've only got a few minutes before security—"

"I only *need* a few minutes." Restrictive as this position was, Zoe's fingers could still reach Warren's belt buckle. She took full advantage of that.

Nothing was happening fast enough. The more she felt of Warren, the more she wanted and she wanted it now, sooner than now. She despised his jeans, the button-front fly—*Who came up with that idiotic invention?* She loathed every item of clothing on his body and her own; they were nothing but barriers, time wasters.

Between the two of them, though, they managed to peel away the essential layers, push them aside or worse—Zoe felt her skirt rip at the waist, the button flying off—as the alarm shrieked, drowning out the sound of their frantic breathing.

When Warren was finally inside her, it was like regaining one of her senses. Zoe started to cry out. He put a hand over her mouth and whispered, "Someone might hear," his breath hot and ragged against her collarbone. That did it. She groaned into his palm, pressing her hips to him as a current shot through her, all the way up her spine and into the base of her scalp, just as she felt him release. *Perfect timing*. She collapsed onto him, not just spent but drained. Filleted.

At that exact moment, a deep voice emanated from the elevator's speaker system. "Security."

Zoe and Warren burst out laughing.

"Are you all right in there?" said the voice.

"We're fine!" Warren called out. He kissed her gently, and she opened her eyes to his—pure and blue and content. Briefly, Zoe remembered the look in Warren's eyes when she'd mentioned the cross in his closet, and a chill rippled through her, a prickling of the skin that stretched across her shoulder blades. She used to call it *hinky*, that feeling, back when she was a crime reporter and couldn't get enough cop slang. But whatever she called it then, whatever she felt like renaming it now—this unease, this sketchy sense of dread . . . It didn't stick around long enough to matter.

THREE

Warren snored. It wasn't of the log-sawing variety—it was more like a purr. Zoe found it endearing, which showed how bad she truly had it for him now. She liked the sound of his snore.

It was close to midnight. As soon as they'd gotten into Warren's apartment, he'd gone online and bought her a round-trip ticket to León Airport leaving Monday night. He'd given her his user's code ("In case you decide to say screw your boss and change your ticket for an earlier one."), and then they'd gone to bed.

Zoe and Warren had time now and so they'd taken it, the sex so slow and languorous that each sensation seemed to reverberate. When they came—eyes open, gasping together—tears rolled down Zoe's face, yet she couldn't say a word. It occurred to her that she might have lost her ability to speak forever—and that if she had, it would have been worth it.

"Where did you learn how to *do* that?" she had asked, once her voice returned.

"From you," he'd said. "Just now."

Zoe rested her head on Warren's chest, listening to him snore, feeling his heartbeat against the side of her face, until she realized she'd never get to sleep this way, not with how she was feeling.

She had to tell Steve she was going to Mexico.

Zoe crept into the living room, where her phone was charging, flipped it open and tapped in his number. She fully expected to get his voice mail; Steve was on weekend shift at the *Trumpet* this month, meaning he had to be in the office by eight the next morning and was probably home asleep.

To her surprise, though, he picked up after one ring: "It's about time you called."

Zoe heard voices in the background, Gwen Stefani yodeling over a massive speaker system, some guy shouting, "No way! Dude! No way!" so earsplittingly loud, you'd think he was trying to flag down a rescue party. "Don't tell me you're still at Katie's," Zoe said.

"Ran into a bunch of *Trumpet* people! Everybody keeps buying me drinks to celebrate!"

"Celebrate what?"

"Desiree talked. She even put me in touch with an ex-employee who'll go on the record. Your advice totally worked, Zoe. You're a genius."

Zoe smiled. "Hey, listen, speaking of celebrating . . ."

"You dumped the douche bag actor!"

"No, we talked and . . . Believe it or not, he and I are in a great place."

No reply, so Zoe went on. "Warren says he and Vanessa St. James are just friends."

"And you believe him?"

"Under the circumstances, yes. He invited me to his place in Mexico, Steve. Gave me a key to his house and everything. . . . I'm leaving Monday—"

"*This* Monday?"

"If I can get the three weeks out of my boss . . ." Zoe shuddered. "That reminds me. Please don't tell any of your *Trumpet* friends about this. If it gets back to Kathy I'm in San Esteban with Warren Clark, she will *freak out*. She might even fire me for not tell—"

"San Esteban." Steve's voice sounded strange, hollow. "That's where his place is?"

"Have you heard of it? Mountain town, about three hours south of Texas. Lots of American hippies, retirees who think they're artists . . ."

"San Esteban," he said, "is where Jordan Brink was killed."

"Jordan Brink?"

He spoke very slowly. "The kid from Queens? The one who got his heart cut out."

"*What?*"

"You didn't hear? It was on the cover of every paper last weekend."

Zoe's breath caught. "Last weekend?"

"Happened last Friday night. It was in the *Post*, the *News*, the *Times*, bottom of the front page. . . . The kid was on drugs in the desert, and somebody got him and . . . I can't believe I have to *tell* you about this!"

Zoe squeezed her eyes shut. "I . . . I don't read newspapers, Steve. You know that."

Steve didn't say anything. Zoe heard a deep voice yelling, "Sorensen! Get off the phone and have another drink!" a group of women shrilling along with Gwen, the echo of countless indistinguishable customers laughing and fighting and shouting to be heard, customers who were drunk and oblivious to some random killing in Mexico. "Hello? Steve?"

Finally, he spoke. "It's bad enough you threw away the

best job in the world to go work at a fanzine. Now you're sabotaging that job to shack up with a—"

"I'm not sabotaging—"

"Okay, maybe that's an exaggeration. But I can't believe he didn't tell you about the murder. Jesus, it happened *one week ago!*"

"He probably didn't want to upset me. Or maybe he didn't know."

"*Everybody* knew."

"I didn't."

"Stop sounding so *proud* of that!"

Zoe said nothing, just breathed into the phone.

"You need to get back in the real world, Zoe," Steve said. "You've got to stop blaming yourself for what happened with—"

"I don't want to talk about this."

"You *need* to talk about it."

"Don't tell me what I need."

"It was five years ago," he said, "and what he did to those women *was never your fault to begin with*. You were an awesome reporter—the best—and you just threw it away because of—"

"That's enough."

"You're going to a goddamn *crime scene* with some dickhead you barely know and—"

"I said, that's enough!"

"It's all because of *Daryl Barclay*."

Zoe's breath got shallow at the sound of the name. Her fists tightened as in her mind, a plank gave way and she began to sink. "I'm going to hang up now, Steve," she said quietly. And she did, before he could say another word.

Jordan Brink, said a voice in the darkness. *That one in San Esteban wasn't me, wasn't my style. You know that. . . .* Zoe couldn't see, but she knew who was speaking. After all, that was all he'd ever been to her—a voice on the phone, calling her pet names, sneaking into her nightmares. . . .

Daryl Barclay. The Barber-Butcher. Her last exclusive.

Boys aren't me, kitten. Mexico isn't me. And besides . . . The voice turned to hot liquid and seared her face. *I'm on hiatus.*

A bright light flipped on and she saw Barclay at the foot of the bed. His head was shaved, as it had been in the court room, his skin pale gray, like the skin of his victims. He smiled wide—wide enough for Zoe to see that gold tooth . . . the one he'd told her about. . . . *Melted down a lady's ring to make it. My first lady. For a while, I kept the finger, too.*

"You're not real," she whispered. "Go away."

I'd like to show you something.

Zoe wanted to close her eyes, but she couldn't. She watched Daryl Barclay's tattooed arm swing around from behind his back, his big fist stopping inches from her face. She watched the fist open. At the center of Barclay's palm was a human heart, still beating.

Pa-dum-pa-dum-pa-dum . . .

Blood coursed out of it, spilling over the hand, splashing onto the floor in thick globs.

Check out the top.

Zoe stared at the thing stretched across the top of the heart, piercing it in places. She began to shake.

Looks familiar, right? Art imitates life, right? RIGHT?

It was a crown of black thorns.

Wonder what else your man keeps in his closet!

Zoe's eyes sprung open. Her pulse was beating so hard, it constricted her throat, made it hard to breathe. Her gaze darted around the room, and for a few panicky seconds she had no idea where she was. "Okay," she said out loud. The sound of her own voice calmed her a little, brought her back to reality. She heard the echo of car engines on the West Side Highway and felt filtered sunlight on her face, and she knew she was in Warren's bed and that it was morning. *A dream.* Zoe hadn't dreamed about Daryl Barclay in four years.

Listening for Warren's snore, Zoe heard nothing. She stretched out to touch him, but instead of warm skin, she felt a tangle of small, sharp . . . *Thorns.* She let out a thin gasp, then made herself turn, look . . .

On Warren's pillow was a bouquet of long-stemmed red roses.

Zoe let out a burst of laughter—pure nerves. Then she took a few breaths, picked up the note that lay next to the bouquet.

Off to the airport. See you in two days.

I.L.Y.,
W

I.L.Y? Zoe gaped at the initials, her pulse quickening for different reasons. Had Warren just told her he loved her?

"Goodbye, Eddie, Goodbye" from Brian DePalma's *Phantom of the Paradise* jolted out of the living room. It was Zoe's ring tone—a birthday present from Steve; she still couldn't figure out how he'd ever found that song. Zoe scrambled out of bed, hoping it was Steve calling to apologize over the Barclay thing. Maybe they could get a cup of coffee, try the conversation again when he wasn't drunk in a bar. But when she flipped the phone open, she saw the *Headquarters* number on her screen. Who was calling her from work on a Saturday? "Uh . . . hello?"

"Breaking news, sweetie," Kathy said. "I need to see you at the office. Now." Her voice sounded cheerful enough.

But the "breaking news" part troubled Zoe. Kathy in the office on a Saturday bothered her, too.

And *sweetie.* That was never a good thing.

Kathy Kinney had taken the job of *Headquarters'* editor-in-chief one year ago, after spending sixteen years as a senior reporter for the world's sleaziest supermarket tabloid, the *Asteroid.* Kathy was slender and blond, with an elegant, Grace Kelly–ish way of moving and the kindest blue eyes Zoe had ever seen. If there was one thing she didn't seem like, it was a tabloid reporter.

Until she started talking.

"Fuck took you so long?" said Kathy, as soon as Zoe walked into her office.

"Subway was late."

Kathy nodded. "Have a seat."

Kathy's office was crazily feminine. She'd inherited it from the previous editor-in-chief—a vanilla cupcake of a woman by the name of Marcie Gordon—and had never gotten around to redecorating. Love seats covered in rosy chintz, whispery pink draperies, Monet prints of haystacks, white wicker like it was going extinct . . . The place was bubbly spring water to the boiling oil that was Kathy Kinney. It made Zoe laugh—well, it would have, if she wasn't so nervous every time she got called in here.

"So what's the breaking news?" Zoe said.

Kathy smiled—a cheerleader's smile, the bright blue eyes sparkling as they took in Zoe's outfit—a tank top and skirt she'd gone all the way back to her apartment to switch into. Kathy took a sip from the bottle of water she always kept with her. (Zoe had heard Kathy drank so much water so she'd have to go to the bathroom a lot. Apparently, she got her best scoops from women's restrooms.) "Too bad you didn't bring a change of clothes." Kathy winked. "You would have gotten here a lot sooner."

Zoe felt the color draining out of her face. Her mouth was instantly parched. She didn't like that wink, didn't like it at all. . . . "What do you mean?"

Kathy smiled. "Tell me something, sweetie. When were you planning on letting me know you've been playing hide the kielbasa with the biggest star on daytime?"

"I don't know what you're talking about!" Zoe said, without missing a beat. Unfortunately, her voice was a full octave higher than its usual range.

Kathy got up from her desk, circled around Zoe's chair. "You're really going to make me do this."

"Do what?"

She sighed heavily. Like everyone else at *Soap Opera Headquarters*, Kathy had a TV in her office—a large flat-screen that hung on her wall, over a white wicker dresser with a DVD player on top. Kathy walked over to it. "When I heard Warren Clark was leaving because of a woman," she said, "I figured, why not find a source of my own?" She slid open one of the top drawers and removed an unlabeled DVD. "I found me a security guard."

As she placed the disk inside the player, a deep cringe overtook Zoe's body—an embarrassment so powerful she couldn't move, couldn't speak. *A security guard . . .*

Kathy hit PLAY, and the screen sparked to life—grainy black-and-white surveillance footage of the inside of an elevator. Warren's elevator. Yesterday's date flashed in the lower left corner of the screen. Zoe managed to croak, "Kathy—"

"Sssh."

Before long, they were watching images of Warren and herself . . . black-and-white, yes. Grainy, yes, but oh, so very, very identifiable.

"I don't know what to say."

On-screen, Warren removed his black T-shirt and mercifully threw it over the lens. "Not much *to* say," Kathy snickered, "when you're starring in surveillance-camera porn."

"I'm so sorry," she said. "I . . . It really hasn't been going on for that long, and—"

"Save the details for the cover story, sweetie."

"The *cover story?*"

"We're gonna call it 'My Red-Hot Nights with Warren Clark.' A thousand words. You can write it under a pseudonym, but I want every detail down to his shoe size . . . and I want it by Monday, so his leaving the show will still be hot news. We'll turn 'Matthias's Shocking Death' into a sidebar and . . ."

Zoe stared at her.

"What? Don't like the hed? I'm not married to it. How about 'My Steamy Trysts with Warren Clark'?"

"Kathy," Zoe said, "Warren and me . . . That's nobody's business."

The sparkling eyes narrowed. "I sincerely hope you're joking."

"I . . . I know it was a conflict of interest. I didn't intend for it to happen."

"The heart wants what it wants."

"That's . . . that's *right.*"

"Know who said that? Woody Allen. Right after Mia Farrow caught him screwing her daughter."

"Look, Kathy. I have real feelings for this man, and he's very private. I can't just *write* about—"

"Let me explain something to you," Kathy said. "What you've been doing with Clark is highly unethical. It's grounds for dismissal. I'm giving you a chance to make it all right again. You don't take that chance— fine, that's your prerogative." Without removing her gaze from Zoe's face, she drained the rest of the water bottle and tossed it in the trash. "But it is my prerogative to fire you."

Zoe swallowed, blood thrumming in her ears. *Five years,* she thought. *Half a decade of working here, and it comes down to this.* "You don't give me much choice."

Kathy nodded. "I'm glad you under—"

"I quit."

Zoe walked to the DVD player. She removed the surveillance tape, placed it into the jewel box and slipped it into her purse. "I can't believe this," Kathy said.

Neither could Zoe. But she tried not to let it show on her face. "Bye, Kathy," she said. "It's been interesting." And with that, she walked out of the offices of *Soap Opera Headquarters* and left her job forever.

Within two hours, Zoe was all packed and had changed her travel arrangements online. Within three, she'd stopped her mail, canceled any plans she had for the next three weeks, called her parents to let them know she'd be gone and left a message on Warren's voice mail, asking him to pick her up at the León airport at seven o'clock that evening.

Within four, she was in a cab, and within six, she was on a plane bound for Mexico. Only then, when the seat belt sign went off and she lifted the little plastic shade and peered down at the clouds, the rays of the setting sun spilling through them like blood—only then did she think, *What the hell am I doing?*

FOUR

If there was one thing that Steve found more irritating than a slow Saturday in the office, it was a slow Saturday in the office with a hangover. He shouldn't have had so much to drink the previous night, but when the executive editor is buying—which he was, repeatedly—it's hard to say no.

Steve was due to meet Desiree and her on-the-record ex-stripper friend at a nearby Starbucks after work. (The ex-stripper was apparently a huge *Star Wars* fan; her stage name had been Padmé.) But even though this was the first break he'd had on the bribe scandal in over a month, Steve's heart wasn't in it. He kept thinking about Zoe—Zoe, who never read news anymore. . . .

It was around five and Steve sat in the newsroom in front of his computer. For the hell of it, he ran a Nexis search—Jordan Brink + Warren Clark. But it yielded only one abstract, from a two-month-old *Soap Opera Headquarters* article written, ironically, by Zoe: *American Idol* winner **Jordin** Sparks is slated to guest star on *The Day's End*. "We're thrilled to work with her," says **Warren Clark** (Matthias). "**Jordin** is on the **brink** of international stardom."

Nexis was such an asshole sometimes. Steve would've rolled his eyes if it weren't for the hangover.

"Doing something on the Brink murder?"

Without turning, Steve recognized the reedy Southern accent. Glen Campbell. Not *the* Glen Campbell, of course. This Glen was a new reporter, fresh out of Northwestern's journalism school and annoyingly eager to please. Glen was Steve's new BFF since the previous night, which was Steve's fault. At the height of his intoxication, he'd asked Campbell to sing him a few lines of "Wichita Lineman." Glen had laughed hysterically, even though it was obvious he had no idea what Steve was talking about. Then he'd spent the whole night sitting next to him, hanging on his every word. If Glen had been a woman, Steve would've been trying to chew his own arm off this morning for sure.

"Kinda busy right now, dude." Steve hated it when people read his screen, and here, Campbell was ogling his Nexis search like it was Swedish porn. "What are you doing in the office, anyway? You're not on weekend shift."

"Thought I'd see if anybody needed any . . . Wait. Warren Clark? Are you serious? You're thinking Warren Clark the soap star had something to do with Jordan Brink?"

"Clark has a place in that Mexican town, and he was there when it happened—that's all. Thought I'd try and find some leads, see if maybe they knew each—"

"Celebrity angle. Good thinking. That's why they pay you the big bucks!"

"Yeah, I rock. Anyway . . ."

"I want to help."

Steve sighed. "That's nice of you, but I've got this one under control."

"No . . . I mean I've got a great source down there. My

roommate from NU—he works at an English-language paper in Mexico City, and they were all over the Jordan Brink story. You want me to call him, see if he knows anything?"

Steve glanced at him. "Sure. Why not?" At the very least, it would get Glen away from his desk for a few minutes.

After Glen left, Steve looked at his watch. Less than an hour and a half from now, he'd be meeting Padmé. It occurred to him that he had no idea what kind of person she was, what type of approach would yield the most information about her ex-boss. He checked to see if maybe she had a MySpace page, but no such luck. . . . *Talking to sources is like dating, Steve. You get a lot farther if you have something in common.* Steve called up Google and started researching all five *Star Wars* movies, wishing that Zoe had half a clue how good she was.

After about ten minutes, Steve heard, "You're not going to believe this!"

He turned to find Glen, grinning like the proverbial sated cat, so keyed up he was practically bouncing. "Are you about to tell me that Warren Clark *did* know Jordan Brink?"

"No."

Steve exhaled. "Okay, well then—"

"I mean, he might have. . . . But this is even *more interesting.* . . ."

"What?"

"The thing is, we can't run it yet because no one will confirm. My friend thinks she paid off the cops to keep her name out of the press. But listen. . . . *She was questioned by the police in the Brink investigation.*"

"Who is *she?*"

Glen's smile got even bigger. He glanced around the room to make sure no one was listening. Then he leaned in close, brought his voice down to a whisper. "Ever hear of Vanessa St. James?"

* * *

Naomi rapped on her aunt's bedroom door. "Would you mind turning the music down, Aunt Vanessa?" she said.

No response. Her *Sweet Baby James* CD kept playing at top volume. Naomi sighed. Back when her mother was alive, Naomi would never in a million years have guessed that this was where she'd be when she was going into her senior year of high school—stuck in a foreign country, surrounded by adolescents in their fifties and sixties who knew as much about raising kids as they did about . . . God, anything.

James Taylor's voice shook her aunt's closed door. " 'I've seen fire and I've seen rain!' "

Big whoop, sweet baby James. I've seen a boy with his heart cut out. And really, that was what annoyed Naomi more than anything else about her aunt. Here she was, wrecked—both her body and her mind. Her sunburned skin was peeling off in sheets. It stung whenever she bent her knees and her lips hurt so much she could barely manage a glass of water. And while she was okay when she was with other people because she had to be, every time she shut her eyes, she had these nightmares, these awful visions. . . .

Vanessa had taken Naomi to the doctor's today. She herself had heard Dr. Dave say the visions could be post-traumatic stress and yet still . . . *still* Vanessa had managed to make this *all about her.* Naomi's aunt could be self-absorbed, yes, but this was insane.

It made Naomi think, *There's something about Jordan she isn't telling me.*

By all accounts, Vanessa had completely freaked out when Corinne and Sean had come by the house the morning after the bonfire, asking if Naomi had ever gotten home. Vanessa had bribed and badgered a couple of police officers until they'd taken her into the desert in their squad car, and when they'd finally found Naomi, the look of relief on her aunt's face had been so pure and Naomi's head had been so screwed up that at first, she'd confused Vanessa for her mom. Naomi had fallen on Vanessa, never happier to see another human being.

When she'd taken Vanessa and the police to Jordan's body, though, Vanessa had acted strange. She'd gone white and still—which was understandable, considering what she was seeing. *But*—and this was what got Naomi—Vanessa wasn't looking at the maggots. She wasn't looking at the darkly dried blood, or the gaping hole in the chest, like a cannonball had gone through it, or even the heart, which lay a foot up from Jordan's head like a gruesome idea bulb. What she was looking at, what she was *staring* at, was Jordan's hands.

They had been placed at his sides, palms open to the sky. Naomi hadn't noticed this when she'd found the body but following Vanessa's gaze, she saw . . . in each palm, someone had placed a long, daggerlike leaf. The spine of a century plant. As the police officers approached Jordan's body and radioed the station—*Es un muerto . . . Un joven . . . Diez y nueve o veinte años . . . corazón sacado . . .* Vanessa had stood behind them, staring at those spines without moving, without blinking. And then she had mouthed a word: *Grace.*

James Taylor was singing about lonely times when he could not find a friend, the bass in his voice vibrating the terra-cotta floor under Naomi's feet. What was Vanessa *doing* in there? Naomi pressed her ear up to the door. It was the most delicate pine, tailor-made for eavesdropping, yet still Naomi heard no words, no movement . . . nothing other than her aunt's beloved JT, and how he always thought that he'd see you again. . . .

Aunt Vanessa, did you just say "grace"?

I don't know what you're talking about, Naomi.

It sounded like you—

I told you. I said. Nothing.

"Aunt Vanessa? Are you okay in there?"

Not a sound. Not even the creak of the bed. Naomi tried the door. It swung open easily, and the next song, "Blossom," knocked her back like a tsunami. *Who listens to James Taylor at this volume?*

"Aunt Vanessa, that *is not good for your ears!*" shouted Naomi, amazed that she was actually saying this to anyone, let alone her legal guardian. It took her a few seconds to register the room—which was empty. Naomi turned off the stereo. "Vanessa?"

She walked to the master bathroom, knocked. . . . The door drifted open, but there was no one there either. *"Vanessa!"*

Naomi heard a rush of movement on the first floor, someone jogging up the staircase. She hurried into the hallway and ran right into her aunt's tiny maid, Soccoro. *"Su tía se fue,"* Socorro said, catching her breath.

"She *left*?" said Naomi. *"¿A dónde se fue?"*

Soccoro shook her head. *"No sé."*

"You don't know?"

"Dijó que va a regresar en dos o tres horas"

Naomi looked at Soccoro. If her aunt had decided to leave the house for at least two or three hours, why hadn't she told Naomi? Why had she left the stereo on?

As if she was reading her mind, Soccoro told Naomi that Vanessa had received some kind of urgent phone call, she thought maybe from *Señor Clark.*

Naomi rolled her eyes. If anyone could make Vanessa jump and run, it was Warren. "Figures," she said.

"¿Cómo?"

"No es importante." But then Naomi thought, *Maybe it is.* . . . Would Warren be able to tell her why Vanessa was acting so weird? Would he understand what she'd meant by *grace*?

Naomi pictured herself asking him these things and cringed. She found Warren hard to talk to—there was something about him that scared her a little. But maybe she could suck it up, give him a call. . . .

Like a comeback, every telephone in the house shrieked. Soccoro started for the one in Vanessa's bedroom, but Naomi told her that was okay. She'd get it.

The landlines in this town didn't have caller ID, but that didn't stop Naomi from looking at the phone anyway before she picked it up. A habit from her old life with her mom, back in Chicago—she still had a few of them. "*¿Bueno?*"

The voice on the other end was male, and spoke English with a thick Spanish accent. "Vanessa St. James?"

Naomi started to say *No, this is her niece*, but the caller didn't seem interested, or maybe he didn't understand. "I am calling about Jordan Brink," he said, all coldness, all business. "I am with the police."

The flight to León was long and irritating. Zoe had a window seat, but she was stuck next to a teenage boy who seemed to believe it was his God-given right to take up as much space as was humanly possible. For the entire flight, he sat with his legs four feet apart and his hands clasped behind his head, his thick arms fanning out like elephant ears, his right leg pressed into both of Zoe's knees. She had to scrunch down in her chair in order to avoid the elbow in the eye, which she would have complained to him about, if he weren't sound asleep.

No sooner did the plane take off than this mammoth teen started snoring—not a soft purr like Warren's, but a phlegm-fueled locomotive, annoying everyone in the vicinity and making Zoe the object of countless pitying looks.

After trying to negotiate her way around the kid's limbs in order to reach the in-flight magazine, Zoe finally gave up and fell into a light, troubled sleep, her dreams filled with surveillance tape images and bloody human hearts. . . .

She woke up to an alarmingly bumpy descent, the plane riding the clouds like an eighteen-wheeler. No fan of even the mildest turbulence, Zoe pushed the teenager aside, yanked her seat belt tighter and gripped the armrests, as if this were any type of defense against plummeting toward earth, trapped like canned meat in a doomed, helpless piece of metal.

The teenager yawned and stretched, his forearm thwacking Zoe in the mouth. "We there yet?"

Man, she wanted to sock this kid. *"Not. Yet."*

After a seemingly endless series of bumps and jolts, the plane touched ground and rolled to a halt. There were gasps and applause. And when the captain said, "Welcome to Mexico," Zoe was filled with an overwhelming sense of gratitude.

"I really hope you have the most wonderful trip," she told the teenager, who looked at her as if she'd just sprouted another eye.

She couldn't help it, though. Surviving bumpy flights always brought out the George Bailey in her, and today, after quitting her job and hopping on a plane bound for a place she'd never been to stay with a man who had just told her I love you (in so many initials, anyway), the feeling was particularly strong. *It's a wonderful life, and today is the first day of the rest of it.* As they all stood up, the woman in front of Zoe asked her where in Mexico she was going. "San Esteban," Zoe replied.

"Oh, I hear it's beautiful there," said the woman. That was it. No mention of Jordan Brink. Zoe wanted to hug her for that. She turned on her cell phone as everybody started to file out of the plane, and immediately, she heard "Goodbye, Eddie, Goodbye." Steve's number was on the screen. "You've got some timing," said Zoe.

"I've been trying to call you for hours," Steve said. "Where have you been?"

"On a plane, going to Mexico."

"What?!"

"Changed my ticket for tonight," she said. "I didn't feel like sticking around. I quit my job today."

"*What?*"

"You sound like a broken record. Wait—does anybody really use that expression anymore? Would it be cooler if I said you sound like a bad download?"

"You're serious. You're really in Mexico right now."

"Yep."

"Is *he* with you?"

"Warren? No, I'm just getting off the plane." Zoe took a breath. "Listen, Steve. I know this must sound crazy to you, and it probably is, but I survived the flight, and there's no turning back. So spare me the warnings and just let me enjoy my vacation. Okay?"

Steve sighed heavily.

"Thank you." They were disembarking now. Zoe noticed the stubby potted palm trees and deep green aloe plants lining the gate area, the mariachi music playing over the loudspeakers and how, even at night in an airport, everyone seemed to be moving slower, smiling more. She felt a million miles away from New York City, and she liked that feeling a lot.

Steve said, "Can I just tell you one thing?"

"Sure."

"Vanessa St. James was questioned in the Jordan Brink murder."

"*What?*" Zoe's smile dropped away and she froze, causing the tall man behind her to walk straight into her back. She threw an apology at him and moved against the wall. "She was? *Why?*"

"I don't know. I got the info from Glen Campbell and—"

"*Glen Campbell?*"

"One of our younger reporters. He swears his source is good, but apparently the cops down there won't confirm or deny. They're really close to a break in the case."

Zoe breathed, in and out. *She's been having some family troubles. . . .*

"Warren didn't mention it, huh?"

"Not in so many words."

"Don't you think that's weird? Huge murder, his *friend* is questioned. He invites you down, without even a 'by the way'?"

Zoe cleared her throat. "I guess he figured it was none of my business."

"Let me tell you something. If he is planning on introducing you to Vanessa St. James while you're there, it is *absolutely* your business. You don't just let your girlfriend hang out with a murder suspect without—"

"Okay, hold up. You know as well as I do that being *questioned* and being a *suspect* are two entirely different things."

He sighed. "You're right," he said. "I guess I got a little carried away."

"A *little?*"

"Just ask him about it, okay?"

"I will," Zoe said, though she wasn't sure she wanted to. She recalled the flatness in Warren's eyes, the way he had glared at her when she'd mentioned the cross in his closet— something he hadn't planned on telling her about, and come to think of it . . . never had.

Steve said, "Zoe?"

"Yeah?"

"Be careful."

"I always am."

"No," he said. "No, you're really not."

After they said goodbye, Zoe made her way through customs and thought it all through. Her mood lifted a little. Steve was being overprotective, as usual, and overcritical of Warren for some reason. When all was said and done, Warren really hadn't had time to tell Zoe about Vanessa and the Brink murder. They'd been together less that twenty-four hours before he'd taken off again—and they'd had other, more pressing concerns. . . .

He was probably planning on letting her know once he showed her around town and she settled in a little. What was the hurry? She had three weeks to meet Vanessa St. James.

By the time she got to baggage claim, Zoe felt a lot better. She scanned the dozens of faces waiting to greet arrivals. She searched for Warren, hoping he'd gotten her voice mail message because she really didn't feel like negotiating a cab right now. Most everyone was Mexican, though—except a tall, blond couple who stood at the back of the group, embracing as if he'd just come home from the war. *Get a room,* Zoe thought . . . until the couple separated, and she saw the man's profile and her heart dropped. *Warren.*

He spoke animatedly to the blond woman for quite a while before he finally caught sight of Zoe gaping at him. Warren rushed over to her and threw his arms around her and lifted her off the ground. "I'm *so* glad to see you," he said, into her neck.

A frisson went through her, but that just made her mad—his ability to turn her on, even when she had just seconds ago seen him . . . Doing what, exactly?

Warren put her back down and asked her how her flight had been, but Zoe said nothing. The woman he'd been holding so tightly was about ten feet behind him, her back turned, talking on a cell phone. Zoe heard her say, *"Está Señor Rafael allí? No? Qué lástima . . ."*

Zoe tapped her on the shoulder. "Hi."

"Mas tarde," the woman said into her phone, then closed it and turned. "Zoe, right? Look at you! You're just as lovely as Warren said you would be."

Zoe took a few steps back, her knees weakening. She recognized the smile, recognized the face and the body and the cross around the neck, and before she could stop it, the woman's name came flying out of her mouth. "Vanessa St. James."

"Hope you don't mind my tagging along," Vanessa said. "Like I told Warren, I just couldn't wait to meet you."

FIVE

Warren drove a Jeep Cherokee. Although Zoe was no fan of SUVs, she could forgive him for it in this mountainous desert region, where the roads were winding and steep enough to merit four-wheel drive. Of course, she didn't have much choice but to forgive him—for the gas guzzler and for Vanessa St. James. For the duration of the bumpy ride from León to San Esteban, Zoe was stuck with both.

Right now, they were rounding the curve of a mountain path. The moon was nearly full and very bright. It gave the dry terrain a grayish cast, turned the dead-looking patches of vegetation velvety black and made the mountain rocks glow silver. It reminded Zoe of how she used to imagine other planets might look—hostile and beautiful at the same time. There wasn't a sign of human life, either; it had been miles since they'd seen a streetlight. Zoe would have found it all very romantic were it not for the chattering supergroupie in the backseat. Whether the purpose was to calm Zoe or herself—or if Vanessa just loved the sound of her own voice—

Zoe wasn't sure, but since the ride began, Vanessa had been nonstop with the inane questions. "Tell me," she was saying now. "How did you know that Warren was 'the One'?"

Zoe glanced at Warren. He hadn't said much during the ride, but she was hoping he might ask his dear friend to stop auditioning to be the next *View* cohost so Zoe could enjoy the scenery.

She expected him to at least *look* irritated, but no. Warren smiled out at the road as if he were listening to his favorite song from childhood. Zoe thought about the way he'd been hugging Vanessa in the airport, like he hadn't seen her in years. What was that about anyway, when they had come to pick up Zoe together? "I *still* don't know if he's the One," Zoe said.

Vanessa laughed.

"That wasn't supposed to be funny."

"What is going on with you, Zoe?" said Warren.

"*Me?*"

"Yes." His voice was cold. "Ever since you got here, you've seemed determined to be miserable."

Zoe started to tell him that she'd quit her job today—that reality was setting in—that she had at most three months' rent saved up and this was the absolute worst time to take a vacation. But though all that was true, it wasn't her real problem. She turned around in her seat and gave Vanessa St. James a long look. She sensed the confusion in the woman's tigerlike eyes and, behind that, a budding anxiety. "Why were you questioned in the Jordan Brink murder?"

Vanessa's mouth dropped open. "That was . . . No one was supposed to . . ."

Warren said, "How do you know that, Zoe?"

"A friend of mine told me."

"What friend?" said Vanessa. "Was it someone in the press? I specifically told them . . ."

"It's not going in the press. My source told me off the record."

"Your *source?*"

Warren said, "You aren't acting like yourself."

Zoe stared at Warren. "If you want me to act like my-self," she said slowly, "try telling me the truth."

He glared out at the road. "I did tell you the truth."

"What, that Vanessa was having *family problems?*" she said. "If there's just been a brutal murder in the place where I'm going on vacation, don't you think I deserve to know—"

"She *was* having family problems."

Zoe stared at him. "What are you talk—"

Vanessa interrupted her. "My niece discovered Jordan Brink's body."

"Your . . . niece?"

"I didn't want it in the press because they had been doing peyote together earlier that night. She's a young girl—just seventeen. Her mother passed away two years ago, and she's got nobody except me, and I'll be the first to admit, that's not a lot."

Zoe looked at her, the fine frown lines between her arched brows deeper now, her eyes downcast. Zoe felt very uncomfortable with herself, as if she'd just punched Vanessa in the gut for no reason.

"I felt awful enough for letting her go into the desert with those kids," Vanessa said. "The least I could do was protect her privacy."

"I understand."

"And besides all that," said Warren, "we just heard that someone confessed."

"You did?"

"Local drug dealer—Carlos Royas. Says he did it because Jordan stole the peyote from him."

Vanessa nodded. "It's a shame because I know Carlos's mother, and she's a dear woman. She works in the *farmácia*."

"But all the same," said Warren, "at least he's off the streets."

"The police called and told me just as your plane landed," Vanessa said.

"That's why you were hugging each other."

"I didn't know you saw that." Warren grabbed Zoe's hand. Startled, she turned back around, and when she looked at him, she saw the most tender smile. "I would never put you in danger, Zoe," he said. "You need to believe that." He brought her hand to his lips and softly kissed it, then turned his eyes back to the road.

Zoe watched his face, a warmth rising up inside her, her heart seeming to swell . . . until she noticed the two deep slashes on the back of his wrist—one about two inches long, the other half its size. She touched the wound, and he flinched a little. "What happened?"

"Cut myself," he said. "No big deal."

Zoe said nothing. The two slashes formed a perfect cross.

Naomi didn't know Carlos Royas that well, but she'd met him. He was very thin, with nails he'd colored black with indelible pen out of boredom and dull black hair that spiked up in back—not from products, but from greasiness and neglect. He was probably twenty, but he looked and acted more like twelve.

There was a large green park near the far side of town. Its official name was El Parque de Pancho Villa, but the locals called it Parque de las Lavanderas because there were a series of long public sinks at its edge where women would bring their washboards and gossip while doing their laundry. Carlos hung out at the other edge of Parque de las Lavanderas, near a thick line of jacaranda trees. He was mostly alone, except when he was with his friend Alejandro—a shy, chubby kid about Naomi's age who went to the Catholic boys' school—or when he was talking to gringos who wanted to buy drugs.

Sean bought pot from Carlos when he was in town. Corinne rarely went along. Carlos creeped her out, she said. But it wasn't because she saw him as physically threatening.

Corinne thought Carlos Royas had so much bad luck that he shed it—that misfortune just flew off his sad, dirty body and attached itself to whoever got close. In her mind, Carlos was why Alejandro's father had died in a car accident; Carlos was to blame for his baby sister's asthma, his parents' divorce, his own sorry poverty. More than once, Corinne had discussed this theory of hers, and each time, it made Naomi embarrassed to be her friend.

But now . . . Naomi didn't know, maybe Corinne had a point. Carlos Royas was about five feet five inches, maybe 110 pounds. He looked like he'd have trouble standing up in a stiff wind, and Naomi was supposed to believe he wreaked *that horror* on a strong boy like Jordan? Over some stupid peyote?

Bad luck, though, or maybe evil spirits. *That* she could believe.

Corinne and Sean had gone back to the States after Jordan's death, but Corinne knew about Carlos's confession. The police had contacted her family before they'd called Vanessa and Naomi. It was close to eight now, and Naomi couldn't remember who had discovered whom online, but she and Corinne had been IMing for over an hour about Carlos, Jordan and that night by the bonfire.

Jordan BOUGHT the peyote from Carlos, Corinne had just typed. **He didn't steal it. Jordan never stole.**

Naomi typed: **Then why did Carlos say he did?**

Maybe the Federales asked him why, and that was the only *why* he could come up with.

Naomi thought back to Jordan by the fire, the troubled look in his eyes. . . . *There's . . . weird stuff going on, stuff I'm guessing you don't know about. . . .* **Or maybe there was a different *why*.** *You're young. You need to be careful.*

Huh?

Naomi typed: **Did Jordan say anything to you about being young?**

The screen said **TexCori91 is typing.** It said that for a long while. Naomi waited and it still said it, so she waited some more, thinking, *What is she going to tell me?* But when Corinne finished typing and her reply finally came through, it was this: **No.**

A chill seeped through Naomi's shoulders. She recalled that feeling she'd had, sitting next to Jordan, alone by the fire—the cold burn of someone watching them. It was hitting her again. She could sense the killer's eyes, the way a doomed animal would sense a hunter. . . . Naomi started to type **Are you sure?** But she didn't finish, didn't hit SEND because her hands were frozen. . . .

Naomi gritted her teeth and shut her eyes tight, trying to ward it off—another one of those flashbacks. She wished she had some anxiety pills that worked, but all she had were stupid herbal capsules. She hated this town sometimes, the whole self-help, New Agey, you-have-the-power-to-change-your-own-life-ishness of it. *Some problems are real, you know. Some things can't be cured with chanting and herbs. . . .*

She breathed deeply and gripped her chair. Again she could feel the hot sun on her neck; again she could hear the hum of those flies. . . . *You are not in the desert. You are home. You are alone. . . .* Corinne's typed words flashed on her screen: **You still there?** Naomi started to tremble. Silence rushed into her ears. . . .

She saw the angel from her desert dream—a figure in a dark hood, standing before her. She heard the angel's voice. *You are safe* . And then she heard a real voice, saying her name.

"Naomi . . ."

She spun around. Less than a foot away stood Corinne's grandmother, Jordan's great-aunt Patty. The vision washed away. "Mrs. Woods," Naomi breathed. "You scared—"

"The housekeeper let me in." Her mouth was a penciled line. Her eyes were two pieces of sea glass, pinpricks for pupils. All grief. She glanced at Naomi's screen and said, "Corinne?"

"Yeah. Do you want to—"

"Please don't tell her I'm here."

"Okay."

"I need to see your aunt."

"She's out," she said. "She should be back soon, though."

Mrs. Woods nodded, her gaze softening. "I'm sorry, honey. I never asked how you're feeling."

"Me?"

"Awful isn't it, finding someone like that?"

"Yeah." Naomi closed her eyes for a few seconds, took a breath. "I . . . I'll be okay, though."

"No, you won't."

"Excuse me?"

"You might feel like you're over it in time, like you barely even remember what he looked like . . . the blood, the hands, that awful smell. . . . But it'll be like having a pin stuck permanently in your finger. You'll go on with your life because you have to. Maybe you even forget it's there, but the minute you catch sight of that pin again and focus on it, the way it's sticking through your skin, those images will come back to you. It will hurt just as much as it did when you first got stuck."

Naomi swallowed hard. She had to look away if she was going to keep it together, but she couldn't. "Mrs. Woods?"

"Yes?"

"Why did you say 'the hands'?"

"Pardon?"

"You mentioned Jordan's hands. How did you know there was anything strange about his—"

"I don't know. Lately, I've been saying a lot of things I don't mean."

Naomi looked into Patty's sea-glass eyes. She knew the woman was lying. She might have pressed her, were it not for that hurt, floating off her like vapor. "Jordan was such a cranky baby," she said. "Back when we lived in the States, Charlie and I would watch him sometimes and he'd just scream nonstop. Didn't matter how many times we changed his diaper and fed him and played with him. But then finally, through trial and error, we discovered the one thing that could calm him down."

"What was that?"

"Jimmy Cliff! We'd put our *Harder They Come* record on, he'd stop crying, fall right asleep. Could you imagine? A little baby reggae fan."

Naomi smiled a little. They heard the front door open, then Vanessa's musical voice, asking Soccoro in Spanish how everything was.

On her way to the door, Patty stopped, gave Naomi a long, sad look. "This town," she said, "is no place for young people."

Before Naomi could ask what she meant, Jordan's aunt had left the room.

Vanessa's house—*house* was an understatement; it was more of a hotel—was located at the top of a hill, at the western edge of San Esteban. Enormous, pale pink and artfully lit, it sported a tropical rooftop garden that was visible from below and obscenely lush, considering the natural topography of the region. "You guys need to work on your carbon footprints," said Zoe when she and Warren stopped to drop Vanessa off. But all she got in return were blank stares from both of them.

"You're going to love San Esteban, Zoe," Vanessa said. "I bet you'll decide you don't ever want to go home." And then she headed for her door and Warren took off, Zoe's gaze lingering on the rearview as the door opened, a small Mexican woman gesturing frantically at Vanessa.

When Zoe looked back at the road, the paved highway had turned bumpy, and they were headed into San Esteban. Warren had never described the town to Zoe—not in much detail, anyway. And since the rush to pack and make it to the airport had precluded the Google image search she'd been planning to run, Zoe had been left to use her own imagination, which had conjured something sleepy, flat and sunbaked—the type of place you'd see on a mural in a Mexican chain restaurant.

But now, with San Esteban twinkling and winding before them, she realized how wrong preconceptions could be. To Zoe, it looked like an illustration in a fairy tale book, the streets narrow and twisted and made of thick cobblestone, tall adobe town houses pressed up against one another, their doors painted such bright colors they made you blink, even by the dim light of the streetlamps. As traffic increased and Warren drove slower, Zoe got a closer look. Sprouting off the tops of most of these buildings were strange stone fixtures. Some looked like screaming gargoyles, some wide-mouthed fish. . . .

"Those are gutters," Warren said, when he noticed Zoe staring at one—a pointy-eared dog, its mouth wrenched open. "They're quite a sight during rainy season—all these strange creatures screaming water."

"I can imagine," said Zoe.

"It's fun seeing this place through your eyes," said Warren. "I don't notice things like the gutters anymore."

There was a big Gothic church, with curvy turrets like a rush of tears. Across the street was a well-lit central square bordered by food stands and metal benches and stunning-looking trees with graceful trunks and blooming purple flowers. "That's called the *jardín*."

"Those trees are amazing."

"Jacarandas—they normally don't bloom this time of year. I think they're trying to impress you."

Zoe smiled. "Kiss-ass trees."

A large white stone cross stood at the center of the *jardín*. There were four outdoor lights aimed at it, but Zoe had the sense that even if it weren't illuminated, it would still glow. Odd for an inanimate object to have that power, that charisma, but Zoe could feel it, even from inside Warren's car.

"You're looking at La Cruz de San Esteban—the cross."

"How did you know?"

"How could you not?"

Zoe peered at the cross. There was a carving on its face. From the car, it looked like a large angry bird, shrieking in profile.

"It was made from the ruins of an Aztec temple. Some of the older people here, the Catholics, they avoid La Cruz because they think it's cursed," Warren said. "Me, I feel just the opposite."

She watched his face. "You think it's blessed?"

"Yes," he said. Dead serious. She glanced at the cross-shaped cut on his hand, and the hairs on the back of her neck prickled.

He turned to her, smiling. "Almost home."

Zoe's ears clicked. She was sleepy, and her head felt sort of cottony inside. The altitude—higher even than nearby

San Miguel, Vanessa had said—was making her loopy, a little paranoid maybe.

"Warren?"

"Yes?"

"In that note you left me, what did *I.L.Y.* stand for?"

"What do you think?"

Zoe's heart swelled. As Warren drove past the *jardín*, heading up another steep street and then another, Zoe thought, *I'm driving into a fairy tale with Prince Charming by my side.* The evil monster had been captured by the police. And if anything seemed a little strange—about Warren, about this beautiful town, about the way Zoe was reacting to both—it could easily be blamed on the thinning of her blood.

SIX

Warren parked the Grand Cherokee on the street in front of his place—a three-hundred-year-old, three-story town house located about five blocks north of the *jardín*. Like most all the other homes here, Warren's was fortresslike, with a white stucco facade, small windows protected by wrought-iron bars and an imposingly large and heavy door—mitigated somewhat by the fact the door was painted cantaloupe orange. Zoe peered up at one of the house's gutters—a shrieking hawk with the scaly body of a snake. "Now that is truly gruesome," she said.

Warren looked a little hurt. "I had the gutters specially made." He put his key in the front door. "Let's see if you like the inside better."

On the ride over, Vanessa had said, *The houses here are like people—so surprising, once you break through the exterior.* Zoe hadn't quite gotten it at the time, but when she saw the inside of Warren's home, she did.

"I had it renovated," he said.

"Yes. Yes, you did."

The door opened onto a huge courtyard, which, carbon footprints be damned, was breathtaking. Zoe wasn't much of a gardener—she'd lived in New York City apartments her entire adult life—but if her mother had seen this place, she would've fallen to her knees. Luscious ficus trees, papery white orchids, thick, sensuous succulents the color and texture of jade . . . Even the cactuses had burst into bloom, their flowers bright as Halloween candy wrappers. Judging from the glass-paned doors lining the courtyard walls, every room had direct access to the garden, which was probably even more stunning by daylight. She didn't want to leave it, even to go inside. "You must have a massive water bill," she said.

"Actually," said Warren, "water has nothing to do with it."

Zoe caught a heady scent that made her think of her mother's garden back in Tarrytown. She followed it to two blooming lilac bushes. She grasped a cluster of the blossoms, held them to her face and inhaled. *Lilacs in the desert . . .* "Incredible."

Warren said, "Do you like it here?"

"My God, Warren, this is . . . it's paradise."

He put his arm around her waist and pulled her to him. With the crook of his index finger, he tilted up her chin. She caught that ache in his eyes, and fully understood the expression *weak in the knees.* "Speaking of water," he murmured, "I've got a hot tub."

He took her hand and led her to the stone staircase at the far end of the courtyard. They climbed the stairs, the stars and moon shining down on them as they passed more glass-doored rooms; then they walked through an equally stunning garden on the second floor to take yet another staircase to his rooftop patio.

The patio was well lit but wonderfully private, with red roses climbing up the high wall that faced the street. *Roses in Mexico* . . . Under a trellis covered in orange bougainvillea, Zoe saw a woven blanket laid out with silver platters of cheese and fruit and an iced bottle of champagne. "The maid put that out for us. But she's gone now—we're all alone." Zoe followed him past the picnic spread, past a line of potted hibiscus and camellia to a cedar hot tub. He flipped on the jets and kissed Zoe deeply.

"Paradise, huh?" he said. And she knew he was about to bring new meaning to the word.

TexCori91: Hello? Are you still alive?

It took Naomi a while to see the words on her screen. She was too busy trying to hear what Mrs. Woods was saying to Vanessa at the foot of the stairs. She caught, "need to talk," from Mrs. Woods and "Not now," from Vanessa, and then "important." After that, though, she couldn't make out anything, other than emphatic rushes of breath as the women whisper-argued.

Naomi typed: **Sorry. V came home.**

Did she bring Brad Pitt? Naomi had to smile at that one. Brad Pitt was the code name they used for Vanessa's sometimes-boyfriend, Rafael. He was a sixty-year-old American artist with a studio in town and *so* not Brad Pitt— but the retired ladies fell all over him like he was. Actually, pretty much all of Vanessa's friends acted like Rafael was God's gift.

It was good to see Corinne attempting a joke. It made Naomi feel like maybe things could go back to normal, no matter what Mrs. Woods said about pins stuck in fingers.

She typed: **LOL! No—she's Pittless tonite. ;)**

From downstairs, Naomi heard Vanessa say, "Fine then. My room." **Gotta run! Later!**

Naomi moved over to her door, pressed her ear against it and listened to the hard rustle of clothes as Vanessa and Mrs. Woods hurried upstairs. When Vanessa's door closed, she waited for a full minute, then crept out into the hall, making her way toward Vanessa's room.

Before she was even there, Naomi heard their voices. She couldn't differentiate words, but she knew it wasn't a friendly conversation, and when she finally got her ear to the door, the first thing she heard was Mrs. Woods saying, "Grace."

Naomi put a hand to her mouth.

Vanessa said, "I wish you wouldn't say her name. It isn't good."

Grace. It's a name, not a word.

"You said it yourself. You *told* me Jordan's hands were just like hers, the heart . . ."

"I didn't say her *name*. We made a vow."

"My nephew was *ripped open*, Vanessa. Forget about vows and names!"

"*Carlos Royas did it*. It's tragic, but he was the killer. He confessed."

"You can't possibly believe that. How would that boy have known to put his hands like that, with the maguey spines? Exactly like—"

"Did you tell the police?"

"What?"

Vanessa's voice pitched lower, its edges laced with threat. "Did you tell the police about . . . Grace?"

Silence.

"Jesus, Patty."

"What could happen? You and I didn't do that to Grace. It was four years ago, and it's not as if we're all meeting anymore. . . ."

Naomi realized her hands were balled into fists, every

muscle in her body tensed. Silence rushed at her like a truck—the beginning of a flashback, she knew. She squeezed her eyes shut. *Hold on, hold on and keep it together.* . . .

Mrs. Woods said, "Oh, my God."

"Patty—"

"You are still meeting, aren't you? All these years, after we promised. You're *still meeting.* You probably still have a cross in your closet."

"That's not—"

"And whoever cut Grace's heart out is still doing it, too. *One of you* did that to Jordan. And that . . . that *one* will do it *again.*"

"You don't know what you're talking about. You're grieving. Carlos Royas, a known drug dealer with a criminal record—"

"How would you feel, Vanessa, if Naomi was next?"

"Don't you ever say that, Patty. Don't you ever *fucking say that to me!*"

"I will say it, Vanessa. Naomi. Who else do you know who is under thirty-five?"

Naomi backed away from the door. She pivoted, walked quickly back to her room, her head down. *Don't think about it, don't think about it, don't think . . .*

Vanessa's door slammed. Naomi heard footsteps thudding down the hall, then the stairs. She closed her eyes and gritted her teeth: *Grace. A name, not a word. The name of a dead girl. A girl who was killed in the same way Jordan was.*

This town is no place for young people.

There was a soft rap on her door. Naomi dug her fingernails into her palms and breathed in and out. *Act normal, act normal.* . . . "Yeah?"

Vanessa cracked the door open and poked her head through. "Hi, honey. Sorry I just ran out like that. I was at the airport. Warren's friend Zoe decided to come two days early."

Naomi forced a smile. "No worries."

"Listen, I'm heading out for a little while."

"Where are you going?"

"Just over to Rafael's studio."

"Okay," Naomi said. "See ya."

Vanessa stopped for a moment, then looked into Naomi's eyes in that bright, questioning way she had. Naomi's fists clenched tighter.

"Isn't that great news," Vanessa said, "about Carlos Royas confessing? I feel safer now, don't you?"

"Yeah."

Vanessa smiled. "Love you."

"Me, too."

Then she left—Naomi's aunt Vanessa, who said, "I love you," to her every time she went out of the house, who brewed Naomi herb tea and sent her to Catholic school and who, self-absorbed though she could be, always took Naomi's moods so personally . . . Vanessa, who had paid off every police officer involved in Jordan's case to ensure Naomi's identity was never released to the press, and who had once told her, "You look so much like your mom it makes me want to cry." Vanessa, her mother's oldest and favorite sister, whom Naomi had known since she was born and knew too well and didn't know at all.

She heard the front door close, but she didn't move until she heard Vanessa's footsteps moving toward the garage, the Land Rover's engine revving. . . .

With a surprising calm, Naomi got up from her desk. She walked down the hall and into her aunt's unlocked bedroom. And then she opened Vanessa's closet.

At first, she didn't see anything but clothes, but when she pushed a few of Vanessa's shirts aside, she noticed a strip of dark wood hanging behind them. *Why keep a cross in the back of a closet?* Naomi lifted the cross off its hook and pulled it out. It was large and heavy. She held it in front of her eyes. And when she saw what had been painted on it, her hands started shaking so bad that it dropped, clattering on the tile floor.

"Should I turn off the jets?" Warren asked.

"Mmm . . . ," said Zoe, who had lost all ability to form vowel sounds. She leaned back against his strong chest and rested her hands on the edge of the Jacuzzi and inhaled the sweet smell of all those moist, healthy plants. Once Warren switched off the jets, she could better hear his breathing, and Zoe closed her eyes for the full effect. On a basic, sensual level, she was so content, she barely felt human. It was doglike, this pure delight in sensations and sounds and smells, this inability to speak.

Warren was such a good lay. She'd known that for a while, of course, but sometimes it scared her. When they made love, she forgot who she was. She didn't want for anything, didn't question anything. For hours after, it was as if Warren could take her to a cliff and push her over the side, and Zoe would go willingly, smiling the whole way down. . . .

From somewhere on the street below came a blast of gunfire. Dogs howled in protest and Zoe's whole body tensed up, but Warren just laughed. "Fireworks."

Zoe exhaled. "Did you arrange them?"

"Don't need to," he said. "They set them off here nearly every night—saints' birthdays, revolutionary heroes, a wedding, a funeral. . . . Any excuse to celebrate, San Estebanses will take it and run with it."

"How do you know it's not a gun?"

"Guns are illegal here—except for the police."

Zoe smiled. "That's nice," she said, the last word drowned out by another explosive burst as the sky lit up red, green and white.

She tensed up again and gasped; she couldn't help it. Zoe had always worn her nerves close to the surface—an odd trait for a onetime crime reporter. Loud noises made her want to coil up and jump out of her skin.

Warren said, "Wait a second." He left the tub and Zoe heard a softer pop and then he was back again in a terry cloth robe, holding two glasses of champagne and an extra robe for Zoe. "You think of everything." Zoe slipped out of the tub and took one of the glasses and drank the champagne—very dry, with a soothing little burn from the bubbles that eased the pinch in her shoulders, warmed her throat. She let Warren wrap the robe around her, pressing his powerful body against her as he tied the belt. "I meant what I said in the car, Zoe. I would never put you in any danger."

"I know."

"I'll always protect you, always keep you safe." Zoe turned and looked at him. The candlelight softened Warren's chiseled features, and it was with utmost gentleness that he stroked her cheek. But what struck Zoe most was the way he was looking at her—such fierce caring in his eyes. *A healing gaze.* It wasn't a thought she'd ever had before; they weren't words she would normally choose. But then again, she'd never been looked at in quite that way. Warren said, "I know about Daryl Barclay."

A scattering of fireworks punctuated the sentence. Zoe's jaw dropped open. She backed away. "You . . . How do you—"

"Don't be upset."

She said nothing—just stared at him, questions racing through her mind.

"About six weeks ago," he said, "Kathy Kinney was talking about it at a *Day's End* fan event. My ears perked up when I heard your name."

Zoe's voice came back. "What the hell does Kathy know about it?"

"She said you used to be a crime reporter. Covered the Barber-Butcher murders for the *Daily News* under the name Zoe Jacobson."

She nodded. "Yeah, Greene is my mom's maiden name. I changed it after I left the *News*. . . . Kathy never told me she knew that."

"She said, before he was caught, Barclay started calling you, giving you exclusives because he'd read your pieces and was obsessed with you. I know how that feels, Zoe. . . . You should see some of the fan letters I've gotten."

Zoe shook her head.

Warren looked at her, a question in his eyes. He sat down on the blanket and she sat beside him.

"It wasn't him that was obsessed," she heard herself say. "It was me."

"I don't understand."

"I wrote about the murders, yes. Do you remember them?"

Warren nodded. "In the Village, right? Young women, their heads shaved . . ."

"Their whole bodies shaved, their throats slashed. After the third one, the cops came out and said it was a serial killer. I had amazing police sources. I got all sorts of exclusives. They interviewed me on the local FOX affiliate a bunch of times, and before too long—"

"Barclay was your fan."

"At first, yeah," she said. "He started calling me at work. The calls couldn't be traced because he always used one of those disposable cells. I would tape record the conversations, turn them over to the police. If they told me we could, we'd run parts of these interviews in the paper." Zoe's stomach constricted. She swallowed more champagne.

Warren watched her, nodding slowly.

"I . . . I started to look forward to the calls," she said. "The more I heard from him, the more curious I got. How does someone become a killer? How do they live from day to day? When they close their eyes and remember the things they've done with their own hands, what exactly do they see? It was like talking to pure evil, like interviewing the devil or something. He answered all my questions. He was . . . proud of his work."

Warren put a hand on hers. For a second, she thought he was going to tell her that she didn't have to speak anymore, but he didn't. She saw it on his face. He wanted to know.

"One day, he told me he'd seen me on the news. He complimented me on my lipstick, asked what the shade was called. It was one of the few questions he'd ever asked me, so I told him. Revlon, Deep Berry. Then he says, 'You know, kitten, I feel like I owe you something special.' "

Zoe's eyes were welling up. She took a deep, shuddering breath. "I didn't think that much of it. He said crap like that to me all the time. Two days later, there's another murder, then another, then another. . . .''

Warren nodded.

"The first three killings had happened over the course of three months, Warren. The second three in *one week*. These women weren't just shaved and slashed—they'd been brutally sexually assaulted, both before and after they were killed."

"Right. Wasn't it the DNA that got him caught?"

Zoe nodded. A tear trickled down her cheek. "All three wore lipstick. Revlon Deep Berry." She started to cry, then sob, the sobs racking her body. Warren put his arms around her and held her tightly. She didn't tell him how Barclay had stared at her during his sentencing or how, when the judge said, "Death," Barclay had given her a wink she'd seen in so many dreams since then—the type of wink you give some-one when you've made good on a deal. She didn't tell War-ren what she'd known at that moment: He'd left the DNA on purpose. He'd given himself to the police for her, yes. But he'd slaughtered three innocent women for her, too.

During that final phone call, just before he'd hung up, Barclay had said, *You've made me a star. I'll always be grateful.*

She didn't tell Warren that, either. But tonight, with fire-works popping and blazing in the sky, Zoe had told him more than she'd ever told anyone about the guilt that still ripped at her, that had made her give up real news of any kind. And from the way he pulled away and watched her face . . . he understood. He understood in a way that no one else ever had. It surprised her, frightened her just a little. . . . Warren took her by the shoulders, stared into her eyes. "You didn't cause those murders," he said. "You couldn't have prevented them." His grip tightened. *"You are not a killer."* He said it with passion, hanging on to each word as if he wanted to keep it for himself.

SEVEN

Glen Campbell was diligent—Steve had to give him that. And annoying though he could be, Glen was also, as it turned out, a genuinely good guy.

After five hours and five cups of coffee at Starbucks with his bribe-scandal source Padmé, Steve had gone home, typed up all his notes, drunk three beers and watched the whole of *Lisztomania* just to get to sleep—only to be awakened at six Sunday morning by Glen, calling to inform him that a small-time drug dealer named Carlos Royas had confessed to Jordan Brink's murder. Glen could have easily kept that information to himself. He could have taken the Brink story and run with it, telling the metro editor it had been his idea to follow through and contact his roommate from J school. But he hadn't. He'd given Steve his former roommate's work and cell numbers and let Steve ask the questions himself. Really, *really* good guy. Steve hadn't told Glen yet, but he was planning on sharing the byline with him. (Truth be told, he couldn't wait for his own friends to see it: BY STEVE SORENSEN AND GLEN CAMPBELL.)

The ex-roommate was a Mexican-American kid by the name of Miguel Guzman who spoke fluent Spanish, and Steve had already talked to him a few times this morning. Guzman knew most everything about the arrest—he'd given Steve all the details and a cop to talk to for an on-the-record quote, and he'd e-mailed him a dozen pictures of Royas, telling him the *Trumpet* could use any of them. He was looking into the dealer's previous convictions, he said, and would get back to Steve as soon as he heard anything. Guzman had also told him (deep background, under penalty of lawsuit) that Vanessa St. James had been questioned only because her niece had found Jordan's body.

Steve was glad Zoe's boyfriend had no connection to the murder—and that her "romantic vacation" would be just that, nothing more. But still, something bugged him about Warren Clark. He'd read several interviews with him online yesterday, and they hadn't left him with the best impression.

In a way, Clark reminded Steve of some of the guys he used to play hockey with—the ones who'd pray before games, as if God were up there saying, "Hold up, starving people in Africa! I've gotta make sure Cornell kicks Princeton's ass!" and who'd beat the crap out of anyone who dissed their skating. Steve never got that. Yeah, hockey had earned him a scholarship, but when it all came down to it, it was sliding on some ice, knocking a rubber disk into a net. It wasn't *saving lives*—and neither was walking around shirtless, pretending your evil twin had amnesia. But Clark seemed to think it was. In one of the articles, he'd even referred to acting on daytime TV as "my craft."

Zoe usually laughed at guys like Warren Clark—pretty boys who took themselves oh so seriously. Was she really that hard up—or was Steve really that clueless about what made Zoe happy?

Steve pushed the thought out of his mind. He was at his desk at the *Trumpet*, the Royas pics lined up on his computer screen like a virtual poker game, and a deadline of just a few hours from now. He needed to concentrate on the story.

Man, what a pathetic kid . . . Steve wasn't sure what he'd expected Jordan's killer to look like—a sick twist to the features, maybe; a Charles Manson gleam in the eye. He *knew* he hadn't expected the Royas that he saw in these photos. There was one of him standing in front of a bull ring in San Miguel de Allende, a baseball cap shielding sad eyes; another of him sitting on a couch next to his mother—a nervous-looking woman with his same frail build, a baby in her arms. There was one of him at church in an ill-fitting suit and one in baggy black swim trunks and a long-sleeved T-shirt at a public pool and one with a fat kid in a park, both of them smoking cigarettes. In every single one of them, Royas had the look of someone going to his own funeral. Steve stared at the swim trunks one—the defeated slump of the shoulders, the wan, poster-child face . . . and what was with the long-sleeved shirt? He pictured this boy ripping a young man's heart out, blood spraying everywhere. Somehow, the image was even more terrifying than if Royas had been a Manson type. There were no warning signs in his appearance. Nothing to scare you away until it was too late.

Unless he didn't do it . . .

Steve's desk phone rang. He picked it up to the voice of Miguel Guzman. "Got Royas's arrest history." He sounded kind of strange, tentative.

"So?"

"Just a sec. I'm calling it up."

There was a pause, during which Steve continued to look at the pictures. He stared into the huge eyes of Royas's mother. How was she able to get up in the morning? How was she able to take care of that baby in her arms without thinking, *What's the point? Look how the other one turned out.*

Unless Carlos Royas didn't do it.

"Lot of drug arrests," said Guzman. "Looks like he stole a whole bunch of nitrous oxide from the hospital, along with some sedatives and muscle relaxants and crap."

"Pretty routine."

"Yeah," he said. "But . . . Okay this is the part that's weird. This one happened in 2004. He was just sixteen years old."

"Violent crime?"

"No," he said. "Grave robbing."

Steve sighed. *J school grads.* "That's not all that weird actually, Miguel," he said. "Lots of poor kids steal jewelry off dead people. It's kind of gross, I know, but—"

"You don't understand."

"What's to understand?"

"He didn't steal jewelry. He stole the *people*."

Steve's breath caught. He stared at Royas's sad eyes.

"He was living in a trailer next to his parents' house," Guzman was saying. "Police found a woman's corpse in there that had been missing from a cemetery in Queretero."

"Jesus."

"He later confessed stealing three other bodies from the same cemetery. He said he burned them after they got too old. Wouldn't say what he used them for when they were, you know . . . fresh."

Steve cleared his throat. "He did that alone?" he said. "This skinny kid was stealing bodies all by himself?"

"That's what he claimed. Of course, the skinny kid killed Jordan Brink alone, without even a fight," Guzman said. "Did I tell you? The police say there were no defense wounds on the hands or arms. No sign of a struggle."

"No," he said. "You didn't tell me."

"I'll call you if I hear anything else," he said.

Steve thanked him and said goodbye, thinking about that saying: *The eyes are the windows to the soul.* What a load of crap that was. *Guess you can't tell much about someone's strength from the size of his body, either.*

He was about to close the screen when he noticed something in the bullring picture. Royas's baseball cap.

Steve blew the photo up 50, then 100, then 300 percent, until finally, he could clearly read the white logo that was stitched over the bill.

There had to be a logical explanation for it. Royas had probably just found the cap somewhere, and even if he hadn't . . . *You arrest somebody for a murder. He's wearing an Ozzy T-shirt. Do you question Ozzy? Of course you don't.*

Which was all well and good, but the fact remained: The logo on Carlos Royas's black baseball cap wasn't for Ozzy or Metallica or any of the newer death-rock stuff that Steve had never heard of, but that a sullen, nihilistic teenage boy would probably love.

It was the logo for *The Day's End.*

Warren had a skylight in his bedroom. Zoe had missed that detail the night before, but waking up in the morning, bathed in sunlight, she appreciated it as much as she appreciated everything else in this room, from the king-sized cherrywood bed to the crisp sheets to the walk-in closet to the enormous windows—of *course* they were enormous—overlooking that otherworldly rooftop patio. Still no personal photos on any of the walls, but everything else met with her approval, particularly the man who was sleeping next to her. . . .

Zoe stretched out to touch him, but felt only the cool, bare pillow. And sure enough, when she rolled onto her side, she saw she was alone in bed. Zoe sighed. This was getting to be a habit with him. Only no roses this time. No plane to catch, either.

"Warren?" she called out. "You in the bathroom?"

No reply. Maybe he was downstairs.

Zoe's stomach growled. What time was it, anyway? She grabbed her watch from the bedside table. Last night, Warren had told her the altitude might make her sleep longer, and when she looked at her watch, she saw how right he was. *One in the afternoon.*

She'd slept away half the day, but she'd probably needed it. Last night had been so intense, she still felt sort of wrecked.

She remembered the way Warren had looked at her when he'd asked her about Barclay—that healing gaze. And how, after she told him what had happened, he'd seemed not only to understand her pain but also to *feel* it. Looking into his eyes, she had seen her own emotions mirrored back at her—that wrenching guilt, that yearning to be a different person, that feeling of *If only* . . . And when she thought she could no longer take it, Warren's gaze had softened, and he'd slipped his hand into her hair so gently, it had made her feel . . . *Special* was the wrong word. *Precious. Treasured.*

I will fix you, he had whispered. *I will make you strong again.*

She got out of bed. She still hadn't even unpacked, although Warren had brought her suitcase up to the bedroom. She unzipped it, got out a clean pair of jeans, some underwear and a tank top. No use bothering with shoes just yet. After she was dressed, she wandered into the master bathroom and splashed cold water in her face. She felt better now, last night's pain fading with the memory of Warren's gentle touch. She noticed the enormous marble tub, candles placed around the sides. It was a tub bursting with possibilities. . . .

Jesus. I'm turning into Jenna Jameson.

She heard movement in the bedroom, and smiled. Good.

He'd just been downstairs. "Warren," she said, "you think maybe you could come in here, show me how the tub works?"

No answer.

"Warren?" She opened the bathroom door to find a silver-haired Mexican woman stripping the sheets off the bed.

The woman stopped what she was doing and gave Zoe a disdainful look. For a second, Zoe felt like a bimbo from an old Dean Martin movie—the wall-eyed blonde in the baby-doll dress who gets shoved into the closet when the nice girl knocks on Dean's door. "Uh . . . *¿Hola?*"

"Hello," said the woman in accented English. "Señor Clark has gone out for a little while. I am the housekeeper, Guadalupe." She stuck out a hand and smiled warmly, which made Zoe think she might have just presumed the how'd-the-slut-get-in-here glare.

Zoe shook her hand. "I'm Zoe," she said.

"I know."

"Warren told you I'd be coming?"

She nodded. "It isn't often Señor Clark has a visitor."

Guadalupe turned back to the bed, and it hit Zoe how little she still knew of Warren, how much she wanted to know. She thought of the lack of personal pictures on his walls, how the only information she had about Warren's past (he'd grown up in Westport, Connecticut, was an only child, had gone to New York's High School of Performing Arts) she'd obtained via *Headquarters* interviews. It brought to mind a song Zoe had once heard on the radio. *You're a mystery, my mystery.* . . . "How long have you worked for Warren?"

"Ten years."

"Since he first bought this house."

"Yes."

Now here's a source. Here's a real, bona fide insider. "Can I ask you something?"

Guadalupe stopped working. She looked at Zoe's mouth rather than her eyes—a sign of trepidation, according to a body-language course Zoe had once taken at the Ninety-second Street Y to improve her interview technique. Zoe gave her a slight smile and mirrored her stance, which disarmed the woman a little, brought her gaze back up. "When did Warren last have a visitor?"

"You mean, from the U.S.?"

"Yeah."

Guadalupe thought. "Ten years ago."

Zoe stepped back. "Whoa. That *is* a while."

"Yes," Guadalupe said quietly. The gaze returned to Zoe's mouth.

"I mean, a beautiful place like this, I'd want to show it off to my friends back home. Wouldn't you?"

"I . . . suppose."

"You keep it so clean, too. Too bad Warren couldn't bring you up to the States. His New York apartment is a *disaster*."

She smiled, returned to Zoe's eyes. "*¿Verdad?*"

Zoe nodded. "Dust all over everything. The silver's so tarnished it looks like lead. Men don't notice these things, you know?"

Zoe laughed, and Guadalupe laughed along with her—an easy, childlike laugh that relaxed her face, made her seem much younger.

Zoe said, "Who *was* that visitor, anyway?"

She stopped laughing. Before answering, she glanced up and to the left—a cue, according to Zoe's course, that she was about to lie. "I . . . I don't remember his name."

"His? The visitor was a man?"

Guadalupe nodded very slowly, a look on her face as if she'd inadvertently screwed her best friend out of a promotion. It made Zoe feel as if she were taking advantage. Guadalupe was such a dignified-looking woman—no makeup, spotless clothes, a gold saint's medal around her neck. She probably saw all this as gossiping about her very private boss, which, frankly, it was.

"Well, it was very nice meeting you," Zoe said. "I'm going to go out for a little while, explore the town."

Guadalupe broke into a smile—pure gratitude. "It was nice meeting you as well."

Zoe unplugged her cell phone from its charger and tossed it into her purse, then grabbed a pair of flip-flops from the outer pocket of her suitcase.

"You might find the cobblestones difficult in those shoes," Guadalupe said.

Zoe shrugged. "I'll take my chances. I'm not sure where I put my sneakers, and I don't feel like digging through my suitcase."

"*Hasta luego, señorita,*" she said. "Enjoy San Esteban."

Zoe stepped out onto Warren's rooftop patio and inhaled the mountain air—sweet corn and cinnamon and the perfume of fresh flowers. . . . Pretty much what heaven must smell like, she figured, except one of those scents—the corn one—was making her weak from hunger.

She hoped she wouldn't be too long in finding a place to eat. And once she got out the door, she saw there would be no wait at all. The source of the sweet corn smell was a tiny storefront tortillarilla, right across the road from Warren's town house. About half a dozen street dogs were sleeping outside it—and for street dogs, they looked pretty well fed. Zoe figured that must be a good sign—the San Esteban version of trucks parked outside a highway diner.

She bought a half kilo of corn tortillas from the smiling, ancient woman behind the counter, and moments later, she left with a stack of them, wrapped in moist butcher paper and so warm they nearly burned her hands. After devouring a few, she rewrapped the stack and slipped it into her purse, then headed down the hill toward where she remembered the *jardín* was.

As it turned out, San Esteban was meant to be viewed in bright sunlight. The creamy stucco town houses with their sherbet-colored doors, the pink-tinted cobblestones, the clotheslines full of red, green and white paper snowflakes atop so many of the roof gardens—as if the whole town were decorated for a party . . . She hadn't noticed any of that the night before. Someone seemed to have waved a wand over San Esteban, made it 50 percent more enchanting. Even the bizarre gutters looked fanciful. What with the dry heat and the sluggishness Zoe still felt from the altitude, she might have been moving through an unusually pleasant fever dream.

The only problem was her shoes. The hill was so steep that with every step, her foot would slide past the edge of her flip-flops, the thong part ripping into the tender skin between her toes. Before long, her feet were cut up and killing her. She considered going barefoot, but what with all the street dogs in this town, she'd have been risking a major case of E. coli.

A woman in a brightly embroidered white blouse, a matching head scarf and a skirt the color of fresh watermelon walked past, pushing a wheelbarrow full of fragrant mangoes. She matched the town. *"Buenas tardes, guera,"* she said, which Zoe knew from high school Spanish meant "Good afternoon, white girl," but in a nondisparaging way.

How interesting to be a foreigner, which made her think of Warren's last foreign visitor. *A man. Ten years ago.* She stored that information in her mind, wondering what Warren would say if she were to ask him about it. Probably something like, *Have I ever told you how much I love your smile?*

He really was a terrible interview. Maybe she could find an independent source. . . .

Zoe's feet hurt enough to pull her away from her thoughts. What kind of a dumb *guera* was she, taking the cobblestones in flip-flops? She really didn't want to go back to the house, though. The idea of walking back up that hill without a full lunch and a beer or two in her was beyond daunting. Plus, she didn't feel like forcing herself on Guadalupe again.

As Zoe approached the *jardín*, she caught sight of La Cruz de San Esteban. It yanked at her attention in such a powerful way, it was almost a slap. She stopped walking and just stared at it, the traffic sounds around her muffling, even her foot pain fading a little. What was it about that cross?

She moved closer. In the trees around her, birds shrieked, the leaves shuddering with their movements. When she was about ten feet away from the cross, she peered at the Aztec bird carved into its face—the same bird, she saw now, as on Warren's custom-made gutters, only without the snake's body—and for a second, she could have sworn she felt an energy radiating out of it, an actual *heat*.

They avoid La Cruz because they think it's cursed. Me, I feel just the opposite.

Zoe wanted to touch the cross, but someone else got there first—a man in a white hemp shirt and jeans, his salt-and-pepper hair pulled back in a ponytail. She didn't see his face, but he was quite tall and, Zoe guessed, American. The man waited a moment, then spread his arms, placing each of his hands on opposite arms of the cross. He bowed his head, stood perfectly still. And then his body began to vibrate.

Zoe watched, transfixed. She wished she could see his face, but his back was to her and his head was bowed—a crucifixion in reverse, with an electric current running through it. *How very, very strange.* And then, in an instant, he backed away, went about his walk as if he'd never stopped there in the first place. Zoe caught a glimpse of the man's profile—a kind, weathered, largely sane face, with a broad, open smile.

"Wait!" she called out. He turned to her. The smile disappeared. He didn't look quite so kind anymore. His eyes were a very pale gray with a steeliness to them that was unnerving. For a second, she flashed on the look in Warren's eyes, when she'd mentioned the cross in his dressing room closet. "Were you talking to me?" the man said. "Do I know you?"

"I . . . Sorry. . . . I thought you were someone else."

He nodded and walked away, leaving Zoe standing there, wondering if maybe La Cruz de San Esteban really *was* cursed.

What a weird train of thought for an agnostic Jew. If Zoe's parents only knew she was wandering through Mexico, crosses and energy and evil curses running through her mind.

Hell, if *Steve* only knew . . .

Take a rain check on the cross. You need protein. With some difficulty, Zoe turned away from La Cruz and started toward an inviting-looking restaurant called Las Enchiladas, across the far corner of the *jardín.* But she didn't get far before she turned her ankle and fell to the cobblestones, catching herself with her hands, and then rolling to the side.

"Are you okay?" said a voice. Zoe looked up to see a tall, sunburned American girl—very young, especially for a gringo in San Esteban. . . .

"I'm okay," Zoe said.

The teenager held out her hand and Zoe took it. But as she stood, she realized that, while her ankle was fine, her left wrist was in major pain—she could barely move it. "Must have landed on it funny."

"The cobblestones are really dangerous," said the girl. "I'll take you to the doctor."

"You don't have to—"

"No worries. I was on my way there, anyway."

Zoe tried moving her wrist again and nearly screamed. "I guess I should get it looked at."

"Yeah," she said. "I know the sun is hot and all, but in the future, you should always wear hiking boots or sneakers."

"Yeah. I've been told." She stuck out her good hand. "I'm Zoe, by the way."

The girl squinted at her. "Not Warren Clark's friend?"

Zoe's eyes widened. "You know him?"

The girl smiled. "This town is so small it's ridiculous," she said. "I'm Naomi Boyd, Vanessa St. James's niece."

EIGHT

Steve had a date tonight. It was one of those dates that Zoe referred to as his *news tricks*, where he'd wine and dine a woman who was obviously interested in him, all so he could get information for a story. It wasn't as amoral as it sounded—the woman was always single, Steve was always a total gentleman, she had a good time, he got the information he needed. . . . Everybody was, more or less, happy.

Tonight's news trick was Debbie Cohn, a former publicist with the mayor's office. Debbie had a big ax to grind against the bribe taker, Ernest Barthel, and an even bigger desire to get with Steve. She'd told him as much, repeatedly. Debbie was hot, too, with shiny black hair and great legs and a sexy, knowing laugh she'd used frequently during the course of his asking her out. But by the time Steve had said, "Pick you up at seven," and hung up the phone, he was already looking for excuses to cancel. First, Debbie loved Andrew Lloyd Webber musicals and Steve . . . did not. To impress her, he'd scored two tickets to a Broadway revival of *Joseph and the Amazing Technicolor Dreamcoat*. But now that he knew this would actually be *happening* in five hours, Steve realized he'd rather stick pins in his eyes.

That wasn't the real problem, though. Steve and Debbie could've had box seats for the Rangers with a cooler full of Grolsch, followed by a Ken Russell retrospective at the Ziegfield and a room at the W, and *still* he wouldn't want to go.

All he cared about was Carlos Royas's baseball cap.

Warren Clark had been in San Esteban during the time of Jordan Brink's murder. The alleged murderer was photographed wearing a cap with the logo from Clark's show. Why was a grave-robbing Mexican drug dealer who confessed to a brutal killing wearing a baseball cap from an American soap opera? Yeah, he could have gotten it at a San Esteban flea market or maybe he was even a *Day's End* fan—but Steve couldn't get past the idea that Clark and Royas might have known each other. He was even entertaining the possibility that Warren Clark had something to do with the killing.

In his more rational mind, Steve had to admit—he was taking an Olympian leap of logic over one stupid cap. If he were to talk to a shrink about this, the shrink would probably tell him he was overreacting, that he had some kind of paranoid fixation on Warren Clark. It was also a good bet the shrink would add, "Are you really worried about your best friend's well-being—or are you pissed off that she's found happiness with someone other than you?"

And then Steve would punch the shrink in the eye. See, this was why Steve was not in therapy. Denial suited him just fine.

It was two in the afternoon. He had already filed the Royas story, but he'd asked Glen to keep his ears open for any follow-up info. Press weren't allowed to speak to Carlos Royas, but all day Guzman had been trying to get hold of

Royas's mother, Alma—a pharmacist in San Esteban who spoke only Spanish. When and if he did speak to her, he promised to ask Alma where her son had gotten the cap, and if he had ever met Warren Clark.

Just for the hell of it, Steve ran a search on the Jordan Brink memorial service, and learned it had been held last week. He found a *Post* article about it, but it was short on details as the service was very private. From the start, Mr. and Mrs. Brink had refused to speak to the press—other than to insist, in a statement, that their son did not take or steal drugs. Couldn't blame them for that; much of the reporting had been incredibly slanted. Steve skimmed the *Post* story for mention of them: Morrison and Barbara Brink of Astoria, Queens.

Morrison Brink. Unusual name.

Steve's phone rang. It was Guzman, sounding a whole hell of a lot testier than he had at the start of the day. "I finally talked to Alma Royas," he said. "Asked her your *soap opera* question."

"And?"

"She hung up on me."

Steve's eyebrows went up. "She did? That's . . . strange, don't you think?"

"Not really," he said. "Your son has just confessed to a brutal murder. His life and yours are pretty much over, and some reporter says, 'What's up with the logo on his cap'? How are *you* gonna react?"

Steve sighed. "Good point."

He said goodbye and hung up the phone wishing that Guzman had never asked the question—because now he was more curious than ever. If Alma Royas had said, "How dare you ask me about soap operas at a time like this?" that would have been one thing. If she'd said, "I have no idea what you're talking about. It's just a stupid cap," that would have been another. But *hanging up* on the question . . . That was like scratching a mosquito bite. It just made it worse.

The office of the local, American-born doctor was a few blocks away from the *jardín*, and as she walked there with Naomi, her wrist throbbing with each step, Zoe tried not to flip into interview mode. It was hard, though, because Naomi Boyd was a fascinating subject. A seventeen-year-old girl whose mother—and only immediate family—had died of cancer just two years ago, she'd moved to Mexico to live with an aunt whose most motherly act had involved a session guitarist with a diaper fetish. And then, just when Naomi was finally beginning to have some semblance of routine to her life, she woke up in the middle of the desert to find her summer crush murdered and mutilated. . . . Yet here she was, so very *normal*. If it weren't for the worry that flooded her eyes every so often, Zoe would think Naomi's life had been nothing but smooth sailing.

"The doctor's name is Dr. Dave," Naomi was saying now. "I know that sounds kind of corny, but his last name is Polish, with about fifty thousand consonants in it. It's really hard for Americans to pronounce, and Mexicans just look at it and laugh."

Zoe nodded. "It's nice of you to take me."

She shrugged her shoulders. "Like I said, I was going anyway."

"What for?"

They stopped at the corner while a truck roared past. Naomi gave her a bright smile, but Zoe saw it creep into her eyes again, that worry turning to panic. She understood Naomi's life was the opposite of smooth sailing—and had been for so long that she'd become used to it, adept at ignoring all but the most treacherous waves. "Post-traumatic stress disorder," Naomi said.

Zoe winced.

"No biggie, really. I've been having a few . . . episodes since last Friday and . . ." Her eyes welled up. She blinked a few times. "They gave me these homeopathic pills—well, Robin did. Dave's assistant? They really weren't doing much, so I looked them up online, and they're like . . . chamomile."

"You need something stronger."

Naomi nodded. "Yeah. I mean, I'm not a druggie or anything. . . ."

"You don't need to explain it to me."

"Robin's really nice, but she's so *holistic*. She's way into Reiki."

"What is that—some New Age thing?"

Naomi rolled her eyes. "Most people here swear by it. Vanessa goes for sessions three times a week. It's this healing technique where someone—the Reiki master—holds his hands over you and aims positive energy at the afflicted area. He never touches you, but it's supposed to make you all better."

"And people get paid for this."

"A lot, I think." There was a slight break in traffic, so they hurried across the road. "In fact, there's a Reiki master right next to Dr. Dave's. I bet you anything Robin tries to get you to go to him for your wrist."

"Sorry," said Zoe. "I don't trust anybody who calls himself 'Master.' "

Naomi laughed. "I thought I was the only one in the world who . . ." Her voice trailed off.

They passed a coral-colored building with a deep blue door that read *Studio Rafael* and next to it, a larger, white building with two shingles out front: REIKI MASTER PAUL and DR. DAVID KVORCZYK, MD. "Looks like we're here," Zoe said. But when she turned to Naomi, the girl was staring across the street—at a town house whose roof-top patio bore just a few dead plants. "That's Patty Woods's house," she said, panic floating in her eyes. "She's . . . she was Jordan's great-aunt."

Back in the Summer of Love days when Patty Woods was in her late teens, people used to call her Patty Permasmile. That was because she went through life with her eyes half closed, a grin affixed to her round, freckled face—the flesh-and-blood embodiment of the Have a Nice Day logo.

The thing was, Patty wasn't any happier than the next person. She was just stoned out of her mind most of the time. She would wake up in the morning, grab her water pipe and smoke a bowl before brushing her teeth. She'd keep seven thick doobies mixed in with her pack of Kents, and go about her day smoking one every three or so hours, just to keep the buzz going. She lived in New York City at the time, allegedly attending Barnard but mostly wandering through the Central Park Rambles with her other hippie friends, marveling at the falling leaves, singing Jefferson Airplane at the top of their lungs, laughing at the rats.

The downside to all the smoking, though, was that it made Patty very paranoid. First, she began to think her friends were making fun of her behind her back. Then, strangers were staring at her and thinking evil thoughts. After a while, she got the snaking feeling she was being followed, which turned, very quickly, to a near-constant sense of dread.

One day, Patty became convinced a hot dog vendor was about to draw a gun on her, and she ran screaming out of the park. It was then she decided enough was enough—this wasn't even *fun* anymore—so she threw the rest of her stash down her apartment building's incinerator and went completely clean.

In forty years, Patty hadn't even touched an aspirin. She

had never felt the slightest bit paranoid—especially not in San Esteban, where teenage boys serenaded their mothers on Día de Las Madres, where guns were illegal for everyone except the police, where people smiled and said *hola* as they passed you in the street, where good or bad, she believed she had everyone figured out.

But now, things were different. That dread was back. She *hadn't* had people figured out after all. The group was still meeting, and whoever had ripped out poor Grace's heart had wreaked the same horror on her nephew.

Now she had real reason to be afraid.

Jordan had arrived at her front door unexpectedly, one day before Corinne was due in for her summer break. "I'm sorry I didn't call first," he had said. "I've been traveling around Mexico, and I missed it here." At the first sight of him, Patty couldn't help but smile. He was bigger now—a young man—but he still had that specialness.

She'd hugged him tight and said, "Of course you can stay." And she'd thanked God for how resilient children could be.

But that night, after a day of sightseeing, Jordan had returned to her house changed. *Changed back.* His mouth was tight, as if he were biting back pain. There were clouds in his eyes—not tears, but the threat of them, which was worse.

"Are you still doing it, Aunt Patty?"

"What?"

"Are you still . . . you, Rafael, Warren and the rest . . . Are you . . . ?"

"Jordan—"

". . . still going to Las Aguas?"

"No, honey. I told you. We stopped a long time ago."

He'd watched her, those clouded eyes bearing down on her skin, seeking her face for the truth. There had been a few seconds when she'd almost told him about Grace, how her death had shown them the damage the group could do. But then she'd thought better of it. Grace had been four years ago. No need to bring that up now.

Finally, Jordan had said, "I believe you. You're not doing it."

"Of course not. What makes you think—"

"But the rest of them are."

Patty had thought, *Jordan is just paranoid. He's probably smoking too much marijuana himself.* She'd heard him leaving the house close to midnight, and she'd seen him in the *jardín*, but she'd thought nothing of it. . . . Not until after his death, when she asked Vanessa if the group was still meeting and saw that telling look on her friend's face . . .

After a night full of dreams that were worse than sleeplessness, Patty now knew what she had to do. This morning, she had reserved a one-way ticket back home to Austin, set to leave from León tomorrow at noon. She had called Rafael, told him she had something important to discuss. "Come by at two," he had said, "when I'm through teaching my class."

Patty lit a cigarette—the last one in her pack. She lipped the filter and took a long pull, the smoke sliding down her throat like hot liquid. Patty had quit when she got pregnant with her first child, picked it up after her husband had died, quit again a year later and started again after Grace. Someday she would give up smoking for good, but for now she needed the burn.

In five minutes, she would walk across the street to Rafael's studio and tell him she knew she was the only one who had kept the vow; the rest of them were still meeting. And then she would tell him about the maguey spines that had been placed in Jordan's hands.

The police hadn't cared about the spines. They hadn't cared about Grace. The new *comandante*, in particular, seemed to think Patty was delusional—some aging gringa hippie dreaming up dead women. "We have no record of this Grace's death," he had said, as if *no record* meant no Grace at all. As if she had never existed.

But Rafael would care. Rafael still loved Grace—so deeply that he forbade anyone from saying her name so that she might rest in peace, with no interruption. He needed to know that Jordan's body had been desecrated, not in a similar fashion . . . but *in the exact same way* that Grace's had been.

He also needed to know whom Jordan had met with, the night before his death—his shoulders slumped, his arms hugged to his chest so protectively, as if he'd shrunk back to his sixteen-year-old self. They had thought they were alone, but Patty had seen them from her rooftop patio, in front of La Cruz at midnight. . . . At the time, she had thought, *Just a conversation. None of my business.* But now, more than anything, she wished she could have heard what Warren Clark had been saying to her sweet, strong Jordan. She wished she knew what Warren had done to make him crumple up like that. . . .

She would tell Rafael, and Rafael would listen. He would understand. He would know what to do, and she would leave town with a clear conscience, knowing she had done all she could to prevent another sacrifice.

Patty stubbed out the cigarette and headed out her door. For a moment, she thought about what had been inflicted on Jordan. *Will the same thing happen to me?*

She shook the thought away. Patty could stay safe for twenty-four hours. She was a smart, cautious, sober woman with a house in a busy area and a scream that could wake the dead. She was not like Jordan, who had spent his last night alive hapless in the desert, under the influence of hallucinogens. And besides, Patty trusted Rafael. He would keep her confidence.

Patty crossed the street as two people were entering the doctor's office—Naomi and a much shorter young woman with a delicate build and dark, wavy hair. San Esteban was one of those small towns where it was impossible to go anywhere without running into someone you knew, and realizing she'd soon be rid of that brought Patty a great deal of relief. She knocked on Rafael's door without bothering to get the girls' attention; Naomi would hear about her leaving soon enough, via Vanessa or Corinne.

Within seconds, the door was opened by Rafael's butler, Emilio. *"Buenas tardes, señora."*

Patty smiled. She had always liked Emilio. *"Quiero ver a Señor Rafael,"* she said. "He should be expecting me."

"Sí, Señora," he said. "Follow me. They are waiting in the sunroom."

Patty said, "They?"

Emilio nodded, and before she knew it, she was in the sunroom, her heart in her mouth, the whole group of elders standing before her like a firing squad.

NINE

D r. Dave's assistant, Robin, looked nothing like Zoe had expected her to look. Something about the word *holistic* had conjured images of a blissed-out hippie princess draped in crystals and batik. But Robin was pure New York art house—blue-black hair and clothes to match, red lips pierced with three silver rings, skin the color of heavy cream. When Zoe walked into the office, Robin said, "Dave's not here," without taking her eyes off her computer screen, and it was as if Zoe were no longer in San Esteban—as if she'd been magically teleported to some video rental place on Twelfth and Avenue A.

As soon as Naomi entered the room, though, Robin looked up and smiled. "*¡Hola, chica!*" she called out, and *holistic* suddenly made sense. Robin had a smile like sunshine. It changed her whole face. "How are the Calms Supremes treating you?"

"They're not," said Naomi. "I think I need something stronger than herbs."

Robin's smile dropped away. She looked personally injured. "Have you tried Reiki yet?"

Naomi gave Zoe a quick sidelong glance. "Actually," she said, "Dave should look at Zoe first. She fell on the cobblestones and landed weird on her wrist. We're afraid it might be broken."

Robin looked at Zoe. "Dave's not here."

"Yeah. You said."

"I was totally rude, wasn't I? I'm so sorry. It's just I was reading this really interesting article about echinacea and . . . wait. Your name is Zoe?"

She nodded.

"*Warren Clark*'s Zoe?"

"Uh . . . yes?"

Robin jumped up from her seat. "Which is the good hand?" she said, and when Zoe lifted it, she shook it vigorously. "Oh, my God," she said. "You should *hear* the way he talks about you." Her voice swooped up high enough to make glass tremble, causing a fluffy golden retriever to bound into the dimly lit waiting room, rear up on its hind legs and slam into Zoe's chest.

"Watch the wrist!" said Naomi.

"Awww," said Zoe. "Who's this?"

"That," said Robin, "is the tremendously well-trained Adele. Down!"

"Don't worry about it." Zoe ruffled Adele's fur with her good hand, put her face right up to hers and let her lick her chin. Zoe loved dogs. No mystery to them at all. She glanced at Robin. "So, are you a friend of Warren's?"

"More like an admirer."

"Soap fan?"

Robin shook her head. "Most of us here don't bother with TV," she said. "The cable hook-up is really expensive, and the only thing on local is old *Magnum, P.I.* episodes, dubbed into Spanish."

Naomi said, "You don't have to be so modest, Robin. You're definitely Warren's friend. You guys hang together a lot. He totally confides in you."

Zoe stared at Robin.

"Yeah, well . . . we're pretty much the only two gringos in this town who are under fifty—except for you, Naomi, of course. So he doesn't have much choice."

"But he *confides* in you?" said Zoe. "Because from my own experience, he's . . . very private."

Robin shrugged her shoulders. "Everyone's a little less private when they're at the doctor's."

Zoe was dying to ask Robin what Warren had said about her—not because she needed to know how he felt, but because she wanted to hear what Warren sounded like when he confided in another person.

"You're an actress, right?" Robin asked her. "It must be so exciting to be all made up, in front of cameras all day."

"I'm actually a magazine writer."

"I could have sworn Warren said you were an actress." The smile fell away. Robin's pale cheeks flushed. Suddenly, she looked as if she wanted to bang her head against the wall, as if getting the job wrong were enough to make Zoe hate her forever.

"Easy mistake," Zoe offered, but Robin just sat there, crestfallen. It made Zoe wonder about the other people in her life.

Maybe Zoe was making snap judgments, but there was a quality Robin had. Zoe had seen it before, in certain child soap actors—an eagerness to please that bordered on desperation. The kid would be standing there, answering all your questions as if this were the Little Miss America pageant, until you asked her something she hadn't rehearsed with Mommy and her face would crumble. Then you'd meet Mommy, you'd see that hardness in her eyes and you'd know why.

Zoe glanced around the room for Naomi, and found her standing in front of the far wall, absorbed in a painting of some strange, dark green thing—it looked like part of a plant. Obviously, she'd checked out of this conversation a while ago.

"Robin," Zoe said, "I quit my job at the magazine two days ago, so even if you got it right, you'd be getting it wrong."

"But—"

"And anyway, I'm flattered you thought I was a TV actress."

Robin's face relaxed back into a smile. "No wonder Warren likes you so much."

Zoe exhaled. She sat down on the waiting room couch, resting her bad wrist in her lap. She watched Adele trot over to Robin's desk and wedge her large body underneath it and thought, *At least she's comfortable with the dog.* "Where did you get Adele?"

"She was a street dog. Followed me home eleven years ago, when she was just a puppy."

Zoe looked at the girl. She couldn't have been more than twenty-two. "Eleven years? Did you grow up here or something?"

She smiled. "Now you're just trying to flatter me."

"Oh, come on. How old—"

"I'm thirty-seven."

"No way."

"Actually, I'll be thirty-eight next month."

Zoe stared at her—the full cheeks and lips, the soft brown eyes, guileless despite all the makeup. Not a line on her whole face, even when she smiled. "Man," she said, "I am definitely trying Reiki."

Robin laughed. Adele shimmied out from under the desk and started barking, and it hit Zoe how spry and youthful she was, too, for a big, eleven-year-old dog. "Is Adele into Reiki, too?" Zoe asked.

But Robin didn't answer. Her face went stern and professional, and before Zoe knew what was happening, Robin was up and moving around her desk, Adele on her heels, rushing toward Naomi, who had turned to them, her sunburned face stark white, her knees buckling. With a thud, she collapsed on the floor.

Dr. Dave showed up just as Naomi was coming to. He told Zoe to wait in his office while he tended to Naomi, giving her ice chips and placing a cool compress on her head and stretching her out on the waiting room couch as Robin grabbed her desk phone and called the Reiki master next door, ignoring Naomi's pleas of, "It's okay. I'm *fine*."

Only then did Dr. Dave turn his attention to Zoe. Like Robin, the doctor did not match her preconceptions. It must have been the name *Dr. Dave* . . . but for whatever reason, Zoe had expected a children's show host in a lab coat—a big, jovial guy with personality to spare.

Yet the sallow, expressionless man who bent Zoe's wrist back and forth as if it were a car part, who placed her hand on the X-ray tray, saying, "Keep still," and nothing more . . . this man had the look and personality of a piece of plywood—yang to Robin's colorful, desperately attentive yin.

Zoe hoped there was that type of balance between them—for Robin's sake. Either he defined the word *withholding* or Dr. Dave was in a very bad mood. She half expected him to strap her to the table, trot out the dental tools and start asking, "Is it safe?" like Laurence Olivier in *Marathon Man*.

He left her in the examining room briefly to develop the

X-ray. The room was silent save for the hum of the fluorescent lights—a sound that, while usually easy to ignore, is close to torturous when you're forced to pay attention to it. Zoe looked at the diploma on the wall, from Tufts Medical School. She couldn't help but wonder what brought a dour man like Dr. Dave to this bright, festive town—not to mention what possessed him to hire someone like Robin.

Maybe he really was just in a bad mood today. . . .

Two minutes later, he was back in the room. "Not broken," he said, as he clipped the wrist X-ray to the lightboard.

Zoe said, "That's a relief."

He regarded her the same way a frog might look at a fly—unblinking, emotionless, vaguely predatory. . . . "I'll wrap it."

He opened a cabinet and removed an ACE bandage. Zoe had a tremendous urge to tell him not to worry about it and haul ass out of his office, but then he took her hand and began wrapping the wrist with gentleness and efficiency, and some of the tension eased from his face. "So," he said, "how are you liking San Esteban?"

"It's beautiful."

He gave her a smile that was mild, almost pleasant. It must have taken a lot of effort on his part—the small talk–smile combo. Then he said, "I've been living here close to twenty years and the sunsets still take my breath away," and she almost fell off the table.

"What brought you here?"

"Rafael."

"From next door?"

He nodded. "I used to live in Glendale, California. He was the minister at my church. He moved down here twenty-five years ago."

"A minister-turned-artist."

"Actually," Dave said, "he's always been a little of both."

He brought the bandage around her thumb, crossed it over the back of her hand.

"We corresponded. He mentioned this beautiful town with so many older Americans and not one doctor who speaks English." He glanced up at her. "I know a business opportunity when I see one."

Zoe said. "You must be busy."

"Always."

"Were you with a patient earlier?"

He stopped wrapping. His expression suddenly shifted back to cold. "What do you mean?"

"I mean . . . when Naomi and I got here. . . ."

"Yes?"

"You weren't around."

"Yes." He glared at her for so long she started to sweat at the temples. Zoe felt as if she were under a microscope—an effect that was only intensified by the thickness of Dr. Dave's glasses, the black ice of his eyes.

"Well . . . ," she said, "I was . . . I was just . . . I was thinking maybe you made house calls and . . . never mind."

He started wrapping again. "I wasn't with a patient," he said. "I was at a meeting."

The fluorescent lights groaned. She stared at the diploma until the words made no sense. Then Zoe realized that while the doctor was still holding her arm, he had stopped wrapping her wrist. "Are you enjoying yourself," he said, "with Warren?" He gazed intently at the delicate pale skin on the underside of her forearm, the network of blue veins running beneath.

"Yes, I am. . . ."

"How old are you, Zoe?"

"Thirty."

"Perfect."

"For what?"

Zoe noticed a strange glint in his eyes—a sort of shared joke, only she wasn't the one sharing it. "We don't get many young people." He ran his fingertips over the veins, and she yanked her hand away. Pain shot up her arm, making her gasp, but more important was getting away from Dr. Dave, as soon as possible.

"No sudden movements," he said quietly.

Zoe headed into the waiting room, where she saw Naomi on the couch with an arm thrown over her eyes, Robin's black-clad form blocking a man who stood with his flat hands two feet above Naomi's body and was speaking in some foreign language.

Would you just give the poor girl a pill?

"Does that feel any better?" the man finally asked.

"Yes, much." Naomi stood up. She looked mortified.

Zoe said, "Should we settle up?"

Naomi nodded vigorously. "Thanks, Paul," she said to the man—the same man Zoe had seen in the *jardín*, his hands on La Cruz.

Zoe gaped at him.

"Anything for the niece of my beautiful Lady Vanessa," he said in an aging surfer's voice—all sunlight and cheer, the polar opposite of the way he'd sounded earlier. *Were you talking to me? Do I know you?* "Did you want me to treat you, too?" he asked Zoe.

"Nah." She held up her bandaged wrist. "But I just might take a rain check."

Paul beamed at her. "Awesome! Hey . . . didn't I see you about an hour ago? In the *jardín*?"

"Yes," Zoe said tentatively.

His tanned face twisted into an apologetic wince. "I was kinda harsh, huh? Everybody knows, though, don't interrupt Reiki Master Paul when he's absorbing Cruz energy—right, guys?"

Robin and Naomi nodded.

"Sorry," said Zoe.

"*No hay problema, chica*. You had no idea," he said. "Anyway, if I knew you were Zoe, I wouldn't have been as rude."

"You . . . know who I am?"

"Warren's told me all about you."

She stared at him. *Warren confides in the Reiki master, too?*

"He said you had the perfect energy for San Es. And he was right about that. He's right about everything." Paul smiled, somewhat reverently. "You have a pure white aura, Zoe."

"Uh . . . thanks?"

He opened the side door—the one that led to the courtyard between his and Dr. Dave's offices—revealing a burst of tropical color. What was it with the gardens in this town?

"So much to learn. Warren will teach you." Paul winked—at Robin. Then he walked out the door.

While Naomi was in the examining room, Robin added up the bill. Zoe watched her tonguing her lip piercings as she clacked away at her keyboard. *Warren's confidante* . . . and she wasn't the only one. Reiki Master Paul, Guadalupe, even the intensely creepy Dr. Dave . . . they all seemed to know Zoe, yet she knew none of them. *Maybe Warren isn't really a private person. Maybe he's only private with me.*

And what did Paul mean by *Warren will teach you*?

Robin looked up at Zoe, smiled. "Penny for your thoughts."

"What did Paul mean . . . ," she started, but something in Robin's face stopped her. She cleared her throat. "What did he mean when he said I have a pure white aura?"

Robin smiled. "It's very rare. It means your soul is pure, and you're spiritually open. Adults usually don't have white auras. It means you're . . . young inside."

We don't get many young people.

Zoe shuddered. As if she was reading her mind, Robin said, barely moving her lips, "What did you think of Dave?"

"Well . . ."

"That's everybody's reaction. I'm telling you, though, once you get past the social awkwardness, he's really a good guy."

"He acted sort of . . . strange with me."

Robin sighed. "Sometimes Dave forgets that people aren't lab animals. He's always *studying*."

"Yes, exactly!"

"Used to give me the creeps, but he's totally harmless," she said. "Ask Warren. He's known me and Dave since he moved here, and he comes *here* for his checkups—not New York, and . . . Something wrong?"

"Robin?"

"Yeah?"

"How well did you know Warren when he first moved here?"

"It's not like we dated or anything."

"No . . . No, I'm not asking that. Do you happen to remember him having a visitor from the U.S.? A guy?"

The brown eyes lost some of their softness; the lips went thin. Robin swallowed, her pale throat moving up and down, as if she hated to betray even the mildest confidence. "Did . . . *Warren* say that to you?"

Zoe thought for a moment. Telling her it was Guadalupe who had said it didn't feel like a good idea. "Yes," she said. "I mean, he mentioned it in passing—that I'm the first visitor he's had in ten years."

Robin smiled—a small, sad smile. "Good for Warren," she said. "Yeah . . . I remember the visitor." Her gaze went to the painting across the room, and for a few moments, it was as if she'd escaped herself and melted into the dark green leaves. "Nicholas Denby," she said softly. "He was . . . He was special."

"Was?" said Zoe.

But then Dr. Dave's door was opening and he was ushering Naomi out, and Robin was tapping away at her keyboard, as if Zoe had never asked her anything at all.

Naomi had passed out, Dr. Dave said, because of dehydration. "The sun is very strong and you're still recovering from last week. Get lots of rest. Stay out of direct sunlight. Do not forget to drink water." He also sent her out with a prescription for a low dose of Xanax, to be filled for her by her aunt Vanessa.

Interesting. When he mentioned Vanessa's name, the doctor's tiny black olive eyes lit up a little. Zoe had noticed the same response in Reiki Master Paul—a thrill, just at the thought of her. She mentioned it to Naomi when they got outside.

"Yeah. All the older guys here are in lust with my aunt," she said flatly. "Vanessa laughs about it. She says it's a generational thing—they just want to go where the Allman Brothers have been."

Zoe chuckled. Naomi didn't.

They walked back to the *jardín*, and Zoe bought them two bottles from the stands—spring water for Naomi, bubbly *limonáda* for herself. They sat on a wrought-iron bench, shaded by jacarandas, facing away from La Cruz.

It was siesta time—something the people of San Esteban obviously took seriously. During the time they had been in Dr. Dave's office, the bustling village had become a ghost town—no people, no traffic, all the stores and restaurants closed. Nothing around but the sound of birds, the bells of that great, Gothic church announcing it was three p.m.

Naomi, too, seemed to have shut down for siesta. Ever since the Allman Brothers comment, she'd barely said a word. Zoe figured she was probably still light-headed, so she didn't want to press her.

Zoe put the bottle to her lips and held the sour bubbles in her mouth and enjoyed the lovely natural light, the lack of groaning fluorescents and medicine smell and Dr. Dave. She breathed in the sweet, flowery air and felt a cool breeze on the back of her neck, and just for a moment, she let herself think of that name. *Nicholas Denby.* The first actual *friend* of Warren's she'd ever heard mentioned, and yet, at the thought of him, Robin's face had lost all its brightness.

He was special.

Naomi said, "I didn't pass out because of dehydration."

Zoe looked at her. "You didn't?"

The girl stared straight ahead. Her lips were very pale. "Uh-uh. It was . . . that picture."

"The one of the plant?"

Naomi nodded.

"Why?"

"Dr. Dave painted it," she said. "He takes classes with Rafael, the artist next door? Vanessa does, too. Vanessa just takes the class to flirt with Rafael, but Dave actually paints stuff. There's something new on his wall every week. Whenever I come in, I always look to see what the class has been working on."

"Uh-huh." Zoe wondered where she was going with this.

"This painting . . ." Naomi closed her eyes. "It was a spine from a maguey—they're also called century plants."

"Okay . . ."

Suddenly, Naomi turned and faced her. "Before I say any more, can I ask you a personal question?"

"Sure."

"How close are you and Warren?"

She opened her mouth to say, *Very close*, but reconsidered. "In some ways, very close," she said slowly. "In others . . . not at all."

"If I were to ask you something . . . something about *him* . . . you don't have to answer. But could you promise *not* to tell him I asked?"

"What does a maguey plant have to do with—"

"You have to promise."

"Okay, Naomi. I promise."

"Has . . . has Warren ever mentioned someone to you named Grace?"

Zoe frowned. "No, he hasn't," she said. "But, to be honest, we don't talk much about . . . other people." She stared at her. "Can you please explain to me, Naomi, what exactly you're talking about?"

Naomi cleared her throat. "You know what was done to Jordan, right?"

"Yes."

"Besides . . . that, someone had laid his hands flat, and put a century plant spine in each of his palms."

"Oh . . ."

"When my aunt saw that—the plant in his hands—she freaked out. I heard her talking to Mrs. Woods last night. . . . There was someone named Grace, a long time ago. I think she was killed in that same way. And century plant spines were put in her palms."

"So that drug dealer—"

"No. No, I think maybe someone else killed Grace. I think that same person killed Jordan and it scares me so much because . . ."

"Because . . ."

"I think he's still out there." Naomi moved a little closer, a look in her eyes that made Zoe's breath catch. "He killed them because they were young."

We don't get many young people.

Zoe's pulse sped up. *Keep it together. She is just a kid, a kid suffering from post-traumatic stress and who knows how long peyote stays in someone's system . . . ?*

"Why don't you think Carlos Royas did it? He confessed."

"Mrs. Woods doesn't think he did it."

"She's Jordan's *great-aunt.*"

"So?"

"She's grieving. She's trying to make sense of things, and a drug dealer killing her nephew doesn't make any sense to her."

"Maybe it shouldn't."

"He confessed, Naomi. You don't confess to a crime like that unless you did it."

"That's what my aunt says . . . but the century plant spines. Grace . . ."

"Maybe Carlos Royas killed Grace, too."

"No . . . No, listen. There's some group. A group Mrs. Woods was talking about, and they stopped meeting after Grace, but she thinks they're meeting again."

"What kind of group?"

"I . . . I don't know. . . ."

"Naomi."

"Jordan said there was something weird going on in this town, and I thought he was just wasted, but now I'm thinking he—"

"Naomi. Take a deep breath."

"I'm tired of taking deep breaths."

"You saw an awful picture and it made you remember. Close your eyes. Breathe in and out. Slowly."

She did. "Okay," she said. "Okay, okay . . ."

"Now listen to me. I know how you feel."

"You do?"

"It's a long story, but I was . . . deeply affected by some murders in New York that I was covering for a newspaper. I had nightmares, flashbacks. . . . That feeling of silence roaring in your ears . . ."

"Yes. Yes, that's right."

"I saw photos of victims. Police photos. Every time I closed my eyes I would see those images. I would hear his voice. . . ."

"Whose voice?"

"The killer's."

"Oh, my God. You talked to—"

"Interviewed him, yeah. You come that close to evil, Naomi—you get right up against it like I did . . . like *you* did—it's going to rub off and work its way under your skin and mess with your head. Really badly."

Naomi stared straight ahead. "He was watching me."

"Who?"

"Jordan's murderer. When I was talking to Jordan by the fire that night, I could . . . feel it. . . ."

"I understand."

"Sometimes," she said, "I feel it still."

Zoe caught a chill, but she ignored it. "I get that, too. My phone rings sometimes, I get this sense . . . like I'm going to pick it up and hear the killer's voice. He's been on death row for four years. I moved. I changed my last name so he couldn't write me or call me, even if he tried, but still, five years later . . ."

Naomi looked at her. Her eyes were wet. "What am I supposed to do?"

"Live with it," she said. "It's all you *can* do."

Naomi started to cry. Zoe put both arms around her and held her as if she were a child—this young woman, at least eight inches taller than she was—and let her cry until her tank top was wet with Naomi's tears. She said, "It's okay. It's okay," even though it wasn't and never would be. It was what Naomi needed to hear, and so Zoe said it, again and again, until finally, Naomi caught her breath. "That . . . that was the first time I've cried since it happened."

"*Really?*"

"Yeah," she said. "I mean, I screamed when I found him and all, but since then . . . I guess I kind of kept it in."

"You can't keep it in, Naomi—that only makes it worse."

"Did you cry after . . . ?"

"Yeah," she said. "But in all truthfulness not very often because once I would start it would be very hard to stop."

Naomi nodded. "Maybe I just misheard what Mrs. Woods was saying," she said. "Carlos wouldn't confess if he didn't do it."

"Why would he?"

Naomi exhaled heavily. "I mean . . . there might not even be a group. I could've heard that wrong, too. I . . . can't trust my own ears half the time. I . . . hear noises, lines from dreams . . ."

"Give it time."

"It's just . . . Mrs. Woods mentioned a cross in Vanessa's closet and so I looked and—"

Zoe stopped breathing. "What?"

"It was probably just some bad art she did. Or one of her boyfriends did. Or someth—"

"What did it look like?"

"It was this awful black cross with a human heart painted on it."

"The heart had a crown of thorns."

Naomi's eyes got huge. "Yes," she breathed. "Oh, my God. Did you . . . does Warren?"

"In his dressing room closet. Yes."

The two of them stared at each other, saying absolutely nothing.

"I'm sure," Zoe finally said, "there's a logical reason why they would both have them." But Zoe wasn't sure of that. Right now, she wasn't sure of anything. "The most important thing is that you stay calm, that you get some rest. . . ."

Behind them, a voice hissed Naomi's name. They turned toward the voice, and Zoe saw a woman of about sixty with haunted green eyes and a deep slash across her cheek.

"Mrs. Woods," Naomi said.

"I'm leaving San Esteban tomorrow," she said. "I'm going home."

Zoe looked closer. It was two slashes, in the shape of a cross.

Naomi said, "I'm sor—"

"Please tell your aunt goodbye. I'll miss her friendship."

"All right."

"And also," she said, "tell her she ought to be ashamed of herself."

The color drained from Naomi's face. She started to say something, but the woman swept past her and crossed the empty street. They both watched Mrs. Woods stalk away in her gauzy blue dress—a furious ghost of a woman getting smaller and smaller and smaller.

TEN

Without considering why, Naomi took the long way home. She walked back up Calle Murillo, the street where she and Zoe had just been. She walked past Rafael's studio and Reiki Master Paul's and Dr. Dave's, and it was like one of those horror movies, where the girl has a bad dream and then she wakes up and she's in the exact same place where the bad dream took place, and then she goes through the whole dream, all over again.

Naomi wished she could wake up.

She looked at Mrs. Woods's house across the street. For about half a second, she considered knocking on the door and demanding to know what she'd been talking about in the *jardín. Exactly why should my aunt be ashamed?* she wanted to ask. *And while we're at it, how did you know about the cross in Vanessa's closet?*

But Naomi knew she'd just get, "Ask your aunt." And there was something else, too. The look in Mrs.Woods's eyes. Zoe had almost seemed relieved by it. She'd said Mrs. Woods had gone crazy with grief and wasn't to be believed.

And, though Naomi wasn't sure about that, she did know this: Mrs. Woods *scared* her now. It was like what Corinne had said about Carlos Royas's bad luck. That look of Mrs. Woods's—and she'd had it only since today—it was more than grief. It was as if someone had taken a vacuum cleaner to her insides and sucked the life out of her. Naomi didn't want to be around that. It might be catching.

As she passed the house, Naomi felt that sea-glass gaze, even from across the street, even through the bars on Mrs. Woods's windows. It chilled her. Naomi remembered the cut on Mrs. Woods's face. Had she done that to herself? On purpose? Or had someone done it to her?

Tell her she ought to be ashamed.

Naomi continued down the road—past a restaurant called El Borracho that was hung with tiny, twinkling Christmas lights all year-round; past El Infierno, a rotisserie place that Vanessa called *Hell Is for Chickens* because roasted chicken bodies were stacked in the windows in a very unappetizing, massacre-like way. . . . She thought of that, of Vanessa singing, *"Because hell, hell is for chickens,"* to the tune of some old song by Pat Benatar . . . and for some reason, it sparked a memory.

She'd seen cuts just like that on Vanessa—not on her face, but on her arms, the backs of her wrists—long, straight scratches that almost looked cosmetic. "Must've happened when I was gardening," Vanessa would say. She would laugh about it, shrug her shoulders, and Naomi would think, *Even her injuries are perfect.* But Vanessa would never look Naomi in the eye.

Sometimes, the cuts were in the shape of a cross.

Vanessa had a black cross in her closet, painted with a bloody human heart. She had weird cuts and Mrs. Woods had a weird cut. Warren had a cross just like Vanessa's, and even if Mrs. Woods didn't have one, too, she'd known enough to ask about it.

Yes, Naomi had been through a lot. She was suffering from post-traumatic stress, and she was still grieving for her mom, and even before the night of the bonfire, she'd been more aware of life's darkness than other kids her age. But still . . . that didn't change the facts.

There was a group. There was a secret group, and there had been a Grace in that secret group who had died, and, while Naomi didn't know whether either Grace or the group had anything to do with what had happened to Jordan, she was frightened. And she was alone in her fear.

There's got to be a logical explanation for the crosses, Zoe had said. Like three times.

Finally, Naomi had replied, *The only logical explanation is that Warren and Vanessa are in the same club. A club they don't want us to know about.*

Zoe had looked at her, and Naomi had seen a change in her face, as if someone had just flipped on the lights. There was this intensity—a curiosity that made her glow. But there was also fear. The fear must have won out, too, because seconds later the switch went off and Zoe's face went calm again. *You know what?* she had said. *I think we could both use a nice, long siesta.*

Naomi had rolled her eyes at the time, and she rolled them again now, just remembering. Zoe was a nice woman, but her problem was this: She was on vacation. It had nothing to do with taking a plane to Mexico, either. She'd been on vacation ever since those murders in New York. Her job at the soap opera magazine had been a vacation and she'd quit that job to *go* on vacation and her whole relationship with Warren was one big, stupid vacation. What had she said? *We don't talk about other people?* Hello?

Naomi had never had a real, serious boyfriend. She had lost her virginity to a boy named Joaquin she'd met two hours earlier, at her first party in San Esteban. It had happened on a scratchy old blanket in the desert, and it had lasted about three seconds and after he took her home, he'd never spoken to her again. But *come on*. Even *Naomi and Joaquin*—during their *two hours* of couple-hood—had *talked about other people*.

Naomi passed a line of Mexican artisans' shops, their doors clustered with marionettes and musical instruments and Day of the Dead masks and tile-bordered mirrors.

She averted her eyes as she walked by. She had real problems with the Day of the Dead stuff now—not so much the papier-mâché masks and candy skulls, but the skeleton marionettes. . . . It was the rib cages.

Most of Jordan's rib cage had been removed with either bolt cutters or a saw. She'd seen it on the ground, about ten feet away from his body—the sternum, half ribs branching off it, caked with dried blood. Like he'd been dissected.

Had Carlos Royas really done that? Would he have even known how?

Naomi reached the end of the sidewalk and headed right. The road she was on now was almost all residential, save for a few small hotels. It was called Calle Parque because it bounded the eastern edge of El Parque de las Lavanderas.

This was why she had taken the long way home. Even though Naomi had told herself she hadn't been thinking about it—that she'd just felt like a little bit more of a walk—she knew that a small, dark part of her brain needed her to go past Carlos Royas's park. It was the same part of her brain where she stored her anger and her sorrow and her pain, where she crammed all the stuff she didn't want to look at so she wouldn't have to cry because crying hurt Vanessa. It made Vanessa say things like, "How can I make the pain go away?" As if she could do that. As if Naomi's pain was that small, that *fixable*.

Carlos Royas used to hang out in Parque de las Lavanderas with his friend Alejandro during siesta every day, stretching out on the grass or leaning against their tree, smoking cigarettes and waiting for business.

Alejandro still did. At least, that was what Naomi had heard.

The park was bordered by thick oak trees and jacarandas, so you couldn't really see it unless you were in it. At the far edge, though, was the break in the trees where the town had set up the long, basinlike sinks for washing clothes, some with hoses running out of them, some with actual faucets. None of the *lavanderas* were here—it was too late in the day—but several of them had left their washboards behind, neatly stacked against the porcelain, waiting for morning. Naomi walked past the sinks and cut into the park, past a series of barbecue pits and picnic tables.

Weird, this place. It wasn't as noticeable when the *lavanderas* were here, but largely emptied out for siesta, you could really sense it. *Bad energy.* Naomi usually found that expression incredibly irritating—Vanessa and her friends used it to describe everything from un–feng shuied living rooms to rude hair stylists. But here . . . it fit. The street dogs that lay sleeping on their sides looked a little meaner. And the occasional groups of people who passed—mostly kids her age—never spoke or even smiled. They just stared.

A lot of missionaries used to hang out here—American teens with big, happy grins and driven eyes. Naomi could spot them a mile away, and even if you were just passing through, even if you were in a hurry, they'd run after you with their Jehovah's Witness pamphlets, asking you what your religion was and if you liked your life. Well, since about a year ago, the missionaries had stopped coming to the park. The Catholics often complained about them, but there had been no town ordinance, no police crackdown or anything that Naomi had known of. You would still see those kids in other places—the *biblioteca*, the *jardín*. But El Parque . . . it was as if the Jehovah's Witnesses had given up on it. The bad energy had won.

Naomi was hitting the southern edge of the park—Carlos and Alejandro's "office." Interestingly, this was the prettiest part. The jacaranda trees were full and healthy, and there were thick-trunked palms, swollen with coconuts, clusters of bright impatiens planted over their roots.

Alejandro was nowhere to be seen.

Funny how everyone had a safe place. Naomi had lots of them. There weren't assigned desks at her school but she always picked the same ones in each class. She went to the same bathroom all the time and used the same stall. She and Corinne had their table at El Borracho and the *jardín* bench she'd shared with Zoe was the one she always chose. Alejandro and Carlos had their safe place, too. It was the second jacaranda on the southwestern end of the park. They would either lean against it, or sit on the grass in front. She wondered if Jordan had had any safe places. Was he haunting them now?

She touched Carlos and Alejandro's tree and closed her eyes, and even though they were both still alive, it was as if they were haunting it. When she breathed in deeply, she thought she could smell their cigarette smoke.

Naomi opened her eyes. She *did* smell it.

She squeezed between the trees and then she was out of the park, on the sidewalk of another, slightly poorer residential street. Standing about five feet away, his back to her, was Alejandro. He was smoking.

His dropped the cigarette to the sidewalk and stubbed it out with his motorcycle boot. Both he and Carlos wore too many clothes—black pants and boots on the hottest days. It was uncomfortable to look at them. Alejandro, in particular, was always sweating, and Naomi thought it was a high price to pay just to look tough. But Alejandro didn't seem tough now, with his drooping head, his big, round shoulders so tense they nearly touched his ears. He looked like a sad boy hiding in black.

"Alejandro!"

He turned and looked at her. His eyes went huge.

Alejandro spoke English, but Naomi used her Spanish anyway. "*¡Necesito hablar contigo!*" I need to talk to you.

Alejandro just stood there, gaping.

There was a time, during Naomi's first few weeks in San Esteban, when Alejandro had had something of a crush on her. Lots of boys did back then—because of her tallness and newness and Americanness and mainly, she thought, because of her aunt. But with Alejandro it was more than that. He had brought her a plant once—strode right up to her as she was walking into Santa Beatriz, and as the girls around her giggled, he had handed it to her—a potted white violet. *You lost your mother,* he had told her in English. *I lost my father. We are the same in our sadness.*

"We are the same in our sadness," she said now, very softly.

"No." He backed away. "Not anymore."

She'd planned a lot of questions in her head on the walk over. They all fell out and splattered on the ground.

Just ask if Carlos really killed Jordan Brink.

She heard herself say in Spanish: *Why did Carlos lie about killing Jordan Brink?*

Whoa. She hadn't planned that one. Alejandro's eyes got even bigger and a look of terror crossed his face. "Go home," he told her.

And then, without warning, he turned and fled.

Zoe returned to Warren's house to find no Warren, no Guadalupe and no note from either. What she did find—

though she couldn't figure out which one of them had put it there—was an enormous bouquet of red roses and greens in a round, cut-crystal vase. It had been placed at the center of the coffee table in the living room and it made Zoe smile. Until she took a closer look at the greens. They were maguey spines.

Okay, okay . . . It's a coincidence. The maguey is an indigenous plant and Patty Woods is a crazy woman and Naomi is suffering from post-traumatic stress and you . . . you, Zoe Greene, are in serious need of a siesta.

She moved through the stunning garden and up the two flights of stairs, determined to forget the day, to escape into sleep, to wake up to Warren and escape in other ways. Zoe moved faster and faster, the bright flowers and thick plants rushing by in a blur, and by the time she rounded the corner of the second flight, it was as if she had a plane to catch. She started toward the bedroom, but then whacked her bad wrist into the banister, sending waves of pain up her arm and down her entire left side.

"*Damn.*" She stood at the top of the stairs, clenching her teeth and cradling her wrist in her good hand, tears seeping from the corners of her eyes. She wanted this whole day back so badly. If she could just rewind to this morning, take an extra five minutes to go through her suitcase and find a better pair of walking shoes, none of this ever would have happened. Where was Warren right now, anyway? Why wasn't he home?

Warren and Vanessa are in the same club. A club they don't want us to know about.

Zoe shut her eyes. She made herself remember the concern that flooded Vanessa's flawless features when she talked about her niece, the way Warren had looked at her just last night—that healing gaze. *I'll always protect you, always keep you safe.* He had said that to her, and she had believed it, and she wasn't going to let a traumatized young girl turn it all on its head. Zoe had been safe for five years—hadn't gotten involved in anything dangerous and therefore hadn't ruined anything. She'd kept her conscience clear. She had found a hot, compelling man and he'd taken her on vacation. And vacation was where she was going to stay.

I'll always keep you safe. She replayed the words and pictured Warren's eyes, his touch . . . until what Naomi had said faded, until it got filed in the back of Zoe's mind—in that crowded place with all those other things she didn't want to think about.

Zoe started for the bedroom, but stopped when she caught something in the corner of her eye. It was on the tall wall at the street-facing end of the rooftop patio, and it was practically hidden by the climbing roses—a small door, about two feet by one, built high into the wall. *A safe?* Impulsively, she tried the knob, but it wouldn't open. She noticed a tiny lock, but there was no key in sight. That was fine with Zoe. If there was one thing she really didn't feel like doing right now, it was unlocking hidden doors.

Zoe opened her eyes to see the skylight glowing a deep, velvety purple. She wasn't sure how long she'd been sleeping, but it must have been a while. She flipped on the switch on the bedside lamp and grabbed her watch. Seven thirty p.m. She got out of bed, and hurried downstairs. The lights were still off. One by one, she checked all the rooms. Empty. Warren still wasn't home.

Zoe hadn't seen Warren in more than twelve hours. *Who leaves a visitor alone for her entire first day in town?* Maybe Warren had been home looking for her while she was at the doctor's, but if that was the case, why hadn't he left a note? Zoe wasn't sure whether to be worried or angry, but worried was winning out. She sprinted back upstairs to the bedroom, grabbed her cell and, with her good hand, pecked out a text message to Warren: **Where R U?** Then she called him, left a message on his voice mail.

Warren didn't have a landline here in San Esteban—no computer, either. So this was pretty much all she could do, outside of heading over to the police station and using her crappy high school Spanish to file a missing-person report about twenty-four hours too early.

Maybe Vanessa knew where Warren was. But that wasn't of much help because she had no idea how to get hold of her. She vaguely remembered that Vanessa lived on top of a hill—but how to get to that hill from Warren's house was a completely different matter. She should have exchanged numbers with Naomi, but she'd been in a hurry to leave town and put the day behind her. Plus, to be painfully honest, she really hadn't wanted to set herself up as Naomi's confidante.

Did Vanessa have a Web site? Zoe could call Steve, get him to send her an urgent e-mail, Zoe's name in the subject line. . . . God, that was a little overinvolved, wasn't it? Why not just check that writing desk in the corner of Warren's bedroom, see if he had an address book? *Get a grip, Zoe. He hasn't been gone that long.*

Warren's desktop was mostly bare, save for a copy of the local English-language paper, the *Amigo*. On the cover was a piece about a street dog adoption drive, another about a Saints Festival. . . . Zoe checked the date: It was today's paper. So Warren had come back at some point—unless, of course, Guadalupe had picked up the paper.

Naomi slid open the top desk drawer. She saw a stack of expensive-looking stationery, another stack of blank post-cards and some stamps. *Great. Letter-writing supplies.* She tried the other drawers—nothing but a stapler and pencils and a hole puncher and boxes of legal-sized envelopes and checkbooks and five or six ballpoint pens with no advertising on them and a penlight and a pack of peppermint gum. Yeah, she knew this was his second home, but never in her life had Zoe seen a desk that was this maddeningly generic. All it needed was a Bible and a room service menu and she could have been in a hotel.

She was about to go downstairs, see if maybe Warren kept a list of important numbers in the kitchen, when she recalled something she'd seen in the top drawer, but hadn't thought much about. She'd been looking for phone numbers after all, but now that she saw how devoid of the personal his desk was, the object took on more significance.

She slid the drawer open again, and there it was, next to the stack of postcards. A small silver key. The type of key that would fit the safe she'd seen on the street-facing wall of the roof garden.

Zoe wasn't the type of person to sneak into the personal spaces of those she was close to, even in her days as a nosey reporter. Getting a story was one thing, but with lovers, if you found yourself picking locks, it was probably time to move on.

She'd never had a lover like Warren Clark, though. And it was nearly eight and he hadn't returned her messages and she had no idea where he was. If he'd wanted her to respect his privacy, he should have tried leaving a note.

She took the key out of the top drawer and the penlight out of the second side drawer, and without mulling over the issue any further, she walked out to the rooftop garden, pushed aside the climbing roses so she could get to the lock, and tried the key. It fit. She opened the door onto a small, metal-lined safe, about twice as deep as a medicine cabinet. She saw no papers inside, no address book or PDA. What she did see was a thick stack of pesos and a men's silver Tiffany watch. She turned it over and shined the penlight. It bore the engraved initials NLD. *Nicholas Denby?*

There was also a silk *Day's End* scarf—she had one herself. They were a promotional gift the soap had given out a few years ago—a sort of fifties tourist's scarf, in pink and green, with a stylized map of Saxon Falls, the town where *The Day's End* took place. *What's that doing here?*

Zoe picked up the scarf. There was a gun underneath it.

Her breath caught in her throat and stayed there. She remembered Warren telling her that guns were illegal in Mexico for everyone but the police. That would explain why he'd hidden it so carefully—but not why he had it in the first place. She picked it up. It was heavy. She held it in both hands and its weight made the wrist pain flare up. She didn't know much about guns, but from what little she'd learned from her old cop sources, this one was a .45 caliber, capable of taking off a good-sized chunk of someone's head. The safety was on and it was a semiautomatic, and when she checked the magazine, she saw it was loaded.

ELEVEN

Zoe didn't know how long she'd been standing there dazed, the gun in her hands, but an explosive ringing shook her out of that fast. She froze. It was like an old-fashioned alarm clock, and it was coming from downstairs. Doorbell. It had to be. *"¡Momento!"* Carefully, she placed the gun back in the cabinet, covered it with the scarf, locked the door. The doorbell rang again and Zoe yelled, *"¡Momento!"* again. She ran back into the bedroom and slipped the key back in the desk; then she hurried downstairs.

"¡Momento!" Was that even the right word?

"Zoe! It's me! I forgot the key!" *Warren.* She felt equal parts relief and creeping dread. *Stop. There has to be an explanation.* The problem, though, was getting that explanation. She remembered the flatness in his eyes, the anger in his voice when she'd mentioned a painted cross in a closet that *he* had left open. How would he react to the news that she'd taken the key out of his desk, opened the safe where he kept his most personal, private possessions? *Like his .45 semiautomatic. And his last visitor's watch.*

She took a deep breath, told herself to calm down and sound normal, which, given the situation, would have to be pretty pissed off. "It's about time!"

"I'm so sorry."

Zoe opened the door to find Warren, in a white shirt and pale khaki pants, his blue eyes full of contrition. He looked like either an angel or a GAP ad, depending on your point of view, and he held two plastic grocery bags in one hand, a bottle of wine in the other. "Hungry?" he said, a little sheepishly. "I brought homemade bread, machengo cheese, Spanish olives, avocados, a roasted chicken. . . ." It was hard to reconcile the demeanor, the look, the grocery list with what she'd seen in the safe, but she tried not to let that show on her face.

"Warren, where have you been?"

"What happened to your wrist?"

"I asked first."

"I told you, I bought dinner."

"All day?"

"I came back, but you'd left. I went looking for you, but couldn't find you, so I went shopping at the *mercado*—"

"Why didn't you answer my text?"

"Forgot my BlackBerry." A flicker of annoyance crept into his eyes, and Zoe thought, *You've got some nerve.*

"Believe it or not," said Warren, "this is more questions than she's asked me in four months."

Zoe thought, *She?* The man behind Warren stepped to the side, and said, "She's right to ask questions." It was then that Zoe realized he'd been there the whole time: a short American man with graying black hair, strong features and arresting amber-colored eyes. "Zoe," Warren said, "I'd like you to meet my dear friend, Rafael."

"As in Studio Rafael?"

"My reputation precedes me." Rafael smiled—a warm

smile that surprised her. Zoe remembered Vanessa at the airport asking for Rafael on her cell phone and Naomi talking about how Vanessa took his painting classes "to flirt." And looking at him now, Zoe thought that it made sense. In a strange way, Rafael was rock star material. He was just a few inches taller than Zoe's five foot three, and he wasn't what you'd call classically handsome. But there was something about his face that was like an effective TV commercial—a brightness that grabbed your attention and held it. He'd been Dr. Dave's minister back in California, and she could see that, too—the preacher's conviction, the righteous glow. . . .

For a moment, Zoe forgot her concerns about Warren and where he had been all day and even the gun. That was how strong a charisma this short, older man exuded.

"Zoe?" said Warren. "Are you all right?"

Rafael's grin grew broader. "Are you the only one she's allowed to stare at?" he said, and only then did Zoe realize she was gawking.

"Oh . . . Sorry. I . . . didn't realize . . ." Her face was hot.

"Nothing to be sorry about." Rafael winked. "You see, I can speak that way to Warren because I've known him since he was an adolescent."

Zoe turned to Warren. "Really?"

"Not exactly. Rafael spent six weeks at the High School of Performing Arts as a visiting instructor. That's how we met." He smiled tightly. "I was eighteen, though. Hardly an adolescent."

"You taught art?"

Rafael shook his head. "Public speaking. How to sway souls with the voice." The amber eyes glimmered. "Warren was my star student . . . as you might imagine."

Zoe watched Warren, then Rafael. Definitely tension between these two. But why? More than twenty years sep-

arating them—former mentor and student, *dear friends* as
Warren had put it, but they seemed more like rivals—two
men competing for the same plum job. "Yes," Rafael said,
"Warren has always been quite adept at stealing . . . I mean,
swaying souls."

Zoe heard herself say, "Why don't you come inside, Rafael? Have some dinner with us?" She could sense Warren's
back stiffening, but she didn't care. She wanted to know
more. She wanted to pour this minister-turned-artist glass
after glass of wine and use every interviewing technique
she'd ever learned to solve the mystery of the man standing
in front of her—the commercially handsome GAP angel of
a man with arms full of groceries and a billion secrets buried
behind his clear blue eyes.

She wondered if Rafael had known Nicholas Denby. She
wondered if he knew that Warren owned an illegal gun.

"Sadly," said Rafael, "I have other plans for the night. I say
sadly because it would be a true pleasure to embarrass Warren
in front of such a charming and intelligent young woman."

Warren laughed. "That's a shame." Zoe could tell he was
thoroughly relieved.

"You never answered Warren," Rafael said, "about your
wrist."

"Oh, right," she said. "I slipped on the cobblestones. It's
just a sprain."

He pointed at the bandage. "Dr. Dave?"

She grimaced a little. "Yes."

"Not much in the way of personality, but a first-rate
medical man," Rafael said. "Let me see it."

"The wrist?"

"Yes."

"Why?"

His smile was magnetic. "Parting gift."

Zoe looked at Warren.

He nodded at her. "Go on, Zoe. You'll be amazed."

"Okay . . ." She held out her wrist, and Rafael took it, cradling it in one of his palms, while placing the other on top. "Close your eyes."

Zoe did. Before long, an intense heat poured out of the top hand like water from a faucet. It coursed into her wrist, and up her arm. It was like nothing she had ever felt before, as if her blood were instantly thickening, strengthening.

She opened her eyes. Rafael looked right back at her, the same heat radiating from his amber gaze. She was transfixed.

He released her wrist. "Bend it."

She did. There was no pain—as if it had never been sprained to begin with. "Unbelievable."

"What did I tell you?" said Warren. "It's a wonderful trick."

It was Rafael's turn to stiffen. "Not a trick," he said quietly.

Zoe asked, "Was that Reiki?"

His gaze shifted from Warren to Zoe, warming as it did. "Close. I studied with a Brazilian shaman years and years ago." Rafael cleared his throat. "My wife had just died. At that point in my life, I became very interested in learning how to . . . take away pain."

Zoe said, "You sure you don't want to stay?"

"Believe me, I would if I could. But I am having a party at my studio tomorrow night, and if you come, I promise you will find out more about Warren than you've ever wanted to know."

"I wouldn't miss it for the world." Zoe watched Rafael as he left, bending the wrist back and forth, amazed at the ease of it, the complete absence of pain. "I wish he could do the same thing with my mind."

Warren tilted her face up and gazed into her eyes and kissed her. "Leave the mind to me."

Steve was getting ready for his news trick, but doing a horrible job of it. Either this new razor sucked beyond belief, or he was too distracted to be trusted with a sharp object, because he now had more than a dozen little pieces of tissue paper stuck to his face. How could he take Debbie Cohn to *Dreamcoat* when he looked like a piñata?

He needed to focus on the bribe story and get the Royas/ Brink/Clark connection out of his mind—whether there was one or not. Steve had Glen calling people in San Esteban, and so far, he hadn't delivered any bombshells. Steve had also found the only Morrison Brink listed in Astoria and had left a polite message on the couple's answering machine about his possibly writing a profile on their late son. No word back on that, either. Outside of calling Zoe in the middle of her vacation and telling her a whole bunch of stuff that she'd say added up to nothing, he had done all he could. It was time to move on.

He just wished Zoe didn't need so much protecting. But even as he wished it, part of him knew he didn't wish that at all.

Steve cut himself again. Blood streamed down the side of his face, and it stung like hell. He got a washcloth, soaked it in cold water and pressed it against his cheek, but when he removed it, most of the little pieces of tissue fell off, and he looked like he'd been attacked by rabid weasels.

Jesus, why did he bother shaving?

The woman next door was screaming, "Why don't you just go back to your little bitch?!" Steve didn't know whether it was directed at her husband or one of her four teenage sons, but either way it was soul deadening. Steve's walls were about as thick as playing cards. If someone had told him when he was a kid that at age thirty-three, he'd be living in Manhattan and working as an investigative reporter for a daily newspaper, he would've been psyched as hell—until he got a look at this godawful scene.

"That's right!" the woman shrieked. "I know all about your little slut of a whore bitch!"

And now the whole world knows. Steve grabbed his iPod, shoved the buds in his ears. It was on shuffle-play, and wouldn't you know it, the so-called entertainment device chose Coldplay's "Swallowed in the Sea," Zoe's favorite song of 2006. He sat down on his bed, and instantly, he was driving his car to Allentown, Pennsylvania, Zoe in the seat next to him. He'd been invited to a press junket at Dorney Park. He'd taken Zoe along because the invite had said, *Bring a guest*, and they both loved roller coasters, and besides, who else was he going to bring?

How amazing and sometimes horrible that music could do this stuff to your head. But all he had to hear was that long, plaintive note on the keyboard, that first line about chopping down a tree, and he could see Zoe, her bare feet propped up on the dashboard, using a half-empty bottle of Coke for a fake microphone as she sang along with Chris Martin at the top of her lungs, completely and painfully off-key. . . .

God, Zoe had a voice like a dog being tortured.

He thought of that horrible singing voice, those big trusting brown eyes and that wicked laugh and the tentative smile she'd give him whenever she asked, "Is everything okay?" He thought of the way she buried her head in his shoulder during the scary parts of movies and how she got into intense political debates with cab drivers and turned into a shark of a pool player when she was drunk and always made Steve ride the Circle Line with her on the first day of spring. He thought of how, after Daryl Barclay was sentenced to death, she'd gone to Steve's place for company and slept in his arms and how right it had felt, hard as he'd tried not to think about that, not to feel that. . . .

Steve's phone rang. He pulled the buds out of his ears and ran for it, hoping more than anything it was Debbie Cohn calling to cancel. Another time, he'd be fine. Just not tonight . . . *Please be Debbie. Please be Debbie.* . . . But when he grabbed the phone and checked the caller ID screen, he didn't see Debbie's cell number or name. No, this was better. It was Morrison Brink.

"So you followed Rafael down here?"

"I wouldn't say that," Warren replied.

"What would you say?"

"I came down to visit him, and I fell in love." He looked up, gave Zoe a sly smile. "With the town. Not with Rafael."

"I figured."

"Did you? Aren't we actors supposed to be ambisexual?"

Zoe smiled. "I like the way you say that word. Say it again."

"Am . . . bi . . . sex . . . ual."

Zoe grinned. They were at the dining room table, finishing dinner and the bottle of wine. Zoe hadn't mentioned the safe's contents yet. She hadn't found the right moment, and truthfully, she couldn't imagine that right moment coming anytime soon. It had been such a perfect meal. Tension with Warren notwithstanding, it felt as if Rafael had laid his healing touch on the two of them. Zoe asked questions; Warren answered them. And, starved for information as she'd been for the past four months, she felt that each benign question was an indulgence, each answer a delicate morsel, meant to be savored.

Where were you born? Syracuse. We moved to Long Island when I was twelve.

What is your middle name? Horace.

Seriously? Yes, unfortunately.

Your first crush? Kimberly Epstein. Kindergarten.

Your first kiss? Jenny Mangione. Fifth grade—party at Matt Kringle's house. We were playing seven minutes of heaven.

First sex? You.

Stop that.

I don't remember anyone else.

Okay, so he was more forthcoming about some things than he was about others, but it was a good start—a wonderful start, considering where they had been before.

"Remember when we first met," he was saying now, "when you were interviewing me in my dressing room?"

"Yes?"

"I knew then that I wanted to take you here. I looked into your eyes and I knew."

Zoe swallowed the rest of her third glass of wine and gazed at him. "And here I thought you just wanted to get in my pants."

"I'm serious, Zoe," he said. "You know, it isn't everyone who makes me think that way. It isn't everyone I invite down here for a visit."

You can say that again. The wine was working. Zoe had to be careful. "I'm really . . . honored."

"San Esteban is a special place and you are such a special person. I could see it in you even back then—that spark, that . . . that aura. You belong here with me."

"White aura. Means I'm young."

He looked at her, curious. "It means more than that," he said. "But where did you hear about auras?"

"Robin and Paul." Zoe smiled a little. "Your confidants."

"They are good people." His eyes bored into hers. "But not like you, Zoe. No one in the world is like you." Warren had always given off a little more heat than the average guy, but since the start of this trip, it was as if he'd turned it up to eleven. Zoe was moved, yet it also made her slightly uncomfortable. Did it always have to feel like this, like he was reaching into her chest and grabbing her heart and twisting? Couldn't the two of them just lighten up sometimes, maybe tell some dumb jokes, watch a little TV?

"You know what my all-time favorite bad movie is?" said Zoe. *"Phantom of the Paradise."*

He didn't reply. The stare grew hotter.

"I like *Showgirls* a lot, too. 'You love doggie chow?' *'I* love doggie chow!' "

Silence.

"Guess you didn't see that one, huh?"

No answer, so she gave up and stated the obvious. "You're staring at me."

Warren said, "I have a surprise for you."

"The roses? Oh, they're beautiful, Warren, and the crystal vase is just perfect. I should have said something earlier. I saw them right when I came in and—"

"It isn't roses."

For a brief, crazy moment, she imagined him pulling that gun. But then he got up from his chair and moved up behind her and slipped his hands down the length of her arms. He kissed the back of her neck, and she turned and met his mouth with her own. His lips were soft and tasted like wine, and Zoe swooned into him, as if her bones were giving way, and she thought, *I surrender. Grab my heart and twist it all you want. It's yours. It's all yours forever and ever. . . .* "Is the surprise in the bedroom?"

He pulled away, shook his head. "I need to drive you to it."

Naomi was still winded. Five hours ago, she had taken off after Alejandro, chasing him up one cobblestone street and down the next in that bleak, unfamiliar section of town. . . . *Five hours ago*, and still, her lungs felt like they had knifes stuck in them.

She'd been amazed Alejandro was able to run so fast. He was such a big kid, and his center of gravity was so low that he always moved as if he was from another planet and found the air on this one to be a challenge. But he'd had a head start this afternoon, plus he knew the streets and he was obviously (if inexplicably) terrified.

So Alejandro had outrun the taller, stronger, faster Naomi, putting a full block between them, then a block and a half, then two, before disappearing into an alley or a house or some waiting car—Naomi had no idea. All she knew was, she'd been left doubled over and wheezing on some crumbling sidewalk in a bad neighborhood next to a hole-in-the-wall cantina that reeked of tequila and dog pee, thinking, *No way in a billion years am I going into that place to ask for directions.*

Luckily for her, Reiki Master Paul had been driving by and spotted her. He'd given her a ride home. "What were you doing in that neighborhood?" he had asked.

When she'd said, "Just walking," Paul had given her a look she didn't like much—the same look he gave people who interrupted him at La Cruz. "Kids and their secrets," he had said.

Why did Reiki Master Paul care what neighborhood she hung out in?

The minute she'd walked through the front door, Vanessa had hugged her so tight, you'd think that Naomi had spent the last five years being raised by wolves. And then Paul had pulled Vanessa into the kitchen, a look on his face like, "We've really got a problem here." Like they were her parents or something. Gross. Naomi had wondered if Paul had one of those crosses in his closet, too, and remembered Jordan saying, *There's . . . weird stuff going on*, and she couldn't even be on the same floor as those two anymore, she was that freaked out. . . .

Naomi had run upstairs to her room. She'd gone online and looked for Corinne, but there was no Corinne—she hadn't been online all day. Her desert dream flashed into her mind: the hooded angel, standing over her, saying, *You are safe*. She wanted to cry but she couldn't.

Ten minutes later, Vanessa was filling her doorway, saying, "Paul tells me you were at Parque de las Lavanderas. What were you doing there?"

"How did he know I was there? The place where he picked me up had to be at least a mile away."

"Don't answer a question with a question."

"I thought he just happened to be driving down that street. Why was Paul following me?"

"Naomi, I told you—"

"If he saw me at Parque de las Lavanderas, he knew what I was doing there. Now you tell me, Aunt Vanessa. Why was *he following me*?"

At that point, Soccoro had come in, telling Vanessa that "Señor Glen Campbell" was on the phone.

"You're kidding," Vanessa had said. "I haven't spoken to Glen in *years*." But not long after she'd left to take the call, Vanessa's bedroom door was slamming and James Taylor was on full-blast.

That had been four hours ago. It was eight o'clock, and Soccoro was cooking *sopa de ajo*, the warm, spicy smell of it wafting out of the kitchen. It was Naomi's favorite—savory garlic soup with an egg cracked on top, with Soccoro's fresh-baked *bolillos* on the side—but still, Naomi was dreading dinner. She couldn't stand the thought of sitting across the table from Vanessa, her head brimming with questions she didn't know how to ask.

That was why, five hours after chasing Alejandro, she still felt winded. She was finding it harder and harder to breathe in this house.

"How would you feel, Vanessa, if Naomi were next?"

"Don't you ever say that, Patty. Don't you ever fucking say that to me!"

Naomi replayed that exchange in her mind. She knew she should probably take some comfort in her aunt's anger, but she couldn't. Not when Vanessa knew what "next" meant— but was so intent on keeping it from her.

She stared at her computer screen. After checking for the millionth time to see if Corinne was online, she'd gone on some medical Web sites and started reading up on post-traumatic stress. *Most sufferers start to feel some improvement after six months,* read the article on her screen. *With proper therapy, however, recovery can begin sooner.* James Taylor bellowed "Blossom come my way today!" for easily the seventh time tonight, and Naomi thought, *Yeah, right, proper therapy,* and suddenly she couldn't take it anymore. She had to let these questions out of her head or else her lungs would shut down and she wouldn't be able to breathe at all.

She got up from her desk, opened the door of her bedroom and walked down the hall to her aunt's room. She pounded on the door. When she heard nothing in response, she yelled, "Aunt Vanessa! I need to talk to you!"

No answer.

"Why did Mrs. Woods have a slash on her face? Does it have something to do with your club? Does it have something to do with the cross in your closet?"

Naomi waited for a few moments. No reply. If anything, the James Taylor seemed to get louder. "Does it have anything to do with *Grace*?"

She held her breath and braced herself, amazed and impressed she'd actually found the guts to say that name out loud. There was still no reply, but Naomi wasn't having that, not anymore. She grabbed the doorknob, turned and pushed.

Her aunt's room was empty. Naomi should have predicted that. Vanessa's new habit—cranking James Taylor and leaving the house. Just to be sure, she headed down to the kitchen and confirmed it with Soccoro. Yep, Vanessa had gone to Brad Pitt's for the night.

Great . . .

As she headed back to her bedroom, Naomi heard the chime of her cell phone and hurried in to answer it. The screen flashed RESTRICTED NUMBER. *"¿Bueno?"*

"Naomi Boyd," said the voice on the other end—a small, shy voice she recognized immediately.

"Alejandro?"

He spoke in English. "Don't come back to the *parque* again. Don't look for me. Don't ask anyone any questions, Naomi. . . ."

"What? Why?"

"I am serving someone. A powerful person. Evil."

Naomi's spine froze up. She opened her mouth to speak, but couldn't.

"You are not in danger right now, but others are. And if you go to the *parque* again, you will be. It can happen to you just like Jordan Brink. Just like . . ."

"Who? Just like who, Alejandro?"

"I like you, Naomi." His voice changed. Naomi sensed a tightness, a wetness. . . . Was he crying? "I don't want it to happen to you. I really don't."

Naomi felt tears coming to her own eyes. She tried to keep her voice calm, tried to stay together. "Alejandro. Who are you serving?"

"You are being watched."

"What?"

"Don't ask any more questions and you will stay safe."

Alejandro ended the call. Naomi sat perfectly still in her desk chair, terror crawling through her, Alejandro's voice melding with James Taylor's and then becoming the angel's voice, from her dream in the desert. *You are safe.* . . . Naomi's body felt numb. She walked over to her bed and picked up her baby toy, her stuffed turtle. She held it to her chest and shut her eyes tight, wishing she was a baby again, a dreaming baby in her mom's arms. From downstairs, she heard Soccoro's voice telling her dinner was ready, and to turn down the music. But all Naomi wanted was to do was feel safe enough to sleep.

TWELVE

"Where are we going?" Zoe asked, still tipsy from the wine.

"I told you," said Warren. "It's a surprise." He opened the passenger's-side door. She got in. He started up the car and said, "There's another festival in town."

"Saint's birthday?" Zoe asked.

"No. It's Presidential Message Day. The president's first big speech of the year—it's always on September first. Kind of like the State of the Union address."

The *jardín* was jammed with people—Zoe and Warren couldn't get within five blocks of it—and the sky was ablaze with smoke and light. "All this for the State of the Union?" Zoe asked.

"That's San Esteban," he said, smiling.

She was feeling a little too loose for her own good, a little too warm and rubbery. Zoe had heard that high altitudes intensified the effect of alcohol and that appeared to be what was happening now. She opened her window, inhaled the scent of gunpowder and listened to the fireworks and the blaring church bells. She gazed at Warren's splendid profile, the way the explosions lit it up like spotlights, and thought, *My vacation, all mine and nobody else's* . . . Warren's hidden safe and its contents crawled into that corner of her mind—right next to Naomi's stress-induced warnings and Patty Woods's tragic green eyes and she thought, *It's going into storage, at least for the night.* "Aren't you going to park the car?"

"Nope."

"We're not going to be able to get closer than this."

"We're not going to *Fecha del Presidente*." He made a sharp right, avoiding the festival. Soon, the street was clear and there was no traffic, the Cherokee bouncing over the cobblestones as he headed east.

Zoe felt a slight pang in the sprained wrist. Some of Rafael's magic was wearing off. Or maybe some of the wine. "Where are we going?" she asked.

"I told you," said Warren. "It's a surprise."

They hit a poorer residential area, with smaller, squatter houses, dogs howling at them from the roofs as they drove past. Soon that neighborhood was in their rearview and the cobblestones turned to smooth highway, and they were out of San Esteban, in the middle of the desert, where there was nothing but the road flanked by sparse clusters of cactuses, boulders scrawled with Spanish graffiti and parched ground, gray as dead flesh in the blazing moonlight. "This the scenic route?"

Warren didn't reply. His silence was beginning to bother her, the effects of the wine evaporating fast as, within her, a vague panic started to build. Why had she agreed to this surprise? "Where are we going?"

"You'll see."

She turned and looked at him. "Warren?"

"Mmm-hmmm?"

"I like you."

"Thanks."

"But this air of mystery of yours is really starting to freak me out."

His smile faded, but still he said nothing. Zoe stared at Warren's tense profile, and all she could think about was how little she really knew about him. Yes, he'd opened up some tonight, but Zoe knew more about Steve than she would ever know about the man sitting next to her. It was unsettling, considering how much she'd let Warren into her life, how much she'd shown him of her darkest fear. Last night, she had told him more about Daryl Barclay than she had ever told anyone, Steve included. She'd revealed the fascination she'd felt for a murderer. And what had Warren given her in return? His first kiss? His hometown?

"Where are we going?" she asked again.

"You'll see."

"You said that."

He didn't reply.

"I don't want to see," she said. "I want to *know. Now.*"

Warren looked at her. "Calm down."

"Don't tell me to calm down." Zoe's voice pitched up. "We're in the damn desert, and there are no buildings or people, and it's the middle of the night, and I want to know where the hell you're taking me!"

"And I said *calm down!*" The car windows shook with his voice.

No, I do not know him at all. . . . Zoe was starting to tremble. The back of her neck was sweating and the muscles in her legs felt weak, as if someone had yanked all the strength out, rendered them useless.

Zoe saw headlights in the rearview mirror. She considered opening her window, throwing her body out the side, signaling to the other driver. She couldn't believe she was actually going to do this while on vacation with the man she thought she might be falling in love with, couldn't believe she was actually putting her finger on the button that opened the window, couldn't believe she was pushing it, but the truth was, he had a gun and his last visitor's watch and God knew what else, and she didn't know him, much as she told herself she did, much as she wanted to. Warren Clark was as real to her as the TV character he'd just stopped playing.

Warren made a hard right onto a bumpy private road, knocking her back into her seat. Her breath caught. Her eyes felt hot. *Don't show him you're afraid.* And again she couldn't believe it, couldn't believe she was having a thought like that. *What is happening here?*

"Zoe?"

She didn't answer.

"Zoe, I'm sorry. I didn't mean to yell at—"

"Why don't you ever take pictures?"

"Huh?"

"You live in two of the most photogenic places I've ever seen, and if your family is anything like you, I'll bet they look great on film, too. Why don't you have pictures of your homes, your family? Your friends?"

"I hate pictures."

"No one hates pictures. That's like hating people. Do you hate people?"

Warren gripped the wheel. He flipped on his brights and stared at the road ahead—a hard stare, as if someone had taken a screwdriver to his face and tightened all his features. "You aren't acting like yourself," he said.

"Actually, I am." The SUV bumped and reeled over the unpaved road, toward some surprise she no longer wanted, but Zoe didn't feel frightened anymore. The wine buzz was long gone and her blood had adjusted to the altitude, but it was more than that.

I am acting like myself.

It was as if a thick and constant fog had momentarily lifted, and she wasn't Zoe Greene anymore. She was Zoe Jacobson. "Who is Nicholas Denby?"

Warren stopped the car, threw it into park. He stared at her. "Who told you that name?" he said.

"It doesn't make any difference who told me."

"Was it Patty Woods?"

She stared back at him, a bright light blazing on that corner of her mind. *There's some group. A group Mrs. Woods was talking about . . .*

She swallowed hard, made herself ask it again. "Who is Nicholas Denby?"

Warren took off his safety belt and turned his whole body toward her. Zoe was afraid he might yell again . . . or worse. But when she looked into his eyes, they were soft, sad. "He was a friend."

"A friend."

"Yes."

"So . . . why the secrecy?" she said. "Why all the concern over who told me his name?"

Warren sighed. He pinched the bridge of his nose, as if he were trying to stave off tears, and when he looked at Zoe again, his eyes glistened, just a little. "I never wanted to keep Nick Denby from you," he said. "I just wanted to tell you on my own."

She watched him.

His gaze shifted away from Zoe's face. He opened his mouth, then closed it, then opened it again, and Zoe saw how hard this really was for him, relaying personal information. What made someone this way—so emotional in front of cameras, so passionate in bed, but when it came to simply telling a true sequence of events, he was in pain?

Zoe said, "It's okay, Warren. Take your time."

"Nick Denby was my best friend in high school," he said. "Great guy. Looked a lot like me, so we often went out for the same parts, but we were never rivals, you know? If we got into a fight, it was like fighting with your brother. There was always that understanding it'd blow over, we'd still be friends no matter what."

He leaned back, gazed up at the car's ceiling as if it were a sky filled with stars. "Anyway, after high school we sort of lost track of each other. He went off to Pace, I moved to the city and started auditioning for stuff. . . . Flash-forward five years. I'm in some audition—not sure what is was for. . . . And there, waiting to be called, was Nick Denby."

"What a coincidence."

"Huge one," he said. "We became friends again. Saw each other a few times a week, caught up." He looked at Zoe. "I was doing pretty well with episodic roles and commercials, and I'd saved up some money, so I went down to San Es, like I told you, fell in love with it, bought the house. I invited Nick down to visit. He stayed at my place for a week. Then . . . he disappeared."

"What?"

"We had an argument that Friday night—not a big one. I don't even remember what it was about, but we were drunk at some bar and it escalated and it got physical. Two grown men in a public fistfight . . . Even as it was happening, I felt like a jackass. Anyway, I woke up Saturday morning, and all his stuff was gone. I knew he was planning on traveling on to Oaxaca after he left San Es, so I called the hotel down there— no sign of him. A day later, I filed a missing-person report. It was like he had dropped off the face of the planet."

"He was never found?"

"*Never*. The police said maybe some banditos got him on the road, disposed of his body by . . . burning it or . . ." Pain washed through his features. His jaw tightened.

"I'm so sorry."

"There were people here," he said. "Terrible people. Rumors started to spread that I had something to do with it. Could you imagine? People saw us fighting, and they thought I . . ."

"That's awful."

He nodded. "There's nothing worse, Zoe. Nothing. You're . . . you're confused and scared out of your mind that something horrible has happened to your best friend. You can't even grieve because there is no body. He's just vanished. . . . And then people start accusing *you* of . . ." He closed his eyes. "I started getting anonymous phone calls, threats on my life. Once, when I came home, my door had cow's blood splashed all over it."

"Why didn't you leave? Sell the house and just—"

"Because that would have been running away," he said. "I don't run away from anything. Ever."

Zoe gazed at him. "I understand now," she said softly, "why you have the gun."

Warren's back straightened. His mouth went tight and his eyes closed off—thousands of steel doors slamming behind them. "How do you . . . ? How could you . . . ?"

"Don't be upset," she said.

He turned away from her, stared out the window.

"I was worried because you weren't home," Zoe said. "I was trying to find Vanessa's phone number. I thought maybe you kept papers in the safe. I found the gun in there." She watched his profile. "I found Nick Denby's watch."

Warren rested his head on the back of the seat and closed his eyes. He was quiet for a long time, and Zoe did nothing. A sad calm ran through her—the lightening that comes after confession. He put his hands on the wheel, and she thought, *He's going to drive home now.* But he didn't start the car, just kept his hands there, resting. "The watch," he said, "was the only thing he left behind. I probably should have sent it to his family, but it felt like . . . like . . ."

"Admitting he was dead."

"Yes." He lifted his eyes to her face. "Yes, that's it."

"I understand."

He nodded. "The gun though . . . I don't know where it came from. I don't want to know."

"How could you not know? You have it."

He inhaled sharply. "About . . . a month after Nick disappeared . . . the same time as the threats, I got this package. It wasn't sent. Someone had put it on the sill of my first-floor window, just in front of the bars. God knows why, but I took it inside. I opened it. . . . The gun was in there, and a note that said, *Para tu protección.*"

"That's all?" Zoe asked. "Just . . . for your protection."

"It might have said my name, too. I don't remember."

"But it didn't say the sender's name. You didn't know who it was from. Didn't recognize the handwriting . . ."

"It was typewritten. I . . . I burned it."

"You burned it?"

He nodded.

"Why didn't you bring it to the police?"

"I . . . wasn't on the best terms with the police at the time, Zoe. People were saying bad things about me. They would have taken any excuse—possession of an illegal firearm—and I didn't even know who the gun belonged to. What if it had been used in a crime?"

"So you just . . ."

"I would have thrown it out, but I was afraid someone might see me with it. So I locked it up. Never touched it again, just like you do with a bad memory—you put it away, shut the door on it. After a while it's like it never happened."

Zoe stared into Warren's eyes. They were like glass. "That's what you do with bad memories?"

"It's what I do with most memories, Zoe." Gently, he touched the side of her face, traced her closed lips with the tip of his index finger. "I have no use for the past." He cupped his hand under her chin and brought her face to his and kissed her gently. His touch was soft and his eyes glimmered with care, and Zoe was no longer afraid. But still, she didn't believe him. He had use for the past. He remembered.

"Warren?"

"Yes?"

"Why did you ask if Patty Woods was the one who told me?"

He pulled away.

"She was one of those people, wasn't she? The ones who spread the rumors."

"Yes," he said.

"I met her today," said Zoe, "when I was in the park with Naomi. She said she was leaving San Esteban. She seemed mad at Vanessa."

He shook his head. "And Vanessa has never been anything but kind to her. Don't get me wrong—I'm sorry for what happened to Patty's nephew, but . . ." His glare pressed into the window, the blue eyes burning cold. "Now she knows what it's like to have a visitor disappear."

Zoe's mouth dropped open. "What are you saying, Warren?"

He shrugged his shoulders. "It's just karma, Zoe. That's all."

"But Jordan Brink didn't—"

"I know. Let's drop the subject. Like I said . . . the past is worthless." He took a breath, smiled at her. "We're here, you know."

"Huh?"

"Your surprise." He started up the car, drove about thirty more feet—to where a flowered arch, illuminated by outdoor lights, stretched over the road—fresh daisies spelling out two Spanish words on a background of dark green leaves.

"Las Aguas?" Zoe asked.

He nodded. "I reserved the mineral baths for the night."

Morrison and Barbara Brink lived in a brick duplex on a small square of trimmed lawn with white rosebushes blooming against either side of the doorway. When Barbara had asked Steve over the phone if he'd wanted to come by tonight, he'd spent about all of three seconds deliberating before he'd said yes. He had called Debbie Cohn, told her he had the flu, and she agreed to a rain check, so long as he let her keep the *Dreamcoat* tickets.

Then he'd called the metro section editor and gotten her to accept a feature on Jordan Brink—a piece that would show him, not as a doomed tourist who stole drugs, but as a real human being, with grieving parents who were willing to go on the record for the first time.

All this, just to see if that poor kid had had any disputes with Warren Clark.

It was hard for Steve to find the house. Nearly every residence on the street was brick and similarly shaped, and the addresses weren't prominent. Barbara had told him to look for a green Volvo, but that was gone—Morrison had left "because we needed more milk" she said when Steve was finally at the door.

"Okay. Well, I hope it's still okay for—"

"I'm lying. Morrison just wanted to get out of the house. He thinks I'm an idiot for speaking to the press."

"Mrs. Brink. I promise I will be fair to your son."

"I know," she said. "I have no idea why I do but . . . anyway, come in." Barbara was a tiny woman. She wore jeans and a black T-shirt, no makeup that Steve could notice, and as he would have expected, her eyes were red-rimmed, dark circles pressing against the bridge of her nose. She had short, spiky brown hair like Laurie Anderson, and large, questioning eyes. College professor, maybe an artist—that was what he would have guessed she was in the real world, back when she was just a regular person and not the mother of a murdered boy.

Barbara led him into the living room, which seemed to be the largest room in the house. There was an overstuffed floral-print couch, where she sat down, a glass-topped coffee table and two chairs covered in soft gold cloth. The walls were lined floor to ceiling with books—mostly philosophers, first editions. "You guys teach or something?" Steve asked.

She shook her head. "Those books belonged to Morrison's dad," she said. "He taught at SUNY New Paltz. My son used to love him. Jordan loved books so much, loved anybody who liked to read. . . ." She cleared her throat. "Can I get you anything? Coffee?"

"No, thanks." Steve sat on one of the chairs. He noticed the cluster of photographs on the table—a dark-haired boy in a rugby uniform; the same boy, shorter and skinnier, in a graduation gown and mortar board. Barbara and the boy, waving from a canoe, and standing in front of the Lincoln Memorial. In another, they were posing with an elephant at the circus next to a man—it had to be Morrison. He had Jordan's exact same face.

Steve glanced up, and saw Barbara watching him. "Is . . . was Jordan an only child?"

"Yes."

He winced. "Any pets?"

"We used to have a dog. We got him when Jordan was three. He named the dog Brother."

"That's cute."

"Brother died a year ago." She pulled a Kleenex out of the dispenser, but she didn't use it, didn't cry . . . just held it between her fingers, a sort of safety net, and he could almost hear her thoughts. *I'm not going to cry in front of a reporter. I'm not going to cry over a damn dog.* "Jordan was very upset when I told him Brother had passed away. He was at NYU, and he'd just started classes, but he took the subway home and we had a burial in the backyard."

"I used to have a dog when I was a kid," said Steve. "Chihuahua. I named him Peanut."

Barbara raised an eyebrow at him. "You don't seem like you'd have a Chihuahua."

He smiled. "Guess I wasn't one of those people who looks like his dog. Of course, I wasn't quite as big back then."

She nodded.

"Man, was I sad when Peanut died, though. I cried and cried. And my mom told me . . ."

"Peanut's in a better place."

"Yeah." He looked at her. "That's exactly what she said."

"We've got a cat now. . . . She hides in the closet twenty-three hours a day, only comes out to eat, and even then, she's very skittish. Morrison keeps saying, 'That is not a healthy cat.'" She raised her gaze to meet Steve's, and her eyes clouded over. "I don't think she likes it here."

Her eyes started to well up, and for a few seconds, Steve locked on to them and saw it: Barbara's life now, the pain—the deep, constant, overwhelming pain no one should ever have to feel. He looked away. "That sucks."

"Yes," she said. "It truly does."

After about a minute, he said, "Do you want to do this interview? Because, if you don't, I understand."

"Anybody ever tell you that you're an exceptionally nice guy?"

"Thanks, but—"

"Turn on the tape recorder."

Steve took a microcassette recorder out of his pocket, switched it on and placed it on the coffee table. "Tell me about your son," he said. And Barbara did. She told him about Jordan, from her difficult birth all the way through grade school and high school and college; told him about all Jordan's girlfriends, all the phases he had gone through, from jock to emo to poet to film student. She talked about all the traveling he used to do, how sometimes, he'd just take the car and drive until he ran out of gas, then call his parents from his end point. The farthest he got was the outskirts of Albany. "His father, in particular, hated that game," Barbara said. "But I think that was the point."

"Did he like to travel?"

"More than anything. When he wasn't traveling, he would surf the Net, post on overseas message boards." She smiled. "He said it was the next-best thing."

"Had he ever been to San Esteban before?"

"Just once," she said. "He visited his great-aunt Patty there for a summer, when he was sixteen." Her expression darkened.

"Was it a good trip?"

"I . . . I don't remember."

Steve knew she wasn't telling the truth, but he didn't want to press her. "Did he mention any . . . famous people who lived there?" He looked at her. "Warren Clark, maybe?"

"I have no idea who that is."

"He's a soap opera actor."

At that, she actually laughed a little. "Far as I know, Jordan had no interest in soap operas."

Steve laughed along with her, not because he thought either one of them had said anything particularly funny, but because it was a relief. Before long, though, Barbara's amusement faded and her gaze drifted to the window, and it was as if she'd left this house, this interview, her own body. "The odd thing is," she said, "I hadn't thought he was planning to go to San Esteban this time around. He started off in Guadalajara and then he just . . ." She snapped back into herself. "Oh, that reminds me." She walked into the other room and returned moments later with a beat-up-looking backpack. "The police sent this to me, after this Royas boy confessed. They've been through it already and . . . It's his . . . his travel bag. I haven't even been able to open it." She handed it to Steve, gave him an imploring look.

"You want me to?"

"Yes," she said. "Please."

Steve unzipped the backpack. It smelled musty inside, like old sand. He opened it, saw a few T-shirts, shaving equipment, a toothbrush. He found a worn paperback copy of Carlos Castaneda's *The Teachings of Don Juan*. From the cover art and all, it looked as if it had been published in the seventies, and when he checked the copyright, he saw that, indeed, it had been. 1978. The book was ten years older than Jordan, and it had wound up outliving him.

He was putting *The Teachings of Don Juan* back when a stack of six or seven photographs fell out along with a small spiral notebook. Barbara stared at the photos, then at Steve. Without looking at them first, he held them out to her, and she took them, sighing a little when they touched her hand.

She peered at the first one. "This is his cousin Corinne," she said, and handed it to Steve—a picture of a smiling, stocky blonde in a University of Texas T-shirt. "This is . . . I guess it's the market or something. I've never been to San Esteban." She handed him a picture of two Mexican toddlers posing next to a tiny dog, another one of Jordan and Corinne smiling with a group of mariachi players. All the photos had been taken with a digital camera, and they all had a date on top: 8/25/07. The date of Jordan Brink's murder. Steve wondered if Barbara had noticed the date, if she'd imagined her son snapping photos like any other tourist, downloading them, printing them out, not knowing that, hours later, he would be dead. Worse than dead.

"He looks happy." Barbara was holding the picture of Jordan and Corinne, her hands trembling a little.

"He does."

"He didn't steal drugs."

"I know."

She looked at him. "I really think you do."

The spiral notebook lay in Steve's lap. It looked like a reporter's notebook, only smaller, something you'd maybe use for grocery lists. And when he opened it, he saw Jordan had written up a list. At first, he had a hard time focusing on the words. They didn't make much sense to him. And he couldn't get past the handwriting. . . .

Steve's own handwriting was a hideous scrawl. If you were to see any of the steno pads he used to take notes during interviews, it would have been hard to tell what language it was. Not when he was younger, though. Not when he was still in school.

Jordan's letters were thin and spidery—he wasn't going to win any calligraphy contests. But it looked as if he'd spent extra time on them, as if he'd tried that much harder to make sure they were legible. At the time of his death, Jordan Brink had been at an age where penmanship still counted, and that got to Steve. Maybe worse than the pictures.

"What is that?" Barbara asked.

Steve cleared his throat. "I'm not sure . . . looks like a list of names. You want to take a look? See if you recognize any of them?"

Barbara read through the two pages, then shook her head and handed the notebook back to Steve.

At the top of the page were the initials SPLV. Jordan had drawn a black cross next to the initials with a red dot at the center. "Was he religious?" Steve asked.

Barbara shook her head. "We took him to church. He usually fell asleep."

On the line under the initials, Jordan had printed in all caps, IT IS STILL HAPPENING!

What followed were two columns of names—one of which had an X at the top, the other, a question mark. The X column had just two names. Question mark was much longer and started with "Me." None of the names on either list meant anything to Steve. But then he turned the page, where the second column continued. He saw the last name on the list and his mouth went dry. "Do you . . . do you mind if I borrow this, Barbara? I can messenger it back to you tomorrow—I just want to Xerox the page."

"Sure," she said. "Why?"

He kept his voice calm. "There's just one thing I want to look into." He'd wanted to say that to Barbara, but he couldn't stop staring at the name—the last name on the question-mark list and, barring the world's biggest coincidence, the Brink/Clark connection, spelled out in Jordan's labored capital letters:

TIFFANY BAXTER.

THIRTEEN

Warren drove through the arch and into the parking lot of Las Aguas, which, save for one pickup truck, was completely empty. "I can't believe you reserved the whole place for us," Zoe said.

Warren winked. "I've got influential friends."

As Warren opened the door, a very thin Mexican man sauntered out to greet him. He was probably in his mid-sixties, small boned and benign, except for the enormous, mean-looking hawk that sat on his shoulder. *"Buenos noches,"* said the man in a deeply soporific voice—he could have been a jazz deejay, Zoe thought. Then the hawk screamed, causing Zoe's nerve endings to freeze solid. She backed up until she was more or less hiding behind Warren.

"This is Xavier," said Warren. "The hawk . . . *¿cómo se llama?*"

"Pio."

"Pio is the hawk's name. It means *pious.*"

Zoe stared at the daggerlike beak, the eyes trained on her

like bullet tips. "Thanks for telling me that," she said. "I feel much closer to him now."

Xavier spoke to Warren in rapid-fire Spanish. Warren smiled and nodded. "*¡Claro!*" He turned to Zoe. "We can go on in."

They followed Xavier and Pio out of the parking lot, Zoe lagging a few steps behind for fear the hawk might suddenly decide she was crowding him and go straight for her eyes. "Don't worry," Warren whispered. "Pio is very well trained."

"He's a predator," said Zoe. "How do you train a predator?"

An odd look passed through Warren's eyes. "Good question."

Xavier flicked on a flashlight, and led them through a dewy green lawn that, like Warren's and Vanessa's gardens, had no place in a desert region. "Take your shoes off," said Warren, and they both did, the grass soft and cool and sensuous against the soles of their feet.

At the edge of the lawn were a series of stone steps leading down the side of a hill to a landscaped area—bright pansies circling fragrant patches of sage, oregano and cilantro. Xavier raised his arm and there was a great flapping of wings as Pio took off for the trees. They walked down, padding on more soft grass until finally they reached baths.

Zoe had expected something like the Russian steam rooms on the Lower East Side—clinical and therapeutic, surrounded by white tile. This was more like the season finale of *The Bachelor*. A long, narrow natural pool wound into a cave, reflecting the moonlight, candles flickering around its edges. It was achingly romantic.

Warren said, "The water in the mineral baths is very warm, and if you swim in them naked, it's believed to make you young forever."

Xavier left, as if on cue. Zoe looked at Warren. "Should we test that out?"

Warren pulled her to him, hooked a finger through one of the straps of her tank top and said, "No. No, I don't think that would be right."

Zoe grinned. "I agree." And within moments they were submerged in the soft, warm, soothing water, all their clothes—including Zoe's ACE bandage—at the water's edge.

Enough had been said for the evening, so Zoe and Warren used lips and tongues and hands, but not voices. They didn't think, either. They just moved.

Afterward, Zoe and Warren slipped out of the water and padded over to a picnic blanket by the side of the baths, on which someone had placed a tray of chocolates, champagne, two large, thirsty towels . . . and a small velvet box. Zoe's pulse quickened. "What is all this?"

"The rest of your surprise." She wrapped the towel around her body, popped a delicate piece of dark chocolate into her mouth and lay on her back, savoring the flavor and feeling the perfect air on her skin, gazing up at the stars. "This is wonderful," she said. But in the back of her mind, she had a strange feeling, as if someone was watching. Pio screamed at them from the trees, but this was something else: the feeling of human eyes, trained on her. . . .

"He was watching me."

"Who?"

"Jordan's murderer. When I was talking to Jordan by the fire that night. I could feel it. . . ."

Warren said, "Don't you want to know what's in the box?"

Zoe shook off the feeling. "Yes, please."

"Close your eyes."

She did. Soon, Zoe felt something smooth and delicate against her bare chest, Warren's fingertips on the back of her neck as he fastened a chain.

She opened her eyes, and saw a thin black cross resting between her breasts, a red stone glistening at its center.

Zoe's mind reeled as she gazed at this strange, sleek pendant, the same size as Vanessa's silver cross, the same color as the dark wooden cross on Warren's dressing room wall, the red stone in place of the red thorn-crowned heart. . . .

"Do you like it?" said Warren. "It's ruby and obsidian."

The pendant looked so strange on her—that strangeness compounded by Zoe's heritage. Warren knew she was Jewish. Why had he chosen this for her?

"I love it," she said.

"I knew you would." Warren slid around in front of her, and kissed her deeply. She made herself stop thinking of crosses and secret clubs, or eyes watching them in the darkness. She made herself forget that moment in the car, when Warren had said of Patty Woods, *Now she knows what it's like to have a visitor disappear.* Zoe made herself forget looking at his face and not liking what she saw.

She forgot all of that, thinking only of Warren's soft lips and the gentle lapping of the water and the cool obsidian against her skin. She had no use for the past.

Zoe heard the sizzle first. Then she smelled smoke and only then did she feel the burn. It wasn't supposed to work this way, but it was a dream, and Zoe was sleeping lightly enough to know that. That didn't stop her heart from pounding, though. It didn't stop her blood from running thin and cold like water as she looked down and saw the cross Warren had given her, saw it glowing orange, burning its shape into her chest like a branding iron, burning all the way through to her beating heart.

Zoe's eyes flipped open, and her hand went to her chest, even though she knew she wasn't even wearing the cross. It was on the nightstand, coiled up next to the clock, which read one a.m. Warren had told her not to wear the cross until Rafael's party the next night. And she hadn't asked why.

Why hadn't she asked why?

Warren was sound asleep. Zoe listened to that purring snore and watched his chest rise and fall with each intake of air, thinking how peaceful he looked, even after tonight. He had confessed to her. Warren, who never even talked about past girlfriends, had laid open his soul and revealed to Zoe the most difficult time of his life. He had told her about losing a friend—literally *losing* him—and blaming himself for his disappearance, just as she had blamed herself for the Barclay killings.

At the time, she had been so grateful, she'd felt so close to him. But now . . . now, in the middle of the night with Warren asleep, clouds were parting in her head, and all she could think of was the coldness with which he'd talked about Patty Woods.

Warren had this hold on her—this crazy, puppeteer-like grip—and it was only away from him that she could begin to see the strings. It was the sex—yes, of course it was the sex. But it was more than that. It was the way his gaze drilled into hers, the way he seemed to be able to climb into her head and bend her thoughts. He had told her he could fix her, and she had thought, *Good!* and *When?*

Not *How?* Or *What the hell are you talking about?*

Odds were, tomorrow morning they'd make love, and again, the strings would disappear. But now, Zoe thought, *How could he hide a gun that long without knowing where it came from?*

You may not have use for the past, Warren. But I do.

Zoe crept out of bed. She held her breath, padded over to Warren's desk as lightly as she could, as if she were made of crepe paper, listening to his snore the whole while. As she slid open the top drawer, she heard a slight catch in his breathing and froze. But before long it was regular again.

In one fluid movement, Zoe slipped the key out of the drawer, pulled her cell phone out of its charger and slid the drawer closed again. Then as fast as she could, she stole out of the room. It wasn't until she reached the roof garden safe that she realized she'd forgotten the penlight. But it was okay. There was enough light. It was the night before a full moon.

Steve was at a Broadway show with Debbie Cohn, but it wasn't *Joseph and the Amazing Technicolor Dreamcoat*. It was a production of *Phantom of the Opera*, starring Warren Clark as the Phantom, Zoe as that chick the Phantom had a thing for—Christine? Was that her name?—and Glen Campbell, the singer not the reporter, as a tap-dancing clown. Clark was on his knees, center stage, belting out a tour de force version of "The Music of the Night," as Glen Campbell did a soft-shoe and Zoe stood off to the side in a bright red gown watching Clark, her hands clasped next to her face like Olive Oyl watching Popeye. All of a sudden, Clark stopped singing, pulled a switchblade, rushed up to Zoe and stabbed her in the heart. "Now that's what I call a plot twist," Debbie whispered as Steve watched horrified, wanting to save Zoe but unable to move.

Then Debbie started singing, "Tommy, Can You Hear Me?" and Steve said, "Hey, that's my ring tone," and he realized it *was* his ring tone and then he woke up.

He looked at his clock. Two in the morning. Who the hell was calling his cell phone at two in the morning? He looked at the screen and saw Zoe's cell number. He remembered Jordan Brink's list—a bad list, he was sure—and his blood went cold. "Zoe? Are you all right?"

"Yeah, Steve. I'm fine."

He exhaled. "Jesus. You scared the hell out of—"

"I know. I'm really sorry. I was just wondering if you could do me a favor." She was whispering. It was hard to hear.

Steve rubbed his eyes. "Sure."

"Can you get one of your police sources to run an NCIC check for me? I've got a serial number."

He sat up. Zoe hadn't asked a question like that since she had police sources of her own. "Are you serious?" he said. "What . . . did Clark pull a gun on you?"

He'd been joking, but Zoe didn't laugh. "Nothing like that," she said. "It's a girl I met here. She found it in her boyfriend's things and she told me the serial number. Asked if I had any reporter friends . . ."

"Sure, Zoe. Gimme the number. I'll call my buddy at the Sixth, John Krull."

"You're the best ever. It's 074764."

"Got it. Easy to remember.

"Oh, and it's a forty-five caliber. Semiautomatic. Glock."

"You bet. Hey . . . Zoe?"

"Yeah?"

"How come you called me about this at two in the morning?"

There was a brief pause, then, "I miss you, Steve." And before he could ask any more, she ended the call.

Steve probably thought she was nuts. Zoe knew this as she hit END, but if you took every troubling thought that was worming its way through her brain right now, and you lined them all up and weighed them against one another, Steve thinking she was crazy was the lightest by far.

The heaviest was the sound of movement she heard through the open bedroom door. Warren was awake. He was getting out of bed. "Zoe?"

Gritting her teeth, she put the gun back in the safe. Then she placed the scarf back on top and locked the door. "I'm out here!" she said.

"I know."

She turned around. He had been standing right behind her. For how long, she wasn't sure. She swallowed. "Oh, hi," she said. "You scared me."

"Who were you talking to?"

"Huh?"

He pointed to her cell.

"Oh, right. I was . . . just calling home. Checking my machine."

He stroked her cheek, gazed into her eyes. "Come back to bed."

"Okay." She kissed him and followed him back to the room, her heart racing, the key a sharp secret in the palm of her hand.

A mile away, in a four-poster bed on the top floor of Studio Rafael, Vanessa lay with the Master, awake and worried. She had come by hours ago, unable to say anything other than "I need you."

The Master had obliged. The Master always obliged, making love to Vanessa for hours, filling her so completely that it was transformative. There was no other like him, no one in the world.

Rafael was filled with light. It poured out of his eyes and his hands and his mouth and his skin, and when he was inside you, it was like the sun being inside you. It was almost too much for Vanessa to bear.

It wasn't often that she needed the Master, but she had

needed him tonight. She needed him still, only in other ways, and for the first time since she had arrived, she turned to him and spoke. "It's happening. The press knows about SPLV."

Rafael shook his head. "Patty told us she wouldn't say anything. She promised, no matter what—"

"I got a call from a reporter, Rafael," she said. "He started innocently enough, asking about my friendship with Warren, about what life was like in San Esteban. Then . . ." She brushed a hand against the side of his face. "He asked me how I knew Jordan."

"Vanessa."

"Not if. *How*. The way he said it . . . He asked how Warren knew Jordan—and if he might have been angry with him."

"Warren?"

"Yes . . . I told him that Warren had never even met Jordan, but he didn't seem to believe me. Everything he said had Patty Woods written all over it."

"Are you sure?"

"He asked me . . . He asked if I was worried for Naomi."

"Oh, my poor dear."

"You don't understand," said Vanessa. "Patty had asked me the same thing. Used the same words that Glen . . . that this reporter did. *Are you afraid that Naomi might be next?*"

Rafael stared at her. Until she had met Rafael, Vanessa had always thought it was David Bowie who had the most mesmerizing eyes she'd ever seen. Rafael's eyes were astounding—amber globes with lit candles inside. But in all seven years of gazing into those globes, she had never seen them like this. It frightened her.

He parted her lips with a finger, and his touch was so gentle. The opposite of his eyes. "I will," he said softly, "take care of this."

FOURTEEN

When Patty was fifty, she'd had a lump removed from her breast. After a biopsy, it was determined noncancerous, and Patty had experienced a palpable sense of relief, a glorious, daylong sigh. Interestingly, though, it wasn't the biopsy results that had made her feel that way—it was the lumpectomy.

Cancerous or not, the thing's presence on her body—its attachment to her—had upset her so much, she couldn't sleep. She began thinking of the lump as a breathing entity, sucking the spark out of her moment by moment, in some kind of awful science fiction way.

Being rid of the lump freed her. It made her think she could start over. It made her feel . . . not young again, but more alive than she'd felt in a while. And that was what she hoped it would be like when she was free of San Esteban.

Patty needed a new lease on life so badly.

They were still doing it. She had been right about that much. They were still taking young adults and bleeding them dry, stealing their spirit and sucking out their hope and using it for what they claimed was a greater good—but was it?

She remembered the way they had all stood in front of her yesterday—the coven elders. All of them wearing the same cold stare. Warren Clark's stare. She'd planned on just speaking to Rafael, but she'd gone through with it nonetheless. She'd come this far; there was no turning back.

"Maguey spines were placed in my nephew's hands," she had said, her voice much frailer and older than it had been in her imaginings. "He was killed and laid out exactly like Grace."

Oh, how they had all gasped at the word *Grace*, as if saying her name were worse than what had been done to the poor girl, to poor Jordan. . . . Listening to those gasps, Patty had felt something snap, deep within her. The fear dissolved. Anger poured ice-cold through her whole body, freezing her toes, her hands, her face, making her numb and strong—a glacier. She stared directly at Warren Clark. The words crashed out. "What were you saying to Jordan in front of La Cruz?"

"What?"

His stare didn't frighten her, the cruel twist of the mouth. "You heard me. I saw you talking to my nephew by the cross at midnight. He was murdered twenty-four hours later, and *I want to know what you said to him.*"

Rafael said, "Is this true, Warren?"

"I have no idea what she's talking about."

"You must be mistaken, Patty," Rafael said.

"I'm not—"

"She needs to be punished," Warren said, "for saying the name of G."

Patty had said, "You can't be serious." But Rafael had nodded and Vanessa had nodded.

"Yes, it must be done," she had said. Vanessa, that weak-willed bitch. And every last one of them had stood there, silent. They had let Warren Clark take Rafael's obsidian knife and cut Patty's face with it. They had let him spit on that cut and walk away, and they had done *nothing*.

Not a shred of sympathy for a grieving woman.

Patty closed her eyes. *Cut it off. Throw it out. Forget them all. You'll have a new life soon.*

Patty was standing in her bedroom. Her bags were all packed. She hadn't called the car service yet, but she would. She had time. It was nine a.m., and her plane didn't leave till twelve thirty.

Patty heard her doorbell ring, but she didn't answer it. Could have been Jehovah's Witnesses or the peanut-and-corn man or the mango girl or Vanessa, stopping by to say she was sorry. Patty had no desire to see any of them.

She waited until the doorbell stopped ringing, then maybe ten, fifteen minutes more before she walked out into her courtyard, and climbed the two flights of stairs to her rooftop patio. There was a small white wrought-iron table up there, a few dying plants and a metal arbor festooned with tiny white Christmas lights that Patty never turned on anymore.

When her husband, Charlie, was alive, there had been different plants up here—potted white hibiscus and impatiens and even a few camellias—their petals reminded Patty of melted strawberry sundaes. Every night at twilight, the two of them would sit at this table. Charlie would turn on the Christmas lights and pour himself a glass of pinot grigio, give Patty a cup of her favorite tea. Together they'd watch the breathtaking sunset, holding hands, feeling so lucky it was shameful.

Until one day, when they were walking home from the *mercado*. Charlie was carrying home a bag of avocados, and suddenly, he started complaining about how heavy it was.

His face turned bright red and he got to feeling so winded he couldn't stand up. The numbness in the left arm came next, and Patty knew enough to realize what that was.

At the time, the town had not yet built a cell phone tower, so Patty banged on the nearest door and asked for the *teléfono*. She called the hospital, explaining in her terrible Spanish what had happened, but by the time she got back outside, her husband of thirty years was on his back next to the spilled bag of avocados, his eyes closed. Patty put her ear against his chest and heard . . . nothing. She might as well have been putting her ear to the ground. She looked at his face and even that was different. Charlie wasn't in there anymore. Patty tried to scream, but she couldn't breathe. Charlie was gone, and it was as if the air had suddenly turned to water and she was holding the body he'd left behind, sinking with it. . . .

That was fifteen years ago. One year later to the day, she had met Rafael.

Patty's throat clenched up a little. She felt tears coming and choked them down, closed her eyes until they went away because these were the worst kind of tears. The ones that you cried over what might have been. If only you'd done things differently. If only you'd said no instead of yes. *If only, if only, if only* . . . As Charlie used to say, *What's done is done. Life doesn't have an eraser.*

Patty walked to the edge of her rooftop patio and looked down at the sidewalk below. Two hopeful-looking street dogs were trailing a Mexican family, the little boy laughing, telling a sister, *Soy muy fuerte.* I am very strong.

Patty said it herself. "*Soy muy fuerte.*" *I am very strong. I will survive.*

"Patty." It was a whisper so thin, it seemed to come from within her mind. But she knew it hadn't. Someone was standing on the roof behind her.

She turned around, confusion overtaking her in a wave. She looked at the intruder. "What are *you* doing here?" Patty said. "Why are you whispering like . . . ?" Her mouth kept moving, but her voice faded away. She felt rough hands on her, surgical gloves. But all she could do was stare at the hypodermic needle, feel the sting as it drained into her arm.

Finally, she snapped out of it. She started to scream, but realized quickly that she couldn't open her mouth. This was not the result of fear or nerves. She was physically unable. What had been in that needle?

She tried to run, but her legs wouldn't move. The only movement she had seemed to be in her shoulders. She tried to propel herself forward, but it was impossible. Her arms flopped and flailed at her sides, useless growths. Her hands couldn't grasp; her elbows couldn't bend. She wanted to gulp air, but she could only manage shallow breaths. Her legs buckled. She saw a large black bag on her patio tiles as she fell.

What is going on? What do you want from me?

Patty was laid on her back with a surprising gentleness. "It's called pancuronium. It isn't legal in the States anymore, but in Mexico, it's easy to get hold of."

She stared up into that familiar face. *Why?*

"It's a muscle relaxant. Since I gave it to you subcutaneously, it took a little longer to set in. But by now, you shouldn't be able to move anything. You're able to breathe, but not deeply. You should know that if you try too deep a breath . . . you might choke." The intruder unbuttoned and took off her blouse, removed her bra, and again she thought, *Why, why?* Patty felt the sun on her bare chest, those eyes on her skin, cold and appraising. It was humiliating. She wanted to fight back, wanted to scream, wanted to push those hands away . . . but she could not. She couldn't even cry.

"You understand you've done wrong, Patty. This is your punishment."

Punishment? Patty couldn't move her shoulders anymore. Her hands were laid flat on the tiles, palms facing up. Out of the bag came a gleaming black knife and two maguey spines. The knowledge barreled through her. *No, please, no. I didn't do anything wrong! All I did was tell the truth, and I won't tell anyone else, I swear!* She screamed the words within her closed trap of a body, its mouth still, its eyes open and focused, its skin feeling . . . everything. One spine was placed in her left palm, the other in her right. The thorns scratched her skin, and then the face was close. She felt warm breath on her eyes.

If only she could close her eyes.

"Pancuronium is only a muscle relaxant." She watched the knife coming toward her. . . . "It's not a painkiller."

Patty felt the blade slicing into her chest. Her mind roiled—terror, then explosive, unbearable pain. Her bladder released, soaking her immobile legs.

"It's interesting, how this type of trauma separates the body from the mind."

Stop, stop, please stop, please. . . .

"Two people can have the exact same ugliness inside. They can hurt others with very similar words and actions. But when the punishment takes place, each of their bodies will respond in its own unique way." The knife came away. Patty's killer regarded her with curious eyes. "Jordan didn't wet himself. But you did."

Jordan. The police had said he never fought back; there were no signs of a struggle. At the time, Patty had thought that was good. At least he had been unconscious when it happened. . . .

He was conscious.

"There's no fighting it, Patricia Anne. It's karma. All you

can do is take the punishment you deserve . . . and let the body react." The knife was back, cutting deeper, and she wished her mind could conjure a kind face, a place she could escape to. But it would not.

As her agony escalated and darts of white light shot through her eyes, Patty thought about the name she'd been called. Patricia Anne. She hadn't been called Patricia Anne since her first communion, and it was strange, hearing that name from the last voice in her life. She held on to the thought, just for a few moments. Then the gloved hands went into the black bag. And they pulled out the bolt cutters.

For the second morning in a row, Zoe woke up alone. This time, there was a note on the pillow. But all it read was, BE BACK SOON—W. No I.L.Y. Zoe wondered if Warren was mad at her. What if he had seen her locking the safe last night after all?

Zoe stretched. If he knew, wouldn't he have confronted her? She checked the bedside clock. Eleven thirty a.m. A little better than yesterday, but not much. The altitude was still taking its toll on her sleeping habits. She sat up . . . and that was when she saw it glistening next to her pillow. *The key.*

Oh no, no, no . . . She remembered: After they'd gone back to bed, Zoe had lain next to Warren for the longest time, awake with her eyes closed, waiting for his breathing to turn into a snore so she could sneak back to the desk and slip the key back in. *Snore, Warren, snore* . . . , she had thought, the chant running through her head. *Snore, Warren, snore.* . . . But the snore had never come and the chant had lulled her asleep and she'd passed out until eleven thirty a.m. with a stolen key in her hand.

Damn, damn, damn, damn . . .

Maybe he hadn't noticed. Maybe he'd just showered and gotten dressed and left hours ago. The desk drawer was still closed. No reason to believe that he knew she'd opened his safe again, that he had noticed the key on the sheets.

Zoe was short of breath. Her heart slammed in her chest as if she'd been running, and her palms were starting to sweat. This was the worst thing to Zoe—the not knowing. It was like that ride to Las Aguas—staring out at a blank road, no idea where she was going, no idea what was running through the mind of the person sitting next to her. . . .

At least he left a note.

She picked the paper off the pillow and peered at the letters, trying to figure out if they looked like they'd been written by an angry person. But when she realized what she was doing—attempting handwriting analysis on her boyfriend—she put the note down fast. She'd crossed the line. This was officially pathetic.

"Goodbye, Eddie, Goodbye" poured out of her cell phone, and she hurried across the room to answer, but it wasn't Warren calling. It was Steve. She took a breath, made her voice sound normal. "Hey."

"I heard back about your friend's gun."

"What, no foreplay?"

"I figured you were anxious to know."

"Yeah, I . . . My . . . my friend is anxious, yeah."

"You okay, Zoe? You sound a little—"

"I'm fine."

"Upset."

"I'm fine, Steve. What about the gun?"

"You can tell your friend the Glock is totally clean. It was legally purchased in San Antonio, Texas, twelve years ago."

"No crimes committed with it?"

"Nope, and it was never reported stolen."

"Great." Zoe cleared her throat. "What was the name of the owner?"

"Garrett Christopher."

"Who?"

"Kind of confusing—first name for the last, last name for the first. Easy to remember, though." Steve coughed. "Not the boyfriend's name, huh?"

"Not even close," she said. "Thanks, Steve. You're the greatest."

"Yeah, I rock. Listen . . . Zoe?"

"Yeah?"

"Do you have a minute to talk?"

She headed over to the bed and grabbed the key. "Sure. What's up?"

"I'm gonna give you a hypothetical, okay?"

She walked to the desk, put the key back in the drawer. "Go crazy."

"Say there's a soap star," he said. "She's not giving interviews, but your editor says she wants a profile, like, yesterday. What do you do—talk to the soap star's friends, family?"

Zoe sat on the floor, thinking, *Now that's an unexpected question.*

"Or do you do the whole disgruntled employee thing? Do you look for former assistants or bodyguards or . . . Do soap stars even *have* bodyguards?"

She stared at the phone.

"Zoe, are you there?"

"Yeah, I'm here," she said. "I'm just kind of amazed you're asking me about interviewing soap stars. Did Kathy offer you my old job?"

"No!"

"I'm kidding, Steve."

"Oh, right," he said. "Well, the truth is, I . . . I needed

some extra money, so I got some freelance from *TV Guide*. Their Web site."

"Okay. Well . . . no to both your questions."

"Really?"

"If the star isn't giving interviews, it's a waste of time to talk to loved ones. And a disgruntled employee is going to be lopsided and inaccurate and very often . . . a little nuts."

"Publicist?"

"Please."

"Who, then?"

"Old-timer."

"Excuse me?"

"You find the oldest actor on the soap—the 'daytime legend' who's been on since 1962, and you set up an interview with her."

"But what if the star you're interested in is young?"

"Doesn't matter. The old-timers always know everything that's going on. They're the ones everybody confides in because they're not competition. They're like Grandma."

"Interesting."

"Veteran actors are usually a lot more articulate than the younger ones, too. They don't take themselves as seriously. They tend to have fewer scheduling conflicts. Plus, this is the best part: When you reach a certain age, you realize life is too short to mince words, so you feed that nice young reporter the hottest dish of her life."

"Great!"

"That help you?"

"Definitely."

"So . . . are you going to tell me what this is really about?"

"What?"

"It's not for a freelance piece," she said. "You hate soaps, Steve, and you're a terrible liar."

Several seconds of silence, then: "So are you."

"Meaning . . ."

"Meaning, you tell me why you're upset, I'll tell you why I'm asking about soap stars."

Zoe heard footsteps, coming up the stairs. "I've gotta go, Steve."

"Okay," he said. "Then we'll both take a rain check."

After they hung up, Zoe braced herself. She pulled her pajama top around her, and turned toward the bedroom door. The footsteps moved closer, but Zoe realized they were lighter than Warren's, and then she saw Guadalupe striding up to the glass door, opening it.

"Hello, Señorita Zoe," she said.

"Have you seen Warren downstairs? Is he back?"

"No," she said. "I let myself in."

"You speak such good English, by the way. Have you ever lived in the States?"

Zoe had only said it to make conversation, maybe squeeze a smile out of her. But a look passed into Guadalupe's eyes— a look Zoe didn't like. "No. Señor Clark taught me," she said. "He is a wonderful man." She averted her gaze, but that look stayed with Zoe—a wariness, a distrust. "Are you enjoying your stay?"

"Yes! I had a great time in town yesterday."

Guadalupe smiled. "I am glad," she said. But still she wouldn't look at Zoe, and when she went about her cleaning, she started with the desk.

As quickly as she could, Zoe pulled an outfit out of the closet—underwear, skirt, sleeveless blouse. Then she headed into the bathroom, grabbed her soap, toothbrush, toothpaste, shampoo, towel. "There's a shower in the second-floor guest room, right?" she asked.

Guadalupe gave her a tentative yes. Zoe felt the housekeeper's cold stare on her back as she walked out of the room.

*   *   *

Zoe headed directly for the guest room on the second floor, thick beige shades drawn over the glass doors. She turned the knob, pushed one of the doors open. The air within was still. It felt as if the windows had been shut for a long time—years, maybe—but the room was clean, the bathroom spotless. Zoe showered quickly. Only after she'd put on her clothes and headed back into the bedroom did she consider the very strong possibility that this was where Warren's friend Nick Denby had spent his last night alive.

Zoe let her gaze linger on the perfectly made bed, the walls bare save for a mirror, the tall, plain wooden armoire. Compared to the other rooms in the house, this one was unusual—all function, no decor. It seemed neglected. She remembered what Warren had said about bad memories: *You put it away. Shut the door on it. After a while it's like it never happened.* Did Warren think of this room as a type of bad memory? Yes, Guadalupe cleaned it. But had Warren set foot in here since Nicholas Denby's disappearance?

She ran her hand over the thick bedspread. Then she moved toward the armoire, opened the door.

Zoe saw it immediately—the only other thing in the closet besides a stack of folded blankets. A cross, hanging in the shadows, on the back wall, painted with a bleeding, thorn-crowned heart. *Just like the one in Warren's dressing room, only . . .* Something was tied to the bottom.

As if her arms were working on their own, Zoe lifted the cross off the wall. She held it against her forearms and stared at the thing that had been tied to the cross with thick string, and her breath went fast and shallow like the breath of a small, frightened animal.

It was the browned spine of a maguey plant, its thorns thickly coated with dried blood.

Zoe swallowed hard. *There has to be a logical explanation. . . .*

Carefully, she placed the cross back on its hook and closed the closet door. Her heart was beating so hard that the whole room seemed to echo with it, with the rasp of her breathing. *Nicholas Denby's room. Maguey spines coated with Nicholas Denby's blood.*

No, stop. There has to be a logical . . .

She whirled around, so anxious to leave this room that at first she didn't feel eyes on her. She didn't notice Guadalupe, standing in the doorway, glaring at Zoe as if she'd just robbed a grave.

FIFTEEN

"Hey, Steve," said Enid, the city editor, "what's your ETA on the Brink mom story?"

"When do you need it?"

"I don't know . . . three hours ago?"

Steve winced. "Sorry." He never turned in anything late—especially something like this Barbara Brink interview, which he'd had to fight to get in the paper in the first place. (Enid did have a point. Exclusive or not, Jordan's grieving mom saying he didn't steal drugs wasn't what you'd call *news*.)

But he'd wanted the story in so badly. Barbara Brink had allowed him into her home and talked to him for half an hour, and it was the least she deserved. When he'd explained that to Enid, she had said, "Okay. Three inches. And make it fast."

Three inches. Steve could turn around a three-inch story in ten minutes, easy. But here he was, hours after arriving at his desk, staring at his computer screen like some poet with writer's block.

It was that damn list Jordan had made. A list that meant nothing to Barbara Brink and would have meant nothing to Steve forty-eight hours ago, but now it was crowding his brain to the point where he couldn't do his job. He'd close his eyes, try to envision a lede for the Barbara Brink story, but all he'd be able to see, in Jordan's spidery pained handwriting, was the last name he had put in the question mark column:

TIFFANY BAXTER.

He'd recognized the name from all the Nexising he'd done on Warren Clark. She was the little girl who played his daughter on *The Day's End*. How old was she anyway, fourteen? A child actress on a New York soap opera, and somehow, her name had been printed on a list by a murder victim in Mexico.

As far as Steve could see, there was only one possible connection. . . .

When he'd gotten to work that morning, the first thing he'd done was called *The Day's End*'s studios and asked for publicity. The receptionist had hooked him up with a woman named Dana LeVine.

"Hi, Dana, this is Steve Sorensen, calling from the *Trumpet*."

If Steve had said he was George Clooney calling to tell her she'd just won Megabucks, Dana LeVine couldn't have sounded happier. "I adore the *Trumpet*! What can I do for you, Steve?"

"I was wondering if you could set me up with one of your young actresses."

"Absolutely. Which one?"

"Tiffany Baxter."

There had been a brief pause, and then her voice had come back with about 80 percent of the happiness wrung out of it. "Can I ask what this is about?"

Steve had started to think of a line to feed her—a feature article about child stars, a profile describing Tiffany as the Miley Cyrus of daytime TV—but that tone change of Dana's had kept him from that. He wasn't going to get an interview with Tiffany Baxter, no matter what, he knew. At this point, the best thing he could get out of Dana was a fast, honest reaction.

So Steve had been honest and fast himself: "It's about Warren Clark."

Click.

Got my answer. Tiffany Baxter and Warren Clark were definitely connected . . . in ways that their show's publicist did not want to discuss.

The next task was trickier—*how to get to Tiffany*. He'd been drawing a big blank on that one until an idea had flashed in his head: *Call Zoe and ask her advice.* And then Detective Krull had called him back with the NCIC info on the gun, giving him an excuse. He'd spoken to Zoe. And she'd given him good advice—advice that, while she didn't know it, would ultimately help her. (And from the way she'd sounded, she could use a little help.)

The only problem was, before he could do anything in terms of locating an "old-timer" to ask about Tiffany and Clark, Enid was on him like eczema.

He called the Brink transcript up on his screen and made himself focus, finding his lede in Barbara's claim that her late son's only true addiction was reading. He tore through the story, finished it in ten minutes and told Enid it was done. She read it quickly and said, "See? That wasn't so bad, was it?" indicating she no longer wanted to push him out of the thirtieth-floor window.

Then, and only then, did he call up *The Day's End* on the Internet Movie Database, and find the name of the longest-running character: business titan Wellington Hardy, played by Andrew Fennimore since 1965.

Steve walked over to Glen Campbell's desk. "How's it going?" he said.

Glen's face lit up at the sight of him. Never before had Steve met a reporter so grateful for half a byline. "Vanessa St. James didn't give me jack," he said, "but I suspect she's hiding something, Steve."

"Me, too."

"I will press on."

"Thanks. Listen, can you do me a huge favor?" Glen nodded of course, and Steve handed him Dana LeVine's number at *The Day's End.*

"This is about Warren Clark?"

"Yeah, but when you speak to her, don't mention his name. I already did and . . . This woman, Dana LeVine . . . she doesn't like the sound of my voice. So, uh, don't mention my name either."

Glen stared at the number. "Okay . . . ," he said. "But you do want me to say I'm with the *Trumpet*, right?"

"No."

"So . . . what do you want me to tell her?"

Steve listened to that reedy, innocent voice, so unexpected from a New York City reporter. Glen also had the type of earnest Southern accent that sounded natural saying *ma'am* and an enthusiasm that was obvious even over the phone. At this particular moment, Steve considered him the *Trumpet*'s best find ever. "Tell her," Steve said, "that you're the world's biggest Andrew Fennimore fan."

Vanessa still wasn't home. It had been more than fifteen hours since Naomi had banged on the door to her bedroom and found the room empty, yet all she'd gotten as far as proof that her aunt was even alive was a phone call—to Soccoro, no less—saying she was "preparing for Rafael's party" tonight and was "busy running errands."

Naomi hadn't been able to sleep much the previous night. Every time she closed her eyes, she heard Alejandro's quavering voice. *I like you, Naomi. I don't want it to happen to you. I really don't.*

You are being watched.

I am serving someone. A powerful person. Evil.

"Who are you serving, Alejandro?" she whispered. "Who is watching me?"

In her mind, Naomi kept going back to what Jordan had said about San Esteban. *I know it's beautiful on the surface, but it is really fucked up.* Naomi would think about those words, *on the surface*, and she'd envision herself floating on the surface of the ocean. She would smell the salt and feel the current, the bright sun sparkling on aqua waves. She would look to her side and see a beautiful mermaid—Vanessa—all glistening hair and clamshells and big, warm smile. Vanessa's boyfriend, Brad Rafael Pitt, would be splashing beside her, and Warren Clark and Reiki Master Paul and Robin and Dr. Dave and God knew who else, all of them would be gliding through the water in unison like the happiest synchronized swim team on the planet . . . until the hooded angel appeared—the one from the dream that she'd had in the desert—only it would be hovering over the waves. Again, it would tell Naomi, *You are safe.* Then it would tie a blindfold over her eyes and push her beneath the surface and Naomi would know that she wasn't safe at all.

The episodes—flashbacks or post-traumatic stress attacks or whatever you wanted to call them—were becoming more frequent. Since breakfast, Naomi had been hearing this noise—not so much a ringing in her ears as a fluttering, like insect wings. . . .

And always, always Alejandro's voice. *Don't ask any more questions and you will stay safe.*

But if I don't ask questions, I won't get answers. She couldn't look for Alejandro; she couldn't go back to the *parque*. But Naomi needed someone, anyone, to explain what was going on. She needed Xanax and she needed answers, and if she didn't get both soon, she'd go insane for sure.

Naomi looked at her watch. It was eleven a.m.—she wasn't sure what time Mrs. Woods's plane left, but maybe she was still around. And maybe if Naomi let her know how scared and desperate and ready to lose it she was feeling right now, she could pull more than an "ask your aunt" out of her. Naomi yanked her cell off the charger. Because of Corinne, she had Mrs. Woods's number on speed dial, so she hit it, waited. . . . No answer. Her machine wasn't on either. *Already gone. Great.*

Naomi could still hear that fluttering. Would it stay with her always? Would she have to just get used to the sound in her ears—live with it, like a scar?

No. That isn't fair. Nobody should be expected to do that. Naomi put on her shoes, left her room, headed down the hall and opened Vanessa's bedroom door. Her Xanax prescription was on Vanessa's vanity table. Her aunt hadn't even bothered to take it with her. Naomi picked it up and hurried downstairs.

Just as she was putting her hand on the door, Soccoro came running up and slid in front of her. "*¿Donde vas?*"

Naomi looked down at her—this tiny woman blocking her way. "*No se.*" Why did she need to tell Soccoro where she was going? Her aunt never did.

Soccoro told Naomi that she wasn't allowed to leave the premises, adding, "*Tu tía me dice.*"

Naomi almost told her she didn't give a flying fuck what her aunt said, and if Vanessa wanted her to stick around the house, she ought to try sticking around it herself. But she knew Soccoro was only doing her job. It wasn't her fault if her employer wanted to make part of that job disciplining her own niece.

So instead, Naomi moved a step closer, using the nine inches she had on Soccoro for all they were worth. *"No comprendo,"* she said sweetly. Then she turned the knob and stepped around her and left the house.

Zoe was approaching the *jardín*. She wasn't sure where she was going, her only plan having been to escape Warren's house as quickly as possible. She'd taken time to find and put on her sneakers—damned if she was going to slip on these cobblestones again—but beyond that, nothing. She needed to get outside, to clear her head. . . .

"Whose cross is this, Guadalupe?"

"I would rather not tell you that."

"Did it belong to Nicholas Denby?"

"Madre de Dios . . ."

"Did it?"

"No, señorita. No."

"Is this his blood?"

"I will not listen to this."

"Stop treating me like I broke into this house. I am staying here. I am living here. I have a right to know."

Guadalupe took a deep breath. "The cross—it is mine."

"What?"

"Please don't tell anyone."

"This blood . . ."

"Mine."

Zoe stared at her. "Why?"

"It is my offering," Guadalupe whispered. *"I bleed into Señor Clark's garden every day."*

At first, Zoe hadn't believed her. She had thought it was some desperate attempt to avoid the topic of Nicholas Denby and to protect Warren's privacy . . . until Guadalupe had shown Zoe her hands—all those scratches. *"Señor Clark is a wonderful man,"* Guadalupe had said, and Zoe noticed how so many of the cuts crisscrossed. She remembered the cross-shaped wound on Warren's hand and what he had said, her first night in the house, when she'd admired his shockingly lush garden.

Actually, water has nothing to do with it.

Who was this man Zoe was sharing a bed with?

She'd let her mind get twisted by pretty words and great sex and an apartment key and more words and more sex and roses on her pillow and a vacation in paradise. . . . And the sad truth was, all she wanted now were still more words and roses and sex—anything to stop her from thinking of crosses and cuts, of housekeepers bleeding on lilac bushes.

Zoe spotted La Cruz. She felt drawn to it, but purposely crossed the street away from it. She sat on the church steps, put her head in her hands and tried to will herself back to the start of her vacation. She couldn't.

There was only so much absolute weirdness she could ignore.

In the past four months, Zoe had asked herself, *Why Warren Clark?* He was so blond and so perfect and so very confident. Not Zoe's type by a long shot, plus a terrible conflict of interest. Why had she fallen so hard for this *soap star*? It wasn't his power or his mystery or his perfect timing, no matter how often she tried to tell herself those things. Deep down, she'd always known what it was.

Since Daryl Barclay, Zoe had tried to avoid reality, to turn away from the news, to stop asking questions. . . . And it had been hard—impossible, really, until she'd met Warren. Warren, who'd been on soaps so long, he'd become a leading man in real life—too intense to be true, astounding in bed, flesh and blood infused with romantic fiction. Zoe had never met any man so thoroughly druglike as Warren. And that was why she'd fallen. He could make her forget.

But forgetting the truth didn't erase it. Daryl Barclay

had lived and killed, and nothing could change that. Jordan Brink had been brutally murdered and so had someone named Grace, and Naomi was not delusional. There *was* a secret club in this town. Vanessa was a member and so was Guadalupe and probably Reiki Master Paul and Rafael, too. Warren was, definitely. The club had something to do with crosses and maguey spines and self-mutilation, and where was Warren right now? Where did he keep disappearing to?

She needed to know.

Zoe closed her eyes. In her mind, she saw the haunted green eyes of Patty Woods. Patty, who had appeared before Zoe and Naomi like a vengeful ghost to tell Naomi her aunt should be ashamed. Patty, who had spoken in private to Vanessa . . . about the secret club. About Grace. Zoe recalled how Naomi had gazed at the house across the street from Dr. Dave's office. *That's Patty Woods's house. She's . . . she was Jordan's aunt.* And it hit Zoe that of all the houses in San Esteban besides Warren's, *Patty Woods's was the only one she knew how to get to.*

Her head spilling over with questions, Zoe stood up and headed for the corner. She crossed the street before Studio Rafael, and moved toward the tall, dark house with the dying plants on its roof.

Patty had said she was leaving town today, but it was only one p.m. Zoe hoped she was still around. . . .

SIXTEEN

For a seventy-five-year-old man—for anyone, actually—Andrew Fennimore had an incredibly busy schedule. From the looks of the latest "Andrew's Fans-and-More" newsletter, which Dana LeVine had e-mailed to Glen, Fennimore had appearances scheduled for every day this month. They were far-reaching, too—emceeing the Miss New York beauty pageant up in Albany, cutting the ribbon on a new strip mall in Fort Lee, signing copies of his self-help book, *Think Yourself Younger!*, at a Greenwich, Connecticut, Barnes & Noble. . . . Steve got exhausted just thinking about it.

Thank God today's appearance was in Manhattan—a fan club "Meet and Eat" at a frilly, lunch-with-the-girlfriends-type restaurant called the Silver Teacup, on Fifty-fifth and Third, just a ten-minute walk from the *Trumpet*'s offices.

Seconds after reading the newsletter, Steve was out the door, in the elevator and racing up the street, weaving around pedestrians like a crazed reality show contestant, heart pounding. Yes, the Silver Teacup was close, but Fennimore's fan club event had been a brunch; it had started three hours ago.

Steve got to the door sweaty and winded, his sports coat hanging on him, his shirt plastered to his back. Really, he had thought he was in better shape than this. He needed to start working out again, hit the rink at Chelsea Piers or something. . . . He took a few breaths, turned to the hostess. No need to get her attention. As it turned out, she was gaping at him already. "I'm, uh, here for the Fennimore brunch."

"You *are*?" she said.

Steve followed her into the back room, where a long table was set up with pitchers of coffee, plates dotted with the sticky remains of a ham-and-egg breakfast, bread baskets now holding just a few neglected danishes, some disemboweled croissants. A couple dozen women in their sixties and seventies—some elegant in pastel suits, others dressed down in jeans or khaki pants and *Day's End* T-shirts—chattered loudly, hoisting back Bloody Marys and mimosas like it was happy hour, a whole group of them clustered around Fennimore, who sat at the head of the table cracking jokes, signing T-shirts and copies of his book. Holding court. Other than Steve and a few put-upon waiters, the soap star was the only man in the room, and he seemed to have no problem with that.

Andrew Fennimore looked exactly the way you'd expect a business tycoon to look—if your only cultural reference was soap operas. He had the photogenic, chiseled features, the perfect shave, the shock of white hair, the red silk power tie. Even soused on Bloody Marys, which he obviously was, Fennimore had an air of dignity. A quality you'd call *presidential*—again, if your only reference was soap operas. Steve took few steps forward. "Mr. Fennimore?"

The actor looked up at him—a challenge of a glare in his gunmetal eyes. "Did Bobby send you?"

"Who's Bobby?"

"Who's Bobby?" snorted a large, silver-haired woman whose T-shirt read MRS. WELLINGTON HARDY in gold cursive letters. "*He* can't be much of a fan!"

Fennimore said, "You're not a lawyer?"

"Uh . . . no," said Steve.

"Oh, thank God." The actor's face relaxed into a thousand-watt TV-star smile. "Sorry. I'm just experiencing a little palimony trauma right now." He stood up and shook Steve's hand. He was quite a bit shorter and slighter than Steve, but his grip made up for that—this guy could crush soup cans. "What can I do for you?"

Steve started to tell Fennimore that he was with the *Trumpet* and interested in an interview. But besides the fact that *The Day's End* publicist now hated the *Trumpet*, as Fennimore was bound to find out, Enid would never go for a story about some soap actor or his antiaging book. And Steve didn't feel right getting an old man's hopes up about something that was not going to happen. "It's . . . personal," he said. "I've got to see you alone."

Fennimore frowned. The woman with the T-shirt said, "Andy, have you been a naughty boy again?" but he ignored her.

"Be right back, ladies," he said, and the two men went in the other room and sat at the bar, Steve ordering a cup of coffee, Fennimore what was probably his eighth Bloody Mary of the morning. "You sure you're not with Bobby?" he said.

Steve said, "Listen, I'm sorry to be so cryptic, but I need to find out some information fast. It's about one of your costars."

Fennimore took an enormous gulp of his drink, ice cubes clinking.

Steve continued. "My friend . . . my best friend, actually . . . she's dating Warren Clark and he took her down to Mexico with him. I need to make sure she's safe."

Fennimore stared at him. Even as the words were leaving his mouth, Steve had realized how ridiculous he sounded. Obviously, this drunken soap actor felt the same. "Let me ask you something. Is your friend a grown-up?"

"Okay, I know I sound like a jackass, but you don't have to patronize me." *Ask the old-timer. What a stupid idea.*

Fennimore blinked several times, trying to focus on Steve's face. "I'm not patronizing you," he said. "The question wasn't rhetorical. You said your friend is romantically involved with Warren Clark. Which leads *me* to ask . . ." He leaned closer. His voice dropped. "Is your friend . . . a *grown-up?*"

Steve's eyes widened. "Oh."

"You understand me now."

"Yes," he said slowly. "Yes. She's thirty years old."

"Good," Fennimore said. "Maybe he's learned his lesson, then." He started to get up.

"Wait," said Steve. "Are you saying Warren Clark and Tiffany Baxter—"

"Sssh." Fennimore sat back down and glared at Steve, the gray eyes turning to knife blades. When he spoke again, very quietly, some of the slur was gone from his voice. "That's exactly what I'm saying." He glanced around the room. "But I am the only one who knows other than *The Day's End* brass and Tiffany's parents and Tiffany herself, who trusted me enough to tell me. Confidentiality contracts have been signed. So if you say one word about this to anyone but your *friend*, if I see even so much as a *blind item on Page Six*, my lawyers will ream you so hard, you will have trouble walking for the rest of your poverty-stricken life."

"Jesus. She's just a kid."

"Have you ever seen Tiffany up close? She's fifteen going on twenty-five."

"Oh, come *on*."

"I'm not excusing what he did. It got him *fired*, for god-sakes. I'm just saying that Clark is not a pedophile, *per se*. And your friend is perfectly *safe* in Mexico with him. Good God, what do you think he's going to do? Turn into a werewolf?"

Steve looked at him. "I have no idea."

He rolled his eyes. "I've got to get back to the ladies."

"Mr. Fennimore, can I show you something?" He reached into his jacket pocket, pulled out Jordan's notebook.

Fennimore hesitated for a moment, then took it and opened it, his gaze moving over the pages.

"I'm going to be totally honest with you," said Steve. "I am a reporter for the *Trumpet*."

"Oh, Christ on a stick."

"No, no, listen to me. I'm not here on business, I swear. . . . That notebook you're holding; it's for another story I'm working on. It belonged to Jordan Brink."

Slowly, Fennimore's gaze moved up to meet Steve's face. "The . . . boy? In Mexico?"

"Yes," said Steve.

Fennimore said nothing, just stood there. "I . . . I didn't know that Tiffany knew Jordan Brink," he said finally. "When it was in the papers, she never said anything—"

"I don't believe she *did* know him," said Steve.

"Then, why—"

"Jordan was killed in the same town where Warren Clark's second home is. Warren Clark was there at the time of his murder." He gave him a long look. "I think Warren connects Tiffany and Jordan. Jordan knew *of* her—I think because of her involvement with Warren."

"What . . . what are these lists?"

"I have no idea."

"Tiffany's on here. He put her on the same list as he put himself."

"Yes."

"And also . . ."

"Also what?"

He glanced away, gave him back the notebook. "I'm . . . I'm not sure. It could be a different name. I need to check. Can I have your card?" His face looked about three shades whiter.

Steve pulled a business card out of his wallet and handed it to him. "Mr. Fennimore?"

"Andy."

"Andy," Steve said, "can you please talk to Tiffany for me? Can you mention those initials—SPLV—see if she knows what they mean?"

He gave Steve a nod, then a sad half smile. "I always told Tiffany she was looking for trouble," he said. "I'd no idea she'd be so adept at finding it."

Patty Woods's house was mostly dark, but Zoe noticed a light on in one of the second-floor windows—a good sign she hadn't left yet. She hadn't shut off her electricity. Even if she was keeping it on so she could rent the place out, she would've at least turned off her lights before leaving town for good, right?

Zoe pressed the doorbell and waited. No answer. She hit it again, and was about to try the door when something knocked into her back . . . a tackle of paws and untrimmed nails. She nearly fell to the pavement again, but caught herself this time, whirling around to the yellow fur, the tongue in the face.

"Adele! Stop that!" Robin shouted from the end of the street.

Zoe put her arms around Adele, scratched her behind the ears, her mood lifting. "Well, hello there, you crazy dog."

Robin came running up, her cheeks pink, panting harder than the dog. "Adele, *down!*" She was wearing a long-sleeved black cocktail dress that seemed inappropriate in this weather, patent leather boots on the cobblestones. It was impressive how quickly she could get around in that outfit. "Hey, Zoe, sorry about that."

"No need to apologize," Zoe said. "I love Adele."

Robin smiled. "Looks like the feeling's mutual. My dog is an excellent judge of character, you know." She winked. "She's crazy about Warren, too."

Zoe cringed a little. "Speaking of Warren," she said, "you haven't seen him, have you?"

"No . . ." Robin glanced at the Woods house and lowered her voice. "You sure won't find him in there, if that's what you're thinking."

Now she knows what it's like to have a visitor disappear. "They don't get along, do they?" said Zoe. "Warren and Patty."

Robin's eyes widened. Her gaze moved up and to the left. *She's going to lie.* "Oh no," she said. "I just meant you wouldn't find him in there because Patty's left town. Warren and Patty get along *great.*" Robin visibly gulped. Zoe thought, *She's almost as bad a liar as Steve.*

"She's gone already? Really?"

"Well, that's what Dave told me." Robin cleared her throat. "Hey, I almost forgot. How was Las Aguas?"

"You knew about that?"

"Knew about it?" She grinned. "Who do you think set up the candles and the picnic?"

"That was you?"

She nodded. "Warren told me he wanted to surprise you, and I kind of . . . took it from there."

"It was amazing."

A smile overcame Robin's face. "Oh, good!" she said. "Listen, I was going to grab some lunch. You feel like joining me?" Next to her, Adele was sitting at attention, tongue lolling out of her mouth, fluffy tail thumping on the pavement. *Both of them, so eager to please . . .*

Zoe thought: *Robin has known Warren for ten years. He confides in her, and loyal though she is, Robin can't lie to save her soul.* Patty might have left town, but as far as reliable Warren Clark sources went, Robin was probably better.

Zoe scratched Adele behind the ear, met Robin's smile with her own. "I'd love to go to lunch with you," she said. "My treat."

Robin's idea of going out for lunch was buying a couple of bollilo sandwiches at one of the stands on the *jardín* (she refused to let Zoe pay) and then taking them back to her desk at Dr. Dave's. "Sorry," she said as they sat down, "but Dave was gone all morning, so I had to turn people away and reschedule. This afternoon is going to be a major pain. . . ."

Zoe looked at her. "Where was he?"

"I have absolutely no idea."

"That sounds familiar."

"Huh?"

Zoe gave her a long look, then started to unwrap her ham-and-avocado sandwich. "Warren was gone when I woke up," Zoe said. "I have no idea where he is, either." She took a bite. "Ever since I've gotten here, I've been waking up alone."

Robin let out a nervous tic of a laugh. "Knowing Warren," she said, "I'll bet he was out buying you presents." She blinked a few times. Zoe could tell Robin was uncomfortable, but she wasn't sure whether it was because of what she was saying about Warren, or because of the intent way that

Zoe was observing her face. Best to back off a little bit. She took another bite of her sandwich and chewed slowly, letting her gaze wander from Robin to the begging Adele and then across the room to the painting of the maguey spine. "Dr. Dave painted that, huh?" she asked.

"I hate it."

Zoe looked at her. She had said it so nonchalantly, while plucking a piece of ham out of her sandwich and feeding it to the dog. But when Robin glanced up and met her gaze, Zoe sensed something in her eyes—a hint of fear. "Why?"

Robin said, "I don't know. . . . I feel like . . . maybe . . . some things shouldn't be painted."

"But, Robin," Zoe said slowly, "it's just a plant."

Robin placed her sandwich on the butcher paper it had been wrapped in and gazed at Zoe's face. "You believe in bad energy, Zoe?"

"Um . . . I'm not sure I—"

"I do. Sometimes, after Dave comes back from Rafael's painting class, I don't want to be around him."

"What do you mean?"

Robin turned to her. "It's like . . . he picks it up in there somehow, when he paints certain things. It attaches itself to him, possesses him in a way. . . . He brought back that painting, it was worse than ever."

"The energy."

"Yeah." Robin took a trembling breath. "You probably think I'm crazy."

"No, I don't."

Robin slid the sandwich away. Her face grew still, her eyes clouded. "He hung that painting on the wall," she said. "Then he walked up to me. He touched my face. Dave does that a lot. He doesn't mean anything by it. . . . He likes to feel the bones—the way they're connected."

"Okay . . ."

"But this time, he touched my face and it *seared*. It . . . it was like . . . evil was touching me."

Zoe stared at Robin.

Robin swallowed hard. Then suddenly she spun around to the side. "Hi!"

Zoe turned to see Dr. Dave leaving his office. His mouth was set in a straight line, his shoulders were slumped and he seemed even paler than usual. If he had been a different person, Zoe might have asked, *Who died?* But it was Dave—eerie, humorless Dr. Dave, the opposite of his jovial name—and so she stayed quiet.

He glanced at Zoe. "You've met Rafael."

"Yes . . . how did you know—"

"Your wrist. Bandage is gone."

"Oh."

"Hey," said Robin, "I didn't even notice . . ." Her voice trailed off.

Dave was touching Robin's face. It was such an odd gesture—neither threatening nor intimate nor even particularly friendly. Just a finger, placed clinically on the hinge of her jaw. "Please call the supply company," he said. "We're low on muscle relaxant." He headed for the door.

"Are you leaving again?" said Robin. "You just got here."

He smiled. "I won't be gone long."

After he left, Robin said, "See? Now that time, I didn't feel anything at all."

"Robin?"

"Yeah?"

"Did you ever feel bad energy coming from anybody else?"

Robin's face darkened, but she said nothing.

"Please. I won't tell anyone. Have you felt it from Warren?"

"*Warren?* God. *No.*"

Zoe hadn't intended to ask that question so directly, but Robin's shock at it provided some relief. "It's just . . . ever since I've been here, I've had this sense that . . . something isn't quite right." She stared into Robin's eyes, searched them for any change, the faintest hint of recognition. "I feel like there may be something weird going on that I don't know about."

"Weird?" she said. "Well, there was . . ."

"What?"

"I shouldn't say."

"Tell me. Please, Robin. We're alone, and God knows I can keep a secret."

Robin took a breath, exhaled hard. "You heard about Jordan, right?"

"Yes."

"He came in here, Zoe. That day. The day he was . . ."

"He did?"

"His cousin Corinne was coming in by bus, and he was on his way to meet her in the *jardín*. . . . He stopped in to say hi. We used to be friends—I teach an after-school English class for Mexican kids at the *biblioteca*, and he'd sometimes help out. But I hadn't seen him since he was sixteen. . . . He came in. He was twenty. A man. Still so good-looking, but . . . troubled. Like he hadn't slept all night. He shook my hand and . . ."

"You . . . you felt the bad energy."

"Adele even felt it. She growled at him," she said. "The thing is, this town is so full of good energy, and we do so much to keep it that way. Reiki Master Paul says the town was built on a bed of healing crystals and La Cruz is the conduit, and that's why it draws so many positive people here like Rafael and Warren and Vanessa and you, so when someone is carrying bad energy, it's really—"

"We."

"Huh?"

"You said, '*We* do so much to keep it that way.' "

She nodded, slowly.

"Who is *we?*" said Zoe.

Robin fed Adele another piece of her sandwich. "This dog is such a little begger. Aren't you, sweetie?"

"Robin."

Robin glanced up at her. "We," she said. "You know, Zoe . . . the people of San Esteban." She stopped feeding Adele and rested her arms on her desk. She gave Zoe that sunny smile, but it went to waste. Zoe was too busy staring at the deep red scratches on the underside of Robin's left arm. "It's all good, Zoe. Lighten up. Come on, you're on vacation with Warren Clark." Robin gazed at her for a moment, her dark eyes flickering with a young girl's wistfulness—the wallflower watching the last dance at the junior prom.

"You would do anything for Warren, wouldn't you?" Zoe asked.

Robin peered at her. "Wouldn't *you?*"

Before Zoe could reply, she heard someone saying her name and turned to see Naomi standing in the doorway, pink faced and breathless. "I'm so glad I found you! Hi, Robin."

"Does your aunt know where you are?" said Robin. "She was in here earlier, asking for you."

The girl's eyes narrowed. "If Vanessa wants to see me," she said, "she should try coming home every once in a while." Naomi was holding a clear plastic bag. There was a bottle of pills inside, and though her face and voice were calm enough, she clutched it very tightly, her knuckles straining against the skin. "You can tell her I was out, filling the prescription she was *supposed to fill for me but didn't.*"

"Jeez," said Robin. "No need to shoot the messenger."

"Sorry. I just need to speak to Zoe. Alone."

SEVENTEEN

Naomi took Zoe to a restaurant down the street. It was called El Borracho, and it was a windowless cave of a place—the most powerful light source the muted bar TV, playing an episode of *Magnum, P.I.* The space was made festive, though, by a galaxy of blinking multicolored Christmas lights strewn across the walls and arranged on the ceiling like a psychedelic chandelier. There were also bright red tablecloths and candles in handcrafted metal holders shaped like stars and fresh gardenias floating in round glass bowls. Zoe would have found the atmosphere enchanting enough to say *Screw it all*, order a margarita and take Robin's advice about lightening up, if she hadn't still been thinking of bloody maguey spines . . . and if Naomi hadn't told her, as soon as they sat down, "Carlos Royas didn't kill Jordan."

"How do you know that, Naomi?"

"His mother, Alma. She's the pharmacist. She told me Carlos was home with her and his baby sister the night Jordan was murdered. She says his confession was a lie. She thinks he was threatened into it."

"Not to be overskeptical," said Zoe, "but wouldn't any mother say that about her son?"

The waitress set a basket of chips and salsa on the table, a cup of strong coffee in front of each of them and a large bottle of *agua con gas* with two glasses. After she left, Naomi opened her bottle of Xanax, broke a pill in half and took it with some of the bubbly water. "Mrs. Royas has proof."

Zoe's eyes widened. "What kind?"

"She didn't feel comfortable talking about it. She said she feels nervous at work—like someone is watching her. She said someone has been calling her there, hanging up. . . ."

"What kind of . . . proof could she possibly have?"

"I don't know. A threatening note, maybe? Recorded phone call?"

"If she has that kind of proof, why wouldn't she go to the police?"

Naomi shrugged. "Maybe they're in on this, too. Maybe the real killer has been paying off the police. The new *co-mandante* questioned me, you know, and I didn't trust him at all."

Zoe looked at Naomi. "Or," she said, "maybe Alma just wants you to think that her son is innocent."

"Zoe," said Naomi, "this is really hard to explain because you didn't know Carlos. But I know he didn't do that to Jordan. I've known it from the start. He's a weird guy, yes. He's even robbed graves."

"He has?"

"Yeah," she said. "But there is a massive leap between Carlos's type of weirdness and what was done to Jordan."

Zoe sipped her coffee and felt the warmth of it. She took a breath, and then she spoke slowly, as if she was trying to convince Naomi and herself at the same time. "I believe what you said about the secret group."

"You do?"

"Yes. Not to go into detail, but I've . . . seen a few things that have made me think . . ." She exhaled hard. "Okay. I found another cross at Warren's house. And his housekeeper said it was hers."

Naomi stared at Zoe, her face going so pale that Zoe figured, *Best to stop here. Best not to bring up cutting or maguey spines . . .*

"I know there's a group," Naomi said.

Zoe nodded. "I think Carlos Royas was in it. I think he went crazy and maybe took some of the group's . . . beliefs . . . too seriously. I think he killed this Grace person, and when Jordan stole his peyote, he snapped and killed him the same way."

"No," said Naomi.

"The weird stuff Jordan told you was going on—that probably had to do with his stealing the drugs from Carlos and Carlos threatening him."

"You don't unders—"

"It is disturbing to think you've breathed the same air as someone capable of that," she said. "It almost feels . . . catching, I know."

"Yes. Yes, that's true—"

"It's not catching, Naomi," she said. "It scars. Bad. But it isn't contagious."

"I know what you're saying, but that's not it. Mrs. Royas is very much like Carlos, and when you see her, you'll get it."

"What do you mean? When am I going to see Mrs. Royas?"

"She's going to meet us here after she's done with work." Naomi looked Zoe in the eyes, her gaze hard and serious and much older than the rest of her. "She's going to bring the proof."

Steve was sitting at his desk, calling Zoe's cell for the fifth time in a row. He got her voice mail. Again. He hit END. Again.

Either her battery was dead or she'd turned off her phone, but regardless, he didn't feel comfortable leaving a message about Warren Clark and Tiffany Baxter on Zoe's voice mail. In fact, he wasn't even sure whether he wanted to tell her over the phone at all. What he wanted to do was find out why she'd sounded so upset earlier. If it had nothing to do with Clark, he'd save the statutory-rape bulletin for when she got home. She'd just quit her job; this vacation was all she had. Why ruin it? Like Andy Fennimore had said, it wasn't as if Clark was going to turn into a werewolf. . . .

Steve glanced at the Rangers calendar he kept on the wall of his cubicle and noticed that tonight was, in fact, a full moon. If Steve were a character in a movie, the fact that someone had mentioned werewolves to him just before a full moon would have been incredibly significant. But here, in real life, it was nothing. Just a stupid coincidence. Sometimes—okay, lots of times—Steve wished life were more like a movie. He wished there were a plot to it—one that made sense and where, if you paid enough attention, you could figure it out. Steve stared hard at life, always, and he still didn't get it. What was Zoe doing with Warren Clark? Why was such a bright, kind, beautiful woman with a sleaze-bag like that when she could be . . . she *should* be with . . .

Steve's cell phone chimed. Mike Grady at the next desk called out, "You need a new ring tone, Sorensen. I'm sick of that *Tommy* song!"

"Get over it. It's a classic." Steve checked his screen. He didn't recognize the number. He thought about letting his voice mail pick up, but his curiosity got the better of him. "Sorensen."

"I need to talk to you about Warren Clark." The voice was a half whisper—fast and tremulous and very, very high. Either a child or a scared woman trying not to be overheard. Steve was betting on both.

He said the name. "Tiffany?"

A long pause, then: "I'm at Sixtieth and Third. Where can we meet?"

An hour later, Zoe and Naomi were well into their second cups of coffee and their third order of guacamole. Alma Royas still hadn't shown, even though her workday had ended more than forty minutes ago. Zoe had a feeling it wasn't ever going to happen—that Alma had told Naomi she was bringing "proof" just to bolster her argument, or maybe to get this overpersistent young *gringa* to leave her pharmacy and stop upsetting her with questions.

Zoe wasn't bringing any of that up, though. As it turned out, Naomi and Xanax were a match made in heaven, and she didn't want to wreck that. No longer clutching her coffee cup as if it were some form of life support, Naomi seemed, if not entirely happy, then at least relaxed, able to talk about other things besides Jordan Clark's murder. "Vanessa means well," she was saying now, "but a lot of times, I feel like I'm *her* legal guardian."

"Like she's going through a second childhood?"

"More like she never finished her first." Naomi smothered a grin. "She ties up the landline talking to her boyfriends. When she's upset, she locks herself in her room and turns up the music. Really loud." She started to laugh.

Zoe laughed, too. "It's like you're living with a fifty-five-year-old Gidget."

"Who?"

"Never mind. I watch too much classic TV."

"Vanessa goes out, doesn't tell me where, disappears for hours. Oh, and you should see what she wears to bed!"

Zoe put her coffee cup down. Her smile dropped away. "She . . . she disappears a lot?"

"Not all the time. Actually, it's usually when there's a full moon." She laughed a little. "Maybe she's a werewolf."

"Warren does the same thing," Zoe said. "Here, I mean. During this trip. He's never around when I wake up."

Naomi's face went still. "You . . . you think the group is—" She was interrupted by a loud trill. "Probably my aunt. She called a couple times, but I didn't pick up. . . ." Naomi plucked her cell phone out of her straw bag and squinted at the screen.

Her eyebrows lifted. She flipped it open. "*¿Bueno?*" she said, and launched into a five-minute conversation, entirely in Spanish. Zoe didn't understand much of it beyond "*¿Por qué?*" and "*Pero—*" But from the tone of Naomi's voice and the confusion building in her eyes, Zoe could tell who was on the other line and what was being said.

"Alma Royas?" she asked, after Naomi hit END.

"*Sí*. I mean . . . yes."

"She's not meeting us."

Naomi shook her head.

"She doesn't have any proof."

"She . . . she told me she lied to me. She said Carlos was not home with her and the baby that night. She said . . . she said she saw Carlos in the morning, washing blood off his hands and arms." She lifted her coffee cup, her grip tightening. She bit her lower lip, as if she were trying to keep it still.

"Naomi," said Zoe, "that's good news. It means they arrested the right man, that you don't have to be—"

"She was whispering. Her voice was shaking so bad I

could barely understand her. She sounded really afraid." Naomi took a sip of bubbly water and set the glass down, carefully. "If her son confessed, and her son is in jail . . . I could see her being sad. I could see her being shocked and angry and thinking that her life was totally ruined. . . . But why would she be *afraid*?"

Zoe stared at her. "I . . . have no idea." She'd been going for comforting words. But under the circumstances, that was the best she could do.

Naomi stared back. "I wasn't going to tell you this," she said, very quietly. "But I got this . . . really disturbing phone call last night."

"You did?"

"I . . . I saw him in the park yesterday and . . . it's a long story." She cleared her throat. "But . . . Alejandro called me and said he was serving someone evil and that I should stop asking questions. . . ."

"Who is Alejandro?"

"Carlos Royas's best friend."

"You know him?"

She nodded. "Not that well. He goes to the boys' school, though, and we sort of bonded when I first moved here because of my mom. Mr. Christopher died like ten years ago in a car crash, and Alejandro's still messed up over it, so—"

Zoe felt the color draining from her face. "Mr. Christopher."

"Alejandro's dad was American," she said. "Why are you looking at me like that?"

"Did he ever tell you his father's first name?"

"Yeah, a while ago," said Naomi. "I . . . I think it might have been, like George or—"

"Garrett. Garrett Christopher."

"That's it. How did you know?"

Zoe couldn't say any more. She felt two hands on her

shoulders, and when she turned around, Warren was gazing down at her. "I've been looking all over for you," he said. His eyes were flat.

Steve and Tiffany had agreed to meet on the corner of Fifty-seventh and Third. He'd image searched her on Google first—and from what he'd seen, Fennimore had been right. In the red-carpet shots especially, Tiffany wore clinging, short dresses, lots of makeup and a leer that would drive any father to install an electric fence, bars on the windows, maybe a couple of eunuchs packing Uzis. . . .

But the girl who waited for him on the street corner was very different. He recognized her when he was about a block away. She was wearing a baggy T-shirt and jeans, pacing in tense circles. Her hair was pulled back in a messy ponytail, she wore no makeup and she looked like a frightened kid.

When Steve approached her, Tiffany's mouth formed a sort of half smile, half grimace. "Walk with me," she said.

"Where are we going?"

"Central Park." They headed west on Fifty-seventh, pushing through the thick, humid air, passing groups of people on their lunch hour. "Okay, so I don't know what Andy told you," said Tiffany, "but I'm gonna guess he said my mom caught Warren nailing me on his dressing room couch."

Steve turned and gaped at her. "Uh . . . actually, Andy wasn't that specific."

"Whatever." They moved past a group of skinny women wearing tight T-shirts and velour sweats and enough heavy jewelry to cause injury. One of them called out to Tiffany, asked for her autograph. Tiffany plastered on a smile, signed the woman's Saks shopping bag. "Make it out to Teena. With two *e*'s." She slipped her sunglasses down her nose, took a quick glance at Steve. "Is this your father?"

"No." Tiffany handed the woman back her bag, grabbed Steve's arm and began walking even faster. Steve could have sworn he heard the woman clicking her tongue, and he almost said, *It's not what you think,* as if he cared about the moral opinion of some Saks-shopping plastic surgeon's wife who couldn't even spell her own first name correctly. "What happened," Tiffany said, "was my mom walked in on us in Warren's dressing room, and my shirt was off, and—"

Steve cut her short. "Look . . . this is probably embarrassing for you."

"It's not."

"Well, it is for me. And it's not important. I'm sure Andy told you I've got a friend who went down to Mexico with Warren. What I really need to know is what SPLV stands for, and if you know anything about a black cross with a red dot in the middle."

She cleared her throat. "That was really . . . that was really in the notebook of . . . that guy? Jordan whatever?"

"Yes."

She stopped walking. "Warren gave me a pendant—a black cross with a ruby in the middle."

"He *did*?"

"Yeah, but he took it back when . . . Look, Steve. I'm sorry if it makes you uncomfortable, but I really have to tell you what happened in the dressing room."

He sighed. "Fine."

"All right." She started moving again, faster. "How can I put this? I'm an early bloomer."

"No kidding."

"My mom walked in on me and Warren, yeah. But . . . let's just say she's walked in on me with guys Warren's age plenty of times, and all she usually does is say 'Whoops. Excuse me.' "

They were at Central Park now. "So," Steve said slowly, "what did she see this time that made her . . . ?"

"That's what I need to show you." Tiffany grabbed his hand and pulled him past the statue of General Sherman, to the line of park benches along the brick walkway that led to the zoo. Thick, shady trees arched over their heads. It was cool here, breezy despite the heat. It always was. On slow days at work, Steve would bring his lunch, eat alone on one of the benches just to breathe some natural air. He thought about that as Tiffany pulled him to the last bench, sat him down and eased next to him.

"SPLV," she said, finally, "stands for *Sangre Para La Vida*. Blood in exchange for life."

He stared at her. "Blood?"

"My shirt was off when my mom walked in, but we weren't screwing." Her voice went small and shaky and very young—a grade schooler reciting a poem. "Blood for life, blood in exchange for life. Young blood, to keep the world alive . . . past when it's supposed to end. Will your friend be under thirty-five at the start of 2012?"

Steve peered at her. "Uh . . . she's thirty now, so . . . yeah."

"He needs her blood."

"I don't understand."

"Warren . . . he has this . . . beautiful black knife. . . ." Tiffany glanced both ways, then leaned closer to Steve and yanked down the neck of her T-shirt. She held it there for a few seconds, exposing herself just long enough for Steve to see, to understand. . . .

"My mother saw him . . . doing this." Between Tiffany's breasts were a series of thickly scabbed wounds, forming the shape of a cross.

Steve inhaled sharply. "Oh, my God."

"He told me I'm special," she whispered. "He was going to take me to Mexico."

EIGHTEEN

Vanessa showed up at El Borracho shortly after Warren. She was wearing a sheer white sundress and would have looked angelic, except that her hair was a mess and she was breathing hard and her eyes were sharp with panic. "Oh, thank God!" She rushed to Naomi and hugged her tightly, practically lifting her off the chair.

"Aunt Vanessa," Naomi said, "I've only been out for a couple of hours."

Vanessa stepped back, her eyes calming. "That's a couple of hours too many. I specifically told Soccoro . . ." She glanced at Warren and Zoe, offered a slight, embarrassed smile. "We'll continue this conversation on the way home. By the way, Zoe, either your cell phone is turned off or your battery is dead. Warren was trying to call you."

Zoe pulled her phone out of her purse, looked at it. It had been holding a charge for shorter and shorter periods of time, and sure enough . . . "Dead battery." She turned to Warren. "Sorry."

He didn't answer.

Vanessa slipped a stack of pesos out of her embroidered handbag and dropped it on the table. "See you both at Rafael's party." She gave Naomi a punishing glare and said, "We're leaving now." Zoe half expected Vanessa to yank her seventeen-year-old niece out the door by the ear.

After they left, Warren took Naomi's seat. His mouth was tight, his jaw forming a right angle. His eyes were dry blue stones.

"What's wrong?" Zoe asked.

"You went into my safe again."

Zoe looked at him. She'd forgotten all about falling asleep with the key in her hand, and at this moment, nothing seemed more irrelevant. She heard herself say, "Yeah, I did," in the same tone of voice she might have used for *I took out the garbage*.

Warren seemed a little taken aback. "Zoe, we're never going to work if you don't start trusting me."

"Warren?"

"Yes?"

"Are you completely insane?"

His eyes widened. "What do you mean?"

"Ever since I've been here, you've disappeared more often than you've been around. I found a cross in the guest room armoire exactly like the one in your dressing room closet, and I don't know what the hell either one of them means because you won't tell me."

"Why were you in the guest room?"

"Oh, my God, I can't believe you just *asked me* that."

"I . . . I was asking because Guadalupe said—"

"Guadalupe. Did she tell you I now know your gardening secret?"

He swallowed. "Yes."

"And you are honestly telling me I should *trust* you? Jesus Christ, Warren. You've got more bizarre secrets than Dracula. I uncover a new one every five minutes without even *trying*, and you have the absolute balls to bring up *trust*?"

Warren's gaze dropped to the table. "I wasn't planning on keeping those secrets forever."

"Really?" said Zoe. "When were you going to tell me you encourage your maid to bleed herself out into the potted plants? Next Tuesday, over lunch?"

"You don't have it right," he said, softly.

"What is right?" she said. "Tell me, Warren."

"Some things, you need to see in order to believe." He looked at her. "Some things you need to feel in your heart."

"I'm asking for a simple explan—"

"Last night. What Rafael did, with your wrist."

"Yes?"

"If I were to just explain that to you . . . if I were to describe that in words and you hadn't felt it for yourself, you would have thought I was crazy, wouldn't you?"

She thought about it. "Yeah, I guess I would've."

"Lots of things are like that. La Cruz, déjà vu . . . the way the sun can turn so many different colors in the course of one day." He gazed at her. "The way the body works. The way *our* bodies work . . ."

"But—"

He lowered his voice. "*Sangre Para La Vida* is like that. It's better than an explanation."

"*Sangre—*"

"Sssh."

"Is that your . . . Is that some kind of . . . secret group?"

"I thought it was weird, too, Zoe, but then I saw it—I felt it for myself. Rafael showed me. Ten years ago."

"Rafael? Is that what this party is about?"

Warren reached across the table and took both of Zoe's hands in his. He stared into her eyes and she felt that healing gaze, and despite everything that was going on in her mind—the confusion and the anger and this nagging, nameless fear—something within her began to give way. "When I met Guadalupe," he said, "she was afraid to look anyone in the face. She was married to a violent son of a bitch who made her think she was a failure because she wasn't able to have kids. She couldn't read, couldn't speak a word of English. Look at her now, Zoe. Look at how straight she stands. She left him seven years ago. She is strong and proud and *happy*." Warren took a breath. His eyes were as warm as his hands. *Señor Clark is a wonderful man.* "It's not bleeding into potted plants, Zoe. It's so much more. . . . You'll see. You'll feel it, and you'll know. *You will be fixed.*"

She shut her eyes tightly. *Focus, focus. . . .* "Your gun," she said.

"Yes?"

"It just turned up in front of your house with that note: *Para tu protección.* You have no idea who gave it to you, no idea who owned it before." She opened her eyes. She sensed nothing in his face but confusion, and when she asked him, "Is that the truth?" he did not look up and to the left before answering.

"Of course it's the truth."

Zoe said, "I ran a check on the serial number. It belonged to Garrett Christopher."

"Who is that?" Not the slightest hint of recognition. Yes, he was an actor, but in her five years at *Headquarters*, Zoe had jolted secrets out of enough of them to know that even the most experienced actor couldn't hide true feelings *that* well.

"He was the father of Carlos Royas's best friend."

Warren went pale. "Oh, my God."

"Garrett Christopher died ten years ago in a car crash—around the same time Nick Denby disappeared, and around the same time . . . whoever it was . . . gave you the gun."

"You . . . you think this person may have caused the car crash, stolen the gun?"

"Yes."

"But . . . Carlos Royas would have been too young. He was only nine or ten years old when—"

"Yes."

"So . . ."

"Someone who knew Carlos, his friends . . . maybe someone who knows them, still." She looked at him. "Do you know them, Warren?"

"*No.*" A new emotion filtered into his eyes. He blinked it away and breathed deeply, and it was gone as if it had never been there. But Zoe had recognized it, and she knew it was real. *Fear.* The same fear as her own.

"I will bring the gun to the police tomorrow morning, as soon as the station opens," Warren said, and Zoe believed him. Then he said, "Will you come with me?"

"Yes, Warren. Of course I'll go to the police with—"

"I mean tonight," he said. "Will you come with me, to Rafael's?"

She swallowed hard. "To learn."

"Yes."

"I don't know."

"I would never do anything that would hurt you, Zoe. I only want to make you strong."

She stared at his face. "All right," she said, because she wanted to believe that, too.

On the way back to the office, Steve phoned Zoe's cell, and again, he got her voice mail. "Call me," he said. "It's very, very important. It's about Warren Clark." If he had to leave messages, fine. Steve didn't care anymore. After seeing what Clark had done to Tiffany, he was pretty much convinced: The guy *was* a werewolf.

When he got to his desk, Steve signed on to his computer. He ignored e-mails from Debbie Cohn, Padmé and the mayor's spokesperson and wrote one to Zoe. *Please call me whenever you get this. It doesn't matter when. It is urgent!!* He didn't want to be any more specific than that—what if Clark was checking her e-mail? What if the whole cult was?

God, there was a *cult*. Zoe—Zoe, of the poorest judgment known to womankind—had gone down to Mexico with the *high priest of a bloodletting cult* and had actually told Steve to *let her enjoy her vacation*.

He called her again, yelled at Zoe's voice mail: "Would you just charge your goddamn battery?!"

"You okay?" asked Mike Grady.

"I'm fine!"

" 'Cause that was kind of a self-defeating message you left there. I mean, if the battery is dead, then how can she hear—"

"Get bent, Mike."

"Jeez, *sorry*."

Steve called up Google, ran a search on *Sangre Para La Vida*. Nothing. Of course there was nothing. It was a *secret cult*. Zoe was down in Mexico with a secret cult whose members believed the world would end when the Aztecs said it would, in 2012—unless they fed their own blood to the energy force beneath the earth. The younger you were, the purer your blood, the more you gave.

Tiffany had explained it all.

Giving makes you stronger, she'd said. *The more blood you pour into the earth, the more cleansed you are. It's like you're taking that bad part of yourself—whatever part of you that is weak or scared or mean—and you're giving it back to nature, which transforms it to good energy. Like . . . spiritual recycling. Does that make sense?*

It hadn't made sense to Steve at all. Because he was *sane*.

Sitting at his desk now, staring at his screen, he could only think of the gleam that still shone out of Tiffany's eyes in spite of everything—even her fears that the cult might have been to blame for what happened to Jordan Brink. That gleam had scared Steve to death, made him feel for Tiffany's mother. It made him so worried for Zoe he could barely breathe.

If you'll be under thirty-five at the start of 2012, Tiffany had said, *then you are eligible for* nextlhualli.

What is that?

Debt repayment.

He'd had Tiffany write the word down for him on the back of one of his business cards. He pulled it out of his wallet now, typed *nextlhualli* into the seach bar. After he hit RETURN, he realized he'd accidentally run an image search, and soon, he was looking at a line of illustrations that made his skin freeze. This was more than bloodletting, this was . . .

Every one of the images was an ancient drawing of an Aztec priest standing over a mutilated human body. In one, the priest clasped an offering from the body, held high over his head. Steve read the caption: Nextlhualli, *literally the repaying of debts to the gods, was the Aztec word for human sacrifice.*

The offering was a heart. A ripped-out human heart.

No . . .

When Warren cut me, it was as if he was cutting out all the bad. He was fixing me. Does your friend feel guilty about anything she's done? Do you think your friend feels like she wants to be fixed?

Steve grabbed his cell phone again, called Zoe's number. He got her voice mail again and then threw the phone against the wall of his cubicle.

These cuts were just practice. Real Nextlhualli *can only take place in San Esteban.*

Mike Grady said, "You . . . you sure you're okay?"

"No," said Steve. "I've got to get out of here."

Enid was away from her desk. Without giving the idea any more thought, he forwarded her the e-mails from Debbie, Padmé and the mayor's spokesperson, explaining at the top of the first e-mail that he had a family emergency and needed to leave town, and suggesting Glen Campbell finish up the story. Then he switched screens and reserved the next possible flight for León, Mexico.

NINETEEN

Warren and Zoe enjoyed a leisurely dinner of chicken mole and rice with saffron—food so aromatic, it wasn't eaten so much as breathed. They talked about Mexican cooking and the weather in San Esteban this time of year and their future job plans. Heavy, sensuous food and light conversation—with Warren, it was almost always the other way around. But what with everything that had been said—and with the uncharted night that lay ahead of them—Zoe craved the mundane. Warren seemed to sense that, just like he sensed all of her cravings.

After dinner, he ordered shots of aged Don Julio and sangrito. Zoe said, "I don't know if I'm up for a tequila shot."

"You'll be up for this," Warren replied as the waitress returned with two long shot glasses full of clear liquid and two more full of a deep, thick red. "Now this is the Don Julio," he said, handing her the clear one. "This is sangrito—it's like Bloody Mary mix, only a little sweeter. Start with the tequila, chase it with the sangrito, but remember to sip . . . savor. . . ."

Zoe sipped the tequila—it was surprisingly smooth, elegant even. . . . It blazed a warm trail down her throat, followed perfectly by the sweet tomatoey taste of the sangrito. "You like?" Warren asked.

"God, yes."

He locked his gaze with hers. "I always know what you like."

She smiled.

After Warren paid the bill, they walked out into the glowing purple twilight—Zoe's favorite time of day anywhere, but here it was particularly beautiful. Warren put an arm around her and she leaned against him, loose and warm from tequila. She peered into shop windows at colorful Day of the Dead masks and papier-mâché animals and turquoise and obsidian jewelry and racks and racks of pastel shawls embroidered with bright flowers, and for practically the first time since she'd shown up here, Zoe remembered she was a tourist. She wanted to hold on to that feeling. "Let's go shopping tomorrow."

Warren smiled and said, "Of course," and she smiled back. But that moment—that whiff of normalcy—was like a Styrofoam kickboard in the middle of the ocean. It might keep you afloat for a little while, but it was way too weak to save you. What was this party going to be like tonight? What was this strange group that Warren was involved with?

She started to tell Warren maybe she wasn't up for learning about *Sangre Para La Vida* just yet (*Blood for Life? Was that really what it was called?*) and maybe he should go to the party alone, when she saw it just one door up. Patty Woods's house. Around her shoulders, Warren's arm stiffened.

"That's weird," Zoe said.

"What?"

"Patty Woods's light is still on."

"Still?"

"I noticed it this afternoon, but Robin said Patty had definitely left—Dave had told her." She turned to Warren. "Don't you think that's strange? Patty leaving town and keeping her light on?"

"Patty Woods is a strange woman," he said. "Come with me."

He pulled her across the street, past Dr. Dave's and Reiki Master Paul's. He seemed to want to get away from the house as fast as possible—a little odd, Zoe thought. She knew Warren didn't like Patty, but Patty had left town. It wasn't as if they were going to run into her.

The lights were on at Studio Rafael. She heard flamenco music coming from within. "Seems like the party's started," she said.

"Yes, it has."

"Listen, Warren . . . I don't know about this—"

"Zoe, I told you. I would never steer you wrong."

"I know," she said. "But I'm really tired and—"

"Before you make any decisions, I want to show you something." He waited for a break in traffic, then took her hand and led her across the street to the *jardín*.

"Where are we going?" she said, but the question was barely out of her mouth when she found herself standing in front of La Cruz de San Esteban with Warren directly behind her. She felt his hard stomach against her back and his palms on her bare shoulders and the heat radiating off the cross in front of her, a presence even stronger than Warren's. . . . She stared into the eyes of the bird carved into its face and went breathless.

"Close your eyes," said Warren. His hands slid down the

length of her arms. He pressed his body against her, took her hands in his and placed them up, over her head, on opposite arms of the cross.

She felt it immediately—a warmth, much like the warmth she'd felt when Rafael had healed her wrist, only about a hundred times more powerful. Like a fireworks finale under her skin. She gasped, and fell back against Warren. He held her there, kept her palms pressed to the granite as that heated force turned to something else . . . an overwhelming rush of emotion. Tears sprung into her eyes. Zoe wanted to blame it on the tequila, on the altitude, on some strange scientific phenomenon. Because she had never felt this way. People like her—rational people—did not feel this way. *Awestruck.* If Warren hadn't been holding her, she would have fallen to her knees.

Slowly, Warren released Zoe's hands. Her face was hot; her fingertips throbbed. She stepped back from the cross, and she couldn't stand on her own. She leaned against Warren's chest and breathed, blinking tears away, heat still pulsing through her.

"I told you," Warren whispered. "There are some things you can't explain in words."

Zoe couldn't speak.

"Will you go with me to Rafael's?"

She nodded.

He reached into his pocket, and seconds later, Zoe felt the obsidian cross pendant at her throat, cool and delicate.

He fastened the chain, kissed the back of her neck. "You're ready now."

Warren at her side, Zoe walked through the front door of Rafael's studio. The energy from La Cruz still coursed under her skin; Warren's words scrolled through her mind. *I would never do anything that would hurt you, Zoe. I only want to fix you and make you strong*. She felt his hand at her back, and leaned against it.

Zoe believed Warren. She knew how deeply he under-stood her guilt over the Daryl Barclay murders. He'd been there himself ten years ago, the guilt probably more intense since the blame had been direct. . . . All these years, his friend never found, a gun locked away in his safe that, as he'd just learned, belonged to another dead man. . . . War-ren was surrounded by ghosts. Yet he seemed so strong, so free from guilt. Maybe there was something to this secret group. Maybe Zoe *could* be fixed.

She gazed at the studio. The space seemed weirdly famil-iar to her, but maybe it was because it looked like a movie set. Unlike most of the homes and businesses here, there was no open courtyard—just a clean, dramatic space with very high ceilings; blinding white walls lined with oil paintings of cactuses, snakes and birds; high, track-lit ceilings and a circular staircase—a New York gallery beamed South of the Border, but with one shocking native touch. At the center of the room, a section of the floor had been removed to make way for a monstrous desert plant, each of its spines at least four feet long. "Is that a maguey?" she asked Warren.

"Yes."

She shuddered a little. The spines looked like the talons of a prehistoric bird. *Just a plant. An indigenous plant.*

Zoe focused on the Gypsy music emanating from the very impressive speaker system and scanned the group of revelers, relieved to see that, so far at least, the party was just that—a party. There were around thirty people there, most of them in their late fifties or sixties, drinking, chat-ting and milling about in pale gauze shirts or dresses, silver and gold jewelry glittering against tanned, vacationers' skin. She wasn't sure whether it was the guests' age, the way they were dressed, the beatific smiles many of them wore or the way they seemed to walk—as if they were moving through clouds. . . . But they reminded Zoe of a flock of angels she'd once seen on a cream cheese commercial. All they needed was wings and bagels.

Among the group, she saw Guadalupe, talking with an elderly American man in a white Panama hat. Guadalupe looked a little alarmed when she caught sight of Zoe, but then she saw Warren and her face relaxed, and she and her friend waved. "That's Ned Hayle, the American counsel," Warren said, smiling at the man in the hat. Zoe peered at the counsel's hands. From this distance, she couldn't make out any scratches. As if he were reading her mind, Warren said, "Relax, Zoe. The learning will come later and you will love it. But for now, just have fun. . . ."

Warren slipped an arm around her waist while shouting, "Hello, Mariposa" at a very tall, androgynous creature navigating toward them in a flowing white caftan.

"Where's Rafael?" Zoe asked.

"Rafael," Warren said out of the corner of his mouth, "is always late for his own parties." Warren didn't seem to mind.

From the depths of the crowd, Zoe heard Warren's name being whispered over and over and over. . . . Funny—back in the city, she'd be out to dinner with Warren and he'd occasionally get recognized, a soap fan might shyly approach and ask him to autograph her cocktail napkin. Here, though, in this town where the only thing on most TVs was *Magnum, P.I.*, Zoe might as well have been standing next to Johnny Depp at a *Pirates of the Caribbean* premiere.

Zoe was getting gawked at, too—she was Johnny Depp's date, after all—but the looks she received disturbed her. . . . Everyone seemed focused, not on her face, but on the cross she wore around her neck.

Relax. It's just a party. . . .

Zoe turned away from the maguey plant, closed her eyes for a moment and swatted away the image that had buzzed into her mind—maguey spines in the hands of lifeless, mutilated bodies. *An indigenous plant.*

When she opened them again, Mariposa was kneeling in front of Warren, one of his hands grasped in hers (his?), and peering at it as if he (she?) were looking for a ring to kiss. "I could bask in your energy for the rest of my life," Mariposa told Warren, in one of those smoke-ravaged Bea Arthur/Harvey Fierstein–type voices that brought no new information as to the gender of its owner.

Bask in your energy for the rest of my life? Did I really just hear that?

"Mariposa, I would like you to meet Zoe." Warren smiled. "Mariposa is a very talented sculptress."

A woman. Thank you. Zoe almost said it out loud. "Nice to meet you." She shook Mariposa's large hand. Her grip was weaker than Zoe had expected. Her wrist was thickly bandaged.

"Warren, you have such wonderful taste." Mariposa was staring at the cross at Zoe's neck, and Zoe wasn't sure whether she was talking about her or the necklace. Either way, she didn't take it as much of a compliment.

"Thank you," Warren said, and Mariposa beamed at him as if he'd made her whole day.

Very quietly, she whispered, "The new master."

"Sssh."

Zoe gave Warren a questioning look, but he just smiled at her. It was a red-carpet smile, all teeth with nothing behind the eyes. He turned his gaze to a couple waving frantically at him from around twenty feet away, and cranked up the smile even more. The man bowed deeply, and the woman nearly swooned. "You've got quite the fan club," Zoe said, but Warren wasn't listening to her. *It's as if he's on camera.*

Zoe was beginning to think she'd made a mistake in coming here. Whatever *Sangre Para La Vida* turned out to be,
this party was a huge ego trip for Warren, and Zoe was not
enjoying the ride.

She felt a cold hand at the crook of her arm and nearly
jumped out of her skin. "The guest of honor," said a voice
she recognized.

Warren said, "Dave, good to see you."

Zoe turned. Dr. Dave was wearing jeans and a white shirt
with the top three buttons undone, a gold cross glistening
against a surprisingly hairy chest.

He held a drink in each hand, and while he seemed much
more relaxed than the previous times she'd seen him, Zoe
still hated the way he looked at her—as if she was an interesting new development taking place in a petri dish. She
was also pretty sure he'd been referring to her when he'd
said, "The guest of honor," and she didn't like that much
either, the cool irony of the tone. . . . She smiled politely at
him, thinking, *If you touch my face, I will injure you.*

Dave said, "Pulque?"

"Excuse me?"

He held out one of the glasses, filled nearly to the top
with a thin grayish white liquid. Zoe grimaced at it.

"Fermented maguey," he said. "Undistilled."

"I adore pulque," said Mariposa.

Warren said, "A lot of people do." He looked at Zoe. "It's
like tequila, only thicker and not quite as strong."

Zoe took a sip. It was nothing of the sort. It tasted like
sour skim milk, with a little baby shampoo thrown in to
make foam. A young Mexican man in a butcher's apron
and bow tie walked up holding a tray full of similar glasses.
"Thank you, Emilio," said Warren. Zoe watched him raise
the glass to his lips. He polished the drink off quickly, with a
sense of obligation—the same way Zoe's grandfather would

drink his four cups of Manischewitz on Passover. "Drink the rest of yours, Zoe," Warren said. "You'll see. It's an acquired taste."

"I don't really like—"

"It's better when you drink it fast." He said it in a way that pushed her hand to her mouth.

Reflexively, she drank. To her surprise, she found that Warren was right. This soapy, viscous stuff had a wonderful, sweet aftertaste. When Emilio offered her another glass, she took it.

"Paul makes it himself," Warren said, gesturing toward the Reiki master, who stood just inside the door with Vanessa and Robin, all three of them in white. Dr. Dave said, "He's quite the alchemist." And to Zoe, Paul did look like some sort of Renaissance-era wizard, in his billowing white shirt and pants tucked into fringed suede boots.

Either that, or he had lost his way to the Fleetwood Mac tribute band audition . . . *That wasn't very charitable of you.*

Zoe was surprised. She never chastised herself for sarcastic thoughts. It was as if the pulque was working to erase her cynical streak. A few more of these, and she'd be like Robin, swearing by Reiki and homeopathic pills, judging people solely by the energy they exuded.

After she finished her second cup, Zoe was not so much drunk as different—soothed and energized and slightly more alive. She wasn't annoyed anymore. She wasn't quite so uncomfortable either. In a way, she felt like the rest of the people in the room looked—that same beatific smile overtaking her face . . .

Mariposa moved away and back into the crowd as Warren greeted a couple—German folk singers by the name of Dietrich and Eva. They both watched Zoe with a little too much interest, but at this point, she was used to it. She gazed across the room at the two grown women she knew

in town. Robin wore a high-collared white dress that reminded Zoe of a Victorian nightgown. She looked a little
older than in her usual black—more mature, anyway—and
she didn't so much run up to them as float—a vision, like
Paul, from another era. Vanessa, on the other hand, just
looked hot.

"What a lovely dress, Robin," said Warren.

"Thank you, Warren." She blushed and made some
fast, eager move with her knees and hands that resembled
a curtsy. "You and Zoe found each other," she said. "I'm so
happy."

"I stopped by Dave's office, and asked Robin if she'd seen
you," Warren told Zoe.

Robin said, "He was so worried. He told me that . . .
Dave, I don't really like that."

Dave was touching Robin's face, as if determining the
source of the blush. "You miss Patty?" he asked her. "I know
Warren doesn't."

"Maybe you should go sit down for a little—"

"How quickly the blood comes to the surface of your
skin," he said, "like it's rushing to the door to greet him."

Warren said, "I think a certain doctor has had too much
pulque."

"Patty never blushed for you, Warren," Dave said. "Why
was that? All the other women blush for you . . ."

Warren's eyes went hard, and Robin said, "Please stop,
Dave."

"All right."

The doctor moved away, but the strangest feeling seized
Zoe—a cringe from deep within her. If she didn't put twenty
or thirty feet between Dr. Dave and herself as soon as possible, she was afraid she might scream. *Bad energy*. She had
never felt this way around anyone, except . . .

"Poor Patty," said Dave. "Immune to Warren's charms.

Only one way you could get that bitch's blood to rise to the surface, right, Warren?"

"Excuse me," Zoe said. She took another pulque from Emilio and quickly left the group. Warren didn't ask where she was going. He just stood there, his back rigid, the red-carpet smile long gone, his eyes aimed like lasers at Dave's face.

She could feel more people watching her as she passed an hors d'oeuvre table and moved into the kitchen, downing the glass of pulque on her way there. *Relax.* . . .

The kitchen was huge and modern, with an enormous island at the center and a stainless-steel refrigerator. Servants hurried in and out, holding trays packed with pulque and tapas. Zoe wondered how Rafael could afford all this stuff as a painter of relatively mediocre still lifes. It couldn't be from guest lecturing at high schools. . . .

She saw a polished wood dinette table and, past that, an open door. *"Qué es esto?"* she asked a young female server.

The server frowned. "Sunroom," she said with no trace of an accent. "It's not for guests."

Zoe nodded.

The light was on in the sunroom, though. And the door *was* open. She wondered if that was where Rafael was hiding. Once the kitchen emptied out, she stepped inside, and quietly said his name.

The room was empty. She looked around. Zoe didn't see what the big deal was. It was just a *room*. A lovely room with floor-to-ceiling windows overlooking yet another incredibly lush garden. She thought of Guadalupe and cringed. Zoe would never look at a garden the same way again. She turned away from the window. A fireplace filled one corner of the room. It wasn't lit, but it had been earlier; the scent of mesquite hung in the air.

Zoe moved toward the fireplace and noticed the large

painting on the facing wall—a very young American woman with huge, haunted eyes.

There are times when a painting unintentionally reveals secrets—when it says less about an artist's talent than about his feelings about the subject he is trying to re-create. Zoe couldn't take her eyes off this painting—so different from all those dispassionate still lifes in the studio.

Who is she?

Her prominent collarbones, her delicate rib cage, her small, bare breasts were visible through the fabric that draped her body. The artist had paid such careful attention, every detail perfectly rendered. And her eyes reflected such longing. . . . Zoe recalled Rafael mentioning his dead wife and thought, *He loved her so much.*

A voice behind her said, "She whose name we dare not speak." Zoe turned, her breath catching, the cringe rushing through her once again. Dr. Dave. He reached out, probed her jawbone with his fingertips.

"Please don't do that," Zoe said.

The hand fell away, but Dave didn't move. He stood inches from Zoe, staring at her skin, his voice calm and clinical. "It's interesting," he said. "In previous centuries, so much more meaning was placed on the physical. A high forehead was a sign of honesty, full lips connoted a wasteful, sensual nature . . . The facial bones. The length of the spine, size of the rib cage, the way it all fit together . . . People saw all those things as indicators of a person's character."

"That's interesting, all right," she said. "You know, though, we should go back—"

"Of course we know now it is not true at all. The set of a person's flesh and bones reveals nothing about the workings of her mind. The most perfectly assembled person is often the most treacherous. You," he said slowly, "you're a bit older, of course. Different hair and eyes and not quite as

thin . . . but . . . your bone structure is very similar to hers."
His gaze drifted to the painting, then settled back on Zoe's
face. "I'm sure it's why Warren chose you. Never bothered
to examine the rest of your character before he brought you
here, though, did he?"

"*What are you talking about?*"

"He should have. Bones mean nothing. Patty Woods's
were similar to hers as well," he said. "And so were Jordan
Brink's. His bones were almost a perfect match."

Zoe stared at him, her heart starting to race. "You
knew . . . Jordan?"

His small black eyes were narrowed and a little rheumy.
Warren was right. Dave had way too much pulque in him,
and it seemed to be affecting the doctor in the opposite way
it did everyone else. He smiled. There was nothing beatific
about it.

"You're right," he said.

"Huh?"

"We should return to the party." Dave moved toward the
door. For a few moments, Zoe turned her attention back to
the painting—to Rafael's handsome signature, and then, for
the first time, to a delicate anklet the girl wore.

It was a thin black cross, a red stone glistening at its
center.

Zoe let out a gasp. She turned away to find the doctor
watching her from the doorway. "Her name was Grace," he
whispered. "Ask Warren about her sometime."

By the time they were back in the studio, Rafael had already made his grand entrance. He was moving from group
to group, all in white, an arm hooked possessively around
Vanessa's waist. Following a few feet behind them was Paul,
smiling amiably in his Renaissance garb, as Zoe watched
them from the hors d'oeuvre table, drinking another pulque,

envying their relaxed smiles. *Grace. Rafael loved her, painted her. Grace, who was killed the same way Jordan was.* Why had Dave told Zoe to ask Warren about her?

Grace, with that black cross at her ankle.

Warren was about twenty feet away, a group of women— including Robin and Mariposa—clustered around him like a harem. One of them—a striking brunette Zoe had never seen before—was reading Warren's palm, her fingertips running lightly over his hand. Zoe imagined herself walking up to Warren and asking, *Who was Grace?* Never was there a worse time to ask a question, but she kept thinking of that painting. She kept wanting to know.

Zoe caught Robin's eye. Robin smiled. Zoe gestured for her to join her, and she did, as enthusiastic as her dog. "En-joying the party?" she said.

"Robin," she said, "there's a painting in the sunroom."

She nodded, her smile fading.

"Dave told me—"

"Dave is trashed," she said. "Don't listen to a word he says."

She looked at her. "Okay, but—"

"Seriously. He's terrible when he's drunk. Vicious and mean. I think he has a problem."

"I agree," Zoe said. "But . . . please. I just need to know who Grace was and what Warren has to do with—"

"Zoe. You're new here and there's a lot you don't know, so I am going to tell you this now, and I *need* you to take it seriously." Robin's face was very still. Her eyes were cold, and for the first time since Zoe had met her, she looked her age. "Don't ever, *ever* say her name out loud again."

"But—"

"I mean it. You only get one warning."

Zoe's eyes widened. "Warning before . . . what?"

"That's all any of us get," she said. "One warning."

She put the smile back on and returned to Warren, and Zoe's skin went cold. *I need to get out of here.* . . . But then Warren called out, "Look, Zoe!" and he pointed to Rafael, who was on the staircase alone.

The effect of Rafael at a height was enormously powerful, and the pulque only enhanced that. His pure white clothes brought out his color. His amber eyes burned. Even the women clustered around Warren turned and stared.

And Zoe smiled. It was a smile that didn't belong to her—Rafael's smile, the pulque's smile. She looked at Warren, and he was smiling, too, and so were Robin and Mariposa and Vanessa and Paul. Even Dave, across the room, with devotion shining in his bespectacled black eyes.

Rafael raised a glass and said, "To Las Aguas!" Everyone in the room applauded—including Zoe, her apprehension crumbling, scattering. . . .

Steve was back at his apartment, finishing up packing when his cell phone rang. He had his iPod shoved in his ears in order to drown out the woman next door, who'd been full-on shrieking about the whore bitch for the past half hour. The sound track from T. Rex's *Born to Boogie* had been blaring so loudly in Steve's ears that at first he didn't notice "Tommy, Can You Hear Me?" But it was clear soon enough. He yanked the buds out of his ears and grabbed his phone out of the charger and answered it without looking at the screen.

"Steve. It's Andy Fennimore. You at home?"

"Yeah. Hi, Andy."

"What are you doing?"

"Well, I'm packing, actually. I'm leaving for Mexico in the morning."

"That's probably a good idea."

Steve stopped packing. "It *is?*"

"I have some more information for you." Fennimore's voice was quiet, far-off.

"Information? Is this about Tiffany because she already told me—"

"It's odd," he said. "I've known Warren for ten years and . . . while I've always found him a bit *alpha* for my tastes, I certainly never thought he was a bad person. . . ."

"Andy . . ."

"It's Tiffany, yes. She told me the whole story, which is . . . *unbelievably* strange. But, unfortunately, there's more."

"More?"

"When you showed me the list, I thought it was the same name, but I needed to make sure. I spoke to our executive producer. Turns out I was right . . ."

"Andy, *what are you talking about?*"

"The first name on Jordan Brink's X list. Nicholas Denby." He was quiet for a few moments. Steve could hear him breathing. "I think your friend needs to come home."

TWENTY

Their SUVs formed a long caravan to Las Aguas. A dozen or so oversized vehicles packed with American baby boomers, most of them in white, driving through the night—the virtual negative of a funeral procession. Zoe traveled with Vanessa, Warren and Paul, who had wedged a large cooler into the back of the Cherokee; Zoe figured it was full of more homemade pulque.

Warren opened all the windows and found classical guitar on the radio, and they leaned back in their seats, letting the elegant music and the warm, fragrant air spill over their skin. In the rearview mirror, Zoe saw Vanessa rest her head on Paul's shoulder, as he smiled, thoroughly content. Zoe envied them. While the pulque and Rafael had relaxed her a good deal, there was still that gnawing feeling—like the tiny part of you that knows you're in a dream and keeps telling you to wake up. The name echoed in her mind, *Grace, Grace, Grace. . . .*

Zoe heard herself ask, "Why aren't you allowed to say her name?"

Paul gasped. "Dear God," said Vanessa.

Warren clutched the steering wheel. He closed his eyes for a second and swallowed hard, and when he opened them again, they glistened a little. He didn't say a word, but he didn't have to. "I saw her painting in Rafael's sunroom," Zoe said. "She was very beautiful."

Warren turned to her. His face was calm, but his eyes were wet. "She was a long time ago," he said softly.

"We don't say her name for Rafael's sake," Vanessa said.

"Right," said Paul. "We sacrifice the name so she can have peace. Rafael says it's the least we can do."

Warren said it again. "She was a long time ago." He turned the music up louder and placed his hand on Zoe's, and no one said anything for the rest of the ride.

They arrived to everyone spilling out of their cars, walking through the parking lot toward the baths. The outdoor lights had been turned off, but the full moon made it easy to find the way. Warren helped Paul carry the cooler, while Vanessa and Zoe walked ahead.

At first it seemed like just a continuation of Rafael's party, Zoe wondering if she should have brought her bathing suit, casting a glance at some of the guests and grimacing at the thought that skinny-dipping might be part of the plan. But then she noticed something. . . .

The scuff of shoes on the gravel driveway seemed to echo, and she felt as if she could hear and separate each guest's breathing as they walked. From within the baths, she heard the shriek of Pio the hawk—and then the buzz of a passing dragonfly, like a tiny outboard motor. At first, she thought it was some strange effect from the pulque—and that might have had something to do with it. The main reason, though, was that no one was talking. Thirty people, fresh from a loud party, not a single one of them saying a word . . .

"Vanessa, why—"

Vanessa touched Zoe's arm and put a finger to her own lips. And then Zoe got it. *This is it*, she thought. *This is where I finally learn.*

Dave and Robin passed them. Dave was leaning against his assistant, stumbling a little. But even Dave, drunk and unruly and rude as he'd been, was quiet. Zoe glanced back at Warren. He was silent, too. But he was glaring at Dave, blades in his eyes.

Wordlessly, the guests formed a large circle on the grassy area by the baths. Zoe glanced around at the faces—Mariposa, Guadalupe and the American counsel, Dietrich and Eva, Dave, Robin and so many others, all of them watching Warren so closely. . . . Zoe stood between Warren and Vanessa, holding their hands. Everyone in the large circle held hands. She glanced at Warren. His eyes were closed, as if in prayer.

How different this was from the last time she and Warren had been here. No picnic. No candles. As in the parking lot, the moon was the only source of light. It spotlit the white clothes, the rocks that bordered the baths, the silver hair of some guests, and made them all radiate. If it was possible, the plants seemed fuller, their flowers brighter, the trees darker and more imposing against the light, starry sky. The grass glistened with beads of water and it looked electric.

Pio screamed from the trees. "Sssh," said Las Aguas's owner, Xavier. Dressed noticeably all in black, he stood between Robin and another woman on the other side of the circle, holding their hands—a missing link in a glittering silver chain. His eyes shone.

What is happening here?

Zoe heard a long, clear, plaintive note. It was played on some kind of wooden flute, and then a guitar joined in, and the note turned to a melody, then one of those wistful Indian songs that made Zoe think of mountain peaks and coffee beans and magic. But where was it coming from? A jug of pulque was passed around the circle and Warren's arm went around her waist and Vanessa's did, too, and everyone—the whole circle—began to sway very slowly. The jug came to Zoe. She took a swallow. She found the pulque's sweetness early this time.

Rafael emerged from the trees, followed by the two musicians, who stayed back, still playing while he made his way to the center of the circle. Once again, Zoe's face broke into a strange, involuntary smile.

Then Rafael spoke—the first voice any of them had heard since they'd arrived. "My brothers and sisters." A shudder passed through the circle. His voice resonated more powerfully than any voice in the world outside. It rode the Indian music like a wave.

"You are here because you have been chosen." He gazed out at the guests. "Each and every one of you is special. You have the power inside you. The shine. There is bad within you, but you all know that. It isn't news." He took a deep breath. "It is your type of bad, though, that makes you special—the type that *turns* when it's released from the body. Your weakness can save the world. You just need to *let the world take it.*"

He paused for a few moments, the words hanging in the air. From somewhere in the circle, Zoe heard a whispered "Yes."

"We have all been hurt before. We have been touched deeply by the cruelty of life. We have seen death close-up. *Everyone here has seen death close-up.*"

A sigh. A stifled sob. Heads nodded. "Yes, yes . . ."

"We have had the nightmares, felt the pain. We have identified the bodies. We have seen the police photos." He glanced at Zoe. "We have heard the killer's voice in the darkness."

Her eyes widened.

Rafael's gaze traveled around the circle. "We have ached with sorrow. We have been ruined by illness. We have watched, powerless, as those we loved more than anything in the world let go of that last, frail thread."

Vanessa let out a gasp. Warren's grip tightened around Zoe's waist. "Unable to help, unable to heal. But I am here to tell you . . ." The music stopped. "You've had that power all along! You can heal yourself, heal your loved ones." He threw back his head and shouted up at the sky, his voice expanding until Zoe could feel it along the base of her skull, in the pit of her stomach, at the tips of her toes. . . . *"You can heal the world."*

Vanessa started to sob. Zoe bent down to comfort her, but she waved her off. Warren pulled Zoe closer to him. She looked at his face, and he glanced back at her, his eyes rapt, glowing. More sobs echoed around the circle. Zoe started to choke up.

"Don't hold your tears back," Rafael said. "You give with your tears. We all know the feeling—that feeling of calm, the strange contentment that fills our bodies, but only after we've cried ourselves *empty*."

Zoe watched him, her vision blurring from tears, her head nodding on its own. *Yes, yes, I know that feeling. I know it well . . .*

"That is the earth's *gratitude*. It is thanking you for your tears by transforming them to good and giving you the first taste. *The very first taste.*"

"Yes," Warren whispered.

"And now," Rafael said, "we will give with our tears. And we will give with our voices."

He closed his eyes, took a few steps forward. The flute

played one long, clear note. Rafael found the same note in his own voice and sang it out. Soon, the guests started to join in, their voices getting louder until they became a single entity. . . .

Zoe's heart thrilled to it. It took her a few seconds to realize that she was singing, too, the note coming out of her and filling her at the same time. . . . Then it became a melody and the melody became a song—a song Zoe had never heard, but somehow, she knew it.

Rafael walked up to her, touched her face. She felt that healing energy coursing out of his skin. He stared into her eyes as she sang. The whole circle was watching her. Normally she would hate that type of attention, but now she didn't care. She was moved—physically, emotionally, spiritually. His gaze overtook her, his touch. Zoe stopped singing.

Rafael said, "You hate a large part of yourself."

"Yes."

"You hate your curiosity."

She swallowed hard, stared at him.

"You do, don't you?"

"Yes," she said, "I do."

"People will tell you that it wasn't your fault. That the women didn't die because of your curiosity, your questions, your *deeply flattering* interest in a killer. . . . But the truth is, they *did*. He *did* kill them for you. It *is* your fault, Zoe Greene Jacobson."

Zoe's mouth went dry. Her jaw dropped. She was aware of Warren's muscles tensing next to her. *He told Rafael, told him everything.* Zoe could tell he felt bad about it. He wanted to comfort her, but she didn't want comfort.

Rafael is right. It was my fault. It's what I've been trying to tell everyone, and no one will listen. . . . Tears sprung into her eyes, but with them came a strange relief. She didn't want to close the door on Daryl Barclay, lock him away like one of Warren's bad memories. She didn't want to act as if the murders had never happened. She'd been trying for five years, and it hadn't worked. She needed to confess. "The murders were my fault."

Rafael's touch soothed her, kept the sobs back. "Yes."

"I killed those women."

"Yes, you did," he said. He brought his face close to hers and said it softly enough so only she could hear. "But you will make it right. You will pay your debt. Tonight."

He stepped back from her, addressed the whole group. "We are here to get rid of the fear, to throw out the weakness, to take away that selfishness and hate and petty jealousy and passivity. We are here to throw away our *morbid curiosity*. We are here to *cut it out of our bodies! We will feed it to the earth!*"

Vanessa gasped. Warren's arm went rigid around Zoe's waist.

Zoe heard a few screams and one woman collapsed.

"We are giving back to the earth. We are giving back to the planet. We are ripping weakness out of ourselves and recycling it to good so that the world will not end. Our loved ones will not die. We will be strong and powerful, and we will arise. Arise!"

More gasps. And then silence, save for a rustling of heavy wings as the hawk in the trees beyond them changed perches. "Arise!" Rafael said again.

And the group repeated it, "Arise! Arise! Arise!"

Rafael hummed with the music. Vanessa let go of Zoe's hand for a moment, and when Zoe turned and looked at her, Vanessa was cutting a line into the back of her own hand with the tip of a maguey spine. Vanessa groaned, and clutched her wrist and flipped the hand over, holding it, trembling over the fresh green grass. "Please, please," Vanessa muttered. "Take the bad and turn it good. Hate to love, death to life. Please, please, please, watch over her for me. . . ."

Zoe's gaze shot around the circle, and she saw the people were passing maguey spines like the jug. Everyone in the circle was cutting himself. . . . She found herself staring at a tiny, elegant woman of around seventy with gleaming white hair and a diamond cross at her neck, hacking away at her wrist, crazed, as if the blood wasn't coming fast enough. . . .

What is going on?

She caught sight of Robin, her head back and her eyes closed as Dave took a daggerlike maguey thorn and cut into the soft underside of her outstretched arm. Zoe saw his face, his ecstatic face, and her stomach turned. This wasn't good. This was not good at all. She looked toward Warren. He smiled and kissed her hand. "We're giving back," he whispered. "Isn't it beautiful?"

"Warren, I don't like—"

His other hand held a gleaming black knife. He sliced into her palm. It seared.

"Stop!" She pulled her hand away and stared at it. Blood poured out of the long, deep wound. Pain shot through her arm.

"Don't fight it." Warren smiled, his eyes gleaming in a way she had never seen. Out of the corner of her eye, she saw the hawk, circling low, drawn by the smell of the spilling blood. And one word entered her mind: *Prey.* "You have been chosen," said Warren. "I chose you. You are special. You are mine. Not his. You can give all of us so much. . . ."

She heard herself say, "You chose Grace."

Warren stepped back from her, speechless, a hard anger working into his features. "No," he said quietly, "she was his."

Zoe stared at him.

"I will fix you," he said, moving toward her with the knife. "I can make you strong."

Zoe ran. Turned and ran away from her lover, ran like a doomed, bleeding animal.

"Zoe!"

Her breath sliced into her lungs; she clutched her throbbing hand. "We will take the folly and weakness of youth," Rafael was saying to the group. "We will give it to our creators, and they will strengthen the earth." She slowed down for a moment, swayed by the sound of the voice. And then she felt gentle arms around her. Robin's arms. "It's okay," Robin whispered. "I thought it was weird, too, at first."

Zoe took a breath. Her head was swimming from the pulque. She looked down at Robin's arm, the red rivulets pouring out, staining her white dress.

"You don't understand," Zoe whispered. "Warren said . . ."

Warren caught up to her. "I didn't mean to scare you," he said. "I thought you were ready to know."

This is the secret? This is the group? She looked at him. The strange gleam was gone from his eyes, along with the anger.

"I'm sorry," Warren said. He was holding a white bandanna. "Give me your hand." Reluctantly, she did, flinching as he wrapped the wound.

Robin said, "Take deep breaths, Zoe. Just watch and be. Listen to the Master, and you'll get it."

"Okay," she said. "Okay." She just needed to catch her breath. . . .

"Zoe." It was Rafael. He was looking straight at her. "Let me ease your fear." The musicians stopped. Rafael walked toward Zoe holding two shot-sized vials. One held clear liquid, the other red. *Tequila and sangrito.* "This is Zoe's first time with us," he said to the group. "We all remember how overwhelming it was at first, don't we?"

Several guests murmured, "Yes."

"Let's all help her feel at ease."

Zoe heard applause. She looked around the circle to see them all watching her, knives put away, maguey spines dropped to the grass. All this attention was wearing on her, tiring her out. She remembered Dave at Rafael's party, calling her *the guest of honor*. She understood now, though still she wondered why. . . .

Rafael handed her the vials. *Just what the doctor ordered.* At this point, she needed something strong. She downed the clear liquid in one gulp. It was much sweeter than the Don Julio, with a chalky bite at the end. She grimaced. Terrible, cheap stuff. At least it relaxed her a little. Rafael handed her the red vial, and she gulped that down fast as well, hearing gasps as she did. The red liquid was not sangrito. It was thick and salty and slightly metallic and . . . *It was blood.*

Zoe gagged. The music started up and everyone began to sway, some of the faces pitched in ecstasy. Zoe broke free of the circle. She heard Warren calling her name, heard someone else—was it Vanessa?—shouting, "She's rejecting it." She headed past the baths, through the herb garden, moving toward the trees beyond. Soon she slowed, though. Her vision blurred, everything holding a weird type of sparkle. *What was in the clear vial?* Her skull felt as if it was stuffed with cotton. She forgot how to walk.

She fell to the ground and started to crawl toward the trees, grasping at the grass, dragging her feet behind her, terribly nauseous. Her face had gone numb. She bit her lip and couldn't feel it. Then she heard several voices shouting her name in slow motion.

Her mouth was very dry. Water. She needed water. A few feet ahead of her, where the trees started, Zoe saw Paul's cooler. It was probably pulque, but she would take that. She would take anything. She felt the slippery grass through her jeans and heard the scuff of her hands on the cooler lid, as if someone had put a loudspeaker to it. She heard her name again; then rough hands grabbed her waist as she pulled the lid off Paul's cooler, fighting the hands and her failing vision. "Get her out of there," said a man's voice. It sounded like Paul.

The last clear thought she had was about the cooler's contents. Dozens and dozens of vials, all filled with red liquid. *Where did he get all that blood?* The thought hung there, but only for a second before the hands pulled her away, and the moon rushed into her eyes and the whole world went shocking white.

TWENTY-ONE

Zoe couldn't move. Her arms were held straight out, her legs crossed over each other, as if there were weights placed on top of her hands and ankles. Somehow, she'd been moved to a wooden floor. . . . Was it a floor? She felt planks beneath her. She heard voices around her—human voices—but they weren't speaking. They were buzzing, like flies. Her whole skull ached. She could move her neck a little, but it made her head hurt more, so she turned very slowly, gazed the length of her left arm. Fresh blood coated her wrist, pooled beneath her fingers. Her gaze darted to the other arm and then she saw the metal spikes driven through her hands. It wasn't a floor beneath her. She had been nailed to a cross. But she was calm, peaceful even. And despite the thick spikes through her bones and veins, she was in no pain at all, save for the throbbing in her head.

That was how she knew this was a dream.

The human flies came closer. Each had the outline of someone she knew—the hair, the shoulders, the clothes of Vanessa, Rafael, Robin, Dave, Paul . . . but they all had a thousand red eyes, antennae worming out of their foreheads. "Not ready," the Dave Fly buzzed. "Don't think there was enough in the vial."

"There is only one full moon a month," the Vanessa Fly said. "And we need her tonight more than ever. She needs to be ready. . . ."

They were all buzzing now, their voices blending, words darting in and out of her eyes and ears. ". . . didn't take to the sacred blood. That isn't a good. . . ."

". . . The others didn't need the clear."

"Better that than nothing."

"She didn't take the blood."

"Stop your arguing. It needs to be done. Now."

Zoe said, "Where is Warren?"

"Are you awake, Zoe?" said one of the females.

"No," she said, "I'm dreaming."

The Rafael Fly brought his face very close to hers. The slick black antennae stroked her cheek. His eyes were a hall of mirrors. "Listen to me, Zoe You have been chosen. You will feed the earth with your weakness and you will become strong. You will transcend the pain and feel yourself filled with light."

Zoe looked at one bleeding hand. She said, "What did you use to drive the nails through?"

The Dave Fly was over her now. "How many fingers am I holding up?"

"Where is Warren?" she said. But she realized she wasn't moving her lips, just thinking the question.

"Filled. With. Light." The words oozed out of the Rafael Fly and poured thickly down her neck, stuck to her skin like honey. She was aware of many other human flies in the room. A swarm. She checked her hands again. The blood was still there, the spikes, but then a voice in her head screamed, *Your eyes aren't open. Open your EYES!*

"Her eyes are opening," said Rafael, standing over her as she lay on her back on the floor of a room that smelled like mesquite and church candles. The sunroom. No antennae. No wings. She looked for the painting of Grace, but she couldn't lift her head. Her gaze took in Rafael, shirtless, holding a large knife with a gleaming black blade. He knelt down, began unbuttoning her sleeveless blouse.

"Stop," Zoe said. The word floated out of her mouth. She could see the letters in the air, puffy and red, crowned by black thorns. *I'm still dreaming. It's okay. I'm still dreaming, not nailed to a cross. I must be asleep, in Warren's bed. I had too much to drink and the party was too strange for words, but I'm home and I'm sleeping, and . . .*

Dave said, "Deep breaths, Zoe." Zoe's gaze followed the voice, to his shirtless form, the thick hair on his chest, the cross. . . . "You may feel some discomfort, but that is natural." He was standing on her right hand. She could feel the soles of his bare feet and saw no blood, no spikes. Her eyes were open. She was sweating. This felt like no dream she had ever had.

Zoe's gaze moved from Dave, darted down the length of her left arm. Vanessa was standing on the hand, barefoot as well. The white bandanna had been removed, but Zoe felt no pain in the wound, nothing but the soles of Vanessa's small feet. Her white sundress was sheer as tissue in the candlelight, her hair glowing white, her face a shadow.

Now Zoe glanced down. Paul sat on her crossed ankles, smiling. Her heart sped up. Beyond her, a line of shadows holding lit candles. She could hear them, shifting on their feet, whispering words she couldn't understand.

"She won't remember," said Vanessa.

"If she lives." That was Dave.

Paul said, "Dave, are you sober enough to perform your duties?"

"Yes. Sorry."

Rafael finished unbuttoning Zoe's blouse, pushed it open. She struggled to move. "There is no other time," he said softly, and then another language started pouring out of him, a language Zoe had never heard before, hard and guttural. *"Wewetottle Weetzeelopochee, Tlalock."* He drifted in and out of focus, and Zoe's muscles went lax again. She thought, *It's just a dream, just a dream. It's okay. It's just . . .*

One of the human shadows moved closer, until he was standing directly behind Rafael. A heavyset Mexican man, everything on him big and flat—his hair, his nose, his lips. He was shirtless as well. In his hands he clasped a black cross painted with a a torn-crowned human heart. *Please let this be a dream, please, please. . . .* The man had a deep black mole that looked like a drop of ink on his cheek. Zoe couldn't stop staring at it.

Dave said, "You may feel some discomfort, Zoe. That is natural. Breathe into the pain. Do not tense up."

Rafael straddled her hips. She felt the weight of him, the muscles of his thighs. He spoke, and she could feel the vibration of his voice, his breath on her bare skin. "We give you youth. We give you light. We give you blood." He touched the tip of the blade to her sternum. She felt a sting, felt something trickling down her chest, hot like a tear. She knew it was blood. Her own blood. She stared at Rafael. *This is happening. It is really happening.* Zoe started to scream. Dave said, "Panicking will only increase blood flow. Please try to stay calm. . . ."

Zoe screamed louder, and the man with the mole shoved his fist into her mouth. She bit his hand, struggled to move, but she couldn't. She was paralyzed.

She heard a voice say, "Stop!" *Warren.*

Can you feel cold like this? Can you bleed in dreams? Can someone's eyes—Warren's eyes—seem so real? He stood behind Rafael, his face hard. "She's not ready. Don't you get it?"

"What are you doing here?" said Rafael.

"I *belong* here," Warren said. "She doesn't. Look at her."

Rafael's face moved in and out of focus, and the air suddenly seemed as thick as water.

Vanessa said, "Warren, you're ruining this." But her voice wasn't her own—it was more like a cat mewling.

"It's already ruined and you know it."

Everything turned to cool gel. Zoe tasted the salt of the strange man's skin, yet she was weirdly relaxed.

"Get away!" said Rafael.

Warren's thick arm was around Rafael's neck. The fist came out of her mouth and the man with the mole was moving toward him. Vanessa mewled, "Nooo . . ."

Rafael's eyes rolled back into his head, a stream of those strange guttural words coursing out of his mouth, the knife blade glinting closer as Warren said, "For God's sake, Rafael, look at her. You have to take them unconscious now? *Are you really that weak?*"

Rafael grew quiet. Zoe saw something creep into his eyes . . . a rage turned to hunger.

She looked at Warren, at those clear blue eyes, and thought: *Prey.*

Rafael's face melted, changed. . . . *"Pa-dum-pa-dum-pa-dum,"* he said as the blade sliced a longer line. "This feel okay? This feel okay, kitten? Won't hurt too much, kitten, if you just relax . . ." And Zoe was no longer looking at Rafael. She was looking into the eyes of Daryl Barclay. She opened her mouth and screamed until her throat ripped apart. But the scream was silent—all feeling, no sound.

She yanked her eyes open. She felt for the top of her blouse, found it closed, and touching it, she realized her hands and feet were unbloodied, unweighted. She was lying in Warren's bed, her head throbbing angrily. God, what an

awful dream—an awful dream with such a bizarre night behind it . . .

The whole scene at Las Aguas came rushing back at her.
They cut themselves. They made me drink blood. How could she
talk to Warren now? What was she supposed to say? But
when she rolled onto her side, she saw that Warren wasn't
there. *Disappeared. Again.* For once, she was glad.

She grabbed her watch off the bedstand. Eight a.m. Zoe
sat up, her head throbbing, her whole body parched.

What was that stuff in the vial?

Zoe got out of bed. Where was Warren at eight a.m.?
She went into the master bathroom and brushed her teeth
with sterilized water from the cooler next to the sink. She
refilled the paper cup and drank it in one gulp, then another,
then another. That made her feel a little better. Her hand
stung, so she ran some cold water over the knife wound.
Already it had healed into a pinkish line, and she wondered
if Warren had treated it before putting her to bed. If it was
Warren who had put her to bed. She couldn't remember
the ride home, couldn't remember anything after . . . *Jesus.*
The vials in Paul's cooler. *Where did he get all that blood?
What were they going to use it for?*

Zoe moved away from the sink and sat down on that lux-
urious tub—a tub that, just two days ago, had held so many
exciting possibilities. . . .

No more. It had to end. She cared for Warren. But she
could never go through another night like last. *They cut
themselves. They gave me blood to drink.* Last night, she had
seen too much. *This is how you fix me, Warren? This is how you
make me strong?*

Zoe had an urge to call Steve, to tell him what had
happened and hear the shock in his voice and feel normal
again.

She would tell him about that dream—that awful dream she'd just had with the human flies and the knife on her chest and Rafael speaking in tongues and going after War-ren. Steve would say, *Sounds like a Roger Corman movie,* and she would surprise herself by laughing.

She missed Steve so much. . . .

Zoe started out of the bathroom, but realized pretty fast she needed a shower first. She felt as if she were coated with a thick, greasy film. She turned the water on in the stall shower, pulled off all her clothes, dropped them on the floor and stepped in. She closed her eyes, breathed in the steam and relaxed a little. Then she felt it.

Where the water hit her chest, it stung. She looked down and saw a shallow cut, perfectly straight, from her throat to the center of her sternum. A knife wound.

"It wasn't a dream," she whispered. Then she collapsed to the shower floor.

The sun was too bright. It blazed down on Vanessa's head and back as she walked back up the hill to her house, rub-bing salt in this gaping wound of a morning after. For the first time since she'd moved here, she was out in daylight without sunblock or a hat, without protection of any kind, and Vanessa could feel herself getting burned by it, the poi-son seeping into her skin, sucking out the moisture, making her feel . . . well, her age.

Often, the morning after a ceremony, Vanessa would think about how good she felt—good as when she was in her twenties, riding home in a limo from a five-star hotel. . . . Then she'd remember her baby sister, Lucy, and compare herself. She would recall how, even when she was healthy, Lucy was too busy caring for Naomi or working her job at the dentist's office to feel young like this. It was as if in Van-essa's family, there was only so much youth to go around, and she had gone back for seconds and thirds, leaving the baby with an empty plate.

Now, though, Vanessa's back hurt and her leg muscles ached and her skin felt as dry as paper. She used to wish her sister had been well enough to go with her to a ceremony, to feel for herself the power, the awakening . . . to watch Vanessa cut the bad out of herself and bleed into the ground for Lucy's sake, for Naomi's, for the earth. . . . God, it was hard to believe this morning that Vanessa had ever, in her entire life, felt that way. The only silver lining in the dark cloud of last night was that Naomi hadn't been anywhere near it.

The blood—that had been the Master's idea. He had entrusted Dave with the task of collecting blood from everyone in the group—not with maguey spines or knives but with sterile needles. Dave had drawn it out of followers and put it into the vials, and Paul had placed them all into that cooler and everyone was to take it—accept it like communion wine. "Absorb one another's weakness," Rafael had urged the group. "Grow stronger. Nourish yourself, like the plants, the earth. . . ."

Most of the followers had balked—especially after Zoe's response. And the few brave souls who did gagged and wretched, anything but stronger, the opposite of nourished. . . .

Warren had shouted the question, "Where did the blood come from? He didn't take it from me!" Paul had said, "Me neither!" and soon Las Aguas was echoing with chatter. *Where had Dr. Dave gotten all that blood?*

Vanessa, who suspected that Dave had simply lent his professional name to the blood collection, had a different question: Where had Rafael gotten the blood?

She could still taste it. Her stomach turned. . . .

She remembered the Master's pathetic effort with Zoe in the sunroom. After it was over and everyone had left, Vanessa had given up on her walk home, returned to the studio and gone to bed with Rafael—a last-ditch attempt to feel right again. That metallic taste still in her mouth, she had slipped beside him in bed and asked, "Where did the blood come from, Rafael? If so many of us didn't give, then who did? Who gave that much?"

He had said nothing. He had grabbed her by the shoulders and flipped her onto her stomach, shoving her head into the pillow, grabbing her by the hair. He had stood her up on all fours and thrown himself behind her—all force, a show of brute strength, the light within him gone. And then he couldn't even perform.

"It's okay," Vanessa had said.

"No, it isn't. Nothing is okay anymore."

After the Master had fallen asleep, Vanessa had lain next to him, staring at the ceiling, that B. B. King song running through her brain. "The Thrill Is Gone."

Magic didn't exist if you didn't believe in it, and Vanessa didn't believe, not anymore. She'd been through this before—with EST and TM. . . . There had been that moment with the past-life counselor when it had suddenly dawned on her: How can you have memories from a previous incarnation when memories are stored in the *brain*, which *dies*? But it was never as bad as this. She had thought Rafael was the One, and Warren was the Next One. And, as it turned out, neither one of them was anything but pretty words and charisma. A whole lot of smoke and mirrors turned to dust.

It was all falling apart. The spell was off and the world was still dying. Vanessa's body was speeding toward the finish line, and she didn't give a damn.

Vanessa reached the front door of her house. She thought of Naomi inside. She needed to take better care of her niece. She needed to start listening to her. Naomi was seventeen, and whether the future lasted five more years or a million, it was *her* future. Naomi deserved her turn at the table.

The house was very quiet. Not surprising. It was only eight a.m. and Naomi, like most kids her age, would sleep till sunset if no one woke her. Soccoro was usually making breakfast by now, but maybe she'd used Vanessa's absence as an excuse to sleep in.

Vanessa took the stairs slowly, her muscles protesting with each step. When she reached the top, Vanessa headed for Naomi's room. The door was closed, as usual. Most other days, the closed door gave her some pause. Opening it made her feel like her own nosey, diary-reading mother, possessive and old. But this morning, she wanted to watch her niece. She wanted to see Naomi asleep and breathing softly, holding that stuffed turtle she still slept with—the one Lucy had bought for her when she was a tiny baby.

Quietly, Vanessa turned the knob and pushed open the door.

"¿*Señora?*"

"¿*Soccoro? ¿Qué pasa aqui?*" Vanessa looked around the room. It was empty, save for the housekeeper. The bed was made. "¿*Dónde está Naomi?*"

"*No se.*" Soccoro was standing in front of Naomi's laptop, peering at an opened e-mail. "*No comprendo,*" she said, and Vanessa moved around her, read the screen.

It was from TexCori91.

N,

I'm really worried. My grandma wasn't on her plane. She still hasn't shown up, and we can't get ahold of her. Can you check on her?

Love,
Corinne

Naomi went to check on Patty.

Vanessa recalled the look in Rafael's eyes, back when she told him she thought Patty was talking to the press. She remembered how he had told her, *I will take care of this*, and how he had never answered Vanessa when she asked where all the blood had come from, and it all seemed surreal—scenes sliced out of a bad dream. The Master wasn't capable of murder, was he?

The truth was, Vanessa had no idea what he was capable of.

"I've got to go," Vanessa told Soccoro, all her Spanish dropping away, along with tiredness and age and everything else. She raced down the stairs, taking them two at a time, praying that, if the same thing had happened to Patty as had happened to Jordan, she could at least stop Naomi from seeing the results.

Zoe pressed a towel against the wound on her chest until the bleeding stopped. It didn't take long; it was a shallow cut. She found a box of Band-Aids in Warren's medicine cabinet and slapped three of them over it, then hurried to the closet and threw on underwear, a T-shirt, jeans, sneakers. *Good. I'm dressed.*

That was about as far as her brain would take her right now. Washing, dressing. Basic actions.

Wash. Dress. Pack.

She pulled her suitcase out of the closet, started throwing clothes in. So far, so good. But then words from last night started leaking into her mind, moments from the dream that wasn't a dream at all. . . .

She shuddered. *Can't think about this now.* What she needed to do was pack, quick as she could, then call a cab and head over to León Airport before Warren returned and tried to explain. . . . Zoe thought, *Where is he right now?* It wasn't even nine in the morning yet. *Where do you disappear to at eight a.m.?*

For God's sake, Rafael, look at her. You have to take them unconscious now? Are you really that weak?

Again, Zoe saw the look on Rafael's face—that deepening rage at Warren. She saw Rafael moving toward him as if he were prey. . . .

Zoe's throat constricted, her breathing grew shallow. She wanted to scream, but she didn't have enough breath. She felt each individual bandage pressing against the cut. Panic threatened to overtake her whole body.

No, no, it couldn't be. They wouldn't. They're not murderers. They're weird, yes. But they're not . . . Where had Dave gotten all that blood?

Bloodletting and consuming. Self-mutilation and speaking in tongues and the spilling of blood on the earth . . . *But not that. They wouldn't. They're grandparents.* Zoe put her hands on the bed, feeling for some kind of warmth, an indentation, anything to show Warren had slept in it before leaving that morning. But the spread was cool and flat, the bed perfectly made . . . just as Guadalupe had left it. She ran back into the bathroom. His toothbrush was dry, the counter scrubbed, no sign of any life, other than her own.

What had Rafael been planning to do to Zoe? What exactly was it that Warren had interrupted? She shut her eyes tight, hands balled into fists, legs frozen. How strong had Rafael's rage been?

Zoe thought, *Protection.* Quickly, she made for the writing desk. She pulled out the key and raced out of the room and opened the garden safe. The stack of pesos was still inside. Nick Denby's watch was still inside. *The Day's End* promotional scarf was still inside. But the gun was not.

She heard the piercing *brrring* of the doorbell, and her heart shot into her throat. *Easy, easy* . . . She remembered:

Back in El Borracho, Warren had promised to take the gun—Garrett Christopher's gun—to the police the following morning. He had made good on his word. Relief washed over her.

He'd made good on his word, and he'd forgotten his key again, and now they could say goodbye. . . .

"Zoe? Are you there?" said the voice at the door. "I need your help," the voice pleaded, and Zoe knew she would have to give it. It wasn't Warren's voice, though. It was Naomi's.

TWENTY-TWO

"**S**he never boarded the plane?" Zoe asked. She and Naomi were nearing the *jardín*, half walking, half running to Patty Woods's house.

"It isn't like her, either," said Naomi. "I've known Mrs. Woods the whole time I've lived here, and she's no flake. She would never just disappear without telling her family."

"And the police—"

"They don't care. They told me to wait another twenty-four hours and then I can file a missing-person report. Can you imagine?"

"Wait. . . . When you were at the station, did you see Warren?"

"No, Zoe. I told you. I haven't seen him at all."

Just after Naomi had shown up at her door, Zoe had borrowed her cell phone and texted him: FROM ZOE. BATTERY DEAD. TEXT BACK AT THIS PHONE ASAP!! She'd also left him a voice mail. So far, there had been no reply to either. What was he doing out there with that gun? If Warren was the one who had taken the gun . . .

They were getting closer to La Cruz. Zoe grabbed Nao-mi's hand and yanked her across the street, narrowly avoid-ing a taxi.

"Whoa," said Naomi.

"Sorry. Just a . . . weird reflex."

"A new one." They were in front of the church now. "Zoe?"

"Yeah?"

"Were you with my aunt last night?"

Zoe stared straight ahead. "Yes."

"What did you guys do?"

Zoe inhaled sharply. "You know what, Naomi? I'd like to take this one step at a time. First, let's go see if Mrs. Woods is still at her house. And then we'll talk about last night. In detail." She glanced at Naomi. "Hopefully with your aunt there, too, because I've got a whole hell of a lot of questions for her."

Zoe felt Naomi's gaze on the side of her face. "What?" she said.

"Nothing. Just . . . you don't seem like you're on vaca-tion anymore."

Zoe turned to Naomi. "I guess I'm not."

"I'm glad."

They passed the church and rounded the corner on Mu-rillo, and in spite of all her mounting confusion and fear, Zoe found herself smiling at Naomi, just a little. "Me, too," she said. "I was getting sick of vacation."

Patty Woods's house looked dark from the outside, but Zoe rang the bell anyway. They waited. No answer. Still, Zoe thought she could hear something.

Naomi said, "Is that . . . someone crying?"

For the hell of it, Zoe tried the door. It drifted open. They both stepped in and an awful smell crashed into them, the crying at full volume now. Both were coming from upstairs—the rooftop patio. They heard a long, piercing wail and then the crying got softer.

"That sounds like my aunt," Naomi whispered. "She must have seen the e-mail from Corinne. . . ."

"Get out of the house," said Zoe.

"But—"

"Go across the street and call the police. Tell Robin we need her to bring something stronger than chamomile, and then you . . . wait for us outside."

"But—"

"I will handle this. *Do not come upstairs, Naomi.*" Zoe didn't wait for a response. She tore across the courtyard and up the stairs, covering her nose and mouth as that smell pressed on her, getting stronger and stronger. She knew what it was. She'd sat in on an autopsy once and so she knew. . . .

No, no, no, no . . . Maybe Patty Woods had died of natural causes. Maybe she'd had a heart attack or overdosed on pills out of guilt and grief. What a strange thing to be hoping for, but compared to the alternative, compared to what Zoe somehow knew she would see on the roof—compared to that, an overdose would be a blessing.

When she got up to the rooftop, Vanessa rushed at Zoe and fell on her, sobbing. "I'm so, so sorry, Zoe. I should never have believed in him. I should never have followed the Master. I see that now. I'm so, so sorry, Zoe. I'm sorry. . . ."

"Are you saying Rafael had something to do with . . ." Zoe never finished the sentence. Her skin went cold. For several moments, she could hear nothing but her own pounding heart, the blood rushing into her ears, as she stared at the mutilated thing on the patio floor.

Rafael couldn't have done that. No human could have done that. . . .

"I'm so sorry." Vanessa wept.

Zoe put her arms around Vanessa and held her close. She had never noticed how thin Vanessa was, how frail. She could feel Vanessa's every bone. She focused on Vanessa, the living person. She closed her eyes, too, breathing shallowly through her mouth so she wouldn't gag, wouldn't faint, wouldn't think about what had happened up here, what had been done to a grandmother.

"Patty was right," Vanessa said. "First Grace, then Jordan and then Patty herself. That's what she got for knowing. . . ."

"Knowing what?"

"*Sangre Para La Vida*. Our group. It was still meeting, after what happened to Grace. We kept it quiet—always at Las Aguas, never in town. We kept the cuts small, explainable. But Patty found out. And Jordan did, too. I thought it was Carlos who killed him, Zoe. I wanted it to be Carlos so badly. . . ."

Zoe caught a glimpse of one of Patty Woods's hands—outstretched, palm facing the sky. A small maguey spine had been placed on top. "Oh, my God."

"It's one of us. One of us did this horrible thing to Grace and Jordan and Patty and . . ."

"Vanessa?"

"Yes?"

"What happened to Warren last night? After he told Rafael to . . ."

"God, you remember. I'm so, so sorry. . . ."

Zoe squeezed her eyes shut. "Did Warren take me home last night?"

"No . . . no, Xavier did. I dressed you, and a few of us helped take you to his car, and then he brought you back."

"Xavier? From Las Aguas? With the hawk?"

"He's a good man. The only good one."

"How did he get in?"

"Most of us have keys to one another's homes. . . ." She let out a trembling breath.

"Could Xavier have known about the garden safe? Could he have taken the gun?"

Vanessa said, "I don't know what happened to Warren. Dave told us he went home."

"*Dave?*"

"Oh, God. Oh, Patty . . ." Vanessa started to sob again, and all Zoe could think of was Dave, drunk on pulque, touching Robin's blushing face. *Poor Patty. Immune to Warren's charms. Only one way you could get that bitch's blood to rise to the surface, right, Warren?*

Zoe gritted her teeth and hugged her. She heard sirens on the street, the front door opening and rushing footsteps and Spanish spoken over police radios. Zoe made sure Vanessa was turned away from Patty's body. She tried not to think of the smell or the sight of it. She rubbed Vanessa's back and told her, "It's okay. It's okay." She said the words the same way you'd say them to a frightened child, over and over, as if repetition could lead to believing, and believing could make it true.

Police officers clustered around the body, bagging the flacid hands, the gaping chest cavity, the rib cage—a large portion of which had been removed and placed on the wrought-iron dinette table. Zoe heard one of them say, "*Corazón ausente.*" Missing heart.

Dr. Dave showed up—not Robin. Zoe froze at the sight of him. He took Vanessa to a chaise longue at the far corner of the patio, where you couldn't see the body and the smell wasn't quite as bad. But before leading her there, he glanced at Patty Woods's mutilated body—the bones he had said were so similar to Zoe's—and it didn't escape Zoe, the calm interest on his face.

Dave gave Vanessa two Valium with a bottle of water. Zoe walked over to him. She took a breath, made herself look him in the eye. "Last night, at Rafael's party . . ."

"I don't remember much of that party, unfortunately," he said. "Robin told me I made an ass of myself." He looked at Vanessa. "Breathe deeply. It shouldn't take long for the pill to begin—"

"You were talking about Patty."

"I was?"

"Warren and Patty. You said, 'Only one way to get that bitch's blood to rise to the surface.' What did you mean by that?"

Vanessa stared at him, "You said that, Dave?"

"This is not the time or the place to answer—" Dave started.

"It wasn't the time or place to say it last night, either," Zoe said. "I want to know—"

"Your needs are not my priority. Vanessa's are."

Vanessa said, "I know why he said that."

Zoe stared at her.

"Vanessa, you don't have to tell her—"

"I want to. It's the least I could do, after what we did to her last night. . . ." Vanessa's eyes were calm, the Valium taking effect. "We had a meeting the day before yesterday. Patty mentioned similarities between Grace's death and Jordan's. Warren punished her for saying the name. He slashed her face." She looked at Dave. "That upset you, didn't it?"

"I don't know."

"It did, I'm sure. It upset me. But I did nothing about it because Warren could do no wrong. . . ."

Patty's face floated through Zoe's mind, the cross-shaped slash on her cheek. . . . "God," she whispered. She thought of the way Warren had looked at her—that fierce caring, that healing gaze. She thought of how he said he always wanted to protect her and keep her safe and fix her, and she tried to reconcile that with how Patty had been slashed—a grieving woman. She felt the blood draining out of her face. . . .

"He was observing the Master's rules," Vanessa said. "We aren't allowed to say Grace's name."

Dave said, "You just did. Twice."

"I don't care anymore, Dave. I really don't." She cast a quick glance at the group of police officers. "Look at what his fucking rules did," she said. A fresh tear spilled down her cheek.

A uniformed officer came up to speak to Vanessa. His questions were basic: What time had she discovered the body? Why had she gone to the house in the first place? How long had she known the victim? He asked the questions in Spanish, yet they were so simple Zoe understood them all. The whole time, she felt Dave's cold gaze on her. After about five minutes, the cop took down Vanessa's phone numbers and told her, in English, "Go home and get some rest. I will be in touch." Vanessa looked relieved. "Are you coming, Zoe?" she asked as she and Dr. Dave started out.

"I'll catch up with you," she said.

They began walking downstairs. "Dave?" Zoe said.

He looked at her.

"Did Warren really tell you he was going home last night? Vanessa says—"

"Like I told you earlier, I was in bad shape. I don't remember a word of what I said to anyone. And it appears I'm better for it."

"Okay . . . well, I'll see you later."

"Don't be too long," he said.

Breathing into her hands to avoid the death smell, Zoe moved closer to the police team. They were speaking rapidly in Spanish—she couldn't understand most of it, though she did catch one phrase. *"Veinte y cuatro horas."* She tapped one of the cops on the shoulder. "Are you saying the approximate time of the murder was twenty-four hours ago?"

He turned and glared at her.

"¿Habla inglés?"

"Yes," he said. "I have no comment."

"I'm not a reporter," said Zoe. "I'm a potential witness." But he had gone back to work. She no longer existed in his world.

Another cop was gesturing to the top of a lifeless arm. *"¡Mira!"* he said. *"Un pinchazo de aguja."*

Zoe turned away, knowing no one was going to tell her what those words meant. No one was going to tell her anything, other than "Please leave, señorita." And in the past that would have been enough for her. In the past five years, anyway, she would have just turned and left. But not now.

She grabbed a pen out of her purse, found a receipt inside and wrote on the back of it, sounding out the words: *Un pinchazo de agoo-ha.* Then she slipped the receipt into her wallet.

Maybe she could find someone downstairs who would talk to her. She began to head down, but in the middle of the second flight, she felt rough hands on the backs of her arms and someone yanking her onto the landing. She jerked away, but the hands were on her again, and then he was in front of her, grasping her shoulders, shoving her into the wall. *Dr. Dave.* "I told you not to be too long," he said between his teeth.

She pushed him off and glared at him. "Get away from me."

Dave's face was inches away from hers. His voice was calm, quiet. "Let me explain something to you. You are a tourist. The rest of us are not. What you saw last night may not be *your cup of tea*, but for many of us, it is a way of life, and if it is revealed, it will be destroyed. Do you have any idea how the people here treat alternative religions?" He moved even closer. She felt his dry breath on her skin. "Do you?"

"No, but I don't—"

"Do not tell the police about Grace. Do not tell them about *Sangre Para La Vida*. Do not say a word about what happened last night, and you will be safe."

"Safe from what?"

"Do not ask questions. You don't need answers. Just go back to Warren's, book yourself an earlier flight back to New York City and cut your loss." He smiled. "He's obviously not the right guy for you."

"Listen, if there was someone killed in the exact same way as Jordan and—"

"Grace wasn't killed."

"What?"

"She died of a broken heart."

Zoe stared at him. "You're sick."

"You are not needed here," he said. "He never should have brought you. Go home."

He turned, headed down the stairs. Zoe watched him go, a chill moving through her as she thought, *I'm staying. And I'm asking questions, too.*

In the courtyard by the front door, she saw a group of three bored-looking young officers. One was chewing bubble gum; the other two were smoking cigarettes—all of them silent, as if talking were the most pointless possible thing to do with one's mouth. They wore M16s slung across their hips like guitars. "*¿Habla inglés?*" Zoe said.

The smokers shook their heads, but the gum chewer nodded. He had a thick, glossy black mustache that looked like a sable wrap for a Barbie doll. It bounced up and down as he chewed his gum, and Zoe couldn't stop staring at it. It was such an odd look for a young guy from this century. *Bet he's a* Magnum *fan.* "Terrible crime, huh?" she said.

He shrugged his shoulders, his expression growing more bored, if that was possible.

Zoe said, "Can I ask your professional opinion about something?"

Another shrug.

"Do you think she knew her attacker?"

He narrowed his eyes at her, and she could practically read his thoughts. *Crazy gringa.* Then he shrugged again.

"Look. I may have a lead for you. It's a group that Mrs. Woods used to be involved in and . . ."

He looked like he was going to fall asleep.

"Maybe I could speak to your chief."

"The *comandante* is busy."

She started to leave, thinking maybe she could just find the *comandante* on her own. But then the thought hit her. "*Magnum, P.I.*"

The gum chewer's eyebrows went up. "*¿Cómo?*"

She shrugged. "You look exactly like him. Don't tell me nobody's ever told you that. I mean, I know it's before your time, but it's uncanny."

"You know that show?"

"Know it? I *love* it." She gave him a conspiratory grin. "So you think Higgins was really Robin Masters or what?"

He actually smiled. "Yes. Yes, I do." He stuck out his hand. "I am Mateo."

She shook his hand. "Zoe." Never before had she been so grateful to her parents for placing no restrictions on her TV viewing when she had been in elementary school. "You know, though," she said, "I never thought they gave TC enough airtime." She made as if to leave, and Mateo stopped her. "That is the *comandante*—over there." He gestured at a stocky man standing in a doorway across the courtyard talking on a cell phone, his back turned. "If you wait a little, I'm sure he will see you."

Zoe smiled. "Thanks."

Mateo watched the *comandante*. "I do think she knew her attacker," he said quietly.

"You do?"

He nodded. "The *comandante*—I heard him say there were no signs of forced entry, and there seemed to be no defense wounds. This is very, very frightening because . . ."

"Because . . ."

"Her nephew, Jordan Brink, had no defense wounds either. The murders were identical, except Mrs. Woods's heart was removed from the scene."

Zoe stared at him. His eyes were wide. Zoe saw the hint of fear in them. "You don't think . . . You don't believe Carlos Royas killed Jordan?"

He shook his head. "I know Carlos. We took an English class together. He is—how would you say it—a wuss?"

She nodded.

"He would get beat up, never fight back. One time, a girl in our class cut her finger and he nearly fainted."

"But he robbed graves."

"I am sure he did not do that for himself."

"Seriously?"

"Someone forced him into it—for whatever reason." He looked at her. "It would not be hard to force Carlos to do anything."

"Confess to a murder, for instance."

"*Sí*. But the *comandante* believed his confession, so . . ."

"Bet he doesn't anymore."

Mateo leaned in close. "He *does*. He believes this one is a copycat. Perhaps one of Carlos's friends . . ."

Zoe remembered what Naomi had said: *Alejandro called*

me and said he was serving someone evil and that I should stop asking questions. "His friends can be forced, too."

"No doubt."

Alejandro, whose dead father's gun wound up in Warren's garden safe. "Do you happen to know if an American stopped by the station this morning? He was supposed to be bringing in a firearm."

"No," he said. "We were very quiet until . . ." He was staring at her.

"What?"

"That cross around your neck. Jordan Brink had one. Exactly like it."

Zoe's breath caught. She felt her pulse start to speed up. Jordan, Grace and Zoe. They all had that same cross.

Zoe backed up into a sturdy body. She turned, and found herself face-to-face with the stocky man Mateo had pointed out to her earlier. "Zoe, this is our *comandante*." Mateo said something in Spanish, then turned to Zoe. "I told him you might have a new lead in this case."

The *comandante* looked at her. *"Dígame."* But Zoe couldn't speak. She could only stare at the dark mole on the *comandate*'s cheek . . . *like a drop of fresh ink.* He smiled at the cross around her neck, and her gaze flew to the man's large hands, and she knew their salt taste. She knew the feel of his fist in her mouth.

"Go on," said Mateo.

"He . . . already knows," Zoe said. Barely able to breathe, she headed for the door.

On the street outside Patty Woods's house, the air was fresh and fragrant with flowers and hot food. But Zoe still felt death on her skin, in her nose and her throat and her veins, as if she was oozing death, as if she'd been marinated in it.

Zoe had told Naomi that evil wasn't catching—but

maybe death was. Patty had caught it from Jordan, who had caught it from Grace. And now Zoe was in danger of catching death, too.

But who had been the initial carrier? She was afraid she knew. . . .

Zoe felt Warren's cross around her neck—the same cross Grace had worn, the same one Jordan had worn. And while Patty hadn't worn one, a cross had been slashed into her cheek—by Warren. Warren hated Patty. He had referred to Jordan's murder and mutilation as "karma" and had said, *Now she knows what it's like to have a visitor disappear.* He had called Grace, simply, "a long time ago . . ." Warren, who had had something with Grace that looked like love but maybe wasn't . . .

Warren also had the gun of Alejandro's dead father—and, unless Xavier had inexplicably stolen it when he'd brought Zoe home, then Warren had taken the gun and disappeared with it while she slept. . . .

Warren, who could convince a cynical Jewish woman to wear a cross around her neck and attend a bloodletting ceremony and feel the healing power of a seven-foot piece of granite. Warren could make a love slave out of nearly every woman in this town—and, Zoe was sure, could easily convince a "wuss" like Carlos to take the rap for a murder. Zoe closed her eyes, and she was with Warren again on the roof, during her first night in San Esteban. She could see the fireworks illuminating his clear blue eyes as he told her, *You are not a killer.* She could hear the way he had said it, with such intensity, as if he were speaking, not to Zoe, but to himself. . . .

Now Zoe was on the floor of Rafael's sunroom in the midst of that nightmarish ceremony. Warren was bursting in, stopping Rafael from cutting her. . . . But he'd sounded more intent on humiliating Rafael than on saving Zoe. *You have to take them unconscious now? Are you really that weak?* And if he had truly wanted to save Zoe, why had he left without her? Had Warren really wanted Rafael to stop? *Or had he wanted to be the one with the knife?*

Zoe's muscles tightened. Her stomach seized up and her heart fluttered in her chest and she nearly felt like screaming. *Please don't let it be true. Please, please, please let me be wrong. . . .*

At the end of the street, Zoe spotted Vanessa and Naomi in the *jardín.* They were sitting on the same bench Naomi had shared with Zoe just two days ago. She remembered Naomi telling her that she hadn't been able to cry with her aunt, but she was now, sobbing into Vanessa's chest as the older woman held her tightly. Zoe felt tears spring into her own eyes, and she wanted so much to do that, to relax enough to sob; to be in the presence of someone she could trust; to be able to ask questions and get answers, real answers. . . .

Carlos Royas didn't kill Jordan. . . . Mrs. Royas has proof.

Zoe tore back up the street to the front of the church, and asked a priest in flowing robes where she could find the *farmacia,* hoping with all she had that Alma Royas was at work today.

TWENTY-THREE

The pharmacy was dark, empty except for the one small woman who sat at the counter, rocking a basket, the baby's screams piercing the air. Zoe walked up to her, locking eyes with her as she got closer. "Mrs. Royas?"

"*Sí.*" Her eyes were so dark they looked hollow. Zoe wondered if her son's were the same. As Zoe neared, she flinched, as if she was afraid of being hit.

Zoe tried a smile. She glanced at the baby, still screaming, its face twisted and red, lying on its left side. "*Qué bonita,*" she said. "*¿Cómo se llama?*"

"Dolores."

A baby named pain. Zoe peered at the tiny girl. "Is she sick?"

Alma shook her head, and Zoe thought, *She understands some English.* "It's okay," Zoe whispered to the baby. "It's okay. . . ." Alma kept rocking the baby until finally she quieted down and fell asleep.

"Mrs. Royas," Zoe said softly, "I know your son didn't kill Jordan Brink."

The other woman's eyes went wide. She shook her head. *"No, no, no. Carlos le mató. . . ."*

"I know because there was another woman today, killed the exact same way."

Alma looked at Zoe blankly.

Zoe racked her brain for the Spanish. *"Hay otra persona. Corazón . . . sacado."*

"No," she said.

"Sí. Es verdad. Patty Woods. Le conoce?"

Alma's jaw dropped open, and a new pain seeped into her wounded eyes. *She did know Patty Woods. Very well.*

"Mrs. Royas, did Carlos have any friendships with . . . older Americans?"

"Jordan."

"No. No, I know he knew Jordan. Older. *Mucho más viejo que Jordan.* Anybody who you might think—"

"Mi hijo le mató a Jordan Brink."

"Mrs. Royas, no es verdad y usted. . . ." Zoe racked her brain for the right Spanish words, but finally her emotions took over. *"Mira."* She showed Mrs. Royas the cross around her neck. Alma's eyes went huge with recognition. *"Mira."* Zoe yanked her shirt down, showed Alma the cuts on her chest. "There is a killer out there, Mrs. Royas, *and it isn't your son and you know that."*

"Mi hijo le mató a Jordan Brink." Alma's voice was taut, trembling as if someone were holding a gun to her head. Zoe stared at her. She couldn't figure it out. Even if Alma didn't care who else got killed, even if someone *were* holding a gun to her head, what mother would keep telling a lie like that about her own son?

Zoe shook her head. She opened her mouth, started to tell Alma again that she knew that wasn't the truth, but what was the point? They were talking in circles. *What mother . . .* *"No se comprendo,"* Zoe said. *I don't understand you.* But she didn't know whether the translation carried with it the meaning she intended.

"*Lo siento,*" said Alma. Her eyes pleaded. Zoe started to leave. Then the baby began to cry again, and Alma picked her up, comforting her. That was when Zoe saw it—the metaphorical gun at Alma's head. . . . The baby's right cheek was bandaged, but through the gauze, the wound still oozed blood—two slashes, in the shape of a cross.

Why would she be afraid? Naomi had said back at El Boracho, after Alma had called her, after she'd taken back everything she had said about her son's innocence. *Why would she be afraid?* Zoe's throat clenched up as she pictured the scene—a scene too horrifying for words—that had taken place here, after Naomi had left.

This is why. "Warren," Zoe whispered.

But Alma just looked at her blankly. The baby's crying eased, and Alma placed her back in the basket.

"I'm so sorry," Zoe said. She reached over the counter and hugged Alma Royas. To her surprise, Alma hugged her back. She put both arms around Zoe and squeezed her with a fierceness that seemed impossible for so frail a body. Alma Royas held Zoe like a lifeline, like the last chance she would ever have. She turned her head and brought her lips to Zoe's ear and whispered one word, very quietly. And then finally she pulled away, and began tucking blankets around the baby.

"*Gracias,*" said Zoe, but Alma didn't answer. She didn't even watch Zoe leave. She'd said what she needed to say. She could be quiet, now. As Zoe walked out of the store and into the bright sunlight, that one word echoed in her head: *master.*

When Rudolph Lehman had first placed his hands on La Cruz de San Esteban, he had finally understood the meaning of the words *changed man*. He'd been an unsuccessful rock musician, an unsuccessful artist, and after he'd finally settled down and gotten married and gone to divinity school, he lasted seven years as an unsuccessful minister at a congregation in Glendale before he was falsely accused of skimming money from the coffers and kicked out of his job.

He'd escaped to Mexico with his wife, Lorelle. But no sooner had they settled into their home in San Miguel de Allende than Lorelle was diagnosed with stage four pancreatic cancer and given three months to live.

That cross, though, that magnificent cross . . . Lorelle had been gone two weeks, and Rudolph had taken the bus to San Esteban, just to get away from the medicine-and-perfume-and-vomit smell of their house. The plan had been to find a cantina and drink mescal until he could no longer stand up . . . but he'd stopped at the cross instead. He'd placed his hands on it, and gazed into the face of that Aztec bird and felt his whole body vibrate. He had closed his eyes and Lorelle had come to him in a vision, whispering, *It is your calling* . . . It wasn't until he opened his eyes again and felt the cool breeze on his wet face that he realized he'd been sobbing.

Later, he learned the legend from Reiki Master Paul—San Esteban had been built on a bed of healing crystals and the cross, which had been made from the ruins of an Aztec temple, had been placed there as a conduit. But at that moment, with no knowledge of San Esteban that wasn't sensory, Rudolph Lehman knew he would never leave. At forty, he had finally found his home, his work, his life, *his calling* . . . and not a moment too soon.

That night, he took a cab to Las Aguas. He bathed in the waters and became young again. He took out the obsidian knife he'd received from the Brazilian shaman. He cut out all his weakness, all his sadness and his loss and his powerlessness. He fed the earth with it and saw flowers bloom

before him. He sliced Rudolph Lehman to bits. And he became Rafael.

Since then, all he had wanted to do in life was to help others cut away their weakness and feed the energy source . . .
to help others become as strong as Rafael.

Rafael opened his eyes, the memory still in his muscles—
his first encounter with La Cruz. *"Arise, arise . . . ,"* he whispered. He took a long, slow pull off his bottle of tequila and
gazed at the picture of Grace on the wall of his sunroom
and thought, *How very far we've come since that day. How very
far down.* Rafael didn't like others to see him drink. It was a
sign of weakness, an invitation for them all to take advantage. But today was his butler, Emilio's, day off, and he had
no class to teach. He was alone, completely alone with his
painting and his memories.

Rafael took another swallow, felt the sweet burn as it
traveled down. . . .

God, youth was such a cruel thing. It stuck around just
long enough for you to figure out what to do with it, and
then it up and left, followed by everything you ever loved.
Everything . . . He looked up at the portrait, into the eyes of
his Grace—gone five years, almost to the day. Just eighteen
years old, but such a wise, wonderful soul. Such a beautiful body, such a precious mind . . . The one woman in the
world whom he'd loved as much as Lorelle, and she too had
left him. She had left him twice.

This morning, she had come to him, his Grace. She
had stood before him, so real he could feel her breath.
She had touched his face with her soft, icy hand. *I miss you,*
she had said. And then she had offered him her heart.

He gulped down more tequila, draining the bottle. *Grace,
Grace, Grace. My beautiful Grace, if only I'd had more time with
you, if only my Grace, if only. . . .*

He would never forgive life for bringing him Warren

Clark. Warren Clark had taken Grace away. They thought that they'd been hiding it from him, their affair. But he had known. He had let Grace stray with Warren because it made her happy. But how it had ripped Rafael apart inside. . . . Lying in bed, pretending to be asleep as she snuck in, late at night, telling himself, *They're just physical. We are so much more.* . . . Who the hell did he think he was fooling? It *killed* him. He couldn't help it. He was a man, after all. He'd imagine them together—Warren with his Grace. He would see detailed scenes in his head, and he'd feel tiny parts of himself twisting and twisting until they broke in two.

When Grace had left life altogether, Rafael had blamed Warren for that, too. Warren had grown tired of her, Rafael could tell. He didn't come into town as much, spent more time back in New York. And Grace looked so sad. Rafael would ask her what was wrong, and she would tell him she was homesick or she was thinking of a cat she used to own or she'd just read a troubling passage in one of her books, but he knew. He knew the woman he loved. Warren had moved on, and as much as Rafael hated the thought of them together, he could have murdered Warren for that. Poor, poor Grace . . .

And still, Warren Clark wanted more.

Warren had come to him this morning—in the flesh, following the lovely vision of Grace. "It's time to hand over the reins," he had said.

"How dare you?"

"Everyone wants me, Rafael. Half of them already call me *Master*. And now that I'm no longer working in New York, I can do it. I can take over."

Rafael had stared at him, thinking, *How can he? After all I've done?* But that was Warren. No conscience. No sense of . . . "What am I supposed to do?" he had said, hating the frail sound of his voice.

"Retire. Relax. Paint."

"Get out."

"But, Raf—"

"Get the hell out of my studio."

Rafael struggled to his feet, tequila and age weighing on him, his heart trembling in his chest. He placed his hand over his heart and tried to warm it, but his hand felt frail and cold, and he thought, *Dear God. That's gone, too.* He could no longer heal. The shaman's magic was crumbling within him, leaving him, just like everything else. Last night, he had even failed with Vanessa. . . .

He walked up to the portrait. He stared at Grace's lovely eyes, and he remembered how she had looked at him as he painted her that day—as if he were the only man in the world. He had really captured it, that look. His vision blurred with tears, until he could no longer see her.

I should never have believed in him, I should never have followed the Master. I'm so, so sorry. . . .

Zoe headed back toward Murillo, her heart smashing into her ribs, Vanessa's voice echoing inside her.

The Master. Not Warren or Señor Clark. The Master. Alma had said it very clearly. An English word, uttered by a Spanish-speaking woman who had looked evil in the face and suffered horribly for it. And the more Zoe thought about it, the more sense it made that Rafael had killed all of them. Rafael had lived here for twenty years. He was very powerful. He'd been angry with Jordan and Patty for learning—and threatening to reveal—the secret that *Sangre Para La Vida* was still meeting. He had motivation to kill them both. No doubt he had known Carlos for years. When Alma had seen the cross at Zoe's neck, she knew what it symbolized. . . . If anyone in the world could convince a young boy to confess to a horrific crime he hadn't committed, it was Rafael. Zoe recalled the power, the strange force Rafael was able to exert, even over her. A grown woman, bleeding and terrified and trying to escape from Las Aguas for all she was worth, and the sound of his voice had stopped her in her tracks. *Imagine the effect he had on Carlos. Imagine how Alma had felt when he'd held his obsidian knife and . . .*

No. She couldn't imagine that. Zoe would never be able to imagine that.

He'd had motivation to kill Grace, too—it was obvious she'd been sleeping with Warren. And if Warren was truly missing and had not just disappeared for the morning, Rafael had motivation to do that, too. Years of it. Zoe hoped with all that she had that she wasn't too late. . . .

In moments, she would knock on Patty Woods's door. She would convince Mateo to follow her across the street to Studio Rafael. She would demand that Rafael tell her what happened to Warren, and then she'd leave him to the *federales*.

She passed through the *jardín* without even glancing at La Cruz. She was over it, just like she was over the rainbow doors and the goblinlike gutters and the winding cobblestone streets and the jacaranda trees and the ridiculously lush gardens and everything else about this pretty bloodbath of a town.

When she reached the western end of the *jardín*, she noticed a thick crowd of people starting to gather. She would have thought it was yet another fireworks celebration, only it was still daytime and everyone looked agitated. Over and over again, she heard, *"¿Qué paso?"* She weaved her way through the group. Once she was on the sidewalk, she saw what had drawn them all: about half a dozen squad cars jammed together toward the end of Patty Woods's street, their lights flashing furiously. The cars were clustered at the entrance of Studio Rafael.

Zoe ran across the street. The gallery door was open, and so she rushed in, ignoring shouts of "*¡Permiso, señora! ¡No entres!*" The gallery was empty, but she heard noises coming from the kitchen—men's voices, the crackle of radios.

She ran for it, slamming into a cop as soon as she made it through the door. "*Usted necesita irse ya,*" he said. But then Zoe felt a hand on her shoulder, and when she turned, she saw Mateo. "What happened?" she asked.

He gestured at the floor, and then Zoe saw what looked like a river of blood, pooling out from under the sunroom door. "Suicide," he said.

Of course it had happened in the sunroom. Zoe stood there, next to Mateo, the smell of blood and gun oil and spent ammunition in the air. *Rafael shot himself,* she kept thinking. *Rafael shot himself. . . .*

Zoe was aware of a plainclothes detective asking Mateo in Spanish who she was, what she was doing there. She heard Mateo telling her, "You must leave now," but she couldn't reply, couldn't speak at all. She couldn't stop staring at the suicide note taped to the bottom of Grace's blood-spattered portrait, next to Rafael's signature.

Goodbye, my children. I am sorry.
I ended the lives of Grace, Jordan, Patty and . . .

—R

"Zoe," Mateo said, "you must . . ."

At the bottom of the page was a tiny arrow. Zoe moved toward the note, grasped it with the tips of her thumb and forefinger.

"Do not touch that!" the detective shouted in English. "It is evidence!"

The other side of the note read, *Look in the refrigerator.*

Zoe headed for the kitchen, the detective hurrying past her. He threw open the refrigerator and they saw it immediately—in a plastic sandwich bag atop a paper plate, wedged between the Tupperwared remains of last night's hors d'oeuvres. Zoe's head swam, and she gagged, tasting bile in her throat. She spun around as the detective called out, "I think we have found Señora Woods's heart." The police raced into the kitchen, knocking into her, pushing her aside. Zoe couldn't stay in there anymore. It made no sense, she knew, to be hurrying back into the room with the dead body, but somehow a whole body was easier to handle.

He took her heart back to his studio. He put it in his fridge.

Rafael's bloody, destroyed body was lying in front of the fireplace. Zoe stared at it . . . maguey spines in the right hand, gun in the left, the barrel lolling out of the hole that used to be his mouth.

The barrel of a Glock .45.

Zoe walked toward the body. Without touching it, without looking at the destroyed face, the shattered skull, she simply stared at the serial number: 074764. *Easy to remember.* She began to shake, then tremble. And then she cried.

TWENTY-FOUR

Like everything else in San Esteban, the police station had a somewhat magical look—bright tiled floors, desks carved with images of Aztec birds, glass doors overlooking a lush garden—no doubt fertilized by the *co-mandante* with sacrificial blood. But it was all lost on Zoe. She had just been questioned in the apparent suicide of the man many considered responsible for the town's magic. And she didn't think it was a suicide at all. Rafael was Warren's rival. He was killed with Warren's gun.

But he had left a note, said the detective who questioned her. And there were no signs of a struggle.

Zoe's gaze had gone from the detective to the *comandante* standing in the corner, saying nothing, his eyes downcast, his fists clenched. "There were no signs of a struggle with Jordan Brink," she said. "There were no signs of a struggle with Patty Woods. . . ."

"She is right," the *comandante* had said in English. "We must look into all possibilities."

They were finished questioning Zoe, but she wasn't ready

to leave yet. Where was she going to go—back to Warren's? What if she found him there? What would she say? As she sat on a bench by the front desk, next to Vanessa, who was crying quietly on the shoulder of her niece, it seemed to Zoe as if some kind of curtain had been yanked away. The spell had been lifted, the magic of her four-month relationship literally shot to hell.

Every bench in the place was filled, with many more sitting on the floor or leaning against the walls—Rafael's followers and the morbidly curious, most everyone shell-shocked or gasping from sudden grief.

Dave was leaning against the wall, his face bright red, tears streaming down his face. He looked like a different person—miserable, human. He locked eyes with her. Zoe mouthed the words, *I'm sorry*. He looked away. Robin stood next to him, her arm around his shoulders, tears on her cheeks. Zoe waved to her, but Robin gave her a strange look, her gaze darting evasively, as if she felt guilty for something. . . .

The *comandante* walked into the room, and stood in front of them. "I am very sorry for your loss," he said. "But you all must leave. We appreciate your help, and will call you with any questions, but for now we are considering Señor Rafael's death both a suicide and a confession of murder."

The crowd started to disperse, but Zoe rushed up to him. Amazing how much life could change in a few hours. Last night, the *comandante* had held her down while a cult leader had cut her chest with a knife. Now the cult leader was dead and the *comandante* was her only ally, and she was more afraid of her lover of four months than she was of this flat-featured man who had shoved his fist in her mouth. "I thought you said you were looking into all pos-sibilities," she told him. "I thought you said Rafael would never kill himself. . . ."

The *comandante*'s eyes were sad, resigned. "We have a witness," he said.

"Who?"

"Him." He looked toward the front door, at a slight, black-haired man who stood talking to Robin, Vanessa and Naomi. When he turned slightly, Zoe recognized his face. "His name is Xavier Vega," said the *comandante*. "He runs Las Aguas. He says he dropped you off at your house last night after . . ." He looked slightly embarrassed.

"Yes."

"He says he was about to drive away when he saw another car pull up. He says he saw Rafael go into the house. . . ."

"He *did*?"

Zoe headed toward Xavier. "You saw Rafael going into Warren's house?" she asked. But he just gaped at her.

"Xavier doesn't speak English," Naomi said. "But he just got through telling us the same thing. He saw Rafael go into your house. And he was concerned because of what had happened earlier."

"I'm so sorry, Zoe," Vanessa said.

"And so he stuck around and waited, to make sure you didn't get hurt. But Rafael left about five or ten minutes later."

Xavier nodded. *"Rafael salió de la casa con una arma."*

Zoe stared at Naomi. "Did . . . did he just say Rafael had a gun when he left Warren's house?"

"Yeah," said Robin, who still wouldn't look Zoe in the eye. "That's what he just said."

"Well, then," said Zoe, "I have one question." Her gaze went from Vanessa to Naomi to Robin. "Where the hell is Warren?"

Vanessa said, "We have no idea."

Someone tapped Zoe on the back. She turned to see a familiar-looking young officer—not Mateo, but one of the two smokers who had been standing with him at Patty Woods's house. *"Se llama Zoe Greene?"* he asked her.

"Sí."

He said something to Zoe in Spanish, too fast for her to understand. Vanessa said, "He said there is a man waiting to see you."

Warren, thought Zoe, but then the man emerged from the cluster of people behind them and rushed up to Zoe and said her name himself.

"Steve?"

"You're okay. Oh, thank God!"

Zoe saw the overnight bag he was holding and she was too grateful to ask questions. She started to introduce him to everyone, but she figured that could wait and just threw her arms around him. She buried her head in his chest, and inhaled the clean laundry smell of his oxford shirt, able at last to breathe, really breathe.

Steve was saying, "I went to the police station as soon as I got into town because I was afraid you were . . . God, I'm so glad you're okay. . . ."

Robin cleared her throat, and Zoe pulled away. "This is Steve, who is . . . wonderful," she said.

"Well, we'll let you guys catch up." Naomi looked at Steve. "Can you give me your cell phone number, in case Warren calls Zoe back? Her battery is dead."

"No kidding," said Steve. He handed Naomi a card.

As Zoe and Steve headed out of the police station, Steve said, "Listen, this might freak you out, but I found out Warren is a member of a very strange cult. It's called *Sangre Para La Vida.*"

"Oh, man," said Zoe, "are you ever in need of an update."

Zoe and Steve stopped at a coffee place around the corner from the police station. It was called La Paloma and it was very charming, with embroidered lace draperies and tables of carved wood, but Steve wasn't paying attention to the decor. Zoe ordered them both black coffees, and caught him up, more or less, on the past three days. As she talked, he grew increasingly pale and his jaw tensed. By the time she got to the ritualistic bloodletting and then the discovery of Patty's body, he was looking at Zoe as if he were praying that at any moment, she was going to point out a hidden camera and tell him that he'd just been punk'd.

"Are you okay?" Zoe asked.

"Am *I* okay?" He stared at her, his head shaking slightly in either amazement or admiration or a combination of the two. "I would say my okayness is pretty irrelevant."

"Yeah, well, you know what, Steve? If there's one thing I've learned from all this, it's that if you bury your head in the sand and you don't pay attention to the news and you don't ask questions—especially if asking questions comes as naturally to you as breathing—then . . ."

"What?"

"Then a whole lot of weird shit is going to happen to you."

Steve grinned. "I hate to say I told you so."

"No, you don't hate to say that at all."

Steve started to say something else, but then his mouth snapped shut.

Zoe realized he was staring at her cross necklace. "Oh, this," she said. "Well, Warren—"

"I've got to show you something." Steve removed a small steno pad from his shirt pocket and handed it to her. "Morrison and Barbara are letting me keep it for a few days."

"Who?"

"Jordan Brink's parents."

"*What?*"

"It was found in his travel backpack. He wrote that . . . when he was here the last time."

Zoe stared at the writing. SPLV IT IS STILL HAP-PENING! She stared at the black cross with the red dot in the middle and the two lists of names. "I think I might know," she said slowly, "what these lists signify."

Steve looked at her.

"I think they're sacrifices . . . people under thirty-five who were repeatedly bled out as part of this cult Warren belongs to. I think the question marks lived . . . and the *x*'s didn't, but . . ."

"Look at the last name on the question-mark list," Steve said. "Turn the page."

Zoe's eyes widened. Her mouth dropped open. "Tiffany Baxter?"

"He was going to take her to Mexico, but then her parents found out," said Steve. "That's what got him fired."

"So I was plan B."

"Apparently . . ."

All she could do was sit there, staring at the name. *Tiffany Baxter*. All those months, blushing at the sound of Warren's name, all those months needing him to the point of addiction, of thinking only of him, and at the same time, the exact same time, he was trying to convince a fifteen-year-old girl to let him ceremoniously cut her. "I was really stupid."

"You're never stupid, Zoe," Steve said. "He just never deserved you, that's all." His gaze lingered on hers for a full five seconds. In Zoe's body-language course, she had learned that anything over three connotes romantic interest.

She found herself looking right back.

Steve said, "I need to tell you about the first name on the X list."

"Nicholas Denby?" said Zoe. "He was Warren's first visitor."

"Warren told you that?"

"Yeah. He stayed with him a week, and they had a fight and he disappeared."

"Did Warren tell you about the audition?"

"You mean, the one where they ran into each other after high school? Got back in touch?"

"Yeah. Did he tell you what it was for?"

"He said he didn't remember."

"Bullshit," said Steve.

"Excuse me?"

"It was an audition for *The Day's End*. Dr. Matthias Caldwell."

Zoe gasped, audibly.

"Nicholas got the part."

After they finished their coffee, Steve insisted on paying the bill. "So just to make sure we're on the same page," he said, "Warren's buddy gets the part he wants, then mysteriously disappears. When everybody is hassling Warren, he receives an equally mysterious gift—which happens to be an illegal firearm. Jordan and Patty—neither of whom Warren particularly likes—threaten to tell the world about SPLV, and die horrible deaths. A guy confesses to Jordan's killing, and it turns out his best friend's dad is the owner of aforementioned illegal firearm—which winds up being used in the so-called suicide of Warren's *new* job rival."

"That's about it," said Zoe.

"Can I ask you something?" said Steve. "Is there any murder in this town that isn't connected to Warren?"

"The thing is, though, there's a witness who claims to have seen Rafael taking the gun from Warren's place. I don't know why he'd say that if . . ." An image flashed into Zoe's mind—Warren talking to Xavier outside Las Aguas. The admiring way that Xavier had looked at him, the reverence with which he'd led them both into the baths . . . *Señor Clark is singular.* "I guess he could have been convinced to say that to the police," she said. "Warren can be very convincing."

Steve nodded. "Most cult leaders are."

I slept with a cult leader. "There's one more of those names that I want to check out," she said.

Steve looked at her. She pulled the steno pad out of his pocket, pointed to the second name on Jordan's X list.

"Grace?"

"Yep."

"She's connected to Warren, too?"

Zoe nodded. "I'm pretty sure she was cheating on Rafael with Warren." She handed Steve the notebook back and stood up from the table.

Steve gave her a smile. "You really do have crappy taste in men."

"Don't rub it in," she said. "Anyway, I think we should go talk to Vanessa about Grace. She seems to—"

Zoe stopped. In the rear corner of the restaurant, she saw him—drinking a shot of tequila alone, his glasses on the table. He was no longer crying as he'd been in the police station, but his face was tight with grief. Dr. Dave. She walked over to him. Steve followed.

Zoe didn't say Dave's name. She just stood over him, waiting for him to finish the shot. She remembered how he was when drunk, how he had kept asking Warren about Patty—a hostile drunk, yes. A bad drunk. But truthful.

Dave looked up at her. He said nothing.

Zoe said, "Why did Rafael kill Jordan and Patty?"

Dave swallowed. His eyes were still wet. "He didn't," he said. "He wouldn't."

Zoe glanced at Steve, then back at him. "Who would?"

"Rafael," he said. "Pastor Rudolph. He was a wonderful man. He wanted nothing but good for all of us. But he let the devil into our group, and before he could make it

right again, the devil got them all. Jordan. Patty. Poor Nick
Denby . . ."

Steve said, "Nick Denby?"

Dave kept looking at Zoe. "Rafael shouldn't have drugged
you. He was very sorry about that. *Nextlhualli* only works if
the young person is alert and willing."

"Who is the devil, Dave?"

"If you are willing, it is beautiful. Rafael understood
that. . . . That is why he let Jordan go, because he stopped
being willing. Nick Denby. He was never willing."

Zoe said, "Nick Denby was bloodlet?"

"Yes. Warren encouraged it, and Nick went along, but he
felt humiliated afterward. He vowed to tell the producers of
that soap opera about Warren's involvement in the group.
They fought about it in a bar. . . ."

Zoe's eyes widened. "He never told me that."

"He doesn't tell much, never has."

"Jesus," said Steve.

Dr. Dave looked at Zoe. "Rafael was a wonderful minister and a godly human being, and if I find out for sure that
Warren was the cause of his death or Nick Denby's, then I
will hunt him down and kill him myself. I swear."

Steve and Zoe stared at Dave. His eyes were the tips of
ice picks, his face a mask of hate. "Thanks for letting us
know," Steve said.

They started to walk out, but Dave said, "Wait."

Zoe and Steve turned around.

"Even if he wasn't the cause of anyone's death, you should
know this." His black eyes narrowed, he stared directly at
Zoe. "Warren Clark is the devil."

Warren was dreaming his sheets were covered in short,
wet hair. He stretched out, and felt damp bristles under the
palms of his hands, the soles of his feet, and as his eyelids

started to flutter, he thought, *Grass*. . . . He opened his eyes and felt the sun on his face. He heard the gentle lapping of water on rocks, and he knew, without looking around, that he was at Las Aguas.

He wasn't sure how long he'd been out. The last thing he remembered was that ridiculous conversation with Rafael. He'd been heading out of the studio and over to his car, thinking, *What a stubborn old man he is.*

Just after he'd gotten into his Cherokee, Warren had felt a hand over his eyes and a needle in his arm and a voice had whispered, *This will just make you sleep.* No tone behind the whisper, just air. . . . And then he'd woken up here at . . . He looked at his watch. It was two in the afternoon.

He'd been out for hours. His heart started to pound. *Don't panic*, he told himself. *You never panic.* He jumped up, ran out into the parking lot. His Cherokee was gone. "Xavier!" he called out.

But there was no answer, and Xavier's pickup truck was gone. *Of course he isn't here. What were you thinking, shouting his name like a fool?*

Warren took a breath. *Keep it together. Stay calm.* He was not afraid. Angry, yes. But not afraid. As far as he could tell, this was some sort of elaborate carjacking, and right when he needed to be in town the most. He needed to visit his followers. He needed to stop by the homes of Celia and Mariposa and Avery and Denise and Robin. . . . It was two in the afternoon, and still he hadn't visited them. Not a one. If he didn't visit them every day, if he didn't stoke their fantasies, if he didn't place his hands on them with his healing touch and gaze deep into their eyes and cup their faces and kiss them . . . if he didn't minister to them, if he didn't cut them . . . they might forget. Warren might slip out of their minds like sand through a sieve, and they'd be back to Rafael, and that could *not* happen. . . .

Warren would call the police. That was what he would do. Warren would call the *comandante*.

He walked back to the grass. He plucked his BlackBerry out of his pocket. He was about to call the *comandante* and report his carjacking when he noticed two text messages—one from Robin, the other from Zoe. Robin's said: **Wherever you are, lie low. Do not call police. Will explain later.**

Warren frowned. Then he scrolled to Zoe's message and read it. He texted her back.

TWENTY-FIVE

When Steve and Zoe got to Vanessa's, Robin was there, too. It was just as well—after that look in the police station, Zoe also had questions for Robin. Vanessa poured them all cups of chamomile tea, and they sat around the dining room table, Vanessa sighing over Rafael.

Zoe had a few sips of her tea while Steve asked them basic questions about San Esteban—where he could buy a tooth-brush, for instance; he'd forgotten his. Vanessa was telling him how to get to "the best convenience store in town," when suddenly Zoe just came out and asked her, because she couldn't think of any way to lead in gracefully. "Did Warren have anything to do with Grace's death?"

Naomi said, "Whoa."

"Of course not," said Robin. But Zoe paid attention only to Vanessa's response.

Vanessa said, "No, he didn't."

"Are you sure?" said Steve.

"Warren adored Grace. We all did. Especially the Master." She inhaled sharply. "It was four years ago. A year after . . . Jordan. Grace showed up out of nowhere, took Rafael's painting class. Soon he was painting her himself and then she was . . . she joined us."

"You bloodlet her," Zoe said.

"She bloodlet herself," said Robin.

"That's right," Vanessa said. "Grace believed in Rafael's teachings more than he did. She loved Rafael even more than he loved himself. She was . . . she was special. The more she gave of herself—not just her blood but her singing and her sweetness and her soul—the more beautiful the town became. The more everyone's lives . . ." Vanessa looked at Naomi. "Do you remember, honey? Four years ago? Remember what happened to your mom?"

"She went into remission," Naomi said softly. "The doctors told her she was cancer-free."

"That's right."

"You thought . . . you believed Rafael and Grace had cured her?" Naomi asked.

"I thought we'd all cured Lucy," Vanessa said. "When it came to your mother, Naomi, I was willing to believe in pretty much anything."

Naomi smiled a little. Her eyes glistened. "You're really sweet, Aunt Vanessa," she said. "Weird. But sweet."

Vanessa smiled back. "Yeah, well . . . your mom is why I got involved with SPLV in the first place. She was diagnosed. I was devastated. A day later, I'm walking through town and I see this beautiful young man with his hands on La Cruz, this . . . absolutely charmed expression on his face."

"Warren," Robin said.

"Yes. He introduced me. I met Rafael through him. It was . . . a very special gift."

"I don't understand," Zoe said. "Who killed Grace?"

"She killed herself."

"But—"

"Rafael blamed himself for her death, his ego. She got so into giving of herself that she didn't know when to stop. She slit her wrists and bled to death in Rafael's sunroom. He found her. She was gone. . . ."

Naomi said, "But the maguey spines on her palms . . ."

"After he discovered she was dead, Rafael called us over—the elders in the group. We decided that this couldn't get out. It would mean the end of all of us. Few would believe such a lively girl was capable of suicide. And there were rumors . . . about Grace and Warren. Rafael—maybe all of us—would have wound up in jail. So . . . Dave was to dispose of the body. Isn't that right, Robin? Bring it to the abandoned silver mines in Patsquaro, just outside of San Miguel. Drop it down. . . ."

Robin stared down at her hands. "Yes."

"God," said Naomi.

"It's gruesome, I know," said Vanessa, "but we were at a loss and . . . really, we would have done anything to protect Rafael." She took a breath. "Somehow, during the time when Grace's body was left alone, someone cut her heart out, put the maguey spines in her hands. Like a human sacrifice . . . It was the most horrible thing any of us had ever seen. We vowed to stop practicing. But, God, Naomi, your mom got sick again as soon as we stopped. Warren started to have some troubles with his job. Dave's and Paul's practices began to suffer. . . ."

"Mariposa had a heart attack," said Robin.

"So we took it up again, in secret," Vanessa said. "Some of us were bleeding ourselves out of guilt . . . just to make up for that awful sacrifice. For disposing of that poor girl's body in such a horrible way, and in the back of my mind, Zoe . . . in the back of my mind, I was always terrified that . . ."

"What? It's okay. You can tell . . ."

"I was always terrified Rafael had made the sacrifice."

"Because of the rumors?"

"Yes. Grace and Warren," she said. "Rafael was a very jealous man."

Zoe turned to Robin, who hadn't directed a single word to Zoe since she'd arrived. She sensed the same strange feeling in Robin as she had at the police station, ever since the night of the ceremony, or maybe even before—that evasiveness. . . . "Where's your dog, Robin?"

"In my car," she said. "I wasn't planning on staying long, and Soccoro's allergic." But still, she refused to meet Zoe's gaze.

"I used to have a dog allergy, but I got over it," Zoe said. "On a totally different note, though, there's something you're not telling me."

For the first time, Robin looked at her. She swallowed hard. "Can I talk to you in private?"

Zoe nodded. She followed Robin into Vanessa's enormous kitchen, Steve watching them as they walked. Once the door was closed, Robin leaned up against the counter. "You've probably been wondering where Warren has been disappearing to . . . in the mornings."

"Yes."

Robin gave Zoe a long, pleading look. Then her gaze fell to the floor. "I know where he's been."

Zoe's pulse speeded up. She thought of Rafael and Patty, both killed in the morning, almost exactly twenty-four hours apart . . . both killed while Warren was gone.

"Warren," she said, "has been with me."

Zoe coughed. "He *has?*"

"We've been having an affair."

Zoe gaped at Robin, completely speechless. "You're . . . you're telling me the truth. You're not just trying to protect . . ."

"I didn't feel bad about it at first. I mean . . . we've been . . . we've been kind of together like this for eleven years, and I never felt guilty when he was with Patrice or Juliana or Margarita or even Grace . . . even though no one was supposed to know about him and Grace. He and I are his biggest secret, his longest. Warren calls us a *beautiful secret*. Every morning when he's in town, we . . . hook up in Dave's office, before he shows up for work."

Zoe stared at her. "But with me you've felt—"

"Guilty, yeah. Because I like you. And you like Adele. How could I cheat on somebody who likes Adele as much as you do?" She tried a smile. It didn't work.

"That's it?" said Zoe. "That's the whole reason why you've been acting so strange?"

"Yes. I didn't want to say anything. But with you guys suspecting Warren, you need to know he has an alibi. It's me."

"You know, Robin," said Zoe, "this whole conversation probably would have really upset me a couple of days ago. But as of now, I don't give a damn."

"Oh, thank God," Robin said. "I'm so relieved."

"Yeah." Zoe frowned. "Me, too." She looked at this girl, this child trapped in a thirty-seven-year-old's body. She thought of the worshipful way Robin looked at Warren, and how Warren's first choice to take to Mexico had been Tiffany Baxter, his teenage TV daughter. "Man," Zoe whispered. So maybe Warren had an alibi. Maybe he wasn't a murderer. Maybe it had been Rafael who had killed all those people, including himself. . . . But Warren was, most assuredly, a grade-A, USDA-prime asshole.

Unless Robin was lying about being with him in order to protect him. If that was the case, he was worse. . . .

From the other room, Naomi shouted, "Text message!"

Robin and Zoe hurried out of the kitchen, and Naomi

handed Zoe her phone. *Zoe. Please come to Las Aguas. I need you. Warren.* Zoe rolled her eyes.

"What's wrong?" Naomi said.

"Nothing."

Robin said, "What's he doing at Las Aguas?"

Zoe said, "I have no idea. But I guess I'd better go. . . ."

"I'm going with you," said Steve.

"We need a car."

"I'll take you guys," said Robin.

One big, happy family.

As Robin headed for the door, Steve leaned over, whispered in Zoe's ear, "Let me guess. She gave you an alibi for Warren?"

"Yep."

"They've been screwing."

She looked at him. "Yep."

"I'm . . . I'm sorry, Zoe."

She smiled at him. "Crappy taste in men."

"I want to go, too," said Naomi.

"No," Robin said. "You take care of your aunt. You're safe here." And Zoe and Steve followed Robin to the front door, Robin using her cell phone to call the police. She glanced over at them. "Just in case he's hurt or something."

"We're not complaining," said Steve. "It's a good idea."

"That's my car," said Robin, pointing to a Jeep Wrangler at the end of the road.

Zoe got in the front seat next to Robin, while Steve hopped in the back beside Adele, who was all over him like a new bride.

"Down, Adele," Robin shouted.

"No worries," said Steve. "I love dogs."

Zoe didn't say much during the drive over. Not much to say when you were going to see your narcissistic, philandering, borderline pedophile cult member of a soon-to-be ex-boyfriend with the woman who's been his side action for more than a decade. And judging from the way she clamped the wheel and the nervous, half smile on her face, the side action felt the same way.

Warren Clark. What had Zoe been thinking? But at least he hadn't slashed that baby's face. At least he hadn't done that to Patty. . . . Zoe recalled the group of officers clustered around her destroyed body. She remembered them looking at the top of her arm. She grabbed the receipt out of her purse. "Robin?" she said. "What does *un pinchazo de agoo-ha* mean?"

Robin frowned at the road. "It's like . . . the prick from a needle. Why?"

"Nothing . . . just something I overheard." Zoe glanced in the rearview mirror. An orange VW Bug from the seventies was riding the Wrangler's tail. And, aside from being impressed that such an old car could go so fast, Zoe wondered, *What is that asshole's hurry?*

Robin swerved into the right lane. The VW followed. She shifted back to the left. It did the same. "Jeez," she whispered.

"We're being followed," Zoe said. She and Steve turned around. The Bug was actually close enough you could see the driver—a fat teenage Mexican boy.

"Christ," said Steve. "I know him."

"What?" said Robin.

"I . . . I mean, I . . . I don't know him. I've seen his picture. That's Carlos Royas's friend."

Zoe said, "Jesus Christ."

"Why is he following us?" said Robin.

"Don't ask me."

They were nearing Las Aguas now.

"Drive past it," said Steve. "Lose him."

Robin put her blinker on. "No, Warren needs our help."

"Well, at least don't put your *freakin' blinker on!*"

Robin pulled into the driveway, her tires shrieking, the Bug close behind. She pulled up next to the entrance, opened her door and ran out, taking the key with her. "I need to help Warren!"

The Bug pulled in right behind them. Its door opened. "Where are the fucking police?" Steve said. He leapt out of the back of the car, Adele barking in protest. "Stay in the car," he told Zoe. The fat kid jumped out of the Bug and started toward the Wrangler. Zoe saw the glint of a knife in his hand, but Steve caught him by the shoulder and threw him up against the side of the Bug, the knife clattering to the pavement.

"No way am I staying in the car," Zoe whispered.

After text messaging Zoe, Warren had come up with an idea. *Why stop at Zoe?* he had thought. He could text Celia and Avery and Mariposa and the rest. He could invite all of his followers and create an impromptu ceremony, right here in the sacred place. He had his knife; he always had his knife. He could consecrate the ground with their blood and his own. He could take over from Rafael here and now. On his own time. Whether Rafael wanted him to or not.

Warren had almost done it—he'd even gone so far as to type in Avery's number. But then he remembered Robin's message—the one about lying low and not calling the police, whatever that was supposed to mean. He always listened to Robin because she always had his best interests at heart, and so he'd stayed and waited for Zoe, lying on the grass, holding his knife and feeling like an animal in captivity. Xavier wasn't here, but Warren heard Pio the hawk flapping in the trees and smaller birds chirping like schoolgirls. He listened to the water and gazed around at all the lush, perfect plants and imagined the voiceover: *Man. In his natural habitat.*

He was beginning to get anxious now, though. What if Zoe never showed up? What if someone had told her what he'd been doing in the mornings? What if she didn't understand that it was for the good of the church and acted like a typical woman and left him?

Then what would he do?

He cared for Zoe, deeply—especially in recent days. No other woman had ever made him feel quite this way, like she could leave him if she felt like it, and she would be fine. He liked that, her independence. She would be a wonderful addition to the church, his church. If she stayed.

He heard footsteps on the pavement and the rustling of leaves, and then a woman was moving toward him, some sort of sheer black veil over her head. He sat up on the grass. "Zoe?" he asked. "Why are you wearing that?"

No answer. She moved closer.

"It doesn't matter. I'm so happy to see you. You know, I've been thinking about it, and I've never said it in so many words, but, Zoe, I . . ."

"Love you," the woman said. It wasn't Zoe. She was taller, with a sturdier build.

"Robin," he said.

"I do love you. I will always—"

"Stop."

Robin moved closer. She knelt next to him, brought her veiled face next to his. "You love her, don't you?"

"Zoe?" he exhaled. "I think I might."

"You mustn't. She doesn't love you. Not anymore."

"You . . . Did you tell her . . . about us?"

"Yes."

"You weren't to tell anybody. You were never to tell—"

"Stop telling me who I should and shouldn't tell." Her voice was louder. The veil quivered with her breath. "If it wasn't for me . . . you would be . . . you'd be nowhere. I've saved you so many times, and still I have to keep quiet. Still I have to be hidden. . . ."

"Robin," he said, "why are you wearing that veil?"

"Because," she replied, "I am your guardian angel." She placed a hand on his neck and lifted the veil and kissed him deeply on the lips. He didn't want to respond, didn't think he should. But then her tongue was in his mouth, and Warren's body acted on its own; it always did. She pulled away for a moment. "I have something I want you to see."

He felt her hand on his inner thigh, moving, and his breathing hitched. *Well, maybe just this one time . . .* "What do you want me to see?"

"A sacrifice. For you. I have brought her to you so you can see it yourself. You can see what hard work it is. How much energy it requires to take the offering from the chest. . . ."

Warren went completely cold. *"What are you saying?"*

He heard Zoe's voice, "Help!" and something about the parking lot, and horror overtook him and his veins froze. *"Robin, no!"* he said, and he hoped she would obey him, hoped she would, *please.* . . . And then the needle in his neck put an end to all hopes.

"I need your help!" said Zoe. "I don't give a damn what you two are doing, just give me the key to your car, Robin!" Warren was silent. Not so much as a word.

She ran up to them. "Look, go ahead and stay here for all I care, but I need the key to your fucking car because Carlos Royas's buddy is attacking Steve in the parking lot."

Robin pulled away from Warren. He fell straight back, stiff as a fence, his mouth closed, eyes staring up at the sky. "Oh, my God . . . ," said Zoe. She heard his shallow breath-

ing and then Robin was saying something about muscle relaxants and Zoe remembered Dave telling Robin they were
low on muscle relaxants. She remembered the needle prick
in Patty Woods's arm, and Robin came at her, as fast as a bad
thought, and drained a needle into her neck.

"Do you have your Xanax, honey? Is it in your purse? Nod
yes or no." Naomi was aware of her aunt's voice, but she
couldn't respond. She was having one of those panic attacks,
the worst one yet. . . . It had started just before Zoe, Robin
and Steve had left, and it just kept going. . . .

"I want to go, too."

"No. You're safe here."

Naomi didn't know how many times that simple exchange between her and Robin had been repeating in her
brain, but it wouldn't stop—like a DVD stuck in a player,
the top menu announcing itself again and again in a con-
tinuous loop.

"I want to go, too."

"No. You're safe here." Naomi was on her back in the desert now, that awful sound track still running through her,
but it was ten days ago, and she had run away from Jordan
and passed out in the desert and now she was asleep. *"I want
to go, too."*

"Honey? Should I call Dr. Dave?"

"No. You're safe here." She was asleep. She was dreaming, and that angel was standing over her. *You are safe.* The
angel was wearing a hood, only she wasn't wearing a hood.
Not really. It was . . . it was a black veil. She said, *You are
safe,* and it was the same voice, and it wasn't a dream. It
was . . .

It was Robin.

Naomi was back at the dining room table, her aunt staring at her, asking what she should do. . . . "Robin killed Jordan," she said. "I saw her that night, in the desert."

"*What?*"

Naomi's eyes widened, the vision melting away as real fear took over. "We need to tell the police," she said. "We need to find her before she does the same thing to Zoe."

TWENTY-SIX

Royas's friend was stronger than he looked. Steve didn't want to hit him—he never thought he'd resort to punching some short, fat kid—but it was getting harder and harder to subdue him, and he wasn't answering Steve's questions. He was trying to act like he didn't speak English, but Steve wasn't buying it. He caught a flicker of recognition in his eye when he asked the kid if he knew Carlos Royas and, for that matter, when he asked him if he knew Warren Clark.

"What are you doing here?" Steve said. And then the big kid's hands were up and around Steve's throat, and he was strangling Steve. Strangling . . . Steve saw bright flecks of light in his eyes, and the thought shot into his minds: *Oh, no. I refuse to be strangled to death by some teenage boy in a goddamn T-shirt that says Cannibus U.* And his arms shot up. He caught the kid in the weak part of the forearm, the part that always made you lose your grip and drop your hands if you were hit just right. And then, for good measure, he punched him in the eye. The kid fell to the pavement, clutching his face. "Listen," said Steve, "I'm sor—" but the kid was up, and lunging at him again. He put his face right up into Steve's—got up on tiptoe to do it—so that Steve was staring at the half-closed eye, at the bruise he'd just caused.

"You don't understand. You must stay away. I serve somebody evil."

"Warren Clark?"

He shook his head. "Master."

"The Master? You mean Rafael?"

The kid shook his head again. "*Maestra*. Robin."

Then he was up again, and racing across the parking lot, into Las Aguas, with Steve close behind him. He turned and tackled Steve to the pavement—surprisingly strong, his body coursing with rage. He slammed Steve's head onto the hard ground as Steve looked up at that throbbing black eye, that Quasimodo face, thinking, *I have to get to Zoe. He serves Robin.* He slammed Steve's head into the pavement again, and pulled something out of his pocket and Steve saw the gleam of a switchblade. As the boy brought it to his throat, he thought, *At least I know why the fucking police haven't shown up.*

Ever since Alma had said *Master* to Zoe, one thought had been nagging at the back of her mind: Why would a woman who spoke absolutely no English suddenly use an English word? Why hadn't she just said his name, Rafael? The answer came to her on the grass at Las Aguas as she lay paralyzed, with Warren at her side. She hadn't said *Master*. She had said *Maestra*. Spanish for *teacher*. Robin taught those kids English at the *biblioteca*.

"Carlos was one of my favorite students—always so helpful. He may have had a little crush. Anyway, he completely understood my devotion to Warren. When I told him my plan, to offer up all those who had ever hurt him, he broke into the hospital for me, stole the pancuronium—that's what was in the shot. It's a muscle relaxant. And he got me cadavers from graves, so I could practice.

"Are you both comfortable?" Robin asked. "It shouldn't take very long. I can't leave Adele in the car forever, and besides . . . I only brought one shot." Softly, Robin smoothed a lock of hair from Zoe's face. "Thanks for being so understanding about. . . . You know," she said, "this isn't about that. It's about betraying Warren." She glanced at him. "She betrayed you, you know. Told everyone she thought you were responsible for the murders." Zoe couldn't see Warren's face, but she felt his hand. For some reason, Robin had decided to place her hand in his. She wanted to squeeze it, to signal to him, to say, *If we work together, we might live. . . .* But how could either one of them live when they couldn't even move?

"You know Xavier? I'm teaching him, too. Remember how I told you he was my buddy? Well, he was nice enough to tell the police he saw Rafael at your house."

Zoe heard footsteps coming toward them and thought *Steve, please let it be Steve.* But it wasn't. "Zoe, Warren, this is Alejandro Christopher, Carlos's friend. He's going to assist, aren't you, Alejandro?"

He said nothing, just grabbed Zoe's legs while Robin grabbed her arms, and together, they moved her a few feet away, to where she couldn't see or feel Warren. Zoe thought, *Christopher.* "Alejandro and I became friends after his father died. When was that car crash, Alejandro? Ten years ago? You were such a little boy. . . . What happened to your eye, Alejandro? We'll have to take care of that."

Zoe looked at the boy. His right eye was mottled and swollen like a piece of rotten fruit. The left eye was wet. *What have you done with Steve?*

Zoe began to feel a loosening of her limbs. Her lips were able to move. Then more of the drug lifted off her, and she felt as if she were breaking the surface of water, but she tried not to let it show on her face. Robin regarded her for several moments. "Warren," she said, "just so you know? This one doesn't love you as much as Grace did. I told Grace she ought to sacrifice herself to you, and she did. This one, I have to be the one to do it. . . ."

Robin sighed. "I'm going back to the car to get my medical bag," she said. "Watch her, please. Watch them both."

As soon as she left, Zoe blinked a few times. Alejandro opened his mouth to shout, but Zoe was able to put a finger to her lips. "Listen to me, Alejandro," she whispered. "Believe it because it's true. Robin killed your father. She killed your father, Garrett."

Robin returned from her car, a black bag in her hands. Zoe lay flat on her back, staring up at the bright yellow bloom of a century plant. Alejandro sat beside her, unmoving. Robin opened the bag and produced a gleaming obsidian knife and two thin maguey spines. Wordlessly, she flipped Zoe's hands over, palms facing the sky. "I am your guardian angel, Warren. Watch what I do for you."

Robin placed a maguey spine on one of Zoe's palms, then the other. "Try not to be upset, Zoe Greene," she said, as if by rote. "It's only karma."

Robin moved away for a moment to grab the knife, and Zoe thought, *I'll show you karma, you crazy bitch.* She clutched the maguey spines with both hands. She sat up, and as Robin turned back to her, surprise washing over her face, Zoe raked the spines across her eyes.

Robin fell back. "Alejandro!" she cried out. He did nothing. Then he picked up the knife and ran away. "Not so easy when we're not paralyzed, is it, Robin?" Zoe said. "Not so easy when we aren't afraid." Robin lunged at her. Zoe slashed Robin's face with one of the spines, her chest with another. Where was Warren during all this? Just watching? *Some leading man. Some hero . . .*

"You picked yourself a winner there, Robin. Warren's twice my size. You don't think his shot has worn off yet? I guess he couldn't care less about either one of us, huh?"

"Shut up!" Robin shrieked.

"Probably running away." Zoe slashed her again. "Waste of time, this whole guardian angel thing, don't you—"

"Shut the fuck up!" Robin flew at Zoe, tackling her to the ground, biting and scratching her like a wild animal. Zoe tried to fight back, but she no longer had the element of surprise, and Robin was much bigger and stronger than she was. Robin picked up Zoe's head by the hair, slammed it into the ground. Silver darts shot through her eyes. She couldn't move her neck. Zoe was vaguely aware of sirens nearing the parking lot. She was aware of Robin rearing back to drive the sharp spike into Zoe's heart. . . .

Zoe closed her eyes. But she felt nothing. When she opened them again, Robin was hovering over her, the spine still raised in her hands, as if she'd had a sudden change of heart. Then she went pale and stumbled and fell to her knees. Warren was behind her. He had plunged a knife, his knife, into her back.

Zoe closed her eyes, woozy from the blow to the head, surrendering to the pain. She heard people approaching, voices. . . .Was that Naomi saying Steve's name? As the darkness crowded in on her, and her breathing slowed, Zoe thought about angels and birds. She thought about planes flying home.

EPILOGUE

Daryl Barclay's latest appeal was denied. Zoe heard two people talking about it on the subway when she was going to work—*If it happens, it'll be New York's first execution in thirty years*—and sure enough the newsroom was buzzing with Barclay for the rest of the day. She was back at the *Daily News* now—she'd snagged a reporting job there a month ago, after writing them a first-person cover story on her Mexico ordeal, which they'd headlined TOURIST TRAP. She liked it at the *News*, and troubling as it was today to hear Barclay's name being repeated and repeated, to hear the morbid jokes about close shaves all over again, it wasn't as upsetting as it would have been three months ago.

That was one thing Zoe could say about her experience with Robin, and Warren Clark—it had helped to put everything else in perspective.

Robin Little had rented the top floor of a house that overlooked Parque de las Lavanderas. After Warren had killed her, police had gone into it and found a more or less normal-looking apartment—neat, too, except for all the shedded dog hair. But then they'd opened the bedroom closet.

Once Zoe had gotten out of the hospital, Steve had taken her to the police station and Mateo had shown them the pictures: a single lightbulb, a black cross on the wall painted with a thorn-crowned heart, a large black-and-white head shot of Warren Clark set up on a small altar that contained two candles, a vial of Robin's blood and offerings from each of her victims. The T-shirt Jordan had been wearing on the night of his murder had been placed on the altar, as well as Patty Woods's diamond watch, the wedding ring Rafael had still worn twenty years after his wife's death and a blood-encrusted lock of pale blond hair, which, after DNA testing, was determined to have belonged to Grace Newell, eighteen, reported missing four years ago by her parents in Shreveport, Louisiana. Garrett Christopher's passport was on the altar. There had been something of Nick Denby's, as well—a baseball cap from the show he'd just been cast on, *The Day's End*—but, as Carlos Royas revealed after being released from jail, his *Maestra* from the *biblioteca* had given it to him as a gift. Watches, rings and scraps of clothing lined the base of the altar—taken from the corpses Carlos had stolen for Robin three years ago, corpses on which Robin had practiced the skills she'd learned during her brief stint in an Arizona medical school so that she might one day improve on what she'd done to Grace's body. So that she might one day sacrifice all those with bad energy—anyone who aimed to do Warren wrong or to take him away from her, or both—and it could finally come true . . . the word she'd scrawled in her own blood across Warren's glossy photograph: *Mine.*

Robin had lived for Warren and died by Warren, and if there was one thing she had taught Zoe, it was that, no matter how strong your feelings, it was never a good idea to lose yourself in another person.

It was never a good idea to lose yourself at all.

After Robin's killing was ruled self-defense and Warren was cleared of all wrongdoing, he had disappeared. Like he had done every morning in San Esteban, only no one saw him—not his female "followers," not Vanessa or Paul or Dr. Dave or his agent or the brass at *The Day's End*, which was apparently champing at the bit to bring Matthias back from the dead, now that Tiffany Baxter had left the soap to host the new MTV makeover show, *Pimp My Face*. Not Zoe, either. No one.

Over lunch last week, Kathy Kinney had told Zoe that there were rumors of suicide. Zoe had recalled the way Warren had looked at her after putting the knife in Robin's back—that regret, that guilt—and she didn't want to think the rumors were true . . .

Zoe had a date with Steve tonight. *Phantom of the Paradise* was playing at the Film Forum, then a late dinner somewhere, then paradise for real. She was trying to take things slow with Steve. No keys had been exchanged, no "commitment" conversations, to her mother's chagrin. But Zoe and Steve were more than that. After six years as best friends, they still hadn't run out of things to say to each other. He could make her laugh so hard, tears streamed down her face. The first time she'd kissed him, it had felt like coming home.

After work, Zoe took the subway back to her Fourteenth Street apartment. Steve was coming by in an hour, giving her time to shower and change before the movie. She took the elevator up, opened the door, hung her key on the hook, dropped her purse on the floor and headed for the bathroom, so tired from her day and all the talk of Daryl Barclay that she didn't notice him sitting on the couch—didn't know he was there until he said her name.

"Zoe?"

He was wearing a tired-looking gray T-shirt and jeans. He looked about ten pounds thinner and he'd grown a thick beard, and others might not have recognized him, but Zoe did. "Warren."

He smiled. "You still know me."

Zoe stood there, thinking, *I never knew you.* But the eyes were too sad, the shoulders too slumped for her to say those words out loud. Warren's eyes were still as blue as a pool-company logo and his hair still shone and his teeth were still perfect, but he wasn't the same. He was just a blond guy with a beard—like someone had stuck him with a needle, drained all the magic out of him.

"What happened to you?" said Zoe. "What are you doing here? How did you get in?"

"Let me start with the easiest answer. Your neighbor. Mrs. Lucas. I knocked on her door. She remembered me. She let me in with her extra key."

"Okay . . ."

Warren took a breath. "Please come here, Zoe."

Zoe looked at this man on her couch. This thin, bearded stranger with the defeated eyes. *He's had himself a bad couple of months*, she thought.

She moved closer and sat down on the couch with him, and for a moment, she felt the weirdest déjà vu—sitting with Warren on his dressing room couch. *Your eyes are incredible. . . .* God, the brain had a sick sense of humor.

"I lied to you," Warren said.

"What about?"

"I told you I burned the note—the one that came with the gun."

"Garrett Christopher's gun."

He nodded. He was holding a white sheet of paper in his hand. He gave it to her. "This is the note. I want you to read it."

Zoe unfolded the note. It was handwritten.

W,

I went through great lengths to get this for you, because I know you need it. Do not ask where it came from. It is "para su protección." *That is all you need to know.*

Nicholas is gone and success is yours and I couldn't be happier. Do not listen to what people are saying. They don't know what you mean to the world right now, but they will.

Everyone who crosses you will be sorry. El que pega, paga.

I am yours. Forever.
Your guardian angel

Zoe looked at Warren. "Did you know who this was from?"

"I . . . I'd seen Robin's handwriting. I had . . . been with Robin a couple of times. I'd . . . I'd once told her *You are mine,* but . . ."

"But you were always saying things like that. To women."

He looked away. "Yes."

"So you knew it was Robin who was doing these things. You knew. . . ."

"No. I didn't want to know. I blocked it out of my mind. I said, it must be someone else. Just some strange fan and Robin wouldn't, she . . ." He took a breath. "The night before Jordan died, he spoke to me. We met in front of the cross. He told me he knew that we were still meeting and he would tell. He would tell the press. I told him that would be a mistake. I told him that he might not have been ideal to give, but others were and he was ruining the greater good and . . ."

"Yes?"

"I told him he would pay. I didn't mean with his life. I just wanted him to stay quiet."

"We all say things we don't—"

"The next day, I saw Robin in the morning, and I told her. She smiled. She told me not to worry. She said . . . *El que pega, paga.*"

Zoe stared at him.

"I didn't want it to be her. I didn't want it to be my fault, Zoe. But it was. It is. All those awful murders were my fault."

She shook her head. *This is the price you pay. This is what happens for not taking the blame and for looking away and for thinking you can do no harm.* "I'm sorry for you, Warren," she said.

"I wanted to think it was beyond my control," he said. "I wanted to think it was karma . . . but there's no such thing."

"Yes, there is such thing as karma," Zoe said softly. "It's working on you. Right now."

Warren hugged Zoe. She let him. He left her apartment quietly, and she knew that no matter what he did to try to put his life back together—moving to Africa or writing a confessional book or checking into rehab or disappearing into another TV role—he would never be fixed. He would never be whole. Life wasn't like soap operas. Nothing ever came back from the dead.

An hour and a half later, Zoe and Steve were walking down Sixth Avenue, arm in arm in the crisp fall night, on their way to see *Phantom* at the Film Forum. She pressed into him and he pulled her close. He leaned down and kissed her on the cheek, and she smiled.

"What's wrong?" Steve said.

"Just a weird conversation I had," Zoe said. "I don't feel like talking about it now, but I promise I'll tell you after the movie."

"I'm holding you to that."

"I know.

"Oh, that reminds me—Morrison and Barbara Brink's cat just had kittens. I can't take one because of Adele. But I told them I'd ask you. You might want to give it some—"

"Yes."

"That's it? No, 'Hmm, let me think about this'?"

"I want a pet," she said. "It would make me happy, I love animals."

He nodded. He knew this because he felt the same. Despite all the bad memories that Robin's dog conjured up, she was absolute sweetness, making life in his tiny, noisy, apartment almost bearable. In fact, Adele was the only reason Zoe ever spent the night at his place.

They stopped at a crosswalk, and Zoe said, "Anyway, it's just a kitten. It's not like I'm going to . . . marry it or something."

"And that thought is horrifying to you?"

"What thought?"

"Marriage."

Zoe turned and looked at Steve. He stared right back into her eyes for five, six, seven seconds. . . . Her chest tightened. "Aren't you supposed to make a joke now?"

His smiled a little, touched the side of her face. "I got nothing," he said.